MUKHTAR AUEZOV

ABAI

(Abridged)

PROGRESS PUBLISHERS
MOSCOW

Illustrations by Y. Sidorkin

Мухтар Ауэзов

Абай
На английском языке
© *Издательство «Прогресс», 1975 г.*
Printed in the Union of Soviet Socialist Republics
© *Translated into English. Progress Publishers 1975*

70303—818
A —————— 127—75
014(01)—75

CONTENTS

Page

FOREWORD

It is not an easy thing to write about Mukhtar Auezov (1897-1961). To say nothi g of the role he played in the development of his national literature, to say nothing of his unique talent and amazing erudition, his very personality was so original, striking, and there was so much that was unusual and at times contradictory in him, that one fears that none of the customary words will describe him. In outward appearance he also made a striking figure: he carried his body, that had rather prematurely run to fat, with great dignity, and there was the stamp of individuality on his face with its unusually broad brow and the calm, searching look in the narrowed brown eyes. And one more thing: everyone who knew him and associated with him carries a picture of his own Auezov. I do, too.

I remember those long-ago days well. After the war a lot of very green young men in worn army coats saturated with the smell of gunpowder smoke entered the literary scene. We were all madly in love with Auezov. I suppose our excited imagination made this charming person all the more attractive. As for myself, I felt strangely overawed by him, as a young mountain climber must be when confronted by a breathtaking summit.

What we admired in Auezov especially was the tender affection with which he invariably treated the young. With us he was infinitely understanding, sincere and simple. Young writers calling at his house were sure to receive a beautiful smiling welcome. And the kind words he lavished on them! He would liken them to new grass, or a breath of fresh mountain wind. He regarded it an aspect of his work as a writer to associate with the young generation, with people who wanted to devote their life to this hardest of vocations. And we, basking in the warmth of Auezov's heart, imbibed more and more of his wisdom and became used to his habits, character and voice.

Mukhtar Auezov sympathised with the beginners in their "growing pains", although he himself had never experi-

enced them. From the outset he was a full-fledged writer.
One of his very first stories *An Orphan's Plight* (1921) earned
him the acclaim of a master in this genre.

He handled the first works of the beginners with especial
care and tact. I can quite understand why his hands
trembled when he took up someone's manuscript. He must
have felt what a father feels when his swaddled newlyborn is
first placed in his arms. He was eager to find out what the
new generation was like, what kind of literature would it
offer tomorrow's readers, what ideas, emotions, colours,
words and forms would it carry.

Auezov was as concerned about the future of his national
literature as he was about its present, and with the intuition
of a truly great artist he was quick to recognise talent, and
once he had recognised it he could not remain indifferent to
the young writer's fate.

Much water has flowed under the bridge since that time
People are only visitors on this earth, they come and go
replacing one another, briefly meeting on one of the
crossroads of life and parting again. The more irrefutably it
comes home to us that Mukhtar Auezov is dead, the more
we become prey to brooding, and the more acutely we feel
our loss. Somehow with him there one felt that the future of
Kazakh literature was in safe hands.

Nature had generously endowed Mukhtar Auezov—he
was an outstanding writer, an astute scholar and a brilliant
orator. It was amazing that so many rare qualities could be
combined in one person. Self-complacency was utterly
foreign to his nature, he was interested in absolutely
everything, and his mind and imagination were always wide
awake. In between his novels, stories and plays, he would
write a brilliant theoretical article on literature, a purely
linguistic treatise, or raise a problem such as the work and
living conditions of shepherds. Everything he wrote was
stamped with talent and originality, captivating the reader's
imagination and transporting him into the world of
Auezov's images and thoughts.

Once, I happened to see him at work. I came into his
house, and the door into his study was ajar.

He was dictating the following passage from his *Abai*:
"The horses became a 'destructive force, a steppeland
fire, a hurricane or a flood. The herd moved in the night in
a solid, dark mass that covered the whole field—an
insatiable ravager with a thousand hoofs and thousands of
teeth'."

I forgot what I had come for. My excited imagination flew after the wild herd, I did not even realise that I was witnessing creativity in the act.

A corpulent man with the brow of a Socrates was pacing the room with measured steps, his fisted hands thrust deep into his pockets, his eyes tensely peering into the strange world of human passions that was visible to him alone. In this moment of inspiration he mobilised his powerful talent, all his immense knowledge and memory, and dictated on and on without pausing in his rich, flowing voice. Now and again he coughed a little, as though to hold back the rush of thoughts, feelings and emotions. And behind the furious clatter of the typewriter I seemed to hear the thudding of those thousands of hoofs as the stampede raced madly across the dessicated steppe. An elemental, wild force had broken loose, and there was only this one man who could control it.

I do not want the reader to be misled into thinking that Auezov never found writing difficult, or never experienced the agonies of creation known to other writers. He was very often displeased with himself, he was glum and sometimes bad-tempered, telling his friends in frustration that he had got hopelessly stuck in one place or another. When he had this streak of bad luck, as he called it, he was cold and reserved, but invariably civil.

In the history of every nation there are personalities whose biographies reflect whole periods in the development of the national culture, and in our case we must first of all name the great poets and enlighteners Makhambet, Chokan, Ibrai and Abai. To this day the poetry of Makhambet and Abai remains the fertile soil nurturing the work of Kazakh writers, irrespective of their age, degree of talent and popularity. What gives Makhambet's poems their lasting strength is that even after the defeat of the national liberation movement, in that grimmest period in the history of the nation, their freedom-loving spirit refused to be repressed and they were charged with determination to continue the struggle against the arbitrary rule of the tsar and the khans. Makhambet urged his countrymen to smash and refashion the narrow-minded, decrepit customs, mores and attitudes which hindered genuine progress.

Abai, his follower and enlightener, first raised his voice in the late 1880s. His father Kunanbai, an elder of the Tobikty clan, was a cruel and despotic steppe ruler, and the boy with his tender, vulnerable soul suffered terrribly every time he

came up against his father's insidiousness in one of its many
shapes and forms. Abai sought support from his young
contemporaries, he confided his troubles to them, hoping
they would understand him, and told them about the crime
committed a hundred years ago. "The strong are again
having their way with the defenceless. What laws, what
customs can justify the tyranny that has been thriving for a
whole century? Only the names of the tyrants have changed:
one was called Kengirbai, another Kunanbai, and the
present one is Azimbai. Also the methods of violence. In the
old days they used to stone people to death, and now they
starve them to death," said Abai, painfully aware of his
loneliness and helplessness.

In moments of despair he felt that his strength was
ebbing, that happiness was lost without recall, that he had
no one in the world, and was too tired to go on. But he never
gave up the struggle, and when things were hardest he
mustered his strength and hope. "My strength is my poetry,
my hope is the people. But this hope is still fast asleep and
will not waken. And my poetry? What if people never
understand it? And will I have sufficient patience, sufficient
will power to stand up in my loneliness?"

From the vantage point of today it is easy enough to say
that the poet's doubts in moments of weakness were
unfounded, because we all know the esteem in which his
grateful country holds his work. Since Chokan Valikhanov,
the famous Kazakh enlightener, no poet in this vast
steppeland had tied up his life so closely with the life of the
people as did Abai. His heart ached for his countrymen, and
he carried this pain with him into his grave.

After Abai, already in the Soviet era, there came young
Mukhtar Auezov. He grew up, learnt and matured in the
double cradle of his two great predecessors— Makhambet
and Abai—and his work became an embodiment of the
spiritual potentialities of the Kazakh nation.

As he studied the work of Abai, he felt he was reliving the
tragic epoch himself, and so it is not surprising that in
Auezov we easily find echoes of Abai in the interpretation of
happenings and in its emotional colouring. He held that
new Kazakh prose, developing in the new social conditions,
had to adopt and carry on the realistic and democratic
poetry of the great poet, and symptomatically the influence
of Abai's social, philosophical and aesthetic views are clearly
apparent in all his books. Many of Auezov's early stories
describe the contradictions of the patriarchal village life.

But while Abai was prone to philosophical generalisations when speaking of these mores and manners, Auezov subjected the same phenomena to a thorough analysis.

Compassion for the suffering and love of life were as naturally combined in Auezov as in Makhambet and Abai, and because he had these qualities he was able to feel the aspirations of the people as his own. He knew the mentality of the shepherd as intimately as he knew the nature of the steppe rulers with their great white yurtas, their two or three wives, their herds, their pastures and their water wells. The vast Kazakh steppes could withhold no secrets from him — he was familiar with its way of life, its customs, rituals, the mentality and habits of the people, he knew the happiness and heartbreak of lovers, and understood the grief and misery of young widows. He admired the superb art of the steppe bards, he felt for the poor in their need and the weak in their helplessness, and knew the brutality of the strong.

In the early stages of its development Kazakh prose was largely influenced by folk poetry, and especially epic poems, which can be easily explained. Poetic traditions prevailed in Kazakh literature for several centuries, and its development was consequently very one-sided. In the early 1920s, when prose was making its first timid steps, it very naturally studied composition, plot construction and development from folk epics mainly. The motifs of oral folk art left a deep imprint not just on the construction and composition, but also on the moulding of the characters, the manner of narration and the description of the landscape. As a rule, the language abounded in traditionally grandiloquent comparisons.

Auezov was a strange phenomenon on this scene, he was quite unlike anyone else. Apparently, for some time his effort remained unappreciated even by men of letters, let alone readers. His play *Enlik-Kebek*, written in 1917 when he was twenty, was first staged in the Abai village in two coupled yurtas (one was the stage, and the other was the audience) at the foot of the Chinghistau. And this production actually marks the beginning of the Kazakh national theatre.

In the 1920s and 1930s Auezov wrote a large number of short stories and the novel *Hard Times* (1928). Already then the writer strove for that simplicity and clarity of narration which were to become the hallmarks of his style.

He embarked on his literary career when the two

mutually negating worlds—the old and the new social systems—were fighting for supremacy. Both the pale rays of the setting sun and the bright light of dawn fell on the Kazakh steppe, and so the social contradictions were especially acute and unconcealed in those years. It was the immediate duty of literature to show the struggle between the dying and the nascent. The new Kazakh prose, born in the stormy days of revolutionary reforms, took up the cause at once. Mukhtar Auezov was one of its most consistent champions, and it is not accidental that his early short stories call an echo in the work of his contemporaries—the Armenian writer Shirvan-zade, the Tadjik Sadriddin Aini, and the Latvian Andrejs Upits.

There were more than enough social, ethic and moral problems in the life of the Kazakh nation which had made the gigantic leap from the patriarchal-community way of life to socialism. And it was up to the first generation of Soviet Kazakh writers to show these difficult problems in all their complexity. It was the same in the case of many Transcaucasian and Central Asian literatures whose development also proceeded in leaps.

Auezov's work of that period was not, however, restricted to a critical reflection of reality. He probed into the depth of the involved social relations and tried to evaluate the true worth of the old and the new, the passing and the coming. Admittedly, his early stories ring a tragic note, but in them he enthusiastically extols the strength of the Kazakh people who had come through the centuries of oppression, slavery and feuds unbroken in spirit, and with their thirst for freedom, knowledge and culture unquenched.

In his allegorical story *Ferocious Grey Wolf* (1929), Auezov tells about a wolf-cub whom a man caught and reared. When the cub grew into a big wolf, he escaped, preferring a hungry but proud death in freedom to his well-fed existence in captivity. Written with the inspired pen of a true master, this story remains a peak in this genre of Kazakh literature that none has yet been able to scale.

Auezov was also the first realist writer to explore the history of the Kazakhs' centuries-long struggle for their social independence.

In his books written in the 1920s-1930s he showed the process of class stratification, and the awakening of the people's self-awareness.

He did not simplify the process, as we see in the story *The Happening on Karash-Karash* (1927). With the insight of a psychologist and a sociologist of experience, Auezov traced the long and thorny path travelled by yesterday's humbled labourers, determined to find their rightful place in life.

The short stories of that period combined into a broad epic canvas, presenting a panoramic picture of an entirely new and unexplored world.

Until fifty years ago there was no Kazakh prose, and the fact that today the Kazakhs can be justly proud of their national, developed and progressive literature is largely due to the talent of Mukhtar Auezov. His monumental work *Abai* confirms this statement.

Abai died in 1904, when the contradictions between the new and the old had become exposed rather clearly. At the time Auezov was seven years old, and he was fortunate to see Abai alive. Later, he lived among Abai's numerous friends and foes, relatives and contemporaries, and came to know them in different situations. He attended the sharp disputes of the biys (elected judges) where, apart from everything else, praise was given to orators for their eloquence, wit and resourcefulness, and where the controversies of two or three contending clans were settled. Auezov travelled about the villages, and went hunting with a falcon.

He did not simply live among people who had known Abai and who readily talked about his habits and character, but was exposed in his growing years to the beneficial influence of Abai's songs, poems and philosophical exhortations, living in that same village, not far from Chinghistau, where passions raged unsubdued for centuries, where tribal feuds persisted, where ravishing raids were staged continually, with herds driven off and girls kidnapped.

Mukhtar Auezov was passionately in love with his native land, and the Kazakh nation's moral grandeur and generosity, fortitude and endurance never ceased to amaze him. He also saw the pernicious influence of the tsarist colonial policy which zealously encouraged the tribal feuds, venality, and the cruelty of the family elders. And his knowledge of these contradictory sides of life probably determined the main conflicts most typical for his stories. He wanted to find a finished monumental form, and this is the epic novel *Abai*—Auezov's major work.

Like Abai himself, all the other main personages were living people—Yerbol, Zhirenshe, Baisal, Baidaly, Bozhei, Takezhan, Suyundik, Aigerim and Ulzhan. And this being so, all the happenings described in the novel are nearer truth than fiction. Every novel, of course, reflects the historical truth of its day in one way or another, and the more truthful the book the more historical it is.

When we speak of a realistic reflection of life we have in mind true happenings and authentic facts, never suspecting that there can be a more complex and important "truth" carried in the "nooks and crannies of the human soul". The essential truth lies in the psychology of the personages involved whose individual traits have ended with their lives and are irrevocably lost. Yet without penetrating their psychology it is impossible to recreate a personalised image of these real-life people in a novel. Apart from this generally known difficulty, experienced in equal measure by writers everywhere, Mukhtar Auezov came up against another formidable obstacle, a typical one in the case of Kazakh writers only. This was a complete absence of any historical documents or chronicles.

Before the Mongol invasion, the Kazakhs were considered a people with an ancient culture, and cities like Otrar and Tarasi, which were quite widely known in Europe. Especially Otrar, the flourishing cultural centre of the Kazakhs, with its observatory, libraries, madrasah, and caravansary where rich merchants from distant lands were received. This city was the first to offer a resistance to Genghis Khan's hordes sweeping over the land in a black cloud from the East, and in the effort it was wiped off the face of the earth.

After this defeat, the Kazakhs whose main occupation was cattle-breeding scattered across the steppe, and since then, to quote Auezov, "the desolate expanse has been the home of the poor Kazakh nation. The solitary villages are lost in the vast desert. Loneliness and desolation everywhere. No permanent, lived-in settlements. No cities bubbling with life". There were no libraries, no archives left after the destruction of Otrar where written information about the former life of the Kazakh nation could be obtained.

Auezov probed the secret of history with patience and perseverance, penetrating deeper and deeper into the past by tracing back the evidence of his predecessors, collecting grain by grain the facts handed down by word of mouth by the ancient bards, and sometimes picking up by chance a precious fragment that had survived in the memory of the people. He wrote: "My work on the novel can be likened to the effort of a wayfarer who, arriving too late at the place long left by the caravan, tries to revive the only smouldering coal he has found and fan it into a bright flame with his breath. I had to reconstruct Abai's past life from recollections that have dimmed with time, and from the face of the sixty-year-old Aigerim I had to paint her in the bloom of youth whose loveliness had once enchanted the poet."

Auezov studied Abai all his life. And not merely as the future hero of his novels and plays. He spent no little time and effort on pure research, and published a number of monographs on Abai. What is more, he had a special course of Abai studies included in the university programme.

He was one of those writers who make their own sternest judges. And so he had to be quite sure that he had learnt all there was to learn about Abai—and his knowledge was probably unchallenged—before starting on such a difficult and terrible Odyssey of the Kazakhs. Even so, he did not venture to get down to the book at once. For the occasion of Pushkin's centenary he published a chapter from his future novel, as though to test his strength once more, calling it *Tatyana's Songs in the Steppes.* If we mentally follow the tortuous process of creating the first Kazakh epic, we shall see that Auezov only took up the pen when, to quote Romain Rolland, "he attained complete spiritual oneness with each of his main characters, with each of the most typical personages". Without such complete understanding of the personages' inner world, without feeling about the world as they did, a writer could not have fathomed the spiritual, moral, philosophical and social essence of the nation in one of the most contradictory periods in its history.

Auezov created classical images, and resurrected a whole epoch in the hard life of the Kazakh nation. Thanks to his novel, pictures of Abai's time, which were already becoming dimmed and forgotten, came alive again. Academician K. I. Satpayev called Auezov's novel "an encyclopedia of the Kazakh nation's life in all its multiple aspects during the latter half of the 19th century", and that is, indeed, what *Abai* is. Apart from its obvious literary merits, the book contains a world of valuable information of interest to readers and of help to scholars investigating the history, economy, ethnography and jurisprudence of the Kazakh nation in mid-19th century.

Mukhtar Auezov was a humanist and an internationalist. He invariably preached friendship among nations, as did all the more gifted and best educated Kazakh enlighteners—Chokan, Ibrai and Abai. As far back as the beginning

of the 19th century it had become obvious that without a
real friendship with the Russian people there was no hope
of converting the Kazakhs to European culture.

On closer investigation we shall easily see that the
friendship between the Russians and the Kazakhs has very
old roots. And although the poet Olzhas Suleimanov called
Kazakhstan "a huge hard-labour camp floating on the map
of the Russian Empire", even in those days progressive
Russian intellectuals were paving paths of friendship into
these outlying steppes. Beginning with the exiled Dostoyevsky and ending with the Marxists exiled in different times, a
continuous stream of sick and enfeebled prisoners — victims
of the tsarist arbitrariness — came plodding to Kazakhstan
from the heart of Russia. They did not speak Kazakh, and
the Kazakhs did not know any Russian. But the hearts of the
ordinary people were open to friendship. The Kazakhs did
not shun these emaciated, bearded strangers. The local
cattle-breeders called Taras Shevchenko "akyn tarasi"— a
poet of justice. And Chokan Valikhanov made friends with
Dostoyevsky, they corresponded regularly, and the great
Russian writer advised him to be the "enlightened interces-
sor for his people".

Y. P. Mikhaelis, exiled to Kazakhstan for his suspect
political views, was Abai's close friend and came to stay with
him in his village more than once. The friendship between
these two progressive men, lasting over many years, could
not but leave some trace on the cultural history of the
Kazakh people. Mikhaelis introduced Abai to Russian
culture and literature, and on his advice Abai became a
regular reader of the magazine *Sovremennik*, later finding an
engrossing interest in the works of the philosophers and
classics of Russian and European literature.

A well-known American traveller and journalist George
Kennan wrote with admiration of Abai. He had been told
about one elderly Kazakh named Ibragim Konobai (Ibragim
Abai Kunanbayev) who often came to the library and read
Mill, Buckle, Draper and others. The first time Kennan met
him, Abai amazed him with his request to tell him about
induction and deduction. It transpired that he was greatly
interested in English and West European philosophers.
Once, when they got to talking about Draper's book *History
of the Intellectual Development of Europe*, Abai displayed
excellent knowledge of the subject.

Abai made brilliant translations of Pushkin, Lermontov,
Krylov and Goethe. He composed music to Goethe's poem

Über allen Gipfeln ist Ruh, and also to Onegin's letter to Tatyana from Pushkin's *Evgeny Onegin.*

All his life Abai gratefully remembered his Russian friend Mikhaelis who once took him by the hand, as it were, led him to the top of a mountain, showed him from there the settlements of all the tribes of all the times, and explained to him that all people were really kinsmen. And Abai could, therefore, say about himself: "I am glad that I am not just the son of a Kazakh, but also the son of all mankind."

Auezov chose for one of his main themes the friendship between Abai and Mikhailov (whose prototype was Mikhaelis), well understanding the enormous significance of an international mergence of noble aims.

His work makes one of the most colourful and novel pages in the book of Soviet multinational literature. For the Kazakhs he is more than a writer, as the role he has played in the spiritual revival of the nation has earned him far greater than merely literary renown.

And now that death has claimed this truly great writer, we find it far from easy to determine, objectively and accurately, his place in our literature, in our moral life. This must be because he is still too alive in each of us, he is encouraging and supporting us. We are still living under the lingering influence of his great personal charm, and we try to look upon the world with his eyes.

The entire history of Kazakh written literature is bound up with the name of Mukhtar Auezov, and his vast experience makes a generous source for Kazakh writers to draw from. Each in his own way is Auezov's pupil.

For centuries the Kazakh people, alienated from world civilisation and held in the vise of a double yoke, developed its wisdom, polished its language, collected and stored away its immortal words like precious grains of gold. And, finally, in the Soviet epoch, it splashed out all these riches with the hands of its enlightened son, astonishing the civilised world.

One may safely say that it was Auezov who raised Kazah literature to the highest modern level. His writings and his meditations are esteemed by the people for whose elevation he did more than any other Kazakh. Anyone who makes so bold as to call himself Auezov's pupil must realise his responsibility to the memory of this writer and to his time.

Auezov did not look for an easy way in literature. He dreamed of creating an image of the modern man in work, in everyday life, in struggle and in involved relations, a true hero of the times.

Immediately after finishing *Abai*, he got down to work on *The Young Generation* (1961) which was to be his last novel. He travelled about the villages, collecting material, went to the most out-of-the-way places in the south of Kazakhstan, staying overnight or remaining for a few days. He was no longer young, and his health was failing, but he held his illness at bay with a sheer effort of will.

A meeting was arranged for him with the local shepherds of a large collective farm, to be held on a rise just outside the village. The shepherds sat waiting for their favourite writer, and there he came with a radiant smile on his tired face, nodding right and left, answering the shepherds' greetings. He walked to the carpet laid in the middle of the circle and sat down with his legs drawn up in the manner of Orientals. He swept the hushed audience with his kind eyes and, coughing a little as usual, said:

"Oh, people! My scholarly bald pate may set me apart from you, but in everything else, in my thoughts and intentions, I am one of you!"

And indeed, he was a different person here, little resembling the Auezov we had known all our lives—a refined intellectual with a European upbringing and education. Now he was more like an ancient Eastern sage who had spent all his life in this steppe among these simple and honest men.

Many feats have been performed in the history of mankind which made an example worthy of imitation for generations to come. Flourishing cities may be erased from the face of the earth by invading hordes, languages may become assimilated or even vanish without a trace under pressure of brutal social situations, becoming dissolved in the language of another, mightier people. All this may happen, but the noble feats of the human genius will never dim in the minds of people, and, like the Milky Way, will shine on the world from the abyss of time.

When a writer embarks on a difficult road he has to be strong and courageous, and then he will certainly attain his goal. Mukhtar Auezov taught us this, he taught this to all those who had chosen the fate of a writer and were prepared to take the thorny path uphill, shouldering all the pain, anger, joy, passion, daring and dream of mankind.

A. Nurpeisov

PART ONE

1

The boy was anxious to get home. He was willing to do anything to make this, the third day of the journey, the last. He had wakened Baitas, his kinsman, who had come to fetch him from the town, while it was still dark and begged him to start at the first sign of day. The boy continually spurred his horse on, in order to keep an arrow's flight ahead of his companions.

"He can't wait to get back to the aul!"* Baitas and old Zhumabai exclaimed again and again.

"Poor boy! He must have been dying of boredom in that madrasah** all winter!"

And the two men urged their horses on, trying to catch up with the boy. Zhumabai carried an old weapon under his knee, the black shokpar,*** while Baitas kept a long birch-wood soeel**** in place with the tip of his boot. As they approached the Takirbulak groves, Baitas thought it better to check the boy's fervour.

"Don't ride on alone," he called. "There may be robbers in Esembai Gully!"

"And they may be watching you this very minute," added Zhumabai. "They are probably saying, 'Look at that brave, riding all alone!' And they'll hit you over the head."

"And you? What are you here for?"

"What could we do? There are only two of us."

"And they're a band," agreed Zhumabai. "If they mistake us for kinsmen, we'll get by, but if they don't — things will be bad!" He scowled at the youngster, trying to frighten him.

But his warning only goaded the boy on.

"If you can't do anything anyway, I might as well be alone. I'm off!"

He dashed ahead, lashing his horse, never once looking back until he came to Esembai Gully.

---

    * Aul—a nomad community.
    ** Madrasah—a Moslem religious school.
    *** Shokpar—a club used as weapon.
    **** Soeel—a long pole with a horsehair loop at one end used by riders in battle.

During the first two days of the journey his elders had exasperated him with their dawdling and now, on this last day, he was happy to have found a means of hurrying them up; he would keep well ahead of them all the way to the aul, he decided.

Although he was nearly out of their sight, he still galloped on. It was broken country, all hills and mounds, a region deserted now that the auls had shifted to the Chinghis Mountains. Every hill commanded an excellent view of the road, and the ravines and gullies made very convenient hiding places for a surprise attack.

"Why isn't he afraid? Hasn't he any sense?" Baitas shook his head reprovingly.

Zhumabai, who had also been unable to keep the boy in check, readily agreed:

"The spit and image of his father! A true son of the old wolf, that's clear! There's nothing for it but to keep pace with him."

They galloped on, now one, now the other racing ahead. Baitas was riding the swift black-maned steed of Kunanbai himself, and Zhumabai was on another of his master's horses, the big snow-white stallion Naiman-Kok. They flew through a pass and on to the next one. Emerging on to a ridge, they found that the boy was nowhere in sight. As they began to descend into the hollow, Zhumabai suddenly heard the clatter of hoofs — from the direction of Esembai Pass, or worse still, from the gully itself!

Zhumbai was beside himself with terror. "The devils are loose! They've killed the boy," he thought, "and now they're after us." Lashing his horse wildly, he raced on, afraid to look back. Then suddenly a rasping voice barked the command:

"Close your eyes!"

Zhumabai turned, but the face of his pursuer was covered with a kerchief in the manner usual to the local robbers on a daylight raid. Baitas had ridden off at full speed. So Zhumabai was alone.... "I'll fight him off," he decided and gripped the shokpar under his knee. "But what if he hits me over the head with his shokpar first?" came the horrible thought. Zhumabai flattened himself against the neck of his horse to evade the blow.

The stranger gave him no time to reach again for the weapon. Dashing up, he jerked the old man's wide-brimmed black hat down over his eyes. Zhumabai was afraid to raise his head — he could not pluck up courage to grapple with his opponent and it was too late to attempt an escape.

The bandit tore the shokpar from under his knee. Suddenly Naiman-Kok pulled up sharp, as though he had come up against a barrier. Zhumabai sat up cautiously and pushed his hat back with trembling hands.

Could he be seeing things? There, on the horse before him, sat the boy! So that was the attacker who had disarmed him, stopped his horse and now sat there choking with laughter. There could be no mistake: it was Abai, the "wolf-cub of Kunanbai".

Furious and ashamed, Zhumabai said testily:

"You're asking for trouble with your pranks, my son! And what a place you've picked for them! The very nest of the robbers."

The boy's dark face was ruddy with suppressed laughter. He bent his head and began to put his hat on properly. Like a real bandit, he had turned his hat and cape inside out. It had been easy to overtake Zhumabai and order him to halt in a disguised voice.

Baitas came riding back to them, and it was hard to say whether he had been frightened or not. When he saw what had happened he laughed and seemed to enjoy the joke.

"Just look, he's even covered up the bald spot on his bay!"

Zhumabai looked, and sure enough the mark over the eyes of the boy's horse was smeared over with clay. But the old man was accustomed to commanding respect; he could not afford to become the butt of a joke and tried to laugh the matter off.

"What a little devil—he's just like his father!" he said with a forced smile. "No wonder the Kerei and the Uak are always complaining that the Tobikty* are all thieves and bandits. And well they may, if even this imp knows all the tricks of highway robbery!"

Abai was well aware of his father's esteem for this old man. He did not know exactly why Zhumabai had come to the town, but from snatches of conversation between his two companions he had gathered that the old man had been entrusted with an important mission by Kunanbai himself.

* Tobikty—a large tribe of Kazakhs in Central Zhusa (Central Orda) which inhabited the southern section of what is now Semipalatinsk Region, the entire territory of the Chinghis Range and the steppes to the north. Their neighbours were the Kerei tribe to the south, the Uak to the north, the Siban to the east and Karakesek to the west. The Tobikty were composed of a number of clans of which the Irgizbai, the Zhigitek, the Bokenshi, the Torgai, the Topai, the Karabatir and the Kokshe are mentioned in this narrative. Abai belonged to the Irgizbai.—*Ed.*

He stopped laughing and brought his horse closer to Zhumabai.

"The journey is long and I only wanted to pass the time. Please forgive me, Zhumakeh," he said affectionately and the old man was secretly pleased, though he made no reply. Baitas, on the other hand, began to joke with Abai as though he were quite grown-up:

"First you play a prank, and then you say, 'Forgive me, please!' It reminds me of my song:

> Load a camel for the road,
> And he will bear the biggest load.
> But it frightens me to think,
> How will Oikapa bear with me?"

Abai wondered what he meant.

"Who is Oikapa, Baitas-aga?"

"Don't you remember Oikeh, my wife?"

"Of course I do. What about her?"

"Last year I was away the whole summer, visiting at all the auls and having a gay time with the girls. But when it was all over I just had not the courage to face my wife. So I decided to soften her heart with this little song of remorse. I passed it on to my friends the singers and she heard it from them a full month before my return."

Handsome Baitas was known for his songs, and Abai regarded him with frank admiration. He remembered Oikeh and Baitas's friends whom he had met the summer before. They were all cheerful and tireless singers with wonderful voices. But what was the end of the story? Baitas had talked with him as with a grown-up, and so he ventured to ask:

"And what did Oikeh say, Baitas-aga?"

Baitas laughed, and hastily put on a serious mien.

"What could she say? Could the heart of a poor woman resist a song sent to her from afar, a song pleading for forgiveness? When I rode up to the house, she came out to meet me, put away my horse, and then my song floated off to be heard in all the auls. And that was all." Baitas winked at Zhumabai.

Naiman-Kok had settled down to an even trot and was now in the lead. The boy suddenly realised where they were and homesickness again swept over him. Lashing his horse, he dashed off, though his companions pleaded:

"Now then, son, you'll ride your horse to death!"

"If you go on alone, you may really fall into the hands of the bandits!"

But the boy, having just escaped from the town and the soporific boredom of the madrasah, was so homesick that he scarcely heard what they were saying. And why should he be so afraid of Esembai Gully and the bandits who struck such terror in the hearts of his companions? What, after all, was the difference between them and the other Kazakhs? Only that they wore ragged clothes, had battered saddles and carried soeels.... Abai had seen their kind before. He had heard the stories of the old men, and would not have minded seeing a bandit raid himself.

Sentry Hill, Secret Gully, and all these places were as familiar to him as his native village. Kunanbai's aul camped here for several months every spring and autumn. The ravines, the gorges, the hollows, the places where the foals were kept and the tents put up, the sheep pastures which could be seen from the road, were all well known and dear to the boy. It was from this very spot, from Esembai, that he had been sent to the madrasah the autumn before. That was on Bokhrau* when the sheep were being shorn. It seemed only yesterday that he had been running about these hills with the other boys, racing them on the yearlings and playing at knucklebones. In the town he had often dreamed of the wonderful days spent here in Esembai.

Now he was told that it was teeming with robbers, a place of danger and disaster, but he was not impressed. These were the same yellowish hills and green fields, the same expanses of silvery feather-grass reaching as far as one could see. Abai looked about him with a loving eye—at the boundless steppes, the hills where he was born and had spent his childhood. He would have liked to embrace it all, to press it to his heart. How caressing was the cool breeze, a gentle breath, never violent and never still. It set the great steppes rippling, wave upon wave of silvery feather-grass. Perhaps these were not steppes at all, but a great sea, a fantastic sea.... He could not look his fill. He was overwhelmed by the gigantic expanses, and not in the least afraid of them! If he could have put his arms around them, he would have whispered, "How I missed you! To others you may be terrifying, but not to me. My home, my own steppes!"

And the boy flew on, a speck against the silver green.

* Bokhrau—Russian Orthodox holiday (October 14).—*Ed.*

"Are we to crawl after him like wagon drivers in a caravan?" shouted Baitas angrily. "Let's get on, Zhumakeh, we're being put to shame!" Spurring his horse, he galloped away.

Whether he liked it or not, Zhumabai had to follow, and soon all three were racing through the steppes.

The boy had had his way. Not resting once from the moment they left Korik, they rode hard all day on froth-spattered horses until just before the evening prayers at sundown they approached Kunanbai's aul in Kolgainar, where Abai's mother Ulzhan lived.

The stream that flowed through Kolgainar was renowned for its clear, ever-plentiful waters. Kunanbai's three or four auls usually stopped there on their way to zhailyau (summer pastures) in the Chinghis Mountains. Near Kunanbai's yurtas stood those of his nearest kinsmen.

The evening air of the steppes was alive with sounds. The barking of the dogs mingled with the cries of the shepherds, the bleating of the sheep and the clatter of hoofs. A golden veil of dust rose over the aul as the horses pressed towards the spring. Let loose, the colts whinnied as they pounded about in search of their mares. Smoke from the camp-fires hung over the village in a solid dark-grey cloud. Here were the things for which Abai had longed so much, things which set his heart racing like a restive colt.

The three riders approached the aul on the banks of the stream. The five tents in the foreground were the dwellings of· the two younger wives of Kunanbai — Ulzhan and Aigiz — and their big families. Kunanbai's eldest wife, Kunkeh, lived in another aul.

The newcomers were recognised at once as they picked their way through a flock of sheep straggling towards the evening pastures near the Great Yurtas. The first to see them were the milkmaids who wore big aprons and had the hems of their skirts tucked up in their belts.

"They're back from town! They're back!"

"And there's Abai! Little Abai!"

"Yes, that's him. I must tell his mother!" And dropping her pails, one of the young women hurried away to the Great Yurta.

Ulzhan had been counting the days and the hours since Baitas had set off to fetch Abai. Having calculated the time needed to reach the town and to return, she had been expecting the travellers on that very day. The cries of the women reached her instantly.

Ulzhan's plump, pallid face, still almost without a wrinkle (though she was over forty), was wreathed in smiles as she came out of the tent, gracefully carrying her heavy body and affectionately leading Zereh, her aged mother-in-law, by the arm. Old Zereh had been longing for her favourite grandchild all winter. Not forgetting him for a moment, she had offered up numberless prayers for his safety.

A large crowd gathered to meet the three riders between the Great Yurta and the Guest Yurta.

Abai stood eagerly scanning the crowd; he had quite forgotten that he had outpaced his companions. He dismounted and someone led away his horse. Then he saw his mother and would have flung himself into her arms, but Ulzhan restrained him with a gesture:

"Ah, my son! Look, there is your father! First make your salem to him!"

Turning quickly, Abai saw his father Kunanbai among several old men who stood somewhat apart, behind the Guest Yurta. Embarrassed by his oversight, the boy made for the group. Baitas and Zhumabai too were hurrying towards Kunanbai, leading their horses by the rein. Kunanbai stood before them—tall, thickset, with a greying beard. His one eye, glittering strangely in his pale, stony face, seemed unaware of them. Other riders were approaching him, stout men, handsomely attired and well mounted. These were the elders, and from the attentive way Kunanbai was watching them it was obvious that he had been expecting them.

Before Baitas and Zhumabai could approach, Abai was at his father's side. Kunanbai returned the boy's greetings with a nod, but did not change his position. Merely casting an appraising glance at Abai, he remarked:

"You've grown. Has your knowledge grown as well?"

Was this said in jest, or did it express doubt? Did his father really want to know anything about him? From childhood the boy had been accustomed to watching the movement of his father's brows for a warning, just as a shepherd watches the clouds in the year of the djut.* And it was for this that his father prized him above the other children. Abai could see that Kunanbai had no thoughts for him at the moment and was concerned only with the approaching party. But the boy knew, too, that his father

---

* Djut—a natural calamity when animals perish from hunger, unable to get at the grass buried under the snow and crust of ice after protracted blizzards.

would be displeased if his question were left unanswered and so quietly and with dignity he replied:

"Praise be to God, Father." And then he added, "School is not over, but you sent for me. The khazret* gave his blessing and I have come home."

Next to his father stood Maibasar and his servant. The younger brother of Kunanbai, Maibasar, was the son of one of the four younger wives of Kunanbai's father. When Kunanbai had been elected Aga-Sultan earlier in the year, he had placed his brother at the head of the Tobikty Volost.

"He is quite grown up now... " Maibasar ventured, pleased with Abai's answer.

But he was interrupted by Kunanbai, who briefly commanded, "Go, my son, and greet your mothers!"

Abai had been waiting for this, and as he turned to the women who had been murmuring among themselves as they watched him jealously, his face again took on a happy, boyish expression. With his usual impetuosity he rushed towards his mother, but someone caught him on the way and he was showered with kisses by the old men and women. So they still considered him a child? He flushed, but was not sure whether to be angry or not. There were tears in the eyes of the old women.

Breaking away at last, Abai hurried to his own mother, Ulzhan, who stood at the side of the beautiful Aigiz, Kunanbai's third wife.

"They have smeared their sloppy kisses all over our boy's face and there's not a dry spot left for us!" said Aigiz. With a disdainful smile, she planted a kiss on each of his eyes.

His own mother did not kiss him—she merely pressed him to her bosom and greedily inhaled the smell of his hair—the reserve and coolness of his father having long been imparted to her. Aware of this, the boy had expected no more. But he could feel such warmth and love in her silent embrace that his heart raced.

Ulzhan did not hold him long.

"You must greet your grandmother," she said and turned him towards the entrance of the Great Yurta.

Old Zereh was leaning on her stick and grumbling.

"Ah, the rascal. He didn't come to me first, he had to run to his father!" But no sooner was he in her arms than her rebukes changed to the tenderest of words.

---

* Khazret—the holy one.— *Ed.*

"My sunshine, my little lamb, my dear heart!" she said again and again, tears rising to her eyes.

Abai entered the tent arm in arm with the old woman. He sat there a long time, until it was quite dark. His mothers offered him goat milk, cold meat and tea, but he had no stomach for food, though he had eaten nothing since dawn.

The women and girls plied him with endless questions.

"Have you finished your schooling?"

"Are you a mullah now?"

"Whom did you miss most of all?"

Abai answered in monosyllables, but the last question aroused him.

"Where is Ospan? Where has he gone to?" he asked with such urgency that they knew right away that most of all he had missed his younger brother, that piece of mischief known as Ospan.

"Who knows? He's running about somewhere, the little scamp. We were so angry with him today that Grandmother and I turned him out." Ulzhan nodded toward Zereh who, realising that she was being spoken of, demanded:

"Eh, what's that? What's that you're saying? I can't hear a word."

Abai shouted in her ear, explaining what had been said.

"Granny, you were not like this last year. What's the matter with your ears?"

He embraced Zereh and nestled against her knees. She had understood his words.

"What's there left of your granny, dear heart? Only a bag of bones," she quavered.

Abai's heart ached for the old woman, doomed to loneliness among so many people.

"But perhaps your ears could be cured, if one really tried?"

Old Zereh laughed at him with the others, but to avoid hurting him she said with a tender smile:

"If the mullah would blow a prayer into them, I might hear better. They say it helps."

"That's good," laughed Aigiz, "your grandson is already a mullah; let him blow if it helps!"

But the other women were serious, as though they really believed in the efficacy of Abai's learning.

"Let him blow into her ears!- It will ease her heart at least."

Abai knew very well that this blowing into a person's ears,

just as painting a sore spot with colours washed from holy scripts, or praying and chanting over the patient, were the usual devices of the mullahs, which did not much differ from witchcraft. For a time he sat smiling at his predicament, but suddenly he took the old woman's head between his hands, pressed his lips to her ear, and half murmured, half whispered:

> Her face is lovely, and her eyes like diamonds glow,
> The cheeks are rosy with the flush of early dawn,
> The supple neck is whiter than the whitest snow,
> Her eyebrows the Creator must have drawn....

No one in the tent could catch the words, but the women were convinced that he was praying. The boy kept a straight face and like a proper mullah muttered on:

> But why then, in those moments rare
> When we do meet, I do not dare
> To raise my eyes, or speak a word?
> My heart feels pierced as with a sword....

He half closed his eyes, pursed his lips and blew into his grandmother's ear:
"Su-uff!"
Those were his own verses. He had made them up in the spring after reading Navoi and Fizuli. The women, however, believed that Abai was saying a prayer. To prolong the illusion, the boy spoke in whispers and only at the end did he give the joke away by raising his voice. Ecstatically rocking to and fro like a mullah when chanting from the Koran, he completed the verses in the ritual sing-song:

> She cannot hear a thing, my poor old dear.
> Let her believe my verse will cure her ears....

"Su-uff!" he blew into her ear again, but everyone realised the joke and there was general laughter. The old woman too understood and laughed silently. Pleased and happy, she pressed her cheek to his forehead and patted his back.
Abai maintained his earnest expression, though a glint of merriment lurked in his eyes. Hugging the old woman, he asked:
"Can you hear a little better now?"
"Oh yes, much better. May you live in never ending joy, my little one!"

The boy's jest had evoked laughter, but something of admiration too.

Ulzhan, his mother, did not burst out laughing like the others; she watched him thoughtfully. How he had grown in that year! How manly he had become, what intelligence shone in his eyes! He was not at all like his brothers. A faint smile touched her lips.

"I thought they had made a mullah of you in the town, my son," she said, "but it seems you have taken after my kin!"

The hint was not lost on the others and there was more laughter.

"Why, of course, there's Shanshar* blood in his veins!"

"One can see at once that he's the grandson of Tonteken!"

Someone recalled Tonteken's words on his death-bed: "It's a shame to cheat the hadjis and mullahs of their expectations. I'd really better die, let them at least earn something from the funeral."

"Apa,"** said Abai thoughtfully, "isn't it better to die like Tonteken than be a quack and live on charity?"

"It is well that you think so. How you have grown, my boy," his mother sighed.

The figure of Maibasar's attendant, the bearded Kamisbai, appeared at the entrance of the tent.

"Your father calls, son!"

There was an instant hush, and the mood which had possessed Abai all evening was gone. He left the tent without a word.

The Guest Yurta was not at all like his mother's tent. Even its exterior seemed austere and forbidding. Stepping inside, Abai clearly and, distinctly pronounced his salem. The grown-ups replied. There were not many: Kunanbai, Maibasar, Zhumabai and several elders of the Tobikty tribe — Baisal, Bozhei, Karatai and Suyundik. Of the young men there was only Zhirenshe, Baisal's cousin, who always accompanied him. He was also Abai's friend, though older than he.

From earliest childhood Abai had known that when his father took counsel with such people as these, especially with three or four of the most influential elders, there was something extraordinary afoot. He had never attended such a counsel; this was the first time he had been invited

* Shanshar—the name of a Kazakh clan.— *Ed.*
** Apa— mother.— *Ed.*

by his father, and there must be some good reason for it.

No sooner had Abai seated himself than the old men began to ply him with questions about the town, his studies and his health. Karatai, a garrulous old man with shrewd features, showed an unusual interest in his answers. He mentioned other sons of Kunanbai.

"That Takezhan of yours is a brave fellow," he said, "so agile and clever."

"That's true," added Bozhei, "he can do anything."

"Yes, yes, that boy's sharp as a needle," Baisal hastened to put in his word.

The praises were obviously directed at Kunanbai, but the latter sat silent, impervious to the flattery. Suddenly, as though to spite them, he turned to Abai and said:

"If anything may be expected at all, then expect it from that swarthy brat over there!"

Just then, Ospan, Abai's younger brother, ran into the tent.

How many times had Abai asked for him today! How he had longed to see the rascal!

Ospan did not forget to make his salem, but paying no further attention to his father and the others, he flung himself on Abai's neck. He was five years younger than Abai, and he loved him more than any of his other brothers.

Conscious that he had to bear himself with dignity in the presence of the grown-ups, Abai embraced his brother somewhat ceremoniously and kissed him on both cheeks, as an elder brother should. Seeing that the boys had just met, the old men took an indulgent view of such licence. But Ospan started to play the fool and soon dispelled the favourable impression. When Abai asked where he had been, the scamp only clung to his neck and whispered into his ear some dirty words he had heard from his elder brother Takezhan. Such was Abai's meeting with the brother he had missed so much. He recoiled from Ospan in horror.

"What did you say?" But Ospan flung himself round his neck again.

"Don't tell father! Don't you dare tell!" he whispered fiercely, and suddenly pushed Abai over backwards.

Self-conscious in the presence of the elders, Abai did his best to extricate himself and regain his composure. But stocky little Ospan laid him flat on both shoulders, and taking something from his mouth thrust it, all slippery, down Abai's neck. Abai wriggled his shoulders and tried to get free. Just a minute ago he had been sitting so importantly among the grown-ups and now that little scamp of a brother had gone and disgraced him! Forgetful of his father, Ospan shrieked with laughter.

"It's a frog! I've put a frog down his neck!"

This made Abai struggle all the more.

Kunanbai had at first paid no attention to the boys wrestling behind his back, thinking they would soon quieten down. But now he turned sharply and saw that the sturdy Ospan had pinned Abai to the ground and was sitting on his chest.

Exasperated, Kunanbai caught Ospan with one hand and with the other slapped him soundly across his face. The boy flushed, but stood still, his large eyes flashing. He was not intimidated and regarded his parent calmly, as though nothing had happened. Amazed by the youngster's fortitude, Suyundik leaned towards Baisal:

"He's a little wolf," he said.

"A real Kuzh,"* whispered the other.

Kunanbai motioned to his servant:

"Throw the rascal out!" He pushed Ospan towards the door. The boy tripped and would have fallen had the servant not caught him in time. For a few moments there was silence. Not until people had begun to stir, and someone had coughed did Kunanbai speak again.

2

The earthenware lamp over the low round table in the centre of the tent shed a reddish light, flickering in the draught. Kunanbai sat beside his son, a grim profile against the light.

There was something chilling about him. His masterful face was sombre and cruel. His words, sharp and impressive, fell upon his listeners with ponderous fury. His speech abounded ir parables and proverbs.

The boy could barely follow his father's meaning. What hidden purpose lay behind it? He could only understand a few disconnected expressions. As became an aksakal,** Kunanbai spoke in a roundabout way, circling round his subject like a hawk over his prey. Abai could not make head or tail of it and was utterly confused. If he could, he would

* Kuzh—a legendary giant.— *Ed.*
** Aksakal — old man, the elder of the aul (literally: whitebeard).— *Ed.*

have fled to the tent of his mother, but his father had
summoned him, and it was impossible to leave.

He sat there listening. Some of the words were new and
altogether incomprehensible, and he tried to fix them in his
mind. His father was angry with someone, menacing
someone. In his mind's eye, Abai envisaged a body of
formidably armed men charging across the steppes to meet
the enemy. When the harangue grew meaningless, he just
stared at Kunanbai's face, his thoughts far away.

From childhood Abai had had a habit of staring intently,
unwaveringly, at the faces of story-tellers, bards and all
whose speech attracted his attention. For him the faces of
men had always had a special appeal. But the most
interesting of all were the wrinkled faces of the old men.
The folds of their withered cheeks and foreheads, their
faded eyes and the waves of their flowing beards conjured
up pictures of groves of sparse and straggling saplings or
soft grass rippling over the black earth beneath.... At times
he would find a curious likeness in them to wild beasts or
gentle domestic animals. A whole universe would come alive
for him in the movements and outlines of human features.

His father's head was long and shaped like the egg of a
goose, and his face seemed all the longer because of his thin
wedge of a beard. To Abai it was like a plain on which were
two hills overgrown with the thickets of his eyebrows.
Kunanbai's one eye stood watchfully on guard by the left
hill, a vigilant and tireless sentry. That eye seemed never to
hide behind its lid; large and slightly protuberant, its glance
was sharp and avid, as though devouring everything
around. And it hardly ever blinked.

Draped over Kunanbai's shoulders was a coat made from
the soft, fluffy hide of a young camel. He was speaking
weightily, with conviction, and his single eye never strayed
from Suyundik, who sat opposite.

Suyundik now and then stole a furtive glance at the
speaker, without daring to look him in the eye. His beard
was a dull silver grey, and his features seemed quite dull and
commonplace to Abai. There was nothing behind them.

At first glance Bozhei too seemed quite an ordinary sort
of a man, though with his pale olive skin, black beard and
prominent nose he was certainly the most handsome among
the men present. He had fewer wrinkles too. Bozhei never
once stirred or raised his eyes throughout Kunanbai's long
speech. It was difficult to say whether he was dozing or sunk
in reflection. His lids veiled whatever passed in his mind.

Only Baisal, who sat in a prominent place, was looking directly at Kunanbai as he spoke. Baisal was a tall, impressive-looking man with ruddy cheeks. His large blue eyes were coldly expressive of his reticence, his ability to keep a secret in the very depths of his soul.

The others sat sullenly silent. Comprehension, an understanding of what Kunanbai desired, shone only in the eyes of Karatai and Maibasar.

The circle of aksakals was terminated on the one side by Abai, sitting next to his father, and on the other by the young djiguit* Zhirenshe.

This young man, a relative of Baisal's, hailing from the clan of Kotibak, was not merely a djiguit in the service of Baisal, but a young man of great promise; he was subtle and highly observant. In addition, he was an excellent story-teller and jester. Abai still remembered some of his jokes, and he was the only man there with whom the boy would have liked to have a heart-to-heart talk.

But to all appearances—and maybe sincerely—Zhirenshe was entirely engrossed in what Kunanbai was saying, and seemed to be totally oblivious of Abai and everyone else.

When Zhirenshe stirred at last and frowned, Abai noticed that his father's speech was coming to a close.

"If the infamy of that scoundrel Kodar put me in an awkward position before the other clans, it is a disgrace to our tribe and to all who are gathered here! To all of you!" He turned his piercing eye from Suyundik to Baisal and then fixed it on Bozhei.

Neither Bozhei nor Baisal moved, but there was an agitated stir among the others. The weight of Kunanbai's words lay upon the shoulders of every man present.

"Honour means more than death! An unprecedented crime demands an unprecedented punishment," thundered Kunanbai.

In the flinty tone of his voice rang out an irrevocable verdict. Everyone knew that nothing could make Kunanbai relent once he had reached a decision.

There were but two things for the men to do: to wrangle, show signs of rebellion and risk an open quarrel, or, as Baisal and Bozhei had so often done, to hide their disagreement and let Kunanbai act alone: let him bear all the responsibility and take all the consequences!

*Djiguit—an expert horse-rider.—*Ed.*

When their personal interests were not involved they were usually sparing of words, expressing themselves vaguely and ambiguously. But this time Kunanbai had not left them a single loophole, and each felt himself trapped. The silence grew oppressive.

Abai did not know Kodar, but before him arose the image of Kodar from the song *Kozy-Korpesh and Bayan-Slu.** The fact that his father had called him a scoundrel, too, fitted the Kodar of the song which the akyn** Baikokshe had sung to his mothers in that very tent the year before.

For a moment Abai thought that Kodar was the nickname of someone who resembled the hero of that song.

Karatai was the first to break the silence, speaking smoothly and deliberately.

"That is truly monstrous! And God forbid that such things should happen to our sons or daughters! If Kodar has committed this crime his place is among the infidels," he began.

Then cautiously and evasively, with a question here and a hint there, he expressed his doubts: what they were saying about Kodar was perhaps not true, after all?

Among those present Suyundik alone was a kinsman of Kodar. That was why Kunanbai had kept his eyes on him throughout his speech. If he could convince Suyundik of Kodar's heinous crime, the man would be condemned by his own kin and the entire consequences would rest fully upon Suyundik and his tribe.

But Suyundik was by no means convinced of Kodar's guilt. Karatai's stratagem had showed him the way, and he eagerly caught at the words "... was perhaps not true, after all?"

"If his guilt can be proved," he said, "then let him die now! May his heart be pierced! But who can vouch for the truth of this?"

Kunanbai stiffened. Leaning forward heavily, he said:

"Ah, Suyundik, Albasty*** truly lies in wait for those who are weak! A weak-willed, hesitating leader will bring evil upon himself. You would like us to pledge our souls for Kodar, to swear to his honesty and innocence? You would like us to acquit him, and in the next world take his guilt upon ourselves? No—I have no souls to spare!" And suddenly he shouted at the stupefied Suyundik, "And you,

---

* In this epic poem Kodar perpetrated cruel and treacherous crimes to win the beautiful Bayan-Slu.— *Ed.*

** Akyn—a bard.— *Ed.*

*** Albasty—an evil spirit.— *Ed.*

can you vouch for Kodar? Will you take your oath on him?
Will you pledge your soul?"

This challenge broke down Suyundik's resistance.

"I have no souls to spare either! I only said that we had to
make sure. And I did not come here to sell my soul," he
added sullenly.

It was clear to all that Suyundik was beating a retreat, and
Kunanbai was quick to take advantage of this.

"If you do not believe us," he said, "you should at least
believe the people who are everywhere proclaiming the
infamy of Kodar! Ours are not the only people who say so.
Strangers threw it up at us yesterday at the counsel! They
also know about it. Try and convince them that they are
wrong! Try and shut their mouths! Have you the strength to
do this? Then go and do it: vindicate him, or condemn him!
But do not sit there hemming and hawing!"

Suyundik could find no answer. After a brief silence
Baisal spoke up. Cool and unperturbed as ever, he glanced
at Kunanbai.

"If we find that Kodar is guilty, what shall his punishment
be?" he asked without emotion.

Kunanbai replied:

"So monstrous a crime has never been known among the
Kazakhs. Nor do we know the punishment it deserves. That
will be determined by the Sharia.* Let the law take its
course."

Kunanbai had been speaking in an exasperated, bitter
voice, but now he altered his tone—he too seemed to be
oppressed.

All avenues of argument were blocked, and everyone felt
he had been brought to a halt, like a horse come suddenly
upon a blank wall. Again there was silence.

Bozhei thought to himself: surely the Sharia knew right
from wrong. They could not be going to pounce upon a
man just like that. He dared not speak his thoughts,
however. Kunanbai would have lashed him with a scathing
reply. Bozhei preferred to say nothing.

Karatai, though, was too impatient to remain quiet.

"And what does the Sharia say?"

Kunanbai turned to Zhumabai, who was sitting some
distance away, as though he had just discovered his
presence.

* Sharia—statute book of the religious and secular duties of the
Moslems.—*Ed.*

"I sent Zhumabai to the town to learn the verdict from the Khazret Akhmet-Riza. The penalty is hanging by the neck," he said.

"Hanging?" Karatai was horrified.

Bozhei turned a questioning gaze upon Kunanbai and looked at him steadily. Kunanbai's face was as if carved from stone.

"Is there no other solution? He may be a mad dog, but he is a kinsman of ours," said Bozhei.

Again Kunanbai's voice thundered.

"May all feelings depart from him who feels for Kodar! Who are we to quarrel with the Sharia? If it were not a question of Kodar, but of the happiness of my whole life, I still would not flinch or waver!"

They knew that there was no roping in this wild horse of the steppes.

"If you are certain, then do as you think best," faltered Bozhei.

Baisal did not say a word.

Suyundik took the path indicated by Bozhei:

"It is you who rule over the people, and this evil-doer too is in your hands," he said. "The culprit and his victim alike rely on your wisdom. We demand but one thing: whatever penalty you decide, first establish the truth. As for the rest, let it be as you will."

The other elders echoed Suyundik's words.

"Establish the truth and then do as you will!"

Their acquiescence, however, was only a pretense. An undeclared struggle smouldered on throughout the evening. There were insinuations and evasions, but no one dared risk an open conflict with Kunanbai. Bozhei sensed that this Kodar affair was some manoeuvre on Kunanbai's part and that there was more to it than met the eye. Where would it lead? But whatever the outcome, Kunanbai alone would have to answer for the consequences: no one had sided with him. He probably understood very clearly that the others had left themselves a free hand to continue the struggle.

But while the aul elders secretly hoped to keep clear of the matter, Kunanbai had one or two things left to say: his stratagem had been thought out to the minutest detail.

In the hands of the six elders lay the fate of the thousands of families of the Tobikty tribe, the whole web of tribal and family affairs with its tangle of inter-relations, intrigues and plots. Up their sleeves they had innumerable combinations, surprise moves, a finely woven net of human cunning.

On becoming Aga-Sultan, Kunanbai had risen above the rest. In his hands lay the power. He was linked with the outer world, with the highest authorities, who respected him and valued his opinion. Moreover, he was acquisitive, a man of wealth. He was never at a loss for words, and cut an impressive figure. He never gave up until he had got what he wanted, and adapting himself skilfully to the circumstances, he imposed his will on all who surrounded him.

But if the Tobikty tribe was the source of Kunanbai's strength, it was also the source of his weakness. As an old Kazakh saying has it: "Wings for soaring, and a tail for descending." These elders were both "wings" and "tail" for Kunanbai.

During the past year he had felt their confidence in him waning, until there was an invisible barrier of distrust separating them from him. Kunanbai was acutely aware of this, but no one as yet ventured to risk an open break with him; they all gave in to him. This was important, for strong and vested with authority though he was, he had yet to reckon with another power, the judgement of the tribe. In the eyes of the tribe the elders were no less responsible for the cruel sentence they had passed than he. If Kunanbai were called to account for this, the others would have to answer as well. They would have to prove that the sentence was just—no matter what they thought about it now. And so Kunanbai pretended to suspect nothing.

Though the Tobikty were made up of many clans and families, all the power lay in the hands of the five or six of them whose aksakals were gathered in Kunanbai's tent. They set the tribal course of action, they laid down the law. They were the chieftains of the Tobikty.

One of these, Bozhei, who was sitting on Kunanbai's right, came from the influential clan of Zhigitek, renowned for its crop of dare-devils, fond of raiding, cattle stealing and all kinds of risky ventures. A boisterous, unruly lot, those Zhigitek.

Baisal was the elder of the Kotibak clan. One of the largest and most powerful in the region, it was often compared to a herd of wild horses. The Kotibak were herdsmen, and year by year seized more and more land. Conscious of their strength, they would stop at no crime.

Suyundik hailed from the Bokenshi, the smallest and poorest of the clans. Through its maternal lineage it was related to the small clan of the Borsak. Kodar, the object of Kunanbai's wrath, belonged to this group.

Kunanbai himself came from the Irgizbai clan, which though less numerous than the Zhigitek and Kotibak, was immeasurably richer. From generation to generation the Irgizbai had maintained their influence and leading position among the Tobikty.

Kunanbai was more closely related to Baisal than to Bozhei and Suyundik, and he had always depended on the Kotibak for men and general support. That is why he sought to uphold his influence among this big tribe.

Karatai stood somewhat apart from the others. He was the elder of the ancient tribe of Kokshe, which was remotely related to all the others. And though this group was by no means large, its capable and resourceful leader cunningly availed himself of his kinship with the other tribes. He was always well informed and took part in all the vital decisions of the tribal council.

Everything said or resolved upon by the elders would unquestioningly be accepted by all the Tobikty, old and young alike.

Maibasar, Kunanbai's brother, who now sat at his side, had withdrawn from his friends and even from Kunanbai's nearest relations when he was appointed head of the volost. Though meek as a lamb in the presence of Kunanbai, he was in fact a man of incredible cruelty. He was the leader of those of the Irgizbai who were particularly interested in maintaining Kunanbai's high position and authority.

It was over Maibasar that Bozhei had first fallen out with Kunanbai. Two months before, at the request of the people, who were driven to the extreme by Maibasar's brutality, Bozhei had approached Kunanbai with the demand that his brother be removed from office. Kunanbai had refused. He knew of the atrocities perpetrated by Maibasar, but needed the presence of a man who could serve as a reflection of his own invincible strength and unbending severity. When Maibasar's savage rule could no longer be endured, the people would be compelled to come to him, Kunanbai, for protection. Maibasar, therefore, would serve as a constant reminder that the authority wielded by Kunanbai was no trifling matter.

To turn the conversation from Kodar, Kunanbai asked the old men about their cattle and pastures and told them when to start moving and where to go. It was agreed again to camp that year on the Chinghis Range. True, the pastures on the other side of the range belonged to the Kerei tribe, but the auls could be set up in their immediate vicinity, and then move gradually along the river-banks, in the secret hope of eventually seizing the Kerei's pasture-land.

The tension was somewhat eased, and everyone now spoke freely, without evasions. Zhirenshe winked at Abai and nodded towards the door.

Abai still did not know who Kodar was or what he had done. The word "hanging" had made him shudder and he had looked at Kunanbai with horror at the realisation that his father was quite capable of insisting on such a cruel penalty. The boy had never heard of such a thing happening here. "All that talk about hanging is just a threat," he thought. "Such a thing cannot happen here."

Only now did he guess why Zhumabai had gone to town. He was dumbfounded! They had been together for so many days and the old man had not said a word about it. A messenger of death, with the dread words of the Sharia locked in his heart, he had ridden at his side, raced over the steppe with him, joked and made fun with him! And now Zhumabai sat silent, as though nothing here concerned him at all! Abai stared at Zhumabai and wondered at the strangeness of grown-ups. "If I were grown-up myself," he thought, "I would understand them better. I would know their intentions."

Abai slipped out of the tent to find Zhirenshe, and came upon him hobbling his horse before turning the animal out to graze. In the dim light of the yurta door Zhirenshe saw the boy and quietly called to him:

"Abai, come over here!"

"Oh, Zhirenshe, who is Kodar, the man they were speaking of? And what has he done?"

"Kodar? He's a poor man of the Borsak clan."

"And where is he now?"

"He lives on the Chinghis, at the foot of the Bokenshi Pass."

"And what has he done?"

"They say that when his only son died this year, he took up with his daughter-in-law."

"Took up? What do you mean?"

"Oh, he just copulated with her."

"I don't understand!"

"What a fool you are! Don't you know what I mean? Well, like the camels—the male and the female.... Do you understand now?" And obscene gesture completed the explanation.

Zhirenshe had been bored with the aksakals and was glad
to be out in the fresh spring air. He would have liked to play
with the boy, but Abai was in no mood for games; his face
remained very earnest, for Zhirenshe's words had disturbed
him deeply.

"Is that *really* true?"

"Well, no one knows for sure. But there have been
rumours. That's why Suyundik insists on verifying the truth
of it," replied Zhirenshe.

"Then perhaps it's not true after all?"

"There are many who think so. You see, when
Kuneken* attended the gathering of the Siban tribe,
Soltabai taunted him with it in front of everybody. It
happened like this: Kuneken told him they must drop the
habit of nasibai.**. The man flared up and answered:
'Nasibai is no great sin, and you would do better to curb that
hairy witch who's built a nest of evil on your Chinghis
slopes!' Kuneken was hit hard. As you've seen, he's not
himself even now—as black as a thunder-cloud."

Abai visualised his father, glowering and terrible as he
was when he had pronounced the word "hanging". For a
moment the boy stood frowning. Then with a heavy sigh he
turned sharply and went off to the tent of his mother.
Zhirenshe called him back—he had something more to
say—but the boy walked on and soon disappeared in the
darkness.

3

Kodar was slowly eating the gruel of millet and sheep
cheese his daughter-in-law had warmed up for him.

"Kamka, my dear, is it not Friday today?" he asked.

"Yes, it is Friday, and I must go to the grave and say a
prayer." Sighing bitterly, she added: "I dreamed of him last
night—it was just as though he were alive."

"Oh, merciful God, merciful God," Kodar groaned, and
it seemed that the grief filling his powerful chest gushed
into the open in that one great sigh. Could empty visions
soothe the heart? He too had dreamed of Kutzhan, his only
son. But where was the solace? Kamka seemed to be
comforted by such dreams. Well, let her talk about it. Let
her young heart ease itself this way. He was ready to listen to
her.

*Kuneken—a respectful form of addressing Kunanbai.— *Ed.*
**Nasibai—chewing tobacco.— *Ed.*

"I saw him as he was in life, riding up to our yurta. He dismounted, cheerful and bright as always, came in and said, 'You and father are weeping too much. I often hear you moaning. Do you think I'm really dead? You see for yourself I've come back. Enough, Kamka! Don't weep any more. Cheer up!' That's what he said, and I was so happy!"

The old man and the young woman sat silent, their cheeks wet with tears.

All was quiet around except for a strange howling sound which Kamka had heard several mornings running.

Lifting her pale face, she listened. The rims of her eyes were red, and a blue vein throbbed on her temple.

"It's only the wind on the mountain-side," he explained.

"Why is it moaning that way?"

"It's the roof on that old shed. The rushes have grown loose, and the accursed things sing in the wind," he said to reassure her.

Together they went out.

Their tent, wretchedly dark and patched all over, huddled against a small shed. There was no sign of life in the neighbourhood—not one hut or yurta. The neighbouring auls had long since moved to their summer quarters.

When he was alive and well, Kutzhan had often said: "We don't want to be the zhataks!* Let's move with the rest!" He had always managed to find the two or three camels needed to move his family with the others. They had hardly known what trouble was in those days. There had been no need to worry about pastures or how to make ends meet. "It is good to travel with the aul," Kodar would say. "We shall have plenty of milk and perhaps even borrow a cow for the summer." And they had moved on, nomads like the rest.

But this summer neither Kamka nor the old man had the heart to leave Kutzhan's grave untended, and mourned there all night.

Their herd was small, and even if their animals had grazed day and night, they could scarcely have depleted a hundredth part of the pastures on the slopes of the Chinghis. In the winter, after the death of his son, Kodar had invited an old kinsman to stay with him—poor old Zhampeis, a single man who had neither family nor shelter, and earned his livelihood by labouring for others. "Two halves make a whole! Upon whom should we depend if not

---

* Zhataks—the poorest neighbours who remained behind to look after the property.— *Ed.*

on ourselves? Let us live by helping one another," Kodar
urged him when Zhampeis came to say a prayer over
Kutzhan's grave. And so the homeless old man had come to
stay with them.

Now there was no need to worry about the small herd,
and at home too there was little to do. The two spent all
their days at the grave—the old man bent with age and
trouble and the young woman crushed with grief. Today,
too, they moved quietly towards the last resting place of
Kutzhan.

It was a bright day in May, one that seemed especially
kind and friendly. The steppeland was flooded with golden
sunlight. Only a few strands of white floated in the blue of
the sky. The rolling hills were already covered with green,
and the young grass was thick enough to form the softest of
carpets sprinkled with snowdrops, tulips, marigolds, wild
irises and poppies—a myriad of reds, yellows and blues just
as though a swarm of butterflies were flitting over it. Chill as
ever, the morning breeze from the mountain pass tempered
the heat and refreshed everything it touched.

But all these flashes of life, the turbulent joy of nature's
rebirth, passed unnoticed by the stricken pair, who had eyes
for only one thing—the fresh grave with its mound of
stones on the hillock ahead. It was this alone that drew them
irresistibly. The flowers and the saplings only reminded
them of the spring, when Kutzhan had been alive. And a
fresh wave of anguish swept over them.

Kodar, at sixty, was a greying man of powerful build.
Other than his irreconcilable loss nothing in the world could
have broken him; life pulsated too strongly within him. He
had been a giant of strength in his youth. In those days no
one could vie with him in skill and daring. All his life he had
vigilantly defended the honour of his name from anything
that might sully it. He had never envied those who were
greedy for power or drunk with vainglory.

Always keeping to himself, he had been satisfied with the
little he possessed and had led a quiet and secluded life in
the midst of his family. He had never cared to visit the auls
of strangers or to take part in gossiping and backbiting, and
was scarcely known even to the members of his own aul. He
sought the company of none but his own kinsmen among
the Borsaks and Bokenshi.

Six months before, misfortune—the death of his only son
Kutzhan—had swooped down on him like a hawk and tore
at his heart to this day.

What could he hope for now? Who was there to comfort him? He knew that fate was unrelenting, and that brooding was of no avail, and he must drive away his melancholy thoughts.

His daughter-in-law Kamka was wilting before his eyes, bereft of will, petrified by grief. What was in store for her? His heart was afraid to answer that question. When he thought that she too might leave him and become a stranger, he felt as if he were reliving the terrible hours of Kutzhan's death. It would be a second bereavement. Had he not been a father to them both?

Kamka and Kutzhan had loved each other and lived so well together! A poor orphan of the distant tribe of Siban, she had come to love her new home. Kutzhan had met her while visiting his mother's relatives and had taken her away the very night he first saw her. Kodar was no less attached to her than to his son. He was a father to both.

A few days before, Zhampeis had told him of some dirty gossip he had heard from the other shepherds in the mountains. Kodar understood little of it, but that little was enough to enrage him and he bade his kinsman hold his tongue. Was it idleness that made those smug and sorrowless people invent such tales? They must be out of their minds. "Why does Kodar keep to his home, like a beast to its lair?" they asked. "Why doesn't he ever show himself?" To this others would add with a sneer, "And why does his daughter-in-law stay at home all the time? What is she thinking of?"

These insinuations had weighed heavily upon Kodar. He supposed his kinsmen were anxious to find a husband for her with no bride money to be paid—in other words, they wanted to force an heir upon him who would seize possession of his property and cattle. To think that such treacherous schemes were being hatched by those who called themselves his kinsmen and had pretended to commiserate with him! Estranging himself from everybody, Kodar refused to see anyone. If they would only leave her alone for at least a year! He did not want to think any further ahead. But the evil breath of gossip had penetrated his privacy. It was of little avail that Kodar's poor neighbours, who knew the true state of affairs, argued with the slandermongers in the old man's defence. Someone was diligently weaving a web of lies, so that the talk, far from subsiding, attained such proportions that it enveloped Kodar like poisonous smoke.

Troubles never come singly. Three days before, Suyundik had deliberately sent the chatterer Bekten to him. The latter had called Kodar outside and after going round and round and beating about the bush had at last blurted out:

"Try stopping up all those mouths! Good people sympathise with you, they have tried to put an end to the slander, but it's no use." Here he brought in Suyundik's name and, as though in passing, heaped him with praise. Then after tormenting Kodar with various hints and insinuations, he baldly declared, "They're saying terrible things about you and your daughter-in-law!"

Kodar started.

"Mind your tongue!"

"Well, Kunanbai believes this gossip and is preparing a terrible punishment for you," Bekten continued, unperturbed. "But can Suyundik leave a kinsman in the lurch? He has sent me here on purpose: 'Let Kodar hide somewhere, as far away as possible, until the storm blows over!'"

"Get out of here! Out of my sight! What do I care for Kunanbai's punishment when God himself has not spared me? Get out, you hear me?" Kodar was beside himself with rage.

The insult rankled, and Kodar felt his blood rise when he thought of it. But he would not have dreamt of speaking to Kamka about it, although his fatherly heart was entirely innocent. To him Kamka was as his own beloved daughter. Day by day they had shared their common burden, their grief, their sighs and their thoughts. So close had they gradually become that it seemed at times as if both were old folk who had come through life side by side. They understood each other well, could speak about anything quite frankly and openly. Nevertheless Kodar could not bring himself to tell his daughter-in-law of that monstrous slander—he felt physically incapable of uttering the words.

Slowly they approached the lonely grave. Kodar knew none of the set prayers, nor had Kamka ever learned them. Here they were wont to make up their own, silent prayers, sharing their woes with Kutzhan and gently rebuking him for leaving them.

Many were the times they had sunk to their knees and, clinging to one another, had looked at the grave through their tears. They knew every pebble in the mound. If the wind laid a few withered blades of grass among the stones, they at once cleared them away; if stones or earth slipped from their accustomed places, they heaped them up afresh.

Today too they stayed for a long time by the grave.

Suddenly there was a clatter of hoofs behind them, and some riders approached them, neither Kodar nor Kamka turning to see who they were.

There were five of them: Kamisbai, the messenger of Maibasar, Zhetpis, a distant relation of Kodar, and three djiguits of Kodar's clan. Dismounting, Kamisbai muttered:

"See what he is doing, the hypocrite!"

They had not expected to find Kodar and Kamka at the grave. Other men would have been moved at the sight of these two mourning their dead, and Kamisbai's companions at first hesitated to dismount. But their leader was cunning and cruel: if he had to cut off a hair he would sever the whole head. Maibasar himself was no match for him in cruelty.

"Dismount!" he commanded.

Realising at last that these men had not come here by chance, Kodar turned and quietly asked:

"What do you want, good people?"

"Your presence is required by the chief of the volost!" Kamisbai said nastily. "All the elders have gathered in Karashoky, all the noblest of the aksakals. They are waiting for you!"

"Who are these elders, and who is the chief?"

"The chief is Maibasar and his superior is Kunanbai. You and your daughter-in-law are to answer before them. Get up and come with us!"

"Have you gone out of your mind? What have I to do with you?"

"What's that you say? What have you to do with us? The chief calls you, that's what!"

"May you be damned with your threats!" Kamka sprang up, quivering with anger.

"Be damned yourself, you hairy witch! Come at once!" roared Kamisbai menacing them with his whip. Turning to the djiguits, he commanded, "Seize them and set them on the horses!"

The djiguits flung themselves upon Kodar.

"Oh, God, what more do you want from me?" Kodar cried desperately and struck out at the two nearest djiguits. One of them fell to the ground, but the three others hurled themselves on the old man. Twisting his arms behind him, they tied him securely. Kamka was simply dragged from the grave and lifted on to the horse of Kamisbai, who sat behind her.

Zhetpis sat behind Kodar. The others quickly mounted and the whole party set off at a gallop towards the east, to Karashoky. "The sword has been drawn and the bullet has been fired. Why trouble to talk to these beasts?" thought Kodar. "I'll speak to the chieftain himself." And all the way he said not a word, not even to Zhetpis, his kinsman.

Yet it was Zhetpis and his crafty brother Zheksen who were the cause of this fresh calamity which had befallen Kodar and Kamka.

Of all Kodar's relations these two were the wealthiest, and in the spring, after the death of Kutzhan, people had begun to rebuke Zheksen: Kodar was a near relative, they said. He was poor, he had lost his son, and was utterly alone, but Zheksen was doing nothing to help him. He would not even lend him the draught animals necessary for migration, and had left Kodar behind at the winter quarters. So frequent became these reproaches that Zheksen had begun to seek a justification for his callousness.

"My heart has always been revolted to evil," he said. "It is not that I do not want to help him, but that I am repelled by his infamy." This he had declared at a crowded gathering of the Bokenshi and Borsak clans; and this it was that had started the talk.

Very soon Suyundik had demanded to know what Zheksen's hints implied.

"It appears that he has taken up with his daughter-in-law," said Zheksen. "What do you want me to do? If I take him into my home you yourself will be the first to spit upon me!" And to give credence to his words, he related what Kodar had said in the spring at Kutzhan's funeral, on the seventh day after his death.

Beside himself with grief Kodar had then exclaimed, "No one is left to me! I am alone! God has seen fit to punish me. Very well then! I would rather die a giaour than bow to his authority. If God has chosen me as a victim, I shall try to pay him back!"

"Now what can he do to the Almighty?" and Zheksen had finally insinuated that Kodar had revenged himself on God by living with his daughter-in-law.

In reality, however, Zheksen was concerned with quite another aspect of the matter. Kodar had a small plot of land in the vicinity of Zheksen's winter quarters. "It's all over with Kodar anyway," he thought. "If I can induce the tribe to drive him away, the land will be mine." This was a tempting morsel.

Like flames over dry grass the gossip spread until it reached Kunanbai, and then came the thunderbolt. When the news reached Suyundik, the latter realised that things had gone too far. Once more he visited Zheksen and demanded proof. Not satisfied with this alone, he had questioned the people living near Kodar. These simple-hearted people to whom all intrigue was foreign had not the slightest doubt of his innocence. They could only relate how stricken the old man had been by the loss of his son.

But Zheksen and Zhetpis had insisted that this was not the truth.

"He's only pretending," they said. "When night falls there's something different on his mind."

Once again Suyundik failed to establish the truth. But he was afraid that if the rumours were confirmed, Kunanbai would avail himself of this pretext to descend on the Bokenshi and Borsak, and when talking with the elders of the other clans he stubbornly insisted, "It is slander!" He had intended to defend Kodar at Kunanbai's council too, but there the latter had cut him short.

After the council in Kunanbai's yurta Suyundik had tried to quieten his conscience by urging himself to believe that Kodar was guilty.

Although no one knew anything for certain, Kodar was caught up in a terrible calamity.

4

Karashoky, one of the summits of the Chinghis Range, rose not far from Kodar's winter quarters. Down its luxuriantly wooded slopes rushed a mountain torrent, whose banks were lined with willows, aspen and twisted mountain birch, magnificent in their spring array. There was an abundance of lush pastures, and though these had been held unchallenged by the Bokenshi and Borsak for as many years as anyone could remember, many of the Irgizbai families had long ago fastened a jealous eye on Karashoky, where the aul of Zheksen stood.

The aul consisted of four yurtas shielded from the winds by a great rock overhanging the river. This was the gathering place to which Kodar and Kamka were being taken.

"There they come! There comes Kodar!" many voices
were raised.

All those who had been sitting in Zheksen's tent now
emerged, with Kunanbai at their head. The crowd in the
field beyond the aul rapidly grew, though the djiguits were
still some distance off.

In the centre of the field lay a huge black camel tethered
to a post. Between his humps was a great mass of felt,
topped by a saddle, and a long rope was coiled round the
whole thing.

Kamka, who had not said a word all the way, shuddered at
the sight of the crowd and turned to Kamisbai:

"Listen, you are a human being. What have we done?
What do you intend to do with us? Kill us, if you like, but tell
us first why...."

Kamisbai too had been silent, but now he spoke, and his
words oozed venom:

"Did you not whore with Kodar, your father-in-law? So
today you will be put to death!"

Kamka moaned and began to slip from the horse, almost
dragging Kamisbai from the saddle. Clutching her firmly,
he quickly rode towards the crowd, where Kodar was
already being lifted down from the horse. In the centre of
the field, Kamisbai dismounted, still supporting Kamka with
one hand. He then lifted her down, but she sank limply to
the earth, in a dead faint.

Kodar came face to face with a crowd of a hundred or so:
Kunanbai, Bozhei, Karatai, Suyundik, Maibasar and other
elders of the Tobikty. Behind them stood the aksakals and
other prominent men. None were to be seen who were
poorly or even modestly attired. These were all atkaminers,* the most influential men from the most important
clans.

Kodar, his arms bound, looked at them. He was seething
with hatred, and as he recognised Kunanbai, whose single
eye was balefully fixed upon him, he shook all over. Jerking
forward in a rush of hatred, he shouted:

"Hey, Kunanbai! You think I have not been punished
enough by the Almighty? What fresh vileness have you
prepared for me?"

He was shouted down by Maibasar and the other elders.

"Hold your tongue!"

* Atkaminer—the elder tribal chieftain.— *Ed.*

"Shut your mouth!" There were outraged cries from all sides. Never had anyone been known to address Kunanbai with such effrontery.

Kodar waited for the noise to subside.

"Do you want to avenge yourself on fate for the loss of your eye by bringing shame on me?" he raged.

"Shut his mouth!" roared Kunanbai.

Maibasar ran towards the old man, brandishing his whip:

"You damned grey cur!"

Kodar's voice rose still louder:

"If I'm a grey cur, you're bloodthirsty dogs! Hurling yourselves on people, tearing them to pieces."

With the help of four djiguits, Kamisbai dragged Kodar away, but the old man went on shouting with all the power he could muster:

"Am I guilty or innocent—you don't want to know, you murderers!"

But the noose was already around his neck, and the four djiguits dragged him to the side of the black camel, thrusting a bag over his head. It was as much as six men could do to hold him, to keep him pinned against the camel's side. As he opened his mouth to roar a final curse he felt something stir violently behind him. The camel was rising to its feet. There was an iron grip upon the old man's throat, a grip that seemed to be crushing the very soul out of him. He felt a fearful weight, like a vast rock. The whole world seemed to fall upon him. He saw one last flickering flame of life—and then came oblivion. The silence of death hung over the crowd.

When the camel had risen, Kamka was hanged on the other side. To her death came instantly.

But spasmodic convulsions still gripped Kodar's body. Death could not quickly conquer that Herculean frame. He seemed to have increased in stature and his toes nearly reached the ground. The onlookers stood hushed and awed.

Baisal could not endure the sight, and walked away. Others tried to speak, but could only whisper. Karatai quietly remarked to Bozhei:

"How long the poor wretch is suffering. He just won't die.... Only now I see what a giant he was!"

Bozhei looked at him, his face sombre:

"Your giant has been devoured by a jackal!" He too turned aside.

"Alive!... He's still alive!" There were murmurs in the crowd.

Shudders continued to rack Kodar's body.

Kunanbai could hear the murmur swelling. The torments of the victim moved the onlookers more than the murder itself. Gesturing briefly, he commanded that the camel be forced to its knees.

When the animal had sunk down, Kamka's lifeless body remained standing for an instant and then lay prone. Kodar, still alive, tumbled in a heap. Without giving anyone time to think, Kunanbai pointed to the peak.

"Carry him to the summit, and have him thrown down from there!"

Kamisbai and four others silently flung Kodar across the back of the camel and ascended the peak from the other side, which sloped gently. The crowd, on the point of breaking up, was immediately checked by Kunanbai's fierce command: "Stay where you are! Let no one go away!" and again stood immobile.

Two riders emerged from the woods. They dismounted, tied their horses to a post at the last of the yurtas and walked towards the crowd. It was Zhirenshe and Abai.

Meantime the men carrying Kodar had appeared on the top of the cliff. At a signal from Kunanbai they swung the heavy body and let Kodar fly from the summit overhanging the meadow.

The mighty body flew through the air and struck the earth heavily, directly in front of the crowd, and those on the edge heard the sound of shattering bones.

It was at that precise moment that Zhirenshe and Abai reached the crowd. Following all eyes to the summit, they had looked up and seen the body of a man flying through the air, his billowing garments outspread like the wings of a great bird. Zhirenshe rushed forward. Abai pressed his hands over his eyes and sank to the earth. It was all over.... The unfortunate man was dead.

If only they had come in time, he could have pleaded with his father to spare Kodar. But he was too late, and he could not bear to look at these people. His one idea was to hurry to his horse and dash off somewhere. Just then the crowd came to life:

"Pick it up!"

"Do it yourself!"

"And what are you here for!"

There were shouts from all sides, now mingled in a

general hubbub, one voice rising above the other. Some reached for stones. "A fight," thought the boy.

But no one was thinking of fighting. No sooner had the corpse struck the ground than Kunanbai had given a fresh command:

"There's still life in him. To rid ourselves of this accursed one, let forty chosen men from the forty clans of the Tobikty stone his body. One man from every clan—pick up your stones!"

Kunanbai had himself stooped for a stone and, turning to Bozhei and Baisal, repeated peremptorily:

"Pick up your stones!"

The two obeyed.

"So it is commanded in the Sharia! Throw!" Kunanbai had shouted and hurled the first stone upon Kodar's chest.

That was why some stooped for stones, while others began to quarrel, urging each other to begin.

Going closer the boy saw them throwing their stones, one by one. Zhirenshe prodded Abai and whispered:

"You see that old man? That's Kodar's kinsman Zheksen! You know him? The dirty old dog!"

To Abai Zheksen looked like a real murderer, and the boy rushed towards him. But the man had already raised his arm to throw, and as he shouted, "Perish, you evil spirit!", a big stone struck Kodar.

It was only then that Abai saw Kodar's body. The skull had already been crushed.... Abai's heart bled, and fury welled within him.

"You old devil," he shrieked and struck Zheksen in the back.

Zheksen turned sharply, no doubt thinking that a stone had accidently hit him. But before him stood the son of Kunanbai.

"You mean old cur!" shouted Abai.

Zheksen was taken aback.

"What's the matter with you, boy? Am I alone to blame? If you are so troubled about it, there's your father behind you," he muttered, somewhat at a loss.

Agitation spread among the crowd.

"What's happened? What's the matter?"

But Abai had already run for his horse. As he untied the animal he heard the sounds of sobbing from the last of the yurtas.

Those were the women and children, who had been driven into that yurta before the execution. Some women shook with sobs, others sat quietly moaning. None dared to weep aloud, but none could restrain their tears.

Abai felt as though an arrow had pierced his heart. Leaping into the saddle with one bound, he galloped off into the steppes.

Zheksen had probably complained to Kunanbai, for the boy heard his father shouting angrily:

"Wait, you scoundrel! You'll catch it from me!"

But Kunanbai did no more than threaten. He could not bring himself to call him back.

Abai headed for his aul, with Zhirenshe dashing after him.

"Hey, you rebel! Wait, Abai! Wait, you donkey!" he cried, calling Abai new names as they came into his head.

And the two soon disappeared in the valley.

Having accomplished their task of killing two human beings the crowd dispersed. The elders rode off in silence.

"In the old days one could demand recompense for the murder of a kinsman," Bozhei said with a sigh, as he rode along with Suyundik and Karatai. "But try to do it now. It's better to hold one's tongue! I helped to kill him myself! From forty families we threw stones with our own hands. Try saying a word about it now!"

"The most terrible part of the Sharia's injunction was saved by Kunanbai until the very end," added Karatai. "It seems that there is plenty of room for trickery and cunning in the law! The Sharia seems to work for Kunanbai!"

Suyundik was in low spirits.

"Let us forget all that has happened! I pray God that the matter ends here," he declared.

But Bozhei was a man of experience and understood Kunanbai better than the others did.

"Ends here?" he said bitterly. "Bokenshi and Borsak, mark my words: It was not around Kodar's neck that you placed a noose today. You slipped it round your own necks with God's help!"

All three were sorely troubled. No one cared to speak again and they travelled on in silence.

5

Abai and Zhirenshe were riding back through the woods along the river-bank. An icy chill gripped Abai's heart, and all his feelings seemed numbed with horror at his father's action, at the blood on Kunanbai's hands. It was his own father who was so cruel, so heartless!

He paid no heed to Zhirenshe's shouts, but galloped on at top speed. The hound flew by his side as the two of them raced along the bank and then skirted the slopes of one of the larger ridges. The way was narrow, a path along which one could only ride in single file, and talking was difficult. But Zhirenshe at last overtook Abai and riding close behind talked incessantly. He had managed to exchange a few words with the djiguits in Zheksen's aul and wanted to share what he had heard with Abai. Shaking as though with fever, the boy heard only half his words, but understood their essence.

Two phrases were on everyone's lips. One had served as a pretext for Kodar's accusation and was cited to justify his monstrous execution. Kodar had said, "God has stricken me and I shall pay him back"—so his murderers today declared. The other was the last phrase that Kodar had flung at them before his hanging: "If I am a grey cur, you are bloodthirsty dogs!"

Abai was shaken to the core. He recalled the pitiful, stifled sobbing of the women in the yurta. Unexpectedly, even to himself, he suddenly began to weep. Zhirenshe could see this, although he rode behind.

"What's the matter with you, you scamp, you Tekebai!* What's the matter?" he asked in surprise and lashed his horse so that he could ride beside the boy.

But the latter, too, struck his horse and dashed ahead.

They had already left the ravines behind and were coming into the broad valley. Abai turned his bay towards Kolgainar and urged him on again, not wanting Zhirenshe to see his tears. The young man tried hard to overtake him, but the boy was leading by an arrow's flight, and finding himself alone in the steppes gave full vent to his tears.

He had not wept for years, but now it was as though he were melting—he could scarcely breathe for sobbing. He spurred his horse on, and the steppes rolled by like the wide rivers of spring, turbulent and swift, mighty and exhilarating. The wind lashed against his face and swept away the tears.

Never before had Abai suffered like this. What had he known of human misery? But now he was plunged into its very depths, and his whole being responded with great intensity of emotion. He was overcome with pity for those two guiltless human beings who had died so fearfully

* Tekebai—stubborn little donkey.— *Ed.*

tormented and abused. A great rage and hatred welled up in his breast.

"Father"—what a dear, proud word! There was a voice within him that spoke up persistently for his father, setting him apart from all that was cruel and steeped in crime. Yet another voice kept repeating the story of today's frightful murder. The horror of it confused his thoughts, pitted them one against the other.

He recalled the words he had been taught at the madrasah: "Human tears shall mitigate the sinner's guilt and atone for his crime." Could he believe that his own tears would serve to atone for the murderers? He rejected the idea: "This is not true!"

The murderers had claimed that they were killing to uphold the holy faith, in the letter of the law as laid down by the Imam. So there was no one to whom one could complain? So he was alone in a silent wilderness? He felt helpless, like an orphan with no place to lay his head. And his grief broke out anew, a fresh wave of pain welled up from depths unknown and heavily smote his frail childish spirit. Abai was seized with another fit of weeping, the tears streaming down his cheeks. Sobs broke from him like cries of pain. If only Zhirenshe did not hear! He kept well ahead, his horse hammering the turf.

Perhaps it was the motion of the horse or else his agitation had been stronger than he could bear, but suddenly he was overcome with violent nausea. Body and soul were racked with pain. But he would not check his pace, and clutching the mane of his horse to keep from falling, he continued the mad gallop. Zhirenshe could not overtake him.

Abai dismounted at Kolgainar and made for his mother's yurta. Ulzhan stood at the entrance and her heart shrank at the sight of him. Her son was deathly pale, his face like that of a stranger. Of course it was Abai, but how awful he looked! His horse tethered, he came up to her, and she at once saw that his eyes were red from crying.

"Abai-zhan, my darling, what has happened? What have they done to you?" She asked anxiously, wondering if his father had given him a beating.

They were alone. Abai silently embraced his mother, pressed his feverish head to her breast and stood very still. How could he have forgotten—he had his mother! He was not defenceless and alone!

He began to shake as though in a paroxysm of weeping, but there were no tears in his eyes now.

"Tell me, sun of my life, what has happened? Has your father beaten you?"

"No, no one's beaten me. I'll tell you all about it later.... Apa, make my bed, please, I want to sleep." They entered the tent, their arms about each other.

Ulzhan was patient: she would say nothing more just now. Why worry the boy? She made his bed in the right-hand side of the yurta, near the couch of Zereh, and tucked him in with her fox furcoat.

But Grandmother at once noticed that something was wrong.

"What's the matter, my sweet? Are you ill?" she asked.

"Yes, he is not well," Ulzhan hastened to answer. "Just leave him alone, let him sleep."

"Close the tunduk* to keep the sun out of his eyes," she whispered to her servant, "and let down the screen over the doorway."

Grandmother looked intently at Abai, but he turned to the wall. She clucked in dismay, and then her lips began to move in silent prayer.

Ulzhan wondered where Zhirenshe could be. The dogs began to bark and she went into the open to see. Zhirenshe stood tethering his horse before the Guest Yurta, and she called him to her.

Zhirenshe told her everything.

It was not until evening, when the flocks came back and the aul was filled with the bleating of sheep, that Abai awoke. It was late—the sheep were being milked—and quite dark. There were noises on all sides—and grizzly shapes, dim and indistinct, dancing before Abai's eyes. His head seemed to be splitting with pain, he was very hot, as though on fire, his mouth dry and lips parched. He tried hard to wet them and swallow, but could not.

His mother and grandmother sat by his bedside. Ulzhan placed her palm on his forehead.

"Apa.... Grandma.... Am I ill?" he asked.

"Yes, you're very hot. Where does it hurt?" asked Ulzhan.

As he turned over on his side he felt a sharp pain in his temples.

While he had been asleep Ulzhan had told her mother-in-law what had happened, and both concluded, "He was badly frightened—and so he's ill!" Zereh fumed at

---

* Tunduk—a rectangular cloth covering the upper aperture of the tent.— *Ed.*

Zhirenshe and all the aksakals. Furiously, she spat on the ground.

Abai guessed at once that they knew everything.

"Father!... Father!..." the thought flashed through his mind. Sighing deeply, he passed his hand over his chest and said almost in a whisper, "How cruel he is! How heartless!..."

This was the first time that he had uttered these thoughts which had been crowding into his brain in disjointed and half-conscious fragments.

Grandmother could not hear, and, as Ulzhan said nothing, she prodded her daughter-in-law with her knee. What had Abai said?

"He spoke of his father. He says he is cruel. Why didn't he have pity on them?" Ulzhan whispered to her.

Zereh sighed painfully and, gazing at the boy, went on stroking his head for a long time.

"My beloved lambkin.... He has no pity, you say? He doesn't know what pity means!"

Her old face raised, her eyes half-closed, she whispered:

"Oh, dear God, hear my prayer! Spare this darling of my soul the wrath of his father. Spare the child his cruelty and heartlessness, Almighty God." With trembling fingers she blessed her grandchild.

"Amen," whispered Ulzhan.

Abai too passed his hands over his face.

These were two mothers.... Between them lay a child who had been wounded to the heart; and in that strange twilight, when the forces of darkness range the earth seeking for their victims, these three prayed silently for peace, kindness and love.

To Abai it seemed that he was back in his cloudless childhood with its bright clarity and peace. His heart felt lighter. But the pain in his head increased and he grew more feverish.

In the tent all was still. The bleating of the lambs and sheep died down, and the steppes were unusually quiet.

6

Abai lay ill for a long time. Some said he was stricken with ushik*; others said it was sopka;* still others thought it was typhoid, but no one could say just what it was. Nor did anyone try to cure him.

* Ushik and sopka—two kinds of fever.— *Ed.*

It was only once, on the second day of his illness, that his grandmother ordered an old woman to take him out at sunset and slap him several times with the steaming lungs of a sheep that had just been slaughtered.

"Perish away, you evil spirit! Perish away and depart from my son," she cried and, turning Abai to the setting sun, continued the strange cure by sprinkling water upon him from her mouth.

Abai's knees were giving way. His head was spinning and it had been so difficult to walk out of the tent. Perhaps it was because he was dizzy that the westering skies seemed so queer. Was this a dream? In that delirious world everything was different and strange....

Two days later, the aul set off for the Chinghis. The men in charge of the move had for days been asking all the travellers if the ground had thawed well at the zhailyau site, was it dry and was there sufficient grass? The foothills of the Chinghis thawed quickly as a rule and were soon covered with thick grass. The slopes, on the other hand, warmed up slowly and the green was meagre there. The snow was too deep to melt away quickly.

The broad and well-watered zhailyau of the Tobikty lay on the other side of the Chinghis Range. No sooner had Kunanbai's aul set off from Kolgainar than the neighbouring auls too were on the move. The Tobikty advanced like an avalanche along all the trails and paths that led to the mountain passes.

Had Abai been well, he would have enjoyed these jolly days of merry-making and sport. The spring migration, so difficult a time for the grown-ups—the shepherds, the herdsmen and the "neighbours"—was for the children and adolescents a time of fun and games. In past years all the ten stages of the journey had been one great holiday for Abai.

. The auls this year had set off at the same time, and moved over the steppes together. The wolves ranging this wild region in packs constantly harried the nomads and compelled them to travel as close to one another as possible. Before the journey the wolves had run about the slopes of the mountains preying on mice and other small animals; but now, under cover of dark, they attacked the flocks, which in most cases were guarded by men on horseback from dusk till dawn. Fires were kept going around the camps and noises were made until daybreak. How different were these days fraught with hazards from the usual quiet life of the auls! By day all were on horseback and in movement, the men armed with spears, soeels and pole-axes, somewhat like a great body of armed cavalry on the march.

The journey this year was painfully difficult for Abai. He was no longer in pain, but was still far from well. The slightest attempt to move made him so dizzy that he fell helplessly to the ground. But the migration could not be put off just because a boy was ill.

Kunanbai usually came to see Ulzhan about once every three or four days. He spent most of the time with his youngest wife, the beautiful Aigiz, and often visited his eldest wife, Kunkeh. She had her own aul, and it was with this party that Kunanbai travelled. When Abai had been taken ill he had asked about him once or twice, but had then seemed to forget the boy.

Abai could not ride a horse. He could have been mounted on a camel, but this his mother would not allow. "The pack may slip off, or the camel may trip," she said. "It is too dangerous."

The nomads were not familiar with wagons or carriages, and the only one in the aul, among all the tribes of the Tobikty for that matter, was the blue carriage of Grandmother Zereh and her daughter-in-law Ulzhan, which Kunanbai had bought in Karkaralinsk when he was elected Aga-Sultan. "You will ride in this carriage during the migrations," he had told his mother.

Ulzhan also found it increasingly difficult to ride over the hills on horseback—she was growing old and stout. But now she could think only of Abai. Sacrificing comfort, she placed the boy in the carriage with his grandmother and, mounting a gentle bay mare, herself kept constantly behind.

The journey to the summer quarters took three weeks and it was only at the end of this time that Abai was able to move about and leave the tent without assistance.

His spirits too revived and he might have been expected to recover his former boyish, carefree cheerfulness. But strangely enough, the playing and gambolling of the youngsters did not interest him at all this year, and the games he had been so fond of no longer tempted him. It was as though he had lost his childhood. Was it the effect of his illness, or had the torments recently endured cast a spell over him? Was this the end of his childhood, the threshold of maturity? But he had not yet attained maturity—something had brought him to a halt midway. It was as if he had run up against a high wall and stood confused and frustrated.

This year he turned thirteen, and in appearance, too, he stood somewhere midway, neither child nor youth. He was tall, his arms and legs had grown longer. Formerly his nose had seemed slightly turned up at the end—now it was distinctly straighter. His face was earnest beyond his years, but there was much in his figure that had an unfinished look. He was tall and thin, like a plant that had sprung up in the dark: pale and weak, with a long, fragile stem.

Once his olive cheeks had always been ruddy. Now, either because of his prolonged stay in the town or his illness, his face was pallid and his black hair had become so thin that the skin shone through; it was obvious at a glance that he had been ill and had not been out in the sunshine for a long time.

His nature too had undergone a great change. He could have ridden horseback now, but felt no inclination to do so. He avoided the boys of his own age and found other friends—the best of them, his grandmother, and next his mother.

It was only that year that Abai fully realised what a wonderful story-teller his grandmother was. Her words charmed the ear and gripped the imagination.

Unable to fall asleep for pain one day during his illness, Abai had begged his grandmother to tell him a story. Old Zereh had reflected for a moment and had then begun to speak—and they were not words that she had strung together, but an endless string of pearls.

> *The ages are hidden from us in a haze,*
> *And who has their secrets divined?*

She began in a sing-song. The words fastened themselves in Abai's memory, and on the next occasion he had only to touch her knee and remind her:

> *The ages are hidden from us in a haze,*
> *And who has their secrets divined?*

This came to be his way of pleading for new stories.

Zereh knew many of them: *Edil-Zhaik, Zhupar-Koriga, Kula-Mergen* and other legends. Abai made her tell them to him from morning till evening, even during the journey.

Abai never tired of her stories and hung on her words, with an earnest, absorbed expression on his face. When she was weary and could speak no more, he would go to his mother. Ulzhan also knew many stories, but he liked it best when she recited poems. He knew that she could neither read nor write and that no one had asked her to repeat these verses for many years. And the fact that she had cherished them in her memory astonished and delighted him. For days on end she could chant the zhirs, * the aitises, ** the edifying songs, and humorous rhymes.

Abai often read verses to them from the books he had brought from town. He read the poem *Jusup and Zyuleika*, translating and interpreting the unfamiliar Persian words. This inevitably reminded them of more stories they knew, and Abai became the eager listener again.

But how dreadful were Zereh's stories of forays and plunder, of the horror of raids, of grief and bitter humiliation.

Once, at the height of their story-telling two guests arrived at the aul, travellers from afar: an old man and a young one. Abai knew the younger man very well and was delighted to see him. He was the akyn Baikokshe, who had visited them the year before at the zhailyau camp and for three days had chanted for them the song of *Kozy-Korpesh and Bayan-Slu*. The older man was a stranger to Abai, though Ulzhan knew him well.

When greetings had been exchanged and all questions about family and household affairs answered, Ulzhan turned smilingly to Abai.

"There, my son—you have plagued both Grandmother and me.... But now you have before you a real treasure-store of stories and songs. This is the akyn Barlas."

Barlas's narrow silver beard, his dignity and musical voice at once won the boy's heart. He did not look at all like the other old men who tried to keep everything they knew to themselves. Frank by nature, outspoken and talkative, he behaved from the first like a man who had spent all his life in this aul, as one of the family.

"This is what they say, my son," he would tell Abai with a gentle smile.

> *The akyn's song flows like a stream of heavenly water,*
> *His listener is chalk that thirstily absorbs it....*

"Blessed are those who can tell and hear. If Abai will not tire of hearing, Baikokshe will not tire of telling."

After they had settled in zhailyau Ulzhan often received guests from other auls, and Barlas, who belonged to the

---

* Zhir—a tale in verse, usually dealing with history.— *Ed.*
** Aitis—poetic rivalry, verses composed at poetry contests.— *Ed.*

Siban tribe nearby, had come to visit his old friends. On the way he had been joined by Baikokshe, of the Mamai tribe. The latter, a pupil of Barlas, spent several months every summer in the company of his teacher who wandered from aul to aul.

The hospitality with which they were received at once put both akyns in excellent spirits. In the evening, while the meat was being cooked, Barlas sang the song of *Koblandy-Batir*. Abai felt that he had never heard or read anything so beautiful. He was so stirred that he could not fall asleep for a long time that night.

On the following day Ulzhan urged her guests to stay a little more.

"Why hurry away? Please stay with us a few days," she pleaded.

This request was made at Abai's wish. He had believed that everything wise and instructive was to be found only in books, that knowledge and art lived in the madrasah alone. Was there anything comparable to Nizami, Navoi, and Fizuli, or the subtle lyricism of Shaikh Saadi, and Khoja Hafiz, or the epic of Firdousi? He had not known that the Kazakhs had such poets as Asan-Kaigy, Bukhar-Zhirau, Marabai, Sadak, and such gems as *Kozy-Korpesh* and *Akbala-Bazdik*.

Whether it was the familiar language of their songs and stories, or the manner in which Barlas and Baikokshe now raised their voices, now modulated them to gentle whispers and then sent them rushing wildly away, or whether it was the sounds of the dombra that fell caressingly on the ear — whatever it was, Abai was convinced that he had never heard anything better than the songs of these akyns.

> *Deep is the secret of my thought,*
> *Sad as the mist on the horizon,*
> *With misery my soul is overwrought...*
> *The silver river gleams and shines,*
> *The living water moves along,*
> *It is Barlas who sings these songs...*

"Why is Barlas so sad?" Abai asked his mother.

"There is a great spirit in him," she replied. "He will never stoop to praise that which is unworthy. He will not go from aul to aul to gather gifts. Learn from him and treasure his words."

Abai followed every word of the akyn; he was astonished
and pleased with those verses which were born then and
there, in his mother's yurta. They often bitterly condemned
the evil doings of the rulers of the land.

Abai was glad that his father was away, and he fervently
hoped that he would not return for a long time. Fortunately
he had not come to see them once while Barlas had been
there. He was making the rounds of the auls in the company
of several elders, so that Ulzhan was able to detain Barlas.
When Kunanbai was at home, the akyns and singers could
not stay long and express themselves freely.

Whom did Barlas have in mind when he composed that
song about rulers? He would never say for certain, but Abai
interpreted the verses in his own way. Life furnished him
many living examples.

The boy pleaded with the akyns himself and through his
mother, and Barlas and Baikokshe stayed with them for a
whole month. He grew very friendly with the two, slept
beside the couch of Barlas at night and in the daytime did all
he could to show his veneration. The old man was very
touched by this and one day, when they were alone, he sang:

> You're growing up, Abai, my love and joy,
> What will you be when you are big, my boy?

And gave his dombra to the boy.

"Take it, child, and with it my blessing. I speak from the
heart!"

So moved was Abai that words failed him.

That was on the eve of the akyns' departure. In the
morning when the horses of the singers were being saddled,
Abai called his mother aside.

"Apa, please give them something nice."

To this Ulzhan made no reply, but when the guests had
had their fill of kumiss she raised her head, about to speak.
The others paused and waited politely.

"When my son returned from school he fell ill and could
not get well," she said. "The songs that you brought to us
have cured him. Never were there guests more welcome
than you."

Indeed, Abai had felt well throughout their stay.

"You must visit us more often," she added.
"Grandmother and I will always be glad to see you. May you
have a happy journey! Please accept our thanks and the
modest gifts which await you outside. Think no ill of us, and
let us part friends."

Abai followed the guests into the open. Two handsome horses were led up, a sturdy dun for Barlas and a four-year-old bay for Baikokshe.

Leading the horses presented to them, the akyns started on their way shouting, "Khosh! Khosh!"*

A wave of boyish gratitude swept over Abai. Embracing the heavy figure of his mother he covered her cheeks, eyes and lips with kisses.

THE WHIRLWIND

1

The auls of Kunanbai finished the sheep shearing earlier than usual that year. In the past Kunanbai had never given the order to move from the autumn pastures to winter quarters before the first snow had fallen. But now he suddenly gave the command at the very beginning of October. None of the other elders knew of his intentions, though they were all closely related to the people of Kunanbai's aul.

They reached Kolgainar in seven stages. As they were preparing to make for their various winter quarters, they were suddenly ordered by Kunanbai not to move without his command. Accompanied by Maibasar he rode to the Chinghis Mountains. The distance was not great and the two spent most of the day surveying the district. Returning to the aul at dusk, Kunanbai headed for the yurta of his eldest wife, Kunkeh.

There were only women gathered there that day: the mothers of Kunanbai, the wives of his departed father, the wives of his uncles and the female relatives of two generations. Their auls, some twenty of them, had long since separated from the main body of the Kunanbai household and now wandered independently. They had come to pay the traditional visit and had brought various gifts usual on such occasions.

Twice a year the women of these auls brought such gifts to Kunanbai's yurta—in the spring when the auls reached the spring pastures, and in the autumn before separating for wintering. This meeting of old friends was particularly lively in the spring after their long separation during the

*Khosh — farewell.— *Ed.*

winter. The women then would visit everyone in the aul, and first of all Zereh's Great Yurta.

When the door, respectfully opened by Maibasar, revealed the imposing figure of Kunanbai, all laughter and chatter was hushed.

The men sat down. The only woman who dared to address Kunanbai was Tansholpan, the second wife of his father and second in age to Zereh.

"My son, your mothers and the other elder women here have brought their gifts of the season. We have already paid our respects to your venerable mother, and now we are preparing to go our separate ways."

In Kunanbai's hearing during the past few years Zereh had always been referred to as "venerable mother", and like the others, Tansholpan spoke of her former rival* in this vein. But Kunanbai did not answer. Tansholpan was one of the self-willed mothers of his family. It was said that in her youth she had pursued with spear in hand a group of Kazakhs who had attacked the herd belonging to her aul. Tansholpan had four sons, and younger wives with many sons often grew wilful and daring.

She resented Kunanbai's silence.

"It is not Kunkeh we have come to honour, but you; although you are young, you are our chief," she spoke again. "Tomorrow we shall separate to go to our winter quarters, where we shall stay like animals in their lairs until spring. Such is the fate of women. May the gifts I have brought bring you joy in the coming year. They are an offering for your happiness, my son!"

Kunanbai looked at her and nodded.

"You speak of separating for the winter?" he asked after a silence. "But what if we do not separate? You'll have to prepare a fresh round of presents then!"

He smiled significantly. The women at once returned his smile, though none understood his meaning. Kunkeh, tall and dark, with a thin pale face, decided to make the best of Kunanbai's jovial mood.

"But I told the servants to untie the packs and to set up yurtas for all tomorrow. Are we going to wander on? We are quite confused. No one knows if we are to stay or go." She looked at Maibasar questioningly.

"But you'll have a fresh round of presents," he said with a smile.

*The wives of one husband were called *kundes*—rivals.— Ed.

"Don't order the packs to be undone and the yurtas set up," said Kunanbai. "Tomorrow we travel on."

"Do we, my good son? To what new place will you take us?" asked Tansholpan regarding him intently.

"We shall all wander together. Tomorrow at dawn we'll set off for the Chinghis. We've already surveyed the pastures and found places for the auls. Tell this to the auls. Let them be ready," replied Kunanbai.

All the twenty auls of the Irgizbai set off at daybreak and made for the heart of the Chinghis.

All moved together and without straggling. During the wandering the auls were usually strung out like a flight of cranes or geese. But now they were bunched together like a flock of ducks menaced by a hawk. This extraordinary wandering began in an unusual manner. At the first sign of dawn Kunanbai had commanded:

"Let there be no loitering! Hurry! And I don't want to see anyone fall back on the way! We all move together and there will be no halts," he told his messengers, sending them off to the various auls.

To the left of the route there loomed a high hill. Kunanbai, accompanied by Maibasar and Kudaiberdy, his eldest son by Kunkeh, rode ahead and climbed to its summit. His bay horse appeared against the dawn sky, curiously large, long and tense. Twitching its ears, the animal seemed to be listening, and turned its head as if impatient with the too slow human stream below. On the hill, high above the people, Kunanbai looked as though he were about to address the throng.

The twenty auls had been up and about since before sunrise, packing their animals without noise and shouts. But now that they were on the move, pandemonium broke loose and all the noises of a nomad caravan filled the air: the scream of a camel whose back was hurt by the sharp thongs of a heavy pack, the whimpering of a young camel separated from its mother, the mad barking of the dogs, the shouts of many riders gathering the pack camels somewhere, the weeping of children and the scolding of mothers. The voices of the herdsmen rose over the flocks and herds on all sides.

When the auls were well underway, Kunanbai turned to Kamisbai and Kudaiberdy:

"Summon all the aul elders," he said.

The two horsemen darted off. Tall, well-knit Kudaiberdy and stocky Kamisbai flew down the slopes towards the head of the human train below. Reaching a group of men riding with the first of the auls, they paused a moment and turned back. Two riders at once left the vanguard and made for the hill where Kunanbai stood waiting.

Before Kudaiberdy could reach the last of the auls, Kunanbai sat surrounded by as many as thirty men. It was a windless autumn day and the clear sky reached over the hills, pale and unfathomable. The rim of the great morning sun had scarcely set fire to the distant ranges when riders from all the auls came streaming towards Kunanbai.

Above them towered the rocky vastness of the Chinghis. Its tall ridges were enveloped in a haze, and now a flood of sunshine suddenly lit up the shimmering array of rocks. Roused by the caravan a multitude of larks swept skyward, and the heavens resounded with their songs. A winged procession of cranes barely visible in the heights endlessly reiterated their curious farewell—"troo-troo".

Kudaiberdy and Kamisbai had made a round of all the auls and now returned to Kunanbai, accompanied by three old men. One of these was Zhakip, Kunanbai's half-brother. Returning their salem, the Irgizbai chief spurred his horse and briefly commanded, "Let's go!"

The hill shook with the thunder of hoofs as Kunanbai, in the company of the elders, moved towards the Chinghis. All along their way the nomads crowded together to let them pass, but the riders did not hurry.

Kunanbai rode in the centre, surrounded by his uncles, brothers, cousins and other relatives.

The only son of Zereh, his father's eldest wife, Kunanbai had inherited the Great Yurta, was the possessor of enormous wealth and wielded unchallenged power. In years too he was the eldest, and there were none among the descendants of his grandfather Irgizbai who dared raise a voice against him. In all the twenty auls there was not a man who would have ventured so much as to express dissatisfaction. And if Kunanbai required support, it was unstintingly given. The force of his will, the very voice of his command drove all before him. Whether it was a matter of seizing the lands of others, or of suppressing the unruly clan, each and every one of the aul elders hastened to respond to the least twitch of his eyebrow. Even in family affairs, so complex and fraught with disagreement, his name alone sufficed to silence any quarrel. The wilful rival wives who were ready to tear each other to pieces were afraid to quarrel openly and noisily. Their husbands' brothers and elder relatives hastened to check the passions of the women, both young and old. The obstreperous were quietened with blows.

The twenty auls solidly grouped around Kunanbai were like a pack of wolves from a common lair.

2

Six days later, another caravan of nomads came along the same route. These were the Bokenshi and Borsak. They too had rounded the Kzilshoky and were headed for the heart of the Chinghis.

This party, however, was advancing in a long ragged line, each aul moving separately. There were few horsemen—only the herdsmen and a few women. All the others, the children, old men and women, rode on pack camels. One might have supposed that these auls had already dispatched their herds to the winter pastures and had left themselves only such horses as they needed. Even the men were mounted on two-year-old camels or oxen. The reason for the lack of horses, however, was quite different: these two clans were poor. Only three of their auls were well-to-do: those of Suyundik, Zheksen and Sugir.

Surrounded by a score of djiguits, the elders rode silently, neither jesting nor laughing. Grey men in their old sheepskins and capes, they seemed to have merged with the fog and the autumn sky. Suyundik was gloomy. The people expected him to guide them in decisive action, but this he could not bring himself to do.

"We'll see when we get there. We'll talk to him ourselves. Let him say whether it is the custom or the law to abandon everyone and set off by himself." Thus he evaded the questions of his tribesmen.

Zheksen supported him, but the others, young and old, were discontented. Kunanbai had left the autumn pastures unusually early. Afraid that something was wrong, the other clans, too, had hurriedly sheared their sheep and set off on his trail. The Bokenshi had noticed the Aga-Sultan's lowering glances upon them all the summer. How many times he had sought a pretext to quarrel with them. Thoroughly disturbed, Suyundik had paid another visit to Bozhei, but the latter could tell him nothing.

When Suyundik had set off to follow Kunanbai, the other clans, too, had grown troubled and soon they were all on the move, both the supporters of the Irgizbai and their adversaries, including Bozhei and Tusip.

The winter quarters of the Bokenshi in the Chinghis were

not large. In the centre were Zheksen's quarters, where
Kodar had been killed in the spring. As they approached
the mountains, the nomads separated, each group heading
for its own familiar pastures.

The auls of Suyundik and Zheksen reached the river and
proceeded to move along its wooded banks. Crossing the
lower spurs of the mountains, they at last reached their
destination. There was the field at the foot of Karashoky,
and there the cliff from which Kodar had been thrown....

But what was this? They could scarcely believe their eyes.
The grass in the meadow before the cliff had been mown
and stacked. A large herd of cows and camels was grazing
on Zheksen's land. And nearby stood the yurtas of a
prosperous aul. Smoke was lazily rising from the camp-fires,
and sheep were bleating in the field.

This winter land was no longer Zheksen's, it had been
usurped by another aul.

Higher up, on the slopes, there were horses grazing,
nearly all of them brown and bay—Kunanbai's herd.

"Allah has punished us! Dear Suyundik, what shall we
do?" Zheksen wailed.

"Yes.... This is the proverbial disaster: 'Zhailyau in the
hands of the enemy, and the winter pasture in flames!'"
Suyundik growled and said nothing more.

He had known that Kunanbai was up to something, but
certainly not a step such as this.

"You can be sure that Kunanbai has laid hands not only
on Zheksen's land," said Zhetpis furiously. "You'll see that
he has taken all the Bokenshi's winter land! Better death
than such dishonour!"

Several of the young djiguits darted forward, lashing
their horses. There were shouts from the crowd:

"Our land or their blood!"

"Bokenshi! Are we bastards, or outsiders, or what?"

"This is the price of cowardice!"

"You held us back—and this is the result!"

Suyundik winced. The outcries stung him like whip
lashes. What was he to do? If these djiguits were not
restrained, they would immediately fall upon Kunanbai's
camp. And those who were shouting were not elders, but
the ignorant beggars. God knows what they might do in
their rage. And who would be to blame? Tomorrow they
would all blame Suyundik, saying that he had led them, that
he had incited them! The thought filled him with terror.

Suyundik gripped the reins of his horse and shouted:

"Wait, you djiguits! Stay!"

They drew up around him.

"If you intend to fight, then go. But you'll be fighting alone! I shall not be with you!... Go, there's the road! Do you think that you can frighten Kunanbai with your twenty soeels? If he were afraid of you he would not have done what he has! Where there are twenty of you, there'll be a hundred of them—and if there're a hundred of you, there'll be a thousand of them! Look!" He pointed to the aul.

And sure enough, riders were unhurriedly approaching from the yurtas, from the peak and the nearby hills. They were armed with soeels, which lay in readiness across the saddles of some or under the knees of others, or attached by looped ropes over their arms. There were no less than a hundred of them. They wedged their way through the herd, emerged together and rode towards Suyundik, a neat, compact group.

The Bokenshi became silent.

Now it was Sugir who supported Suyundik. He was the owner of many herds and by far the richest man of the Bokenshi.

"We are not alone," he declared, not too loudly. "We have kinsmen, and finally there are the people. We'll make them restore what is ours! We'll put the matter before the people. But let's not forget ourselves in our anger and do something we shall regret later!"

"Those who start a quarrel shall pay for the consequences with their heads," Suyundik added harshly. "Mark this well!"

Kunanbai himself could be seen among the riders. His large bay moved at an even, dignified gait, tossing its mane. As they came near, the Aga-Sultan waved aside his armed riders and, accompanied only by ten elders, approached Suyundik and his djiguits.

Kunanbai regarded them sternly. "What can you do against me?" he seemed to say by his very bearing. His head was thrown back haughtily. All the atkaminer rulers bore themselves in this manner, but in Kunanbai it seemed especially formidable. Suyundik knew that it was merely a gesture. Had he not borne himself in a similar manner to intimidate others? But now, like the others, Suyundik was abashed before the authoritative silence of the Irgizbai leader.

The Bokenshi were the first to salem. Kunanbai acknowledged their greeting, barely moving his lips. For a moment there was tense silence.

"Mirza,* what riders are those?" Suyundik asked finally (all the elders of the Tobikty addressed Kunanbai as Mirza).

"Those? We were going to brand the horses, it is time to turn them out on the winter pastures. That is why they are here," replied Kunanbai.

There was no more to be said, it seemed. Zheksen turned—the head of the caravan had already crossed the spur of the mountain and was approaching.

"Mirza, those are our auls approaching. We have come to winter, but our quarters have been occupied by others. What shall we do?" Zheksen addressed himself to Kunanbai.

"And who asked you to come here?" was the curt reply. "What conceit made you start off without asking where to go? Your auls will turn back!" The law rang in his voice.

"But it is said, 'The ruler commands the people, the people command the land!'"

"And so you suppose that the ruler must remove himself to the skies? Where is it said that the Irgizbai have no right to winter in the Chinghis?"

"But why do you have to winter in the Chinghis? Mirza, you have plenty of other good land for wintering," objected Suyundik, hoping to negotiate, but Kunanbai cut him short.

"Listen, Bokenshi!" he began as though addressing a general council and presenting his weighty decision before the people. "You are our elder brothers. You grew to manhood earlier than we, and seized the whole of the broad foothills of the Chinghis. The Irgizbai were once small in numbers and younger than you, but you did not give them a scrap of land on the whole of the Chinghis. Now you speak of 'other winter lands'. But what sort of land is it compared with the Chinghis? We are grown men at last, and how much longer shall we endure it? The Irgizbai too need convenient winter pastures. We have grown and are strong. We are not strangers, but kinsmen of yours. Are we newcomers, that you refuse to give us land to which we have as much right as you?"

Kunanbai's speech sounded like both the plea of a petitioner and the verdict of a judge.

"How much of the winter land do you intend to take from the Bokenshi?" asked Suyundik. He wondered just how great Kunanbai's demands would be.

* Mirza—master.—Ed.

"The Bokenshi will leave all the winter land in this region to us."

"And where shall we go?" cried Zhetpis, the brother of Zheksen.

There was a tumult of shouts on all sides.

"Are the Bokenshi to be driven away?"

"Shall we wander from here?"

"Is there no one to intercede for us?"

Kunanbai silenced them in an instant. Glaring at Suyundik with his single eye he loudly commanded:

"Quieten them!"

Still hoping to keep in Kunanbai's good books, Suyundik turned reproachfully to the djiguits:

"I told you not to start trouble, you loud-mouthed fools! Keep quiet!"

The shouting ceased.

"Bakenshi," spoke Kunanbai, "do you believe that if your winter land has been taken you will be left without pastures? If I take something I do not take it for nothing: you shall receive other pastures. I offer you winter land right here, in the Chinghis: Talshoky in the mountains, Karaul in the foothills. Turn about with your auls and go to those places. Such is my decision!"

At that moment riders appeared from two directions. Two of them came from the west, and of these one was the eldest son of Suyundik.

"Our winter land has been occupied by the brothers of the Mirza, by Zhakip and Zhortar. What shall we do?" he asked his father.

A djiguit of Sugir approached from the east.

"Our winter land has been occupied by the uncles of the Mirza, by Mirzatai and Urker. What shall I tell the people? We cannot unload, we don't know what to do," he said.

Groups of four and five aul elders deprived of their winter land now approached from different directions. They were bitterly angry—they seemed to have brought the indignation and curses of all their kinsmen.

The crowd of Bokenshi continued to grow. But Kunanbai sat on his horse unperturbed. Suyundik realised the hopeless position of his people. He was himself humbled, crushed, trodden underfoot by Kunanbai.

"What's to be done? What can I do? If at least we had been wronged by strangers," he began.

But Zhetpis would not let him speak.

"There's no more justice!" he cried.

The crowd again grew restless.

"There's no one to speak for us!"

"It would be better if they had driven us away altogether instead of humiliating us like this!"

Two other parties of riders appeared from behind a hill. The first, numbering about ten, consisted of the atkaminers of the Kotibak headed by the senior of them, Baisal. Approaching Kunanbai, they salemed and greeted him in a most cordial manner:

"Welcome to your new home, Mirza!"

"May Allah grant you joy in it for many years!"

"May your new home bring you good fortune!"

The second party, which was now approaching, was headed by old Kulinshak, the eldest of the Torgai people. He was accompanied by his five sons, known as "the five dare-devils", brave men and skilful with the spear. Halting before Kunanbai, the old man said:

"I hope you're well, my dear Kunanbai! Let me congratulate you on your new home!"

This opened the eyes of the Bokenshi completely: it was not the Irgizbai alone who were robbing them. Kunanbai's rascally actions were supported by all the elders of the Kotibak, the Torgai and the Topai.

And Suyundik had pinned his hopes on the Kotibaks! "Baisal is firm and straightforward. Surely he will take no part in a robbery," he had thought. When had they conspired? Perhaps they were still concealing something? Who could say! It was clear that Kunanbai had won the support of the elders of the largest clans. This sudden arrival of Baisal and Kulinshak was no accident. They had been ordered ᵥto demonstrate their unity before the Bokenshi, Kunanbai had arranged it all.

Suyundik was not the only one who thought this. Zheksen too understood.

"But by all that is holy," he exclaimed bitterly, "this was the winter land of my forefathers! It was here, at the foot of that cliff, that the blood of a son of the Bokenshi was spilt. The land is mine—it has been washed with the blood of my erazamat!"

All were startled by his words.

"It is truly said that grief can derange the mind," Suyundik angrily murmured. "What is the good of recalling such things?"

Kunanbai was somewhat put out by Zheksen's words—he had not expected Kodar to be mentioned. But now he resolved to use Zheksen's thrust to justify the seizure of the land. Ominously he fastened his eye upon Zheksen.

"What is that you're saying? You're probably feeble-minded with old age. A 'hero', you called him, an 'er'! * If he were such, then what are you, the Bokenshi? Kodar was not a hero, but a scoundrel whom the souls of the ancestors of the Bokenshi have renounced! He has been renounced by the whole of the Tobikty tribe! And for this I have distributed this land among others — to efface the last traces of that blasphemer, to wipe his memory from the minds of all! And yours is foolish talk!"

His words were like a slap, a slap in the face of all the Bokenshi. Now they understood the real purpose of Kodar's murder: it had served as a pretext to steal their winter pastures.

Even Suyundik could not contain himself.

"Oh, God," he cried, "what do I hear? Oh, wise Bozhei! How shall I forget your words! How truly you spoke when you said, 'It was not on Kodar's neck that you have placed a noose today. By God, you have placed a noose round your own necks!' Oh, Kodar, my lion who died without guilt! Brave, dear Kodar!"

He could say no more, he was choking. He fell forward, clutching at the neck of his horse.

Zheksen suddenly burst into tears.

"The shame rests with me," he sobbed. "May I be damned! I'm a dog, a miserable dog! Oh, my own, my very own Kodar!" Spurring his horse he dashed away, in the direction of the former winter home of Kodar.

His words were like a spark falling on dry grass. All caught up the funeral cry — "Oh, my own, my very own!" — and turned their horses about to follow Zheksen. Suyundik, too, joined the crowd.

Remaining with Baisal and his attendants, Kunanbai felt somewhat annoyed with himself. But nothing in his demeanour revealed that he regretted his words. Silently he watched the Bokenshi ride away, trying to think of the most plausible explanation for this unexpected flare-up.

"D'you know who's incited them?" He turned to Baisal. "Just prod them where it hurts, and out comes all that's

---

* Kunanbai deliberately distorted Zheksen's words. The latter had called Kodar "erazamat", i. e., male relative, and Kunanbai said merely "er", i. e., brave man, hero. — Ed.

hidden in their hearts! They've been incited by Bozheı! By him and no other! He'd like to lay a trap for me among the Tobikty! You're always talking about our 'unity'. Now you can see what it's worth!"

Baisal said nothing.

"But God is just," Kunanbai continued. "Come what may, I shall endure it." And as though emphasising his trust in Baisal, he concluded, "Tell Suyundik, Sugir and Zheksen that they should not incite the people. Let them set the people's minds at rest. Whatever places I may have chosen for the Bokenshi in the Chinghis, I shall see to it that the elders won't suffer. For the three of them I'll do my best. They can take my word!"

3

The Bokenshi withdrew from the Chinghis, but not to the lands indicated by Kunanbai. Instead, they set up their tents at Kzilshoky, and there they stayed.

The other clans had long gone to their separate winter places and were busy making hay, drying horse dung for fuel, cleaning out the stalls, whitewashing the houses and dug-outs, building stoves and doing other urgent jobs.

The Bokenshi had no such cares as they did not know where they would spend the winter.

Kunanbai's messenger had already passed on instructions to Suyundik: let them pick a place on Karaul; they could also have Koldenen and Shalkar for summer pastures.

Suyundik and Zheksen put their heads together: if their two auls could be the first to reach the Karaul winter land and then occupy the two rivers in the summer, they would have no cause for complaint. They resolved to act at once and, without a word to their other kinsmen, ordered their auls to gather the camels at dawn, and to dismantle and pack the yurtas. But as they were about to desert their kinsmen, another group of some twenty or thirty Bokenshi also mounted their horses.

These were the poor of the Bokenshi. They had been roused by Darkembai, a tall and strong old man who had learned from experience to divine the schemes of the elders. He led the group direct to Zheksen's aul.

"Where are you going?" he demanded. "Are you deserting the people?" he shouted. "You dare not go off alone. You must endure the hardships with the rest of us. Put your yurtas back!"

Zheksen could not find the courage to object. Assuming an injured air, he merely asked:

"Now what are you trying to do, my friends?"

"Better mount your horses," Darkembai said brusquely. "We'll ride to Suyundik and finish our talk there!"

Zheksen and Zhetpis had no alternative but to follow.

The conversation with Suyundik was also brief. Darkembai compelled him to stay.

"Tell me at least what you are hoping for?" Suyundik demanded. "The cold has set in; must we let the old people and children freeze? How long are we to stay?"

"Lead us, you two: you, Suyundik, and you, Zheksen!" Darkembai answered firmly. "Let us ride to Bozhei. We'll talk to our kinsmen. 'You too will come to grief if you desert us now!' we'll say to them. And if the Zhigitek will not help us, then we'll see!"

Bozhei's camp was reached by noon. He was wintering in the splendid Chinghis pastures inherited from his forefather Kengirbai.

When he saw the elders of the Bokenshi he at once sent for Baidaly and Tusip. In a matter such as this, he wanted to have the unanimous opinion of all the Zhigitek.

As before, Suyundik was cautious and reserved.

"They have come to you," he said to Bozhei, "because they want your advice. What is your opinion? What would you advise them to do?"

Bozhei tried to read Suyundik's thoughts.

"Cowardly as always," he thought. "Weak-willed as usual and afraid of Kunanbai." He smiled faintly.

But if Suyundik was timid, the crowd was fairly seething.

"Bozhekeh, we have grovelled before Kunanbai long enough!" Darkembai spoke hotly. "Cowards are always bitten by the dogs and pecked by the hens. We hope that you at least will not urge us to submit! Give us the sort of advice that will at last help our clan to stand on its feet, and stick up for itself!"

This manly talk appealed greatly to Baidaly, who respected firmness and daring and had himself always been one for decisive action. He was a living embodiment of the strength and gripping power of the Zhigitek.

"Oh, Suyundik," he exclaimed, "you should ask Darkembai for advice. Poor as he is, he speaks like a man!"

Before resorting to force, Bozhei decided that an appeal should be made in the name of justice, the law and custom. If possible, he would open the eyes of the people to

Kunanbai's schemes. But first the Bokenshi must be warned
of what awaited them.

"Bokenshi, you are my kinsmen," he began. "He who
wrongs you, wrongs me. My happiness, my fortunes, cannot
be divided from yours. All that Kunanbai has planned is
clear to me. I have heard that he has offered you Talshoky,
Karaul and Balpan. Do you know what all this must lead
to?"

Bozhei's gaze swept over the crowd.

"He wishes the land of the Zhigitek and the Bokenshi to
have a common border. And that usually means an end to
agreement and good-neighbourly relations. He hopes that
living side by side we, too, shall quarrel over every bush,
over every mouthful of water. He wants to sow enmity
between us, an enmity which will be passed on from
generation to generation. It shall not be! My heart remains
with you, my kinsmen. If you are forced to settle at
Talshoky and Karaul, I'll willingly share with you all I have.
That is settled. But first we must try to dispute with him.
We're related equally to you and to them. Who should
intercede if not we?" Here he looked at Tusip. "We shall
try. We'll tell him that the Zhigitek regard his action as
unjust. What is to be done afterwards, we shall see. Do you
agree?"

His decision was approved by all.

"Then, Tusip, mount your horse. Convey our opinion to
Kunanbai and return with his reply today," concluded
Bozhei.

"But tell him everything!" Baidaly added. "Speak your
heart without reserve. We've been cowards long enough!
Even if there is to be a rupture, convey everything that has
been entrusted to you!" Baidaly was angry and determined.
He wanted to encourage, to hearten Tusip.

Kunanbai was resting at Karashoky at the winter home of
his eldest wife Kunkeh. Tusip reached the aul at sunset and
the Irgizbai leader met him on a small hill nearby. They
conferred for a long time. Tusip began very cautiously with
abstract matters, spoke of the necessity for unity and
co-ordination, and at last got to the object of his visit.

"Your action is condemned not only by the Bokenshi, but
by the whole of the Zhigitek," he began, but Kunanbai
angrily cut him short.

"I can see that the Zhigitek intend to take up the cudgels
for the Bokenshi who they claim have been wronged. But
why do they forget their neighbours, the Kerei and the Uak

people, who have also been wronged? And by whom? By the Zhigitek! You have wronged all who live near. It has been said that you seize the cattle of others, that you refuse to restore the hard-earned wealth of your neighbours. Bozhei, Baidaly, and you, Tusip, have been blamed for this again and again by all who know you. First try to justify yourselves, and then speak of the Bokenshi! First put the curb on your own thieves and plunderers!"

"There are plenty of slanderers everywhere, Kunanbai!" Tusip flared up. "Have Bozhei and Tusip ever been thieves? Perhaps you'll invent something else to bring us grief? But whatever you say, our hands are clean and we are guilty of nothing!"

"And I repeat that you are guilty and dishonoured!"

"If that is so, then prove it now at this sacred hour of sunset!"*

Tusip was trembling from head to foot.

"I'll tell you this. Let Bozhei cease laying traps for me! Let him cease throwing darts from behind the backs of others! And if he does not, then let him discharge all his wooden bullets and fire all his guns—he will bear the consequences! He alone will answer!"

Kunanbai concluded peremptorily.

"Tomorrow I shall hold a gathering at your auls; and there we'll hear the complaints of the Kerei and Uak and compel you to return the cattle you have stolen. That's the first thing. And second, leave the affairs of the Bokenshi alone! Go your own way. Don't set yourselves up in judgement in such matters. I have not appointed you to do so and have no need for your judgement. Do not interfere unless you desire trouble! And if you do not obey, then I shall understand that you have deliberately meddled in order to oppose me! Now go and convey my words to Bozhei and Baidaly."

4

At noon on the following day the two messengers of Maibasar, Kamisbai and Zhumagul rode to the Zhigitek and dismounted at the aul of Urkimbai.

Six yurtas stood nearby, and as the riders approached, the dogs barked furiously until they were driven off with whips and curses. Terrified by the angry guests, the children hid

*According to Moslem beliefs, at sunset evil spirits roam the earth in search of victims.—Ed.

themselves like mice and peeped through the mats curtaining the doors.

Urkimbai was entertaining guests in his large grey yurta—Kaumen and Karasha, close relations of Bozhei. Urkimbai's dishevelled little daughter ran into the tent, and pressing her small body against her father, whispered: "Messengers, messengers!"

Even the children knew that messengers were carriers of misfortune. When the two who wore the marks of authority—leather pouches and large brass badges—entered the tent, the little girl hid behind her father.

Urkimbai's greeting was anything but friendly.

"Well, what's all the fuss?"

"Urgent matters! An urgent order!... Set up your yurtas. A gathering is to be held in your aul. The people will gather here, also petitioners from the Kerei and the Uak. There will be talks between the tribes and the thieves will be compelled to return the cattle they have stolen."

"Who says so?" snapped Kaumen.

"And who is going to decide the matter?" demanded Karasha.

"And who will answer for the thieving—the thieves, or will everything again be heaped on innocent people?" Urkimbai asked hotly.

The arrangement of a council always entailed great expense. It would be attended by many—by the petitioners, by those in authority, and by the various visitors brought by curiosity from other clans. Cattle and sheep would have to be slaughtered to feed the fat, voracious biys day and night for a whole month. This was common knowledge. And it was known too that the ruler always held such councils in auls which had incurred his displeasure.

Kamisbai did not for one moment expect that those who sat here would readily agree to receive the council. They would not dare, of course, to complain to the Aga-Sultan or Maibasar, but they would no doubt try arguing with the messengers. He and Zhumagul, however, had received strict orders from Maibasar: no excuses were to be accepted.

"Such is the will of Kunanbai and Maibasar," he said. "It is not my own idea." Defiantly he looked at Karasha. "Talk it over and make the necessary preparations! Gather all the yurtas together and set them up here! Also consider well which animals are to be slaughtered and how many of them. For a start, the Zhigitek are ordered to supply fifty sheep. From what auls are we to take them? Let us discuss it now!"

Kaumen knew it was futile to argue with the messengers. Instead, he turned to Urkimbai and Karasha:

"This affair does not concern us alone: it's a disaster for all the Zhigitek. There'll be no time to speak to Bozhei—he is far from us. But Baidaly lives near. Karasha, take your horse and ride to him. We'll await his answer."

"Good! Go to Baidaly!" Urkimbai approved.

The messengers offered no interference.

Karasha rose quickly and departed. The messengers sat sipping their tea. Urkimbai would not speak—he was too angry.

They had not long to wait. A party of riders soon approached and hurriedly dismounted. It was Karasha who returned from Baidaly. But he had not come alone. He was accompanied by ten djiguits, a band known as "the desperadoes", men who were not unfriendly with the raiders of the steppes.

Zhumagul, cunning and quick-witted, was not at all pleased to see them.

"What has brought you here?" he began, but was interrupted by one of the djiguits.

"It is said that 'when one's father is to be plundered, one should help the plunderers'." There was a challenge in his words. "We have come to rob the Zhigitek of all their livestock and hand it over to you."

"Why all the livestock? Fifty sheep, we said. But if you have so many, you can bring the animals when the petitioners arrive. Why hurry?" Kamisbai asked with a grin.

"Perhaps we should deliver the animals to you?" Karasha asked, squatting next to him.

"And why not?"

"Ah, you blood-thirsty beast! Have you not caused enough suffering? When will you stop tormenting the people?"

"Enough of such talk! Let me be! Now, what has Baidaly answered?"

"I'll tell you. Here is his answer!" And springing to his feet Karasha brought his heavy whip down on Kamisbai's head.

Before the messenger could pick himself up, Urkimbai shouted to the djiguits in the yurta:

"Whip the life out of the dogs!"

Zhumagul and Kamisbai struggled, cursing furiously, but the djiguits were upon them before they could recover.

Both were flung to the ground, and strong knees pinned them down.

"Here's Baidaly's answer! He ordered us to beat you as long as we have the strength and return you to Maibasar half-dead! There! You've earned this," and kneeling on Kamisbai, Karasha showered him with blows.

Urkimbai and the other djiguits attended to Zhumagul with equal zest.

Badly beaten, their clothes torn to shreds, the two messengers found it as much as they could do to return to Karashoky. Without washing the blood from their faces, they appeared before Kunanbai.

The Aga-Sultan sat in the yurta surrounded by Baisal, Maibasar, the tall and mighty Nadanbai and Manas, sons of Kulinshak, and various djiguits. The tent was full.

After hearing the messengers' story Kunanbai did not speak for some time. Then with a grim expression he turned to Baisal and pointed to the bruised faces of the two men.

"See? This is what comes of being a good kinsman. It was not they who were beaten with Bozhei's whips but I!" Beckoning to the djiguits, he commanded, "Go at once and fetch Urkimbai, who had them beaten in his yurta!"

Ten djiguits leapt to their horses and dashed off. Among them rode the sons of Kulinshak.

Reaching Urkimbai's aul in the twilight, they administered a cruel beating to all the men and dragged the owner from the tent. Urkimbai tried to resist, but soon realised that this might cost him a grave injury. White with rage, he gritted his teeth, determined to endure in silence. His hands firmly bound behind his back, he was seated on the saddle before Nadanbai, and with angry shouts the entire band then set off at a gallop towards Karashoky.

The darkness deepened as the djiguits raced along the bank of a river. Soon they emerged from the winter pasture of Urkimbai in the heart of the Chinghis, struck the road on the ridge, crossed the stream and turned west, to Karashoky.

An aspen grove lay in their path, and suddenly a body of armed riders burst out into the open with wild shouts.

"Here they go! On to them!"

"Pull them down! Down with them!"

"Beat them! Flay the dogs!"

Forty men descended upon Kunanbai's djiguits with yells. Shokpars and soeels were brought into action.

The attackers were led by Karasha. Baidaly had warned
him, "You have taken a bold step — now see that you are not
caught unawares! Watch out!" Karasha had then mounted
and kept a sharp look-out over the mountains until at dusk
he had observed the horsemen approaching the aul of
Urkimbai and at once guessed their intentions. In his own
aul he had gathered five djiguits. On his way back he was
joined by Kaumen's djiguits. They were too late to intercept
their enemy at the aul itself and ambushed them in a
convenient spot.

Karasha was a skilful soeel fighter and the djiguits of his
aul were as good as any in a battle.

Kunanbai's men were headed by Manas, one of the five
"dare-devil" sons of Kulinshak. The onslaught did not
take him by surprise and he did not lose his head when the
formidable company burst upon him from the wood. He
snatched his shokpar from under the knee.

"Steady!" he shouted. "What if they are many? Hit out
boldly!"

The two parties madly hurled themselves upon one
another. Manas at once unsaddled two Zhigiteks, but
Karasha fell upon him so swiftly that he had to turn to
defend himself. Bound fast, Urkimbai saw Karasha in the
mêlée and shouted:

"I'm here! Karasha, set me free!"

Karasha wheeled and flung himself upon the horse
bearing the two riders. But this was one of Kunanbai's
chestnut pacers, and it seemed impossible to overtake him.
Nevertheless, Karasha hung on. Having separated Nadanbai and his prisoner from the others, he pursued them hotly
until Nadanbai was compelled to turn in his saddle
for defence. Urkimbai promptly took this chance to slip
to the ground, and was at once set on his feet by his
friends.

The echoes of voices and hoofs reverberated through
the mountains and quickly brought more riders to the
scene.

"Get away! Fight them off as you go! Follow me!" Manas
shouted when he saw that the Zhigitek had freed their
kinsman.

Away they dashed through one of the passes amid the
rocks and soon vanished in the dark.

Both events — the beating up of Maibasar's messengers
and the fight for Urkimbai — inspired the Zhigitek and
strengthened their confidence in their powers.

5

The following day brought a change in the weather, and the first icy breath of winter.

Usually a friendly wind blew from the ridges of the Chinghis. In the spring it carried away the snow, cleared the passes and the groves. In the winter, too, it was the helpmate of the herdsmen. It swept the snow from the pastures and was rarely very cold, as it usually blew from the south. It could be dangerous, of course, for there were times when it hurled great rocks from the heights, uprooted anything that grew tall, and spared only the low shrubs and feather-grass—the best winter fodder for the sheep.

It was in the autumn that the Chinghis wind became an enemy. Its fierce gusts were hard to endure, and it brought on the frosts and draped the skies with leaden clouds.

On this day the wind brought the snow-flakes, the first of the year.

The auls in the passes and valleys had already taken to winter quarters. Though many still lived in their yurtas, a sharp watch had been kept on the weather and this first day of cold compelled all to strike camp and carry their things to warmer shelters. There was such busy activity in Kunanbai's aul at Karashoky that one might have supposed that preparations were being made for a funeral feast.

When Maibasar's djiguits returned empty-handed after losing their prisoner, Kunanbai sent his heralds in all directions. The elders who had come to visit him with Baisal were detained, and were soon joined by other men of the Irgizbai. Wherever the heralds appeared, men quickly mounted their horses. They streamed towards Kunanbai's aul from everywhere.

Ten djiguits headed by Maibasar were sent to the Bokenshi, who had not yet moved from Kzilshoky.

The djiguits brought them strict orders from their chief, which compelled them to move at last. Suyundik and Sugir had long been ready for this and only awaited the signal. They were the first to depart and the others had to follow.

But the Bokenshi were not the only ones who set off that day. Several of Kunanbai's auls were also on the move. Earlier the Aga-Sultan, who desired to keep them all within reach, had not allowed them to wander. With the advent of the cold, however, he could not keep his old mother, Ulzhan, and the children freezing.

Having dispatched their aul, Kunanbai hastened to take advantage of the general disorder that prevailed in the Chinghis during the wandering.

The horsemen summoned by the heralds had been gathering from early morning. By noon they were many—a great fighting force armed with soeels, spears and shokpars, and ready for action.

In addition to the Irgizbai, there were men from other clans—among them the Kotibak people headed by Baisal. Their winter quarters were also near Karashoky.

At noon, Kunanbai, properly arrayed and accompanied by Baisal and Maibasar, appeared before the crowd.

"Mount," he commanded.

All sprang into their saddles. The Irgizbai were the first to seize their weapons.

The wind grew stronger and howled over the peaks. It was beginning to freeze, the snow clung to the men's faces and blanketed the earth. The mountains grew dim and an icy fog crawled over the ridges, covering everything with hoarfrost.

Kunanbai mounted his grey bay and surveyed the scene. The furrows on his brow grew deeper and his one eye reddened ferociously.

Briefly he gave the order to Baisal and Maibasar: "Forward!"

The frozen ground rang with the thunder of many hoofs as the great mass moved towards Tokpambet, the winter quarters of Bozhei. Kunanbai and his party rode in the vanguard. Soon they were going at a fast trot.

The sun was still high when Kunanbai and his force reached the projection which lay not far from Bozhei's winter quarters.

At Tokpambet final preparations were being made for the winter. The chimneys gave forth the dense yellow smoke of sheep's tallow, and many people were busy outside the huts. There were horses tethered to the walls, but not many, as Kunanbai noticed at once. The remaining horses were saddled but hobbled, grazing in the rich pastures.

When they saw the enormous body of riders coming, the people by the huts sprang into motion. There was a general rush for the horses, for soeels and spears. The Zhigitek seemed to be ready for a desperate fight. Within a moment they would all be mounted.

Kunanbai realised this immediately and was prompt to act.

"Olzhai! Olzhai!"* he shouted, lashing his bay.

The entire force thundered forward behind him with the cries: "Irgizbai! Irgizbai!" "Topai! Torgai!" They fanned out over the slopes like swift-spreading flames in the steppes. Their howls and battle-cries and the clatter of hoofs reverberated in the hills and valleys.

Bozhei's men were fewer than those of Kunanbai. The Zhigitek, moreover, had failed to rally—they had been caught unawares. According to custom, the opponent should have made known his intentions, indicated the field of battle and only then sent his horsemen into attack. Kunanbai had done nothing of the sort. He had struck without warning.

Bozhei was surrounded only by those who dwelt in the neighbourhood. It was impossible to warn the auls in the foothills and the Zhigitek on the banks of the river. In the mountains most of the Zhigitek were busy preparing to move to winter homes.

Among those gathered about Bozhei were ten who had been brought by Darkembai. In the morning his suspicions had been aroused by the lines of armed men moving towards Karashoky from the various winter places of the Irgizbai. "Kunanbai is probably gathering his kinsmen to fall upon Bozhei and all the Zhigitek," he thought. Long before noon he had given warning to Bozhei and other kinsmen. On his way he had visited Baidaly, Karasha, Kaumen and Urkimbai and all these had followed him with their sons.

Altogether some forty men had gathered to defend their leader. Among them were the valiant sons of Kaumen and Karasha and other young djiguits well armed and ready to fight for their people. At first they had wanted to throw themselves on the horses grazing nearby, raise their battle-cry: "Kengirbai! Kengirbai!" and meet the enemy with soeels and shokpars in hand. But Baidaly restrained them.

"Stay!... Would you leave Bozhei unprotected? If we must die, let us die together!"

Kunanbai's force was rapidly drawing near. His djiguits came rushing on with Kunanbai at their head, merciless in his intent.

Bozhei was distraught. "What grief has come upon us! He

---

* Olzhai—the name of an Irgizbai ancestor and the battle-cry of the clan.— Ed.

has caught us unawares! Again disaster descends without warning!" he repeated in despair.

His only hope lay in those of the djiguits who had managed to mount. With soeels in hand, they would strike at Kunanbai's flanks in small groups of five and ten. But there were so few of them! The others were still running about the fields catching their horses. Would the enemy strike them down without so much as letting them mount?

Kunanbai dashed on. Without checking his pace, he dispatched two hundred to strike at his opponents from both sides. As his howling horde reached the grazing horses these darted in all directions, soeels smashing wooden saddles to pieces.

A ragged row of the Zhigitek attempted to face Kunanbai on foot, but were overwhelmed by the avalanche of the Irgizbai, whose forces were not even visibly diminished by the two hundred that had been diverted. The Zhigitek horsemen who struck at Kunanbai's flank were quickly felled. Nothing could have been easier, the odds being forty and fifty to one!

Those who could not reach their horses in the pastures also tried to fight on foot. But what is a man on foot against an armed horseman? Short shrift was made of them; a single, well-directed blow sufficed to strike each of them down. A similar fate overtook all who had strayed from the huts. The attackers knew their superiority and their battle-cry rose louder.

"Olzhai! Olzhai! Irgizbai! Irgizbai! Topai! Torgai!" They were calling to the spirit of Olzhai and other ancestors to strike great terror into the hearts of their enemies.

All resistance smashed, the conquerors descended in a solid body upon the houses. The howling of the riders, the clash of their soeels and clatter of the hoofs merged into a general uproar.

Bozhei's small force had not moved from the spot. All raised their shokpars and soeels, a bristling knot of fighters who would not give in. They were hemmed in on all sides.

"Fall back to the houses! Hold the doors! Keep them out! We'll fight to the end!" Baidaly shouted and led the way to the yurtas.

Baidaly and Bozhei took a stand within the main entrance, surrounded by the strongest and bravest of their djiguits, who were headed by Kaumen's two sons.

But the numbers of the enemy were overwhelming. The

Irgizbai horses pranced at the very door, their riders awaiting orders.

Kunanbai, still on horseback, was in the midst of his men.

It was at this moment that Darkembai forced a way between Bozhei and Baidaly and began to take aim from an old flint-lock resting on a support. Where he had found the weapon, it would have been hard to say. The gun was loaded, however, and only needed to be ignited. Breathless, Darkembai called to Bozhei:

"That one-eyed devil has no heart! He's come to jeer at us again, but this will lay him flat! Step aside!" He fumbled with a flint trying to strike a spark.

Bozhei caught his hand.

"Don't! It's not for us to mete out punishment to him. The spirits of our ancestors will smite him!"

Kunanbai's voice now rose above the din:

"Drag them from their lair. Tie them up like slaves and pull them out!"

Headed by Maibasar, the crowd rushed to the door. Kunanbai urged them on as he saw their hesitation.

"Dismount and break down the door! All together!"

Darkembai and those who surrounded Baidaly and Bozhei fought desperately, but the odds were too great. The Irgizbai burst into the house.

Beneath the low ceiling the defenders were unable even to swing their soeels. Within a few minutes they were overcome, disarmed and dragged into the open.

No sooner did Karasha, Urkimbai and the young djiguits emerge than they were struck again by many fists. Blood-stained and battered, they continued to resist, cursing Kunanbai in the foulest language, but their words were lost in the general turmoil.

"Give them a taste of the whip!" Maibasar roared, his eyes blazing fiercely. "Don't spare them! Let them know with whom they have picked a quarrel!"

His djiguits, headed by the two messengers, Kamisbai and Zhumagul, lashed away without mercy.

Kunanbai showed no interest in this scene—he was sharply scrutinising every man dragged out of the house, looking for the one against whom he was nursing his wrath. That one was Bozhei.

At last Bozhei appeared, not at all in the same condition as the others. No one had dared lay hands upon him. His fox-fur hat had not been disarranged and his garments were not disordered or torn. He was not dragged out, but walked alone, the Irgizbai merely accompanying him, moving in a close circle around him.

Kunanbai lashed his horse and came close. Baisal too urged his horse nearer.

"The whip!" was Kunanbai's order to Maibasar.

Zhumagul and Kamisbai hurled themselves on Bozhei and threw him to the ground.

"Give him the whip! Strip and flay him!" raged Kunanbai.

"May your last eye burn in its socket! Ah, Kunanbai, you'll be damned by the spirits of your forefathers," Bozhei cried struggling furiously.

But his cape and fur coat were torn from him, and Kamisbai swung his whip. Bozhei's back was bared, his white body lay under the very hoofs of Kunanbai's bay. A silence stole over the crowd, and no one stirred.

Kamisbai's whip swung in the air, but suddenly a man broke through the crowd and, flinging himself upon Bozhei, covered him with his body.

This was Pusharbai of the Kotibak, a friend of Bozhei.

"Enough, enough, Kunanbai! Arasha!... Arasha!"* he cried.

"Give him the whip too! Hit the dog!" Kunanbai was twirling his whip in a fury.

"Only dare!" A strong and commanding voice rang out, the voice of Baisal. Kunanbai turned sharply and looked him full in the face. The change that had come over Baisal's features augured much, but Kunanbai was unyielding.

"Strike away! Lash the two of them!" he ordered.

Maibasar giving the lead, the Irgizbai responded to the command. Blows rained down on Bozhei and Pusharbai.

Baisal's horse was spurred into sudden action, and his master stooped quickly and flung Maibasar aside.

"Kotibak! Follow me, all Kotibak!" It was the tribal cry, and a swift movement ran through the Kotibak. In a great mass they separated from Kunanbai and went over to the Zhigitek.

Overwhelmed and helpless, the latter could not have been of much use to Baisal, but the fight was not resumed. It was evident that Baisal had been outraged by the treatment meted out to Bozhei, to Pusharbai and his entire people,

---

* Arasha—"I intercede". A man who pronounced this word took the blame of the other upon himself.— *Ed.*

and in his anger and bitterness he had suddenly gone over
to the Zhigitek.

This was plain to the djiguits and Maibasar's messengers
and they were afraid to go on with the beating. Instead they
withdrew and let Bozhei rise.

"Hey, Kunanbai!" Bozhei shouted furiously after the
departing leader. "I saved you from a bullet, and you cast
me into the flames! I won't let you forget this day!"

Kunanbai gathered all who were left to him after the
desertion of the Kotibak and, still surrounded by a
formidable force, returned to Karashoky.

ON THE ROAD

1

The sun had just set, and the night's thickening shadows were creeping from all the corners of the room, rising to the ceiling in a dark indistinct cloud.

Ulzhan's house, in which Abai lived with his grandmother and mother, was the largest one in the Zhidebai winter settlement. This spacious and hospitable home was decorated with rugs, draperies and alasha.*

The lamp had not yet been lit. Most of the family were engaged in various tasks in the open, and the great room seemed all the greater for its stillness.

Abai was kneeling before the window overlooking the Chinghis ridges, his elbows resting on the sill, his chin cupped in his hands. On his right, Zereh sat on a low couch and with her knee gently rocking the cradle of her granddaughter Kamshat, the daughter of Aigiz. As so often before, the old woman was crooning a lullaby. It was an old song, older even than she, the only one who sang it now, and to Abai it seemed as warm and as dear as Grandmother herself: once, long ago, he too had been lulled to sleep by this melody. And nothing had changed in it since—not a word: a good song is as true as a mother's heart and knows no changes. The melody was as serene as the quiet breath of night, and Grandmother's gentle voice seemed to enhance the stillness of the sunset. As Abai listened he felt that old Zereh's singing, so warm and yet melancholy, was lulling him too. He would have liked it to go on for a long, long time, for ever.

Since the day of their arrival, Abai had spent his evenings with his grandmother. He could not have said just why he was so drawn to her. At dusk when the herds were returning from the pastures, he would go to the house of his younger mother Aigiz and pick up his little sister Kamshat. Then he would take her to their grandmother's and play with her.

But that evening Kamshat would not fall asleep. At every pause in the song she opened her black-currant eyes,

*Alasha—a woollen, patterned bedspread.— Ed.

blinking her long lashes and made little sucking noise as though demanding that the song continue.

Abai generally spent the evening hour in solitude. If he were outdoors at the time he liked to climb a nearby hill. The steppes were pervaded with a mysterious, compelling force which strangely affected his thoughts.

And now as he listened to the soothing song, his eyes wandered over the mountains, over the jagged skyline of the Chinghis, to the haze of the farthermost, barely visible, peaks.

The mountains were about fifteen miles from Zhidebai, but they seemed to recede into the gathering gloom. Blue and ominous, the cold outlines of the great ridges looked like giants turned to stone. Immobile and silent, they slowly cloaked themselves in darkness.

What was happening in the mountains? News had not yet reached the aul about the attack on the Zhigitek, but word had come that the Bokenshi had been driven from Karashoky, that they had left their old winter home with bitter tears. Everyone knew that some terrible calamity had descended upon the winding Chinghis Range, and Abai sensed that too.

The cold wind from the mountains was like a breath of the cruel life raging there. But the icy gusts seemed to melt away in the warmth of Grandmother's song. What enormous strength lay hidden in a song!

Startled by the idea, Abai turned his eyes skywards.

A full moon floated there, now touching upon a solitary dark cloud, now hiding behind it and peeping mischievously through. Fascinated, Abai forgot the world.

The moon dived into another cloud below, popped out for an instant and dived again. It seemed to be playing hide-and-seek: one minute it would disappear completely and then, bright and smiling, it would emerge suddenly from behind a dark curtain, only to vanish again in a second. Now it seemed to be winking as though teasing someone, now it floated serenely, a silver disc, and then once more it plunged into the mists. What a frolicsome moon! And when it chose to peep out glittering for an instant, he smiled, fancying that it was playing like a child.

It was such fun to watch, Abai could have gazed at it for hours. But suddenly there was a noise outside, and he heard someone running up to the door. In came Ospan. He must have been teasing someone and as always had taken to his heels. He ran in laughing boisterously, followed by Smagul, the son of Abai's younger mother, Aigiz. Smagul was weeping bitter, angry tears for all that he was as old as Ospan.

Obviously Ospan had been mean to Smagul. Abai sprang up and seized his brother. Then Smagul also made a grab at the bully. But Ospan was in his own home now, and bravely prepared to·fight.

"What d'you want?" he yelled, catching Smagul by the collar.

Abai pulled them apart.

"What has he done?" he asked Smagul.

"He's taken my knucklebone!" and he wailed still louder.

"Have I? You cry-baby," Ospan teased. "He's taken my knucklebone," he mimicked Smagul.

"Give it back," said Abai severely.

But Ospan was determined to resist by fair means or foul.

"He's a liar. He never had any knucklebones!"

Abai tried to search him; but Ospan wrenched himself free, fled to the stove and with his hands behind his back defiantly wedged himself into a corner. A pail of kumiss stood near and he decided that if the worst came to the worst, he could upset the pail and then Abai would be in a fix too. But Abai guessed his intention and did not go for him.

"Show me your hands," he said, unexpectedly catching Ospan by the ear.

Ospan roared, and kicked at the pail. Abai stopped him from upsetting it, but the lid was knocked off. Twisting madly, Ospan threw the knucklebone into the kumiss.

"Oi-bai! See! There's nothing in my hands!" he whined.

Abai had not seen the knucklebone fly into the milk, but Smagul had been watching his tormentor closely. He dashed to the pail, rolled up his sleeve and pushed his dirty hand into the kumiss. The sleeve fell and also went into the liquid, but Smagul zealously went on fishing. Angry with him now, Abai let go of Ospan so that he could pull Smagul away.

Like a hawk Ospan pounced on his half-brother, punched him in the back several times and gleefully ducked his head into the pail. Poor Smagul never retrieved his treasure, for the mare's milk filled his mouth and nose. Choking and spluttering, he went for Ospan.

"You thief," he·shouted, adding a string of filthy words for emphasis.

Abai was disgusted.

"Fool! Who taught you such words, you little pig?"

He boxed Smagul's ears, and Ospan, the instigator, also came in for some rough treatment. Howling at the top of their voices, the half-brothers ran off in different directions: Ospan to throw himself at his grandmother's feet, and Smagul to his mother.

Abai was astonished by Smagul's filthy cursing. Suddenly he heard him whining again—but the sound was drowned out by the angry cries of Aigiz who was obviously coming with her boy.

The door of the Great Yurta flew open. Aigiz pushed her boy into the room and almost before she had crossed the threshold screamed:

"There he is! Claw at him to your heart's content! Tear him to pieces! Eat him alive!" She came close to Abai.

"Kshi-apa...*" he began quietly.

But Aigiz cut him short. Words tumbled from her lips in an endless torrent.

"That's right, take advantage of the fact that you're stronger than he! There are many of you, four from one mother!"

"Kshi-apa, please listen.... If you had only heard the words he used!"

"Why should I hear them? You've grown and want to show your fangs? You beat him up because he's the son of your mother's rival!"

"Heavens, what are you saying?"

"You enjoy beating those who are younger and weaker, don't you? Just you wait. Tomorrow Khalel will show you a thing or two!" Khalel was her eldest son who was away at school in the town.

It looked as though the two auls were preparing for a fray.

"Is that really all that you, our mother, can say to us?"

"Hold your tongue! Enough of that! You're the seniors, and we—tokal.** It's our lot to be humbled and beaten, isn't it?"

Abai was abashed by the open coarseness of his young mother. He turned pale, and trembling with indignation resolved neither to beg her pardon nor to yield.

"Stop this! What sort of a person are you?" he cried angrily and turned to the window, unable to say more.

---

* Kshi-apa—younger mother, a form of addressing the younger wives of the father.—Ed.
** Tokal—younger wife.—Ed.

The deaf Zereh had not been able to hear the whole of the quarrel, but she guessed its meaning by the woman's gestures, and also noticed that Abai was upset. She left Kamshat and rose to her feet.

"Get out of here, out of my sight!" she shouted, approaching her daughter-in-law. "What are you babbling about? Sowing discord among the children, are you? Get out before you come to harm!"

Aigiz retreated before the old woman, but continued her insolent complaints.

"You're against me because I am tokal. You're all against me. But we'll see! Wait till he himself comes tomorrow!"

She meant Kunanbai. Aigiz was his favourite wife, and she could depend on him. Nonetheless, she tried to speak only loudly enough for Abai to hear, not Zereh.

A quiet voice suddenly spoke behind her. It was Ulzhan. She had entered long before, and had been listening silently to Aigiz's shrieks.

"Stop it, for the love of God. Enough! Think of the children.... I've been shielding them from this and you don't seem to care at all," she said.

"You'd like me to endure everything in silence, wouldn't you?"

"Please stop it. Go! I shall never remind you of the things you've said here—but please go away and keep your anger to yourself." Ulzhan's voice was as calm as ever.

Glaring at her, Aigiz took her son by the hand and departed. Ulzhan watched her go, then sighed and removed her coat. Reaching for the flint, she struck a spark and lit the lamp. In the light of the thin reddish flame, almost lost in the big room, she could see the unhappy, flushed face of Abai.

"Abai-zhan, what's the matter with you, my son?"

"Apa! Why does kshi-apa quarrel so often?" he asked.

This question was the question of an adult. Ulzhan preferred to conceal her thoughts from the other children; but she could not bring herself to hide anything from Abai. He could be trusted with her secrets.

"My dear," she said. "Rivals will remain rivals. We spend our lives licking our wounds. How can you know what I feel?"

Deep in his heart Abai understood her, but he could not express it in words.

Somebody laughed at the door. Takezhan, Abai's elder
brother, and the Mullah Gabitkhan came in, bringing a
youthfully carefree, gay mood into the room.

Takezhan was nearly sixteen. An ingenious lad, a great
lover of jokes and witty sayings, he had somehow gained the
friendship of Gabitkhan, whom he treated as an equal
despite the difference in their years. Following the mullah
in, he laughingly teased him for his curious pronunciation.

Gabitkhan was a Tartar. To evade the draft some years
back, he had fled to Karkaralinsk, where he had been
received by the clan of Bertis and had found himself in the
aul of a distant branch of the Irgizbai. Though young, he
was known to be erudite; at a ceremony to commemorate
the death of Kunanbai's father, he had been invited to stay
with the Irgizbai chief.

Gabitkhan still distorted the Kazakh language in a very
amusing way, but his simplicity, gentleness and erudition
won all hearts. Both young and old regarded him as a
friend, and only Takezhan made fun of him.

During the past few evenings Gabitkhan had been
relating the stories from the *Arabian Nights* in the home of
the mothers. After tea, at Ulzhan's request, he began the
thrilling story of the three blind men. The tale, however,
was interrupted by the arrival of a horseman, whom they
saw ride past the window.

"Now who can that be?"

"He's certainly in a hurry!"

The messenger Zhumagul entered the room.

Exchanging brief greetings, he launched on a detailed
description of the fight that had taken place the day before
at Tokpambet, the bruises on his left cheek providing
evidence of his part in it. Speaking loudly for Zereh to hear,
he told the tale of Bozhei's beating with great relish, making
no attempt to conceal his pleasure.

When Zereh had heard the story, she turned quickly to
Zhumagul and made him tell it again. Then, assured that
she had heard correctly, she said with asperity:

"Bozhei's the last of the wise elders in our tribe. You've
lost your conscience altogether! And you, windbag that you
are, why are you yelling about such things in the presence of
the children?"

Perhaps because all of them knew Bozhei as a respected
man of honour, or else because the old mother's authority
had its usual effect, they lapsed into an embarrassed silence.
Only Takezhan approved his father's action.

"Let them know that we're not to be trifled with! He got what he deserved!"

Ulzhan looked at him coldly.

"You'd better hold your tongue! What's been done to him is bad enough," she said.

Satai, an old herdsman, had arrived with Zhumagul. At first he sat listening quietly, but then he too engaged in the conversation, telling the company how at noon that day he had been out in the pastures and had seen Bozhei, Baidaly and others — about ten men in all — dismount at the grave of Kengirbai. They had stood on the hill for a long time, he said, and one of the djiguits had told Satai, "Bozhei and his kinsmen are riding to Karkaralinsk to complain against Kunanbai. They have just paused on the way to offer a prayer at the grave of their forefather."

This reminded Zhumagul of the purpose of his visit: Kunanbai had sent him to fetch Abai. Kunanbai too was going to ride to Karkaralinsk tomorrow and desired to be accompanied by his son.

There was a shocked silence. Everyone was dismayed.

On the following day the entire family turned out to see Abai off on his long journey. Zhumagul stood ready, holding a cream-coloured horse by the rein. On its back was a rich-looking silver-studded saddle.

Abai went up to Zereh first.

"Good-bye, Grandma," he said, taking her small withered hand into both of his.

Zereh pressed her face to his brow.

"May God keep you. A happy journey, Abai, my heart!"

From the others Abai took leave more formally, saying merely, "Khosh, Khosh!"

Ulzhan stood by his horse, having taken the rein from Zhumagul.

"Come to me," she called her son. "Bless you," she said and helped him into the saddle.

Abai gathered the folds of his cloak and was about to set off when Ulzhan placed her long, slim fingers on the animal's mane.

"My son," she said, "the older people often turn from peace to strife. It is said that 'with rivals, even the flakes of their ashes are enemies'. But you must keep out of this. When you see Bozheken, hold him in honour and convey our salem. We have always respected him as a kinsman. Who is right or wrong is not for you to decide. Leave to your father his enmities, but you must be just."

Abai spurred his horse. Again and again he turned to look back—his relatives still stood watching. His mother's words rang in his ears. And Bozhei was near and dear to him, a man who had a claim upon his sympathy.

2

Abai and his father had long arrived in Karkaralinsk. Winter had come, and the ground was thickly carpeted with snow.

Kunanbai had taken up his abode in the centre of the little town, in a spacious wooden house with a green iron roof, which belonged to a hospitable Tartar trader who liked the company of Kazakhs.

The Aga-Sultan had come to town attended by numerous kinsmen and nokers,* who took up residence in the surrounding houses.

When Abai grew bored at his father's, he would ramble from house to house for diversion. After morning tea on this sunny day, he decided to go to Maibasar's residence. The surrounding hills were capped with snow and sunk in the slumber of the cold season. The slender pines on the outskirts of the town were deep in snow-drifts, and the mountains were like old men in hats of furry white.

The day was cold, though the nothern wind barely breathed. As he pulled his fox fur hat more snugly over his ears, Abai thought of his grandmother's advice, never to forget to fasten his hat well. "There's nothing worse than being deaf," she had warned him. "You see the trouble I have." He wondered how she was. "Probably worries about me in every snowstorm and on every cold day," he said to himself, and the thought of all his loved ones at Zhidebai made him homesick.

The frozen surface of the snow crunched underfoot, and now and again Abai's narrow-toed new boots slipped on the icy road. He no longer looked like a boy—he was dressed as befitted a young man. On his head was a hat of fox fur and black velvet. The older folk wore hats made from fox paws and, to distinguish themselves, the youths of the Tobikty had lately begun to wear hats made from the pelt of the fox. As was customary, Abai wore a squirrel coat beneath a broad cloak of black velvet shot with silver grey. The sleeves were not very long. Cloaks with wide armholes and long sleeves were worn only by the Karkaralinsk Kazakhs. The cut of

* Nokers—members of someone's suite, bodyguards, servants.—*Ed.*

their collars, too, differed from that of the Tobikty, and their fur hats were made not of six but of four sections. Young Tobikty men wore scarfs of blue cloth instead of leather belts.

On his way Abai met many of the aul Kazakhs. Most of them were on horseback and heading for the house of Kunanbai. They were the atkaminers who had come with various petitions and the plaintiffs who would sit about the Aga-Sultan's house from morn till night.

In the courtyard of Maibasar's house there was a great gathering in a large open shed. All the Tobikty who lived apart from Kunanbai were here. There were no strangers, only kinsmen and acquaintances—mostly elderly men. Among them stood Maibasar, large and ruddy, with a white lambskin thrown over his shoulders.

Four young djiguits were trying to overthrow a fawn four-year-old mare with prominent withers. From the first day of Kunanbai's stay in Karkaralinsk, Maibasar had been gathering—as presents to the Irgizbai leader—fat sheep and foals, and other choice meat. One of the fattened horses was now to be slaughtered for a feast of the friends.

On the way to Karkaralinsk and in the town itself all the Irgizbai had met with a warm welcome and generous hospitality; and those who had gathered were therefore grateful to Kunanbai who had won such esteem for them. Seeing the fat fawn mare they felt even greater gratitude.

"This journey of the Mirza has been especially successful," began Kunanbai's brother Zhakip.

Following the example of the numerous petitioners and plaintiffs who had arrived in Karkaralinsk, all the Tobikty spoke of Kunanbai as "Mirza".

"Our enemies are green with envy. When the mosque opens tomorrow, the people will sing the praises of the Mirza," said Maibasar importantly.

"And with good reason too! The mosque is splendid!"

"Karkaralinsk has never seen the like," the others chimed in delightedly.

Abai had heard a good deal about this mosque from the townsfolk as well as from his father. The foundations had been laid the previous year and the building was erected at Kunanbai's expense, which had earned him universal esteem and veneration. Today this first and only mosque in Karkaralinsk was to be consecrated and the mullahs in the town and the prominent elders of the auls could not praise Kunanbai highly enough for this house of Allah.

Two days before, Kunanbai had received none other than the Imam himself, the Mullah Khasen Saratau, who was favourably disposed towards the Kazakhs.

"From the plain people you have risen to be a khan," the Imam had said. "In the Koran the mosque is termed 'the dwelling of Allah'. You have erected a home of the Almighty among this ignorant, unenlightened people. You shall find favour in the eyes of the Lord of the Creation!"

Hereupon he had bestowed his blessing on Kunanbai in the sight of the full assembly of atkaminers. For such marks of distinction the Imam, before he left, was duly rewarded by the Aga-Sultan with a mount and a camel.

Abai could see that his father was more powerful and influential than any of the atkaminers. Curious, he watched and tried to understand how this had come about. But the longer he lived with his father and observed his actions, the more of a puzzle his father seemed to him.

The meat of the slaughtered mare was taken to the kitchen. The Tobikty staying elsewhere also came to dine with the head of the volost, and the courtyard grew crowded. Maibasar was already leading his kinsmen into the house, and the guests were ready to take places, when the outer gate was flung open by Karabas, the messenger of Kunanbai.

He seemed in a great hurry.

"Alsheken* will soon be here! They say that Alsheken is on his way," he told Maibasar and Zhakip. "The Mirza calls—hurry!"

Maibasar quickly donned his sheepskin, and Zhakip moved to follow. Abai wanted to stay, but Maibasar told him:

"Abai, you must come with us! He's your future father-in-law and you must give him your salem!" He smiled ironically.

Kunanbai had sealed his friendship with Alshinbai two years ago when he asked the hand of Dilda, Alshinbai's granddaughter, in marriage for Abai. Alshinbai had thus become Abai's prospective grandfather-in-law.

During his stay in Karkaralinsk Kunanbai had already been visited several times by Alshinbai, who was greatly esteemed by the elders of the region. Abai had always heard

*Alsheken—a respectful form of Alshinbai.—Ed.

him referred to as "Alsheken" and never merely "Alshinbai". His clan bore the name of Karakok. Abai's betrothed
Dilda, therefore, came from an ancient and honourable
line, and the kalim demanded for such a bride was
enormous. Herds of horses and camels had already passed
from the aul of Kunanbai to that of Alshinbai. What with
the prospective marriage, and perhaps other reasons, the
two leaders became bosom friends. No sooner did Maibasar
and Zhakip hear that Alshinbai was near, than both were
ready to do his slightest bidding.

Maibasar never missed an opportunity to tease his
nephew about his future bride:

"What a father-in-law you'll have! The most important
man in the region! It's almost impossible to get to him. You
must bow when he comes."

Owing to these jests Abai did his best to avoid a meeting
with Alshinbai. But two days earlier, he had been summoned by Kunanbai and Alshinbai, who had rebuked him
for his undue bashfulness. Although Abai considered
himself a full-fledged djiguit he was overcome with
confusion in the presence of his father-in-law and kept out
of his way. Alshinbai himself was not at all to his liking, and
the endless joking and constant references to his future
parents-in-law, the reiteration of the words: "wedding",
"bride" and "bridegroom" made the thought of Dilda
herself obnoxious.

But now, as they were walking, Maibasar regarded him
earnestly and said:

"There is something I should like to discuss with you
without any joking. And don't pout like a baby! You're a
grown man and should understand that it's not without
reason that so many horses and camels are being driven to
Alshinbai's aul. When the new mosque opens and the
holiday ends we'll talk more seriously."

"Father has probably decided to hasten the marriage.
This time he means it," Abai thought to himself, and his
anxiety was reflected on his face. He could not have said
why, but the thought of marriage evoked a feeling of
hostility. The very name of Dilda seemed to mean bondage
and duty.

He frowned, his eyes flashing angrily, the only sign of
dissatisfaction he could allow himself — he was afraid to
contradict his uncle.

They reached Kunanbai's house and all four entered the
gate. The courtyard crowded with men on horseback and

on foot was unusually noisy. There were litigants and
petitioners standing about everywhere arguing in groups of
five and ten. The same words could be heard again and
again: "The volost chief, the biy ... the investigation, the
verdict ... the conditions, the fine ... the guilt, peace, fric-
tion...." Most of them were of the Boshan people, as could
easily be seen from their capes. The dress of the Tobikty was
also in evidence, as well as the lambskins and peaked hats of
the Kerei.

Abai would have liked to linger on, but his companions
went straight into the house. Zhakip led the way and opened
Kunanbai's door. The four entered together and salemed in
unison.

The large bright room was decorated with vivid, curiously
designed carpets. Hanging on the walls, as was customary in
town, were expensive fur coats, embroidered prayer
carpets, and Arabian fabrics inscribed with proverbs and
sayings. Metal bedsteads glittering along the walls of the
room were heaped with pillows. Silk curtains formed
rustling partitions. At the doors and windows, too, were rich
hangings. Leaning back against soft cushions, Kunanbai and
Alshinbai sat on rugs piled before a low but spacious folding
table. To the clear, respectful salem they replied without
effusiveness, barely moving their lips.

The newcomers seated themselves to the left and right of
the host and his guest. Alshinbai had been speaking, but
before he resumed his discourse he paused to look
questioningly at Kunanbai. The latter reassured him with a
gesture; he could safely resume.

Alshinbai was portly, ruddy and silver-bearded. Over his
beshmet* he wore a fox-fur cloak slung carelessly round
his shoulders. The small, steel-grey Kazakh cap planted
firmly on his skull could not conceal his baldness.

"Baimurin is also dissatisfied," he continued his account.
"He is annoyed and says as much."

Kunanbai turned to the speaker with a frown, but the
other looked at him intently and added:

"This is what he said, 'They say that Kunanbai will be
angry if Bozhei is my guest. Since when have the Tobikty
been in charge of my dinner bowls?' "

"And just why Baimurin chose to take up the soeel for
him, he did not care to explain, I suppose?" asked Kunanbai
sharply.

Abai knew what they were talking about. Two days ago,

* Beshmet—a light silk or cotton robe.— *Ed.*

his father had had a long talk with Alshinbai and had uttered this threat against Bozhei. "He'd better withdraw the complaint against me. If he does not, I shall not rest until he is put in a grey kaftan and sent off to very distant parts!" Negotiations and a biting exchange of pleasantries between Kunanbai and Bozhei were conducted through Alshinbai and Baimurin, the latter being one of the most prominent Kazakhs of Karkaralinsk. Alshinbai had apparently come to tell Kunanbai of the latest thrusts of the opposing side.

Kunanbai had long known that Baimurin was supporting Bozhei, and Alshinbai's words confirmed his suspicions. Kunanbai cared little about Baimurin, who was not his main enemy. Let him be insulted if he chose—this could worry only Alshinbai and not him. And Alshinbai was unlikely to quarrel with Kunanbai over his kinsman Baimurin—the ties between the two leaders were firm and had been repeatedly tested over the past few years. The prospective marriage and their friendship were more important to them than family connections.

"First hear Bozhei's answer to your threat," Alshinbai said after a thoughtful pause. "We can discuss the other things afterwards. This is what he said, 'The grey kaftan was tailored not by the Mirza but by God and it yet remains to be seen who is destined to wear it.' Someone must be urging him on. Baimurin perhaps, or some other."

As they heard Bozhei's defiant words, Maibasar and Zhakip looked at each other and frowned, as if to say, "The man is asking for trouble." All day Abai had been wondering just how Bozhei would reply to the message conveyed to him by Alshinbai and was equally astonished by the answer. "What hatred lies behind those words!" he could not help thinking. "And how bold he is!"

Kunanbai sat silent for some time. His head was thrown back, he stared stonily before him, and his pale, lowering features took on an even more forbidding aspect. Not by word, movement or sound did he give any sign of the turmoil raging within him.

Alshinbai looked away. Even he was somewhat alarmed at the expression on Kunanbai's face.

Everyone was silent. Karabas opened the door gingerly and entered the room.

"The mayir* has arrived, Mirza," he reported.

* As most of the tsarist officials in Western Siberia were military men, the Kazakhs usually called them "major", distorted to "mayir".—*Ed.*

Kunanbai did not stir. The door opened to reveal the enormous bulk of the major. He was followed by the interpreter Kaska, a pale and withered Kazakh with a goatee.

After shaking Kunanbai and Alshinbai by the hand, the major did not seat himself on the floor, but reached for the only chair and sat down to face them. He had a fluffy yellow beard and big blue eyes that squinted slightly. At the nape of his neck lay fat folds of crimson flesh.

Among themselves the Kazakhs usually called the "majors" not by their names, but by descriptive nicknames attached to the title — for instance "the bewhiskered major", "the fat major", while one pock-marked official was known as the "corn-crake major."*

This one's appearance had given rise to all sorts of nicknames. By some he was dubbed the "cross-eyed major", by others "the hairy major" or "the pot-bellied major". Kunanbai and Alshinbai had a somewhat low opinion of his intellect and referred to him as "the piskenbas-mayir" — "the major with the boiled head".

The chiefs of the Karkaralinsk duan (the Kazakhs called a district a "duan", and a district chief "the chief of the duan") were Kunanbai and the major. Kunanbai was considered to be the head of the district, while "the piskenbas-mayir" his deputy. It was this that gave Kunanbai the title of Aga-Sultan. The Junior Sultan, the third in command, was away at that time.

The major had come to see Kunanbai about Bozhei — and the Irgizbai chief, so enraged by Bozhei's reply, was more than glad to see him. He wasted no time on preliminaries.

"Mayir, your forebears were not of the Tobikty, but you seem to have found a kinsman here, in Karkaralinsk. Did I not say that Bozhei must be exiled and this would settle the matter? But you're dragging things out and the affair is hanging on like some lingering disease. What is the matter? Has he settled in your liver,** or has he become a close kinsman of yours? Why do you sympathise with him so?"

Balefully he regarded the major with his single eye, and the latter turned questioningly to his interpreter.

Kaska was horrified, his glance shifted from one to the other. On the one hand, his stock of Russian words was too

*An allusion to the speckled eggs of this bird.— *Ed.*
**An untranslatable play on words: *bau* means both liver and kinsman.— *Ed.*

limited to translate Kunanbai's statement with fluency, and on the other hand, he was simply afraid to convey such irate language from one chief to the other. He hesitated, smiling foolishly, and drew patterns on the rug with his finger.

Kunanbai exploded:

"What an interpreter! Tell him precisely what I have said! Stop fidgeting about like a wagtail!"

The comparison set Maibasar laughing, but a look from Kunanbai silenced him. Abai, too, was amused by his father's expression: the interpreter was so completely at a loss and really did resemble that small fussy bird as it hops over the sand.

Kaska slowly but precisely translated all that Kunanbai had said. But the major was not put out. Unhurriedly, he explained in a loud, calm voice.

"We have no authority to avenge ourselves upon those with whom we quarrel. Bozhei Yeralinov has lodged many complaints. We must look into them. And he is not alone. There are many who support him. For the time being, we cannot exile him."

This was followed by a heated argument in which each sought to outtalk the other.

"Do you want to keep us eternally wrangling? Is that what you are after?"

"This is not merely my personal view," the major replied. "The former Aga-Sultan Kusbek and Zhamantai are of the same opinion. Even Baimurin—Alshinbai knows him—thinks the way I do."

"But who are they? Just a handful! They are the minority! They are just envious. But the people side with me. Can't you see for yourself?"

"The minority? Well, what if they are? Remember, the law has been laid down by the tsar, and all are equal in the eyes of the law. There are witnesses and we must hear what they have to say."

"And you're a judge! No wonder evil-doers grow brazen when you defend them!"

"Kunanbai Mirza, that rebuke cuts both ways."

"I know your little game!"

"Aga-Sultan, you are forgetting yourself! We were both appointed to office by the Corps!"* said the major.

He lit his pipe, rose and began to pace the room, flushed with anger.

---

*The Kazakh name for Governor-General's office.—*Ed.*

Alshinbai saw that it was time to intercede. If the two chiefs were to continue in this vein, the altercation might lead to an actual rupture. This was not at all desirable, and Alshinbai could not let matters take a turn that might be harmful to Kunanbai and also to himself. He had been sitting very still, his elbow on the table, but now he quickly raised his head.

"Listen, Mirza! Listen, mayir! Come to your senses!"

Alshinbai was respected not only by Kunanbai but also by the major, who had conferred with him on various serious matters in the past. Up till now nothing had happened to mar their relations. Though not officially vested with authority Alshinbai was a decisive force in the elections of the volost chiefs, even of the Aga-Sultan himself, and the major was aware of this. He paused in his stride as Alshinbai spoke, and glanced furtively at Kunanbai. The other too seemed to have been affected by Alshinbai's words.

The major resumed his seat. He was breathing heavily and wheezily, as though short of breath.

"You are the chiefs of the duan. How can you quarrel so?" Alshinbai began.

Leaning towards the major, the interpreter quickly repeated the words in Russian.

"You must support each other. If you are in harmony you will govern justly. How shall you rule in discord? Quarrels and wrangling would be fatal. You must co-operate. And if you cannot agree, then consult others. That is my counsel," he concluded, relieved to see that both had cooled down a little. "As for Bozhei," he went on again, glancing at Kunanbai, "it is because of him that I am here, Kunanbai Mirza. Mayir, could you suspend your decision until the evening? Could you put off the matter till then? Tell me yes or no!"

At this point Karabas appeared from the outer room with a tall jar of kumiss. Maibasar, Abai and the others silently spread the cloth and placed a brightly painted bowl before each elder. Maibasar stirred the kumiss with a long ladle of ram's horn, and the thick fluid, given a slightly yellow tinge by the leather bags it had been stored in, did not foam but swirled in gentle ripples. More bowls were brought in, containing fried dough balls. A hot dish was also served—not the usual fried minced meat, but Kunanbai's favourite kidney dish, which he liked to wash down with kumiss.

When Alshinbai had finished, Kunanbai turned to him and the major:

"Let us eat—raise your bowls!" he said briefly.

Then he prayed, covering his face with his hands. Since he had begun to build the mosque and consort with mullahs and khazrets, he had grown very pious. Though he knew no words of Arabic, he observed all the formalities, always covering his face with his hands as he prayed and never forgetting to say "Bismilah".

Alshinbai's speech had been interrupted by the appearance of the food, but there was nothing more to say. As Alshinbai had taken the solution of the problem upon himself, the major saw no reason for further discussion. If difficulties arose, he would see what to do. Otherwise, the affair rested with Alshinbai.

"You are right," he said to Alshinbai, "I quite agree. I shall wait."

The conversation took another turn. The major applied himself to the kumiss and drained five bowls, one after the other. He also had some kidney, and then took his leave.

It was then that Kunanbai unburdened himself of a thought which had been troubling him all the time.

"It seems that the crop of that 'boiled head' has been stuffed with bribes. Do you see how they have primed him? Through Baimurin his belly has been filled by Bozhei and Baisal."

Alshinbai thought much the same, but he could see deeper and a fresh suspicion arose in his mind. He sat for some time brooding.

"My dear Kunanbai," he began at last, "have you ever seen an official who did not accept bribes? Do they not grasp all they can and whatever comes their way, devouring everything like locusts? But then bribery is not the worst of it...."

Alshinbai now broached the subject which had brought him to Kunanbai. The habitual furrows in his brow deepened as he narrowed his eyes and said:

"I have stood by watching all your steps and all their consequences. 'An onlooker can see the game better than the player,' my father used to say. That's true enough and I must tell you this: it is time for the Tobikty to call off the game. If they do not, things may turn out badly for them."

Kunanbai was startled and alarmed.

"Alshekeh!" he exclaimed. "In the steppes Bozhei and Baisal were snapping at my feet, and here, in the duan, they are preparing to seize me by the throat! Why should I not throw everything into the fight after this?"

Impatiently Alshinbai raised his left hand.

"Of course, if you are going to continue the fight, you will throw everything into it! But they too will spare nothing. Don't forget the mayir! And there are not a few who, like Baimurin, will clutch at every piece of gossip and slander. Do you imagine they have resigned themselves to the loss of the Aga-Sultanship for all time? They've been lying in wait for you at every turn and this is a chance for them to drag you from the saddle. Think it over! A lawsuit involving your name can lead to nothing good."

Kunanbai understood. Both the major and Alshinbai knew very well that the struggle between the two large clans had sprung from personal enmity. Who could guarantee that no one would raise the question of how Kunanbai, the Aga-Sultan, could have raided Bozhei's aul, tied up the people and beaten them with whips? Who could be sure that affairs might not take a most undesirable turn? The fires were smouldering here and there: "Bozhei's complaint." "We must look into it." "There are witnesses!" All these were but sparks from the same fire.

Kunanbai watched his partner thoughtfully, but said nothing; he wanted his friend to speak his mind. Alshinbai calmly returned his gaze.

"The mosque will be finished today," he said significantly. "You are placed above all other men, your name is on all lips. There are many who envy you, foremost among them the Corps and the mayir. If you yourself put an end to the quarrel, you will not be humiliated. Everyone will understand that you have forgiven your enemy and wish to unburden yourself of worldly matters, engaged as you are with the consecration of the home of Allah, as the Koran says. Thy kinsman shall not be thy enemy. Do not push Bozhei into the arms of strangers. Try to make peace with him."

Kunanbai thought long and hard. If a man like Alshinbai demanded peace, one had to think well before refusing. Was he not the most influential of the biys in all Karkaralinsk Region? Entire tribes came to him with their quarrels and complaints. Had not Tyure Kusbek been removed from the office of Aga-Sultan after falling out with Alshinbai?

The Tobikty were by no means the strongest or most numerous of the tribes in Karkaralinsk Region, and Kunanbai owed his Aga-Sultanship to his friendship with

Alshinbai....If he continued the feud against Bozhei, the latter would not stop harassing Kunanbai even if he lay prostrated. That was how matters stood. And if one considered who had been wronged, it was clear that he, Kunanbai, had wronged Bozhei. What indeed had Bozhei done to wrong him? Nothing! If Alshinbai desired reconciliation—he would have to agree. His decision did not, of course, imply that he was going to change his tune completely and give in at once.

If it had been someone other than Alshinbai, the Aga-Sultan would not have made up his mind so quickly. But it was Alshinbai who demanded reconciliation—and Kunanbai hesitated no longer.

"Alshekeh," he began, "you speak as a man who had weighed and considered everything beforehand. You speak as a friend. If I fail to appreciate this, the blame will rest with me. I did not want to give way, but how can I disobey you and stubbornly go my way? I shall trust in God and you—please take over the matter and finish it yourself."

The discussion was ended, and Alshinbai retired to his own quarters.

Abai was so happy for Bozhei that he even felt a grudging liking for Alshinbai. The fangs of hatred had been drawn in and all was warm and friendly in the world. He sighed with relief.

He liked to be alone not only when he was sad, but also when he was happy, and so that evening he went wandering about the town.

Abai had crossed three or four streets when he saw a large crowd of people coming towards him, talking and laughing. Not one of them was known to him, but since they were on foot Abai judged them to be townspeople. Among them were young and old men and everyone was so cheerful and friendly that Abai could not help being interested. Smiling, he halted in the middle of the street. They came nearer, their many boots crunching the snow, but none paused to look at him. Now he could see that in their midst was a man of venerable age. He too was laughing, and was obviously arousing merriment among the others.

But why were they leading him in that strange way—supporting him on both sides? And why did he keep his head so erect, never turning to look at whoever he was talking to. On looking closer, Abai saw that the old man was blind.

Abai joined the crowd, as did all who happened to be passing or standing at their doors.

One elderly man, his beard streaked with silver, dropped behind a little.

"Who is that old man?" Abai asked him.

The other was astonished:

"Have you never seen Shozheken? Don't you know him? That's Shozhe, Shozhe the akyn!"

Abai had heard of this famous bard, but had never seen him. He pushed forward, trying to get a better view of the akyn and hear what he was saying.

"Shozheke," an old local man said to the akyn, "you have just arrived in our town. Have you heard our news?"

"No. Tell me what has been happening here? Of what are the people talking?"

There was much to tell. The mosque built by Kunanbai was finished. Alshinbai and Kunanbai were going to hold a feast in honour of the occasion; then there were rumours that Kunanbai intended to make peace with Bozhei.

Abai was surprised; he had not expected to hear his father's name here. "The mosque is one thing," he thought, "but the people seem to know all his business, even his quarrels!"

"Alshinbai can reconcile anyone!"

"Ah, he is simply afraid that Kunanbai may be thrown out of office if he quarrels with everyone."

"And who has brought the Tobikty into such esteem if not he? The respect they receive, the honours! It is to him alone they should be thankful!"

"Alshinbai supports them, to be sure!"

"He does! And the Tobikty devour all that's fattest in the droves and dig out all that's best in the shops!"

"They won't leave until they've devoured all the fattest horses around here."

Shozhe had been listening with a faint smile and suddenly he began to sing in his ringing voice:

The one-eyed Raven and the Cat with thinning fur
Struck up a friendship with the lame old Cur,
And said to him: "To pray for us you are empowered!"
The Cat forthwith gave to the Raven what the people had,
And all of this the Raven then devoured.

There was a burst of general laughter; some clicked their tongues, astonished at the aptness of the words and the old akyn's quick-wittedness.

"The bald Cat is Alshinbai of course!"

"And the Raven's Kunanbai!"

"And the Imam *is* lame, as we all know!"

"That old man has made short work of the lot of them in a single verse," people all around began to say.

Abai flushed and turned away. At that moment the owner of the house appeared and invited Shozhe to enter. The crowd broke up and Abai strode off.

Shozhe's song still rang in his ears; it had touched him to the quick. He remembered the words and involuntarily repeated this verse which levelled two mountains at once.

He whom none had dared to refer to other than "Alsheken" had become a "bald cat" — Alshinbai's bald pate was well known. And his own father, the Aga-Sultan, the Mirza, had become a raven. And what a raven! He, the man who rolled in wealth, the ruler of the great Tobikty, was nothing but a predatory bird tearing with his beak and claws at everything that was most highly prized by the people!

Surely there was nothing on earth stronger than the word? Abai recalled the witty and clever Karatai: "A word can pierce to the core," he had said.

Abai was lost in thought. It seemed to him that he had found the great force destined to shake the world. Unaware of his surroundings or of the passers-by, he strode on.

But as he turned a corner he came upon three horsemen. He looked up and recognised the first as Bozhei. His pale face was sombre under his fox fur hat, and the hoarfrost clung to his moustache. At his side rode Baisal and Baidaly.

Abai was dumbfounded—he had not yet had occasion to meet Bozhei in town. But recovering quickly, he advanced to intercept the riders in the middle of the road. They reined in their horses—either from surprise or because they recognised him.

With great deference Abai raised his right hand to his heart and loudly salemed:

"Assalauma-galeikum!"

At the madrasah he had been taught that such a greeting should be given to the khazret. Perhaps he had remembered the last words spoken by his mother when he had set off for Karkaralinsk? But no, the greeting had sprung from him spontaneously.

The unusual behaviour of the boy astonished Bozhei, and he brought his horse to a standstill.

"Uagalai-kumussalem, my son," he gave the convention-al reply.

But Baisal recognised Abai and frowned.

"So it is he! Let us ride on!" He was about to spur his horse, but was checked by Bozhei.

"Wait."

"Why? Do you think it pleases me to hear a salem from the son of that fiend?" Baisal looked at Abai morosely.

Abai reddened violently. His whole being was aflame. He had not deserved the slight, and now turned burning eyes upon Baisal.

Bozhei divined what was going on in Abai's heart.

"Tell me the truth, my son. Was it your father who told you to salem us, or did you do so of your own free will?"

"My father has nothing to do with it. It was my will."

Abai was still under the spell of that pleasant feeling of harmony and tranquillity with which he had left his father's house.

Neither Bozhei nor Baisal had yet heard anything of Kunanbai's decision to make peace with them. They were now on their way to the house of Alshinbai, who had sent a man to invite them for negotiations, the subject of which was unknown to them.

"If you did this of your own desire and not because of your father's wishes," said Bozhei quietly, "then step up so that I can give you my blessing. I see sincerity in your eyes, my son!"

Baisal frowned again and would have urged his horse aside had Bozhei not detained him.

"This young man promises much, Baisal." Again he turned to Abai: "The future will rest on your shoulders, my son. May God give you all but the cruelty of your father!" He passed his palms over his face.

Abai received the blessing, his eyes fixed on the man's face and his palms upraised. Then he also passed his hands over his face.

"His eyes are like burning embers," Baidaly said to Bozhei as they rode on.

Abai stood thinking for a long time.

Had all this been genuine? Had Bozhei been sincere? Perhaps he had merely pitied him because of Baisal's unkind words? But what had induced Bozhei to bless him so warmly? How had he been able to read his heart in an instant and to divine his thoughts? Bozhei hardly knew him! But old men are experienced, penetrating and wise, thought Abai as he walked on. If Bozhei had seen something that was good in him, then he, Abai, was not as bad as he himself had thought.

The more Abai considered the scene, the more his youthful self-esteem exulted. He felt that his heart was soaring to the heavens on great, powerful wings.

How different this day had been from all the others! There had been his father and Alshinbai in the morning, Shozhe and the crowd in the evening, and now Bozhei and Baisal, who had just disappeared into the darkness. What strange and opposite worlds had come together in this crowded town of Karkaralinsk! What immeasurable gulfs lay between them! They were as far removed from one other as the ends of the earth. The one had power, the second talent, and the third the heart. Why could not these merge into one? What would happen if all these men came together to act in accord?

This idea struck Abai with sudden force, and it seemed to him that no one had thought of it before. "Reason, will.... Power, glory, dignity...." In books he had read of the constant conflict between these things. Now he had seen this conflict in real life. And he reached a fresh conclusion: all these qualities should be combined in one man.

How many and varied were the people he had met in the town, and the thoughts that had come to him here! He had seen and heard the illustrious Shozhe himself!

3

Kunanbai and Bozhei made peace. The negotiations were conducted on their behalf by Alshinbai and Baimurin. Their decision was unusual. They said to the contending parties:

"If you had belonged to different tribes we should have advised you to establish kinship. But you are kinsmen, and kinsmen by blood. You must, therefore, strengthen this tie: let Bozhei take a child from Kunanbai and let him bring it up. Through this child you will become reconciled."

Abai was aghast at the news.

Three weeks later Kunanbai started on the return journey.

Both old and young rejoiced, but Abai had been longing for home more than anyone else. In his dreams during the past few days he had again and again seen his mothers and the aul of Zhidebai. Everyone worked with a will, and everywhere there was jesting and laughter.

The way from Karkaralinsk to the Chinghis Mountains was by no means short and travelling was exceptionaly hard

that year because of the deep snow. Both the hillsides and
valleys were covered with a solid crust of ice. The fierce
winds had not abated. Blizzards raged for days on end and
raised clouds of stinging snow dust. The wind moulded the
drifts into curious undulating patterns, and there was no
path for the travellers to follow.

The straggling column advanced like migrating cranes or
a wandering aul.

Kunanbai led the column, mounted on a well-fed golden
pacer with a white mane. Well-knit and strong, this animal
did not droop its head like the others. This was Kunanbai's
favourite stallion for long winter journeys.

During the day Kunanbai tried to cover as great a distance
as possible, but when he paused for rest at the auls it was
difficult to get away. Everywhere his appearance evoked an
almost worshipful deference, as though he were a hadji returned from Mecca.

One thing, and one thing only, was on the lips of the
aksakals, elders and devout believers in all the auls: "The
mosque! The mosque!" There were old men who flattering-
ly assured Kunanbai, "You have risen from the midst of a
simple tribe to be a khan!" "You have emerged unscathed
from battle!" "You are a mighty nar* in tinkling bells!" The
fount of their flattery never ran dry; and they went to great
lengths to please the Aga-Sultan.

During the winter the atkaminers of many of the auls had
come to Kunanbai in Karkaralinsk for advice in various
controversies. Among them there were some whom Kunanbai had helped to pay off old scores with their enemies and
to recover previously sustained losses. In such auls Kunanbai was inevitably led aside for consultations. Later his train
would be enlarged by extra riding horses and mares
fattened for slaughter.

Two black amblers, a grey and three or four other
stallions were tethered to the horses of Karabas, and some
of the grooms. Though these gifts at first astonished Abai,
he did not think much about them. But the nearer they got
to Tobikty territory, the more numerous became the
presents. There was scarcely anyone in Kunanbai's party
who was not leading a horse by the halter. When they
reached Tobikty land the gift horses were so numerous that
they were driven ahead in a herd.

What better evidence could there be of the esteem the
Aga-Sultan enjoyed on his journey? And if anyone in

_____
* Nar—dromedary, a symbol of strength and power.— *Ed.*

Kunanbai's aul was at that moment foretelling the future from the droppings of the sheep, he must have observed: "The sides of the travellers are fat, and they are laden with spoils," as though returning not from the town, but from the land of an enemy whom they had pillaged.

On the seventh day of their journey Kunanbai and his company reached the western slopes of the Chinghis. He had stopped nowhere except to spend the night—they had not even halted for midday meals.

On that day the column overtook three djiguits who had been sent ahead as an advance party—what for, Abai did not know.

On the slopes three riders could be seen driving a great herd of horses.

"There they are," said Maibasar.

And sure enough—these were the three djiguits of Kunanbai and before them they were driving about a hundred horses. The animals had evidently been picked with care—they were well fed and had high withers.

Kunanbai rode into the midst of the herd to look it over.

An inkling of the truth dawned upon Abai.

"What horses are these? Who is their master?" he asked Karabas as he came closer.

"These are gifts. Gift horses for your father."

"What sort of gifts? From whom?"

"Are you a child? Has your father no people under him? What do you think happened to all the people who crowded around him in the town? Doesn't he deserve something for his efforts on their behalf? Should he work for them without reward?" Karabas was amazed at the question.

Abai asked no more. Now he knew everything. Although he had been with his father so long he had never suspected the source of his wealth.

He remembered Shozhe. Though he dwelt far away, the old akyn evidently knew more about Kunanbai than his own son did. He must indeed have known him well to brand him so aptly. "How awful!" thought Abai, burning with shame—he felt as if the old akyn stood near him at that very moment....

The cavalcade was again on its way and it was hoped to reach Kunkeh's aul at Karashoky before nightfall. Abai would see all his friends and relatives, but even this prospect could not lighten his heart.

The longer he thought, the more he understood about his father's underhand and dishonest affairs. It was from such droves, too, that the fifty horses had been sent to the aul of Alshinbai. The kalim!* And so the payment for his bride was also being collected in this manner?

But what was happening? The clear, unsullied world of his youthful dreams was gone. "Betrothed!" It was a beautiful and sacred word, but it had lost its former meaning. Resentment welled up within Abai against himself and Dilda. It was more than resentment—it was anger....

Extortion was the most heinous of sins, one that could never be washed away. This he had often read in the holy books. It was the sin which for all time had sullied the memory of Kengirbai, a famous judge of former times. Such wealth was shameful spoil torn from the meek, who were trapped by the exigencies of fortune. And "The home of the Almighty", the mosque which was Kunanbai's crowning glory—had that too been built with such money? How could a mosque erected with bribes continue to stand? Why did it not collapse under the weight of its shame? It was monstrous that in such a house the mullah would piously wail the words of the Koran in the exaggerated Bokhara fashion, would cite the commandments and other holy teachings of the Prophet on behalf of Allah!...

They reached Kunkeh's aul towards evening, but Abai did not stay with his father and set off at once for Zhidebai in the company of Zhumagul. He was impatient and rode hard all the way.

Although it was late, Abai's mothers had not yet retired or even begun their evening meal when the two riders came past their windows with the dogs yelping at their heels.

It was a tall, manly youth who entered to salem them. He had the weather-beaten face of a traveller, his step was firm and his bearing dignified. The entire household rejoiced at the sight of him.

"Abai!"

"Abai-zhan!"

"My darling!"

"My lamb, my little black lamb! Abai-zhan!" cried his mother and grandmother. Delight shone in every face.

Everyone was well. Grandmother and Ulzhan felt very well indeed. In turn they fell upon him with their kisses. Ospan too was still up and, shrieking with joy, kept jumping up and down, slapping his thighs.

*Kalim—bride money.—*Ed.*

ABAI   121

"What have you brought? Where are the sweets? Give me, give me!" He would not let Abai exchange greetings with his mothers, Gabitkhan and Takezhan. Quickly he searched in Abai's bosom and pushed his hands deep into the pockets.

For about a week after his return Abai did not leave the house, even for a walk, being particularly anxious to avoid his father. In Zhidebai it was learned that there was a great gathering in Karashoky and that the aul of Kunkeh was crowded, many people having come to inquire about the Mirza's health.

For days Abai related all that he had heard and seen in Karkaralinsk to his mothers and Gabitkhan. His younger mother Aigiz also came to hear the news.

Abai told them about the reconciliation with Bozhei, but said not a word about the agreement to deliver one of the children to him. This fearful decision weighed him down like a constant burden. Let his father tell them about it. He, Abai, had not the heart to mar the joy with which his mothers had received him. How they would take it remained to be seen. If he were to say anything about it now, they would burst into tears, give way to despair and say things they would regret afterwards. He had better not torment them!

On his way to Zhidebai he had decided that this was the best course and has asked Zhumagul, his companion, to say nothing about it to anyone.

Five days later it was learned that Bozhei had arrived.

Kunanbai at once dispatched Karabas to Zhidebai.

"The Mirza sends his greetings," said the messenger to Zereh and Ulzhan. "Many guests will arrive tomorrow. This gathering and the final reconciliation with Bozhei is to take place in the Great House. Bozhei and Baisal will be here. The Mirza has asked you to prepare to receive the guests in a fitting manner."

Ulzhan was not flustered in the least. With the help of Aigiz she had everything ready by the end of the day. She ordered the great carpets and ornate felt rugs to be unpacked. These and the bright draperies enlivened all three houses — Zereh's Great House, the Guest House and the home of Aigiz. Mountains of dough balls were fried, sheep were roasted whole, great quantities of cheese and many other things were got ready. The butter for the feast was chosen from such stocks as were not strongly salted and were therefore tastier.

Kunanbai and Bozhei arrived on the following day, their respective attendants following them.

As Bozhei crossed the threshold of the Great House, old Zereh arose, approached and kissed him with tears in her eyes.

"Oh, light of my eyes! Is your heart embittered with us? But you were always as a son to me, and I as a mother to you!" she exclaimed.

"Oh, zhariktik!* Our gentle mother!" cried Baidaly, Suyundik and other companions of Bozhei, deeply moved by the words of the old woman.

Bozhei himself was moved. Sighing, he embraced her heartily. Without words, by a mere gesture of the hand, he begged her to be seated, and himself settled next to her.

For some moments he was silent, and then turned to the children, first to Abai who sat near his grandmother. He then kissed Ospan and Smagul—wanting to show gratitude to Zereh for her affectionate reception.

Bozhei revered the Great House. To him this was not merely the house of Kunanbai, but of the entire tribe —pleasant and hospitable.

When Bozhei and his companions had been seated, Kunanbai appeared, attended by Karatai, Maibasar and others.

Abai could not bear to see his father sitting next to Bozhei. Room had to be made for the elders, and on this pretext he left the room.

Nor did he return that evening or the following morning. His mother told him that Kunanbai and Bozhei had been polite to one another, but had shown no warmth and had spoken in monosyllables.

On the morrow Bozhei was to leave. The hour had come for the dreadful decree to be put into effect.

Aigiz collapsed, sobbing, on the floor. Karabas took Kamshat from her, dressed the little girl and carried her to the Great House. Tiny and fair-faced, the child regarded the company with curious shining eyes.

"Aga, ata! Ata, aga!" she lisped, lingering over the words.

Ulzhan could not bear to look at the child. Overwhelmed with pity, she left the room. Zereh fell to the floor, weeping silently. To Abai it seemed that the elders exuded a coldness that chilled the heart; he too left the house.

---

*Zhariktik—deferential form of addressing the aged, an expression emphasising their superiority and moral qualities.—*Ed.*

Kunanbai watched the distress and the faces full of pity and compassion, with the piercing gaze of his only eye. He was carrying out the decree of Karkaralinsk—he had taken a child from its mother and given it to Bozhei.

Kamshat sat quietly unaware of her fate. It was only when a strange man picked her up and carried her away that she called, "Apa, apa!... Azheh! Azheh!"* and began to cry.

Her little heart was wrung with fear and she screamed as though her tiny feet had touched hot coals.

Her pitiful voice could be heard for as long as Bozhei and his men were in sight. And the farther their horses carried them, the more pitiful and desperate it grew, like the shriek of somebody drowning or burning at the stake.

* Azheh—grandma.—*Ed.*

Abai continued to live with his mother and grandmother in Zhidebai. He had not left the settlement since the day of his return.

Reading was to be his only occupation until the spring. Having been away from school a long time, he had somewhat forgotten his Arabic and Persian, but he had dictionaries borrowed from Gabitkhan.

Mullah Gabitkhan was a great lover of books. Among his collection were the works of Firdousi and Nizami, of Fizuli and Navoi, the *Zhamshid,* the *Arabian Nights,* the *History* by Tabari, *Jusup and Zyuleika, Leili and Mejnun,* and *Ker-Ogly.* Abai read avidly all day long, and between tea and supper in the evenings he would relate the most interesting passages to his mothers.

"That is a good thing, my son," Zereh said to him when she saw how keen he was on books. "How many there are in this world who think of nothing but eating and sleeping! They waste their lives in idleness—and remain empty-headed good-for-nothings! Don't be like them—don't part with these pages of wisdom!"

Grandmother's veneration for his books delighted Abai and the books engrossed him even more. His fascinating tales, now told daily, were heard by all—by the mothers, the servants and the children. Aigiz, too, came from time to time and sat listening for hours. After Kamshat had been taken from her, she had grown meditative, pale and wan; the shadow of grief had settled on her beautiful features. How well Abai understood her! When she came to listen, he retold the stories with especial zest and care.

Abai was a good story-teller. Even Gabitkhan listened with interest.

Unfortunately, however, all the books had been read by the beginning of spring.

Gabitkhan and Abai obtained other books from the mullahs and the pious book-lovers. On one occasion Gabitkhan visited Kunanbai's aul in Karashoky and returned with a whole sackful of books.

Kunanbai received them in Karkaralinsk through the Mullah. Once, when Abai asked him to let him have these books, Kunanbai had replied, "Stay here with me and read the books aloud. But if you want to enjoy them alone, I won't let you have them." Abai had not wanted to live with his father and so did not get the books. But now Gabitkhan had managed to induce Kunanbai to part with them, and this was a real treasure trove for Abai and the entire household. Unfortunately, however, Abai was soon summoned to Karashoky by his father and had to leave.

No sooner had he appeared at Kunkeh's aul than his father entrusted him with a message for Kulinshak, one of the elders of the Torgai. Abai memorised the message and set off on the same day in the company of Karabas.

The aul of Kulinshak lay not far off. After the seizure of the Bokenshi lands in the autumn, the Torgai had acquired the western slopes of the Karashoky where Kodar had once wintered.

Abai halted at the grave of Kodar and Kamka to say a prayer, the fearful scene as fresh in his memory as though he had witnessed it the day before. He relived all the horror, the pain and the tears once again. And so when they arrived and dismounted at the aul of Kulinshak, the young man was silent and reserved, as befitted a far older person.

The people here were still living in their winter quarters. The yurtas were generally set up next to the wooden dwellings at the first sign of warm weather, but Kulinshak was still in his house.

Being a messenger from Kunanbai, Abai was received as an adult, despite his youth. When the greetings and the usual formalities were over, Kulinshak called to his wife: "Khatin,* prepare something for the guests!"

Of his five mighty sons, known as the "five dare-devils," only Manas was at home. He was truly a giant of a man, young and strong, with a handsome clean-cut face. Now he sat quietly strumming a dombra, casting hostile glances at the visitors.

Tea was soon ready. Manas's young wife spread the cloth and brought the refreshments. She had an oval face, a straight thin nose, and bluish black hair showing from under her headdress. Abai thought her beautiful. There was something winning about her innate nobility, her tidiness and her reserved hospitality. Her every movement

* Khatin—wife.— *Ed.*

was modest and graceful. When she had served the tea, Abai at last spoke of the purpose of his visit.

"Kulinshak-aga!"

Kulinshak turned to him, extracted a small horn, tapped it with his finger-nail, took a pinch of tobacco and sniffed it with pleasure.

"My father sends his salem."

"And may he keep in good health as well."

"He wishes me to tell you about Betkudik fields which used to belong to the Borsak, but have now passed to Akberdy together with the winter houses. Last year you took up these grounds by agreement with the Borsak, but now Akberdy has said to my father, 'What if Kulinshak intends to set up his yurtas there again in the spring? I'd like the land to rest fallow for a time. I shall make hay there in the autumn. Let Kulinshak find another place for his auls.' He asks this of you through my father."

"Akberdy is nothing to me. What does your father think?"

"My father agrees with Akberdy. He's sent me to ask you not to move to Betkudik this year."

Abai's voice was firm. He spoke calmly and to the point, quite like a man. Kulinshak nodded, but his smile was without mirth.

"Let us take tea," he urged.

Abai took up his bowl, waiting for his host's reply.

Two bowls were emptied, and still Kulinshak said nothing.

"Now, my son," he turned to the boy abruptly. "Does your father know how things stood with the Betkudik fields? When they belonged to the Borsak we occupied those grounds by turn and shared the hay equally. Does he know this?"

"Yes, he does. And this is what he says, 'Ownership is one thing, and agreement is quite another. The owners of the grounds were the Borsak. Kulinshak occupied them not as an owner, but merely by agreement with the owners. If he can come to a similar agreement with Akberdy, let him continue to use the land. But he must remember that it belongs to Akberdy,'" concluded Abai.

"In other words, Akberdy is the master of the horse. If it suits him, we can ride behind him—if not, then we can walk. Why not put it plainly and say, 'You must give up Betkudik though it lies directly before you!'" Kulinshak spoke sharply.

Abai sympathised with him and would not have pressed the matter. He had not realised what a disagreeable task his father had given him. Only now he understood from Kulinshak's disturbed expression what a role he had been assigned.

"I have only told you what my father has said. The rest depends on you. Do as you think best."

"It can't be helped," sighed Kulinshak and with a bitter smile he added: "Trouble and Akberdy go together — if not for the one, there would not be the other!"

Kulinshak's remark somehow caught Abai's fancy and he promptly recited:

> Nothing's safe from Akberdy,*
> Not the land and not the water,
> Not the moon and not the stars,
> He's God-given, Akberdy....

The quip made everyone laugh. Manas's wife, who was pouring the tea, clicked her tongue and glanced at him with pleasure. Kulinshak was delighted.

"Well put, my son! May your words reach Akberdy!"

Then he changed the subject, and asked Abai about his family, about old Zereh and Ulzhan.

"Tell me, my son, have you heard anything of the child that was given to Bozhei? They say that poor Aigiz is broken-hearted."

This was a painful subject for Abai. He did not answer, but Kulinshak continued:

"The Zhigitek, it is said, are dissatisfied because they were not properly compensated for their injury, and I have heard that your little sister is badly treated. Poor Aigiz probably suspects as much. How is she?"

"Aksakal, please tell me, why are your sons called the 'bes-kaska'?"** Abai asked. "Aigiz and I were wondering about it yesterday."

"A sharp youngster," thought Kulinshak, seeing that Abai had evaded his question. "He can hold his tongue all right! They've already taught him that." He smiled.

"That's what they think of themselves — five bold fellows! But just whom they've put fear into I don't know. Empty talk! When the Bokenshi refused to give up their winter

---

.* In the Kazakh language Akberdy means sent by God. — Ed.

** Bes-kaska is a play on words, meaning either "five bald men" or "five bold men".

grounds and said they would rather die than leave
Karashoky, I went rushing to the place with all of my five
sons as soon as your father gave the command! I'd hoped to
receive at least a scrap of the land that was to be taken. And
what did we get? A slap in the face—that's all they got, my
five heroes!" concluded Kulinshak, returning to the issue so
embarrasing to Abai.

"But there's a saying: 'From a people who have been
beggared take not so much as a buldergi!'* Who will
benefit from what is taken from the plundered Bokenshi?"
demanded Abai heatedly. "And they are not strangers to
you—they're your kinsmen!"

Kulinshak was of a different opinion. Though Manas and
his wife fully agreed with Abai, he continued to harp on his
wrongs and to complain about Kunanbai to the end of the
conversation. Abai saw that the main reason for Kulinshak's
resentment was that he had been overlooked in the division
of the spoils. Such indecent greediness amazed him.

On return Abai told his father that Kulinshak had agreed,
but said nothing of his annoyance. He described his visit
briefly, in as few words as possible.

Kunanbai then summoned Karabas and, man to man,
asked him for a detailed account. Karabas could not praise
Abai highly enough.

"Your son wasted no words," he said. "He spoke well and
with dignity, as a man should. He was not embarrassed in
the least and talked to Kulinshak as an equal."

Karabas would have liked to go on, but Kunanbai
dismissed him with a wave of the hand.

He was satisfied with his son's conduct and the next day
sent him on another mission. Again accompanied by
Karabas, Abai this time set off to visit Suyundik.

The two reached the Bokenshi chief's aul as darkness was
falling. Driven from its old lands, the settlement was now in
a ravine known as the Camel Humps, in the upper reaches
of the Karaul. The Bokenshi were living in their yurtas—there had been no time to erect sturdier dwellings for
so many.

Suyundik's Great Yurta was warm; on the outside it was
protected by two layers of felt, while the interior was lined
with brightly patterned woollen rugs.

Abai was still wearing his winter clothing—a beshmet

* Buldergi—the leather loop attached to the handle of a riding-
whip.—*Ed.*

lined with squirrel fur and boots with felt legs and he did
not feel the cold. This was the first time that he had entered
a yurta that day, and it was refreshing and strangely
gay—in the early spring he was particularly fond of life in
the tents, where one could breathe the pure air of the
steppes.

A lamp glimmered feebly in the depths of the yurta.
Besides Suyundik, his wife and his two sons, Adilbek and
Asilbek, there was one other creature there—the loveliness
of spring itself. She was Togzhan, the daughter of
Suyundik.

She kept coming in and out from the Small Yurta of her
mother, Suyundik's younger wife. The sholpy* in her hair
tinkled at every movement. The tiny earrings, the small
beaver cap she wore, and the rings on her fingers—all these
seemed dainty and beautiful to Abai. She had such a delicate
face, a well-chiselled nose and dark eyes. Her eyebrows,
long and sharply defined, rose to her temples like the wings
of a swallow. As Togzhan listened, laughed or blushed,
those exquisite brows would one moment rise in a slender
arch and the next relax in a smooth curve. Perhaps they
were the wings of an invisible bird, now spread for flight,
now level for soaring.... A bird? No—rather a spirit,
intangible and swift. It would dart away, high and far and
tempting. Abai could not take his eyes off her. He stared
entranced, unaware that he was thinking of her in images of
the poets he had read.

Togzhan had come to the yurta to look after the guests.
She told the servant to spread the cloth and serve the tea
and herself took a place at her father's side.

"Suyundik-aga," Abai addressed his host, "why is the
lone mountain over there called Karaul?"**

"Who can say, my son," replied Suyundik, adding:
"There was a time when the Tobikty and the Mamai were
constantly at war. This name must have come down from
olden times."

"You suppose that the name came from us, the Tobikty?"

"From whom else? All places here received their names
from the Tobikty."

"What about Chinghis? Was there ever a man called
Chinghis among the Tobikty?"

*Sholpy—a gold or silver ornament worn in a young woman's
hair.— Ed.
**Karaul — watch-tower.— Ed.

"No! You are right. How did that ridge come to be called Chinghis?" pondered Suyundik.

Adilbek was annoyed to see that his father was at a loss and hastened to the rescue.

"They say the name comes from the word 'shinkis.'* The winters have always been very cold here."

"Hardly," objected Abai. "Chinghis was the name of a famous khan."

"That's true. I've heard of him — I can't quite remember what. Tell us about him, my son."

The young man related all he knew of Genghis Khan and his conquests and ventured a few guesses of his own:

"That is, probably, why the ridge is called Chinghis and its highest peak Khan. The other mountain which stands some what apart may have been the site of his camp. That, perhaps, is why it is called the Horde. And it is possible that the name Karaul, too, springs from that time."

Suyundik listened with interest. Togzhan noticed that her father was so engrossed that his bowl of tea had grown quite cold. She herself could not take her eyes off Abai. The older people felt ill at ease, embarrassed by their ignorance.

"No doubt that is how it was," repeated Asilbek and Karabas.

Completely captivated by Abai's tale, Suyundik himself offered him a fresh cup of tea.

"Please help yourself, Abai," he said, proffering the zhent,** the butter and the fried dough balls.

Togzhan was astonished at these marks of attention to so young a guest. Abai more than once caught a glance from her shining eyes, and it was not idle curiosity that he saw there, but deep attention and understanding.

Never in his life had Abai regarded a girl with such interest. Togzhan returned his gaze, but then blushed and looked aside.

Suyundik was deep in thought.

"It is not he who has lived long who knows all, but he who has studied much."

To this Abai said:

"It is from such respected men as yourself that I have learned all I know, Suyundik-aga."

* * *

* Shinkis — real winter (shin — true. kis — winter). — Ed.
** Zhent — cottage cheese mixed with butter and honey. — Ed.

The evening meal was served, and since the guests were kinsmen the entire family was present. Togzhan sat between her parents, quite near Abai. Now he could see her profile. The line of her small, straight nose seemed even more fascinating, and her chin was soft and rounded—a light rosy apple. Her long black braids framed her lovely white neck, and her earrings glittered like tiny drops of water.

Togzhan was in the grip of a new emotion which made her blush one moment and the next turn suddenly pale. Abai again sat lost in admiration.

The hot dishes were followed by kumiss, over which the company sat for a long time. Conversation was lively and time flew.

But Abai spoke so little that his hosts at last decided that he must be sleepy. The men left the yurta while the women prepared beds for the guests.

Abai walked a little away by himself, glad to be left alone. His heart brimmed with a new, unfamiliar emotion.

Beloved.... A stirring word he had heard from others and come across many times in books. Today it had escaped from the songs and the books and appeared before him in all its magic meaning. It had become real for him in the laughter, gestures, smiles and breathing of a young girl with a delicate face, a slender form, and a glance that filled his heart with longing.

Beloved....

Abai raised his face to the stars. A spring breeze blew from the mountains, and he drank it in greedily.

He saw Togzhan's white hands and her delicate throat. She—she was his morning.

The dawn of love, you fill my heart....

It was not Abai who spoke, but his heart. This was its first love song—the song of Togzhan. The words flowed lightly, freely....

The voice of Karabas calling him brought Abai back to earth.

As Abai approached his couch, a curtain stirred suddenly and bells tinkled at the entrance as the graceful figure of Togzhan appeared. She was carrying a silken cover, and moved unhurriedly, even slowly. Her every step made sweet silvery music.

A servant woman had made up a soft and comfortable bed for Abai. But Togzhan, still with the cover in her hands, said quietly:

"Please, make it a little higher at the foot!"

In these few words Abai could feel concern—for himself! What was he to say? He would have liked to say something, but his heart was too full. And he could not find the words.

Togzhan laid the silken cover on the bed and was gliding away, towards the door.

She had certainly shown great concern for him—perhaps it was a silent mark of respect. Was that all, though? Could it really be all? Togzhan did not look back until she reached the door; then with an amazingly lissom movement she turned and smiled—and was gone.

What was behind that smile? Mockery perhaps? Perhaps he had deserved it in some way? Abai was perturbed. Quickly he undressed and slipped under the blanket.

He could still hear that tinkle, growing fainter and fainter—or was it the beating of his heart, loud as the thunder of hoofs, drowning out all other sounds? And then the silvery melody was suddenly gone, as though snatched away by an invisible hand.

Karabas blew out the lamp.

But what did it matter to Abai whether the lamp was lit or not? To him the whole world was bathed in a dazzling radiance. He did not even notice the darkness. Although his eyes were closed his mind raced on, as though caught up in a whirlwind.

He did not fall asleep until dawn, but at the first stirrings in the yurta, he awoke and got up, looking pale and drawn.

Suyundik was up, and came out of his yurta. Abai presented his salem and gave him his father's message. The conversation was brief, and Suyundik led his young guest to tea.

Togzhan did not appear, nor did Asilbek or Adilbek. Anxious to make the return trip while the morning was yet cool, Karabas went off to saddle the horses directly after tea.

But Abai was reluctant to leave. They were hospitable, kindly people who dwelt here, their home was like a warm and cosy nest. "If I were a near kinsman," he thought suddenly, "I would visit them often, very often, whenever I liked...." But it was time to go.

Suyundik asked him about Ulzhan and Zereh.

"Convey my greetings to your mothers, my son," he said.

The baibishe,* who had not spoken a word the night

* Baibishe—elder wife.—Ed.

before, now asked her respects to be conveyed to Ulzhan; then she remembered Aigiz and little Kamshat.

"Tell me, my dear, have you heard anything about the child that was given to Bozhei? How does poor Aigiz take the separation? And how could your people bear to take a weeping child and hand it over to stranger?"

Her words expressed dismay and condemnation. Abai's answers were brief, but this did not discourage her.

"Bozhei's wife is hard-hearted. She has many daughters of her own and is not likely to care much for that poor child," she added sadly.

"But what about Bozhei? Even if she cares nothing for the child, he will look after it," interjected Suyundik to soften her words.

"Oh, I don't know. I've heard that in their aul it is commonly said, 'They had no cattle to spare for us and gave us that chit of a girl instead,' and the child is ill-treated. They took her from her mother, and all to no purpose! Poor Aigiz must be in a terrible state," and the baibishe wept with pity.

Abai was moved. Her sincerity and sympathy were obviously genuine. These rumours disturbed him, and at home, in Zhidebai, the news would cause fresh suffering. He remembered how Aigiz and his grandmother had wept. But then it had only been the sorrow of parting. What would happen when the cold horror of the new tidings assailed their hearts? Yesterday Kulinshak had spoken of it, and today the people of this aul. Everyone was saying that little Kamshat had been abandoned, had been given into slavery, she was humiliated and abused. Surely there must be some grain of truth in it all! In Zhidebai he would tell them all he had heard about little Kamshat. His father could say what he liked, but he was determined to do this.

Before their departure the guests were once again offered kumiss, and were not allowed to go without a last generous meal.

They had taken their leave of the elders at the Great Yurta, and the horses had set off, but Abai still could not take his eyes off the Small Yurta; its tunduk was closed as before.

"Togzhan does not care to see me again! She does not even come to say good-bye." Angrily he lashed his horse, but could not help looking back once more. A woman stood beside the Small Yurta. She wore a black hood and a flowing white garment. Was it Togzhan? Probably she had just got up. It seemed that he could hear the tinkle of the sholpy in her hair; or perhaps it was only his heart singing? But to stop just now would have been impossible.

Camel Humps, the very name of the aul now dear to Abai, was soon left far behind. Skirting the foothills of the Chinghis, the riders moved along the banks of the Karaul River. Abai brought his horse to a walking pace.

Suddenly he heard the pounding of hoofs behind and his heart jumped with hope. Quickly he looked back but the rider was a square-set djiguit, and he was not coming from Suyundik's aul. As he approached, Abai could see that he was very young, with just a faint line of down above his upper lip. His brown mare was shorn in the manner of the three-year-olds. He presented his salem, smiling cheerfully.

He had found it dull riding alone, and had overtaken the two so that he would have someone to talk to. The breast of his mare was steaming, there was foam at her mouth, and her nostrils were dilated.

The newcomer was welcome and the usual introductions were made. The young man turned out to be Yerbol and came from Suyundik's aul.

Karabas was soon chatting with the young man as though they had known each other a long time. Abai listened and felt strongly drawn to the young djiguit. Yerbol was a near kinsman of Suyundik, his mother being a cousin of Togzhan's mother, and he could visit Suyundik's house whenever he pleased. He was talkative, cheerful and immediately won Abai's heart.

There was plenty of game in the area, and Abai observed that the hunting must be good.

"Have you a falcon?" Yerbol responded promptly. "If so, come to visit us. I'll show you where there are plenty of duck and geese."

At home Takezhan had a falcon, and Yerbol's invitation was very tempting to Abai. Almost before he was out of Camel Humps, he had been tormenting himself, trying to devise all sorts of schemes; when and on what pretext could he return? This invitation was a good opportunity.

The subject of hunting brought them quickly together. They chatted like old friends and they seemed all set to go on for ever.

But at last they reached the valley where their ways parted—Yerbol had to go to the right, and Abai and Karabas to the left, to Kunkeh's aul at the foot of the Chinghis Range.

Abai was reluctant to part with Yerbol.

"Perhaps you are not in such a great hurry to get to Kolgai-nar? Why don't you come with us?" he urged.

"How can I? What shall I say if I'm asked what I have come for?" the other said laughingly.

"No one will ask. You'll stay with us for a time, and we'll go hunting with a falcon."

Yerbol hesitated.

"I'd like nothing better." He pondered a little. "But I can't," he announced decisively. "I have too much to do."

He took his leave and set off for Kolgai-nar, as gay and fresh as he had been when they had met him. This was a young man after Abai's own heart. How he envied him—Yerbol could see Togzhan every day if he wanted to. Wasn't he lucky! And Yerbol probably met her quite casually and thought nothing of it. Yerbol was his only hope. They had just been so close, and now he was gone.

2

They arrived in Karashoky after the midday meal. Kunanbai had evidently summoned a gathering, for many horses, their saddles inlaid with silver, stood tethered before Kunkeh's large tent and the smaller yurta which served as a kitchen. By the brands of the animals Karabas knew that all who had arrived dwelt in the immediate neighbourhood.

"They are Irgizbai, Zhuantayak and Topai, the usual gathering," he said, and then added with some bitterness: "Their horses are saddled and they are about to leave. We've missed the dinner!"

Abai entered the yurta and presented his salem. The tent was full. Kunanbai sat beside a high couch, his shoulders towering over the others, the front of his white shirt open to reveal a hairy chest. The guests had already put on their outdoor clothes and were finishing their kumiss as they listened to the final words of their chief. Some had partly risen, and had paused, half-kneeling, their fur hats on their heads. Kunkeh sat beyond the couch, near the door, and at her side stood old Zhumabai, who was stirring and pouring the kumiss. Abai seated himself near them and listened to his father.

"I am told that I am mistaken, that they are not plotting a new feud. Very well, I shall take note of this; I shall believe that it is so, though this may do me harm." He emphasised the last words with solemnity. "I shall be patient until I see

things with my own eyes. And those who are my true
friends,"—his one eye swept the company from end to end
and fixed itself on the elders of the Zhuantayak and
Topai clans—"let them have patience as I have. But be
ready! And when I mount my horse, you must be with me.
If you act so, you will do right in the sight of God and will
find favour with me! I have no other requests, no other
demands," he concluded, as if to say, "Those who are ready
may go."

There was a general murmur of assent.

"So be it!"

"It shall be as you say!"

Abai thought, "This is just like an oath! Father probably
called them together to draw the reins tighter."

Kunanbai had just used the word "friend". Looking
round Abai could not help noticing that these men whom
his father had styled friends were men he did not know at all
or people he knew but slightly. Once his father had
numbered among his friends such men as Baisal, Karatai,
Bozhei, Suyundik and Tusip. Not one of them was here
today. Even Kulinshak, whom Abai had visited so recently,
was absent. There was something curious about this. Who
were these new friends? And where were the old ones? Was
there something new and secretive afoot?

Abai had been confident that the differences and quarrels
had ended in the reconciliation sealed by adopting the
unfortunate child. He had heard no more rumours or loose
talk and paid little attention to the murmurings among the
people.

By now most of the guests had departed, Kunanbai
having kept back a handful of the elders. But even in this
narrow circle he seemed reserved and tense, and it was
difficult for Abai to find an opportunity to tell him about his
visit to Suyundik. But at last he was able to make his report
to his father, and decided to stay no longer, for he was
anxious to get to his mother at Zhidebai. But his father
pulled him up.

"Are you a little girl who plays with dolls?" he demanded.
"Must you always run to your mother? You seem to get on
better with the women than with me. Here you can meet
people, listen to wise speech and learn how to live. What can
you learn there?"

Privately Abai was not in accord. "You are my father, but
she is my mother," he thought. "Sons are brought up by
both." But he dared not contradict.

"I have a falcon at home," he explained hesitantly.
"There's a lot of game about and I thought I'd do some
hunting round Zhidebai."

This seemed reasonable to Kunanbai and he raised no
further objection.

"Just stay another day or two. Tomorrow I should like to
send you to Baidaly, and after that you can go to Zhidebai."

Abai was pleased and relieved, but as he left the tent he
began to ponder.

Kunanbai had first sent him to Kulinshak, with whom he
had fallen out, then to Suyundik whose old differences with
him were known to all. From neither of the old men had
Abai heard anything commendable about his father. Now
he was to be sent to Baidaly, the friend and supporter of
Bozhei.

What was the meaning of this, and why was he being sent
to see these men? It was clear that Kunanbai was
deliberately sending him to those with whom he had
quarrelled. "Let him see that they are my enemies, let him
learn to know them better, and he will understand and
respect me more!" Probably this was his father's idea.

Was it this or something else? Abai became thoughtful
again. What a maze—an impenetrable thicket through
which he, Abai, was compelled by an iron will to blunder,
helpless and unarmed.

Two days later he and Karabas were once more in the
steppes, this time on their way to Baidaly.

Here their reception little resembled the hospitality they
had been accorded at Kulinshak's and Suyundik's.

There was neither a welcome nor a repast. On crossing
the threshold of the enormous yurta they heard the angry,
scolding voice of Baidaly.

The tent was unpleasantly warm, stuffy and in disorder.
Just near the door a servant woman was preparing some
sheep cheese and a cauldron stood boiling in the middle of
the yurta. Baidaly was raining blows on a little olive-skinned
girl.

"Get out of here! You give me no peace, curse you!" He
pushed the child away. Frightened, she nearly fell into the
fire, and burst into tears. She sobbed and screamed, and
then her face turned blue as she choked with her tears.

"Throw out this trash! I can't bear the sight of her!"
Baidaly yelled to his wife, driving the child out of the yurta.

Abai and Karabas entered and presented their salem.
Baidaly reciprocated coldly.

When cheese is being made, the cauldron is occupied, a convenient excuse for those who are reluctant to treat their guests to meat. But anyway Abai felt no inclination to stay in this place of noise and disorder. "If there is no repast, so much the better," he thought and secretly laughed at the plight of Karabas, who loved food more than anything in life. The prospect of a good piece of meat for dinner or supper always meant a great deal to him, and frequently when Abai had been anxious to hurry away from somewhere, Karabas had detained him only because smoked meat was expected for supper.

Black-bearded and grim, their host did not once look at them, but stood glaring at the door. Finally he made a vague gesture to his wife, as if to say. "Shall we give them some kumiss?"

Karabas had already loosened his belt and was preparing to seat himself comfortably, but Abai understood his host's sentiments and had no intention of prolonging the visit. The kumiss was served, and Baidaly himself stirred it up and poured it.

"Where are you bound for?" he asked finally. "And what is your business?"

Abai at once conveyed his father's message.

It was again a matter of grazing land. Before departing for zhailyau the previous year Kunanbai had given the Bokenshi the land bordering on Baidaly's pastures in exchange for the grazing grounds taken from them at Karashoky. Now he begged Baidaly to permit the auls of Sugir and Suyundik to avail themselves of his pastures.

When Abai had finished, Baidaly frowned and for a long time said nothing. He fixed the young man with a piercing stare, but Abai was not to be put out of countenance. His expression was one of unaffected surprise, as though asking, "Why are you looking at me like that?"

Finally Baidaly gave his answer.

"So be it! Let Suyundik and Sugir set up their auls on my pastures. What else can I say?"

It was the decision of one who was courageous and resolute. He had wasted no time in arguing or pleading, though he was obviously seething with fury. Abai finished his kumiss, thanked his host and was about to leave when Baidaly spoke again:

"I have agreed to his proposal, but I have something more to say to your father. Will you convey to him exactly what I say?"

"Please speak your mind, aksakal. I promise to repeat your message word for word."

Baidaly was impressed.

"If I were to give the message to another, there might be gossip and false rumours. To you I can speak as to your father." Again he was silent and thoughtful.

"Was it not yesterday," he began, "before a large gathering in Karkaralinsk, that we agreed, 'Let there be peace and friendship between us'? But what has our peace come to now? If Kunanbai continues to harass me, then in what way does his peace and friendship differ from bitterness and enmity? How have I offended him? How have the Zhigitek offended your father? Our forefather Kengirbai once blessed your forefather Irgizbai to succeed him as biy after himself. Do you imagine he had no sons of his own? And yet he said, 'Irgizbai shall be at the head'. And now Kunanbai stands above us—he has the power and the glory. Why does he not cease to trample our people underfoot? He gives us no peace—he is constantly urging, 'Into the fire with you! I won't rest until I have my way!' He demands an answer, doesn't he? Then convey these words to him, 'If he does not cease to harass us, sorrow will come upon him.' Tell him that this message is not from me alone, but a salem from the entire Zhigitek. As for the land, let him have it! Not these pastures alone, but all of them!"

Baidaly waved his hand.

The yurta was silent but for the crackling of the fire beneath the cauldron. The long tongues of flame kept licking the great vessel in which the cheese was boiling. The sour milk had thickened, there was a mighty heaving, and great bubbles rose slowly to the surface. As Baidaly spoke, Abai stared at the boiling mass in fascination. The fury of indignation long suppressed! Just like that mass in the cauldron it was accumulating everywhere and rising to burst at many spots at once. Kulinshak's resentment, Suyundik's bitter words, Bozhei's hatred. And now—Baidaly....

Baidaly's words were restrained, but how many deep wounds they touched! How many bitter thoughts they evoked—and complications! That brief message was the culmination of years of disagreement, reproaches, and irrefutable accusations that could be proved to the hilt....

Abai's features were composed. He would not let Baidaly see whether he sympathised with him or not, and was intent only on hearing and remembering. Reaching for his

hunting crop and hat, he was about to take his leave, but
Baidaly again moved to speak and Abai put down his
things.

Old men know how to preserve their composure and to
bury the profoundest thoughts in the hidden unknown
depths of the soul, but this sudden change from storm to
calm, this power of self-control was quite new to Abai.
Baidaly, who had just been on the verge of explosion,
suddenly spoke peacefully—even mildly.

"Do you meet Karatai often? He's a splendid man! It's a
pity that he belongs to the poor Kokshe. If he'd been an
Irgizbai he'd have climbed high.

"One day," he went on after a moment's silence,
"Karatai, Bozhei, Baisal and I were talking, when one of us
asked, 'Who is the most generous of all we know?' We
thought this over for a time. Baisal lay blinking at the sun
like a lynx, and it was Karatai who answered, 'Kunanbai.'
Soon there was another question: 'Who is the most
eloquent?' Again Karatai answered, 'Kunanbai.' And we
asked for a third time, 'Who is the best man among us?' And
for the third time it was Karatai who answered, 'Kunanbai!'
But Baisal then raised his head from the pillow. 'Now there,
you fox! What nonsense are you talking? Kunanbai's
generous, Kunanbai's eloquent, Kunanbai's the best! Then
why do we turn up our noses and quarrel with him?' To this
Karatai answered promptly, 'Who cares about Kunanbai's
vices? Do they trouble us? Not at all. He has all the virtues
save one—charity! That's why we live in discord.'" Baidaly
looked keenly at Abai. "You, I see, are a man who knows the
value of words. Perhaps your father has never heard of that
talk of ours. Tell him about it. Karatai has witnessed his
cruelties more than once—many times! And from day to
day the Zhigitek also see and realise what sort of a man he is.
I suppose we shall not live to hear the words 'I forgive' from
him."

Baidaly relapsed into silence.

On his way back Abai had no wish to halt anywhere. What
he had heard was as painful as it was instructive.

"Let's have a race," he proposed, when they were hardly
out of the aul.

Karabas was not at all fond of such games, but in any case
they had to hurry if they were to reach Karashoky by dusk,
and the black mare he rode was as good as Abai's Aimandai.

"Well then, here we go!" He applied the spurs and darted
ahead.

They rode hard for a long time, first one of them leading, then the other, but neither would give way. Karabas would have liked to slacken the pace once he was ahead, but then Abai would be alongside on his Aimandai, shouting, "On, on! Or I'll get ahead!"

"Baidaly has set him aflame, now there's no holding him!" Karabas thought.

Their foam-flecked steeds galloped into Karashoky just before sunset.

There was a rocky hillock beyond the aul, and there Abai saw his father sitting with Maibasar. Springing from the saddle, he threw the reins to Karabas and hurried to his father.

Kunanbai realised at once that his son had come galloping all the way. The bay reared and tore at the reins, his sides heaving, which was enough for Kunanbai's experienced eye.

But this was not what concerned him. Kunanbai was not petty and never plagued his children with such admonitions as: "Now you've ruined the horse." He did not complain even if their horses went lame or collapsed beneath them. Young people would ride fast, no matter what one told them.

Kunanbai was interested in something else—Abai had not gone home, but had come hurrying up the hill, straight to his father. Kunanbai gazed intently at his son. The young man's eyes were blazing, his cheeks were aflame and his nostrils dilated. What a curious change! This was not the usual quiet and reticent Abai.

"What's the matter with you? Why are you so excited? Tell me what has happened?" he demanded as the young man approached.

Surprised to see how well his father understood the state he was in, Abai sat down and related his conversation with Baidaly word for word.

As he spoke he watched his father narrowly. Kunanbai seemed patient enough at first, but at the words, "How have we, the Zhigitek, offended?"—he frowned and stared at his son, wondering what Abai thought about it all.

His father's steady gaze did not disturb the young man, who not only fully conveyed the resentment of the Zhigitek, but even added some conclusions of his own. The hour had come for the father to face his son.

Abai wound up with the Zhigitek salem, so charged with menace. Kunanbai was still silent, and Abai related the story

Baidaly had told about Karatai's words. "He'll have to speak now," thought Abai. "But what will he say?" Impatiently he waited.

Kunanbai divined his thoughts—he knew that he had to answer neither Karatai nor Baidaly, but his son who sat waiting before him. He had to answer if only so that his son might know the worth of his father's enemies.

"Karatai," he said, "is an experienced horseman. He knows when to ride hard and when to go slow. Perhaps he is right. But it seems to me that a man's vices may grow out of any number of virtues. Persistence and perseverance, in my opinion, are man's finest qualities. When I begin something, I go on to the bitter end. It is possible that this has been the cause of my mistakes."

He sat silent for a while with an ashen face.

"A man is but a slave of Allah. And how many are the faults that may be found in a slave?" he continued more calmly.

And Abai suddenly felt that his father really was a big man. Albeit indirectly, he had admitted himself to be wrong. In this he was not like Baidaly, who was quick to accuse others but found it hard to recognise his own mistakes. His father had not spoken for the sake of eloquence: his words were fraught with meaning. Kunanbai's heart was not easy to fathom, it was as difficult as finding one's way through the intricate folds of a mountain range.

The father had his own aims, his own way—and his son had his. Abai went home, his thoughts in the same hopeless tangle.

3

Before returning to Zhidebai Abai asked his father where they were to spend the summer that year. It appeared that the Great Aul was to move first, but this time not in the usual direction. The camp was to be set up beyond the pass, in the Bakanas Valley.

The Bakanas and Baikoshkar were the largest rivers in the pasture grounds of the Tobikty. Formerly Kunanbai's auls had gone in the summer to Baikoshkar, while Bakanas had belonged to the Kokshe. But now Kunanbai had fallen out with Karatai and was apparently determined to seize his summer pastures.

Other calculations also entered into the matter. The three clans—the Bokenshi, Zhigitek and Kokshe—were preparing to spend the summer together. Baidaly's threat, conveyed through Abai, had been no idle one, and it was clear that he was gathering about him those who were of the same mind as himself. Kunanbai intended to get some of his auls into Zhigitek territory—then each of the stratagems of the Zhigitek, each of their secret moves, would reach his ears at once.

It was most advantageous to send the Great Yurta first, as Zereh's tent was known and respected by all the Tobikty. Besides Ulzhan was hospitable, open-hearted and generous—not at all like Kunkeh. She attracted everyone by her friendliness, she knew how to soften hearts and blunt enmity.

Taking everything into consideration Kunanbai ordered the Great Aul to set off for the Bakanas, a place just beyond the mountain pass, and to set up its tents alongside those of the Bokenshi.

Abai could not read his father's secret thoughts. He knew, however, that the migration of one aul alone, unaccompanied by the others, would be rather difficult—and yet he was overjoyed, for riding along the banks of the Karaul towards Bakanas would bring them near Suyundik's aul. He had been so despondent, fearing that his path would never again cross that of Togzhan and that he would not even come near her again. And now the unaccountable ways of fate were again leading him towards her aul!

His thoughts of Togzhan had been so sorrowful of late that he could not conceal his joy, and blushed violently as he heard his father's instructions. Kunanbai noticed this, but said nothing. Abai offered no objections to this strange migration, but observed that he was not altogether certain that it was a good thing for an aul to go all by itself.

But Kunanbai had thought it all out.

"You won't be alone. I've ordered no less than ten other auls to follow," he replied.

Having discussed all the details, Abai returned to Zhidebai.

He would meet Togzhan again. He would see her, and more than once perhaps. What a precious, unexpected stroke of good luck! Now his thoughts were only of Togzhan; visions of her crowded into his mind.

"My only one! My hope!" he repeated again and again. The words came of their own accord, and seemed to keep time with the hoofs of Aimandai under him. Such

moments were never to be repeated. This was winged
youth, aflame with passion!

Abai rode all the way at a fast trot. Never before had this
ride seemed so short, and he did not even notice how he got
to his mother's aul.

In Zhidebai everyone had long moved into the yurtas.
The Karaul River had overflowed its banks that year and
the surrounding meadows were covered with lush grass.
The numerous white yurtas of the aul had such a festive
look as if some very welcome guests were expected. Flocks
of sheep hemmed it in on all sides; lambs were bleating for
their mothers and dogs were barking. Everywhere there
were people, and the aul was busy and noisy. Abai reined in
before the Great Yurta, greeted his mothers, and gave them
his father's instructions. The green grass had appeared
early this year on the zhailyau grounds, and the auls in the
Chinghis had not troubled to move to the foothills but had
at once set off for the summer pastures. The Great Aul,
therefore, must not lag behind.

Ulzhan agreed, her only objection being that she could
not move at once, but needed at least five or six days to pack
and put the winter houses into shape before departure.

Abai was worried. What if Suyundik's aul crossed the
mountains first and got so far ahead that it would be
impossible to overtake them! And how pleasant it was to
travel with the auls of one's friends! To move together and
halt together by day and by night! During the zhailyau
wandering, it was customary to dwell in the small yurtas, in
huts and in light tents. If you were in love, you could meet in
a tent on a moonlit night! Abai had often heard of such
things from the older djiguits.

But his mother's decision was inflexible. In household
affairs Ulzhan always did as she chose, not even deferring to
Kunanbai. Abai had grudgingly to consent.

During the evening meal he told Zereh and Ulzhan what
he had heard about little Kamshat, keeping back nothing
and relating all the details. Let them weep and grieve, but he
could no longer conceal the plight of the little girl.

Zereh sighed and began to heap angry reproaches upon
Kunanbai. Ulzhan sat still for a time and then addressed
Abai:

"Say nothing to Aigiz of this. Her heart is already broken.
Only this morning she told us that in a dream she had seen
Kamshat fall into the fire."

"Suyundik's wife is a real mother," she added after a

moment's silence, "kind and loving. She would not say such things without reason. When we reach the Chinghis, take one of the grown men and go to see Kamshat. When we learn all that there is to know, we shall speak to father. Then we may tell Aigiz."

Ten days later Kunanbai's Great Aul crossed the range and settled in the neighbourhood of the Zhigitek and Bokenshi.

Some ten auls had made the journey—just as Kunanbai had foretold. Right until the last day it had been impossible to overtake the Bokenshi and Zhigitek, who had moved from the Chinghis foothills earlier. The Great Aul had evidently travelled more slowly than the others.

From the very first day of their arrival they were showered with presents of meat and kumiss, traditional gifts to Zereh as a sign of welcome to the Great Aul. Bevies of women kept slipping into the Great Yurta to greet old Zereh. Notwithstanding their quarrel with Kunanbai, all the kinsmen in the vicinity came to present their respects, with the exception of Bozhei, Baidaly, Sugir and Suyundik. Everyone who came to Zereh was warmly received, and those who failed to come were tactfully not mentioned.

On the day after their arrival Abai and Gabitkhan went to Bozhei's aul, which lay across the green hill to the west, on the shore of a fresh-water lake. Arriving during the midday meal, Abai at once saw that this was not a prosperous aul—there were only one or two fine new yurtas, the rest being black with age.

At Bozhei's yurta, Abai and Gabitkhan dismounted. They learned that the master was away, visiting a kinsman across the lake.

As they tethered their horses and approached the tent, they heard a feeble wailing—a pitiful sound that could come only from a sick child.

Abai recognised the voice of Kamshat and his heart grew heavy. Rounding the tent, they approached the entrance, to hear a harsh voice cursing and scolding the child. It was Bozhei's baibishe, and her viciously enunciated words each struck a painful blow to Abai.

"Don't howl! Stop your screech, you blasted foundling!"

Abai parted the curtains and entered with Gabitkhan. The roomy yurta was richer than its external appearance indicated, and there were many valuable rugs and draperies. But everything was in disorder: the floor had not been swept, the beds were unmade and things lay scattered everywhere. A large swarthy woman sat at a spinning-wheel by the bed. Her twitching nostrils and the incessant movement of her lips betrayed her shrewish character.

Bozhei's two daughters sat on the floor behind the bed, busy with embroidery; these overripe maidens, both ugly and clumsy, looked as bad-tempered as their mother.

The child went on crying.

Yes, it was Kamshat. She lay curled up on some filthy rags, with the sleeve of an old coat for a pillow. Her wailing was weak and tremulous, a lament at the callousness and cruelty around her.

The once rosy and chubby Kamshat was thin and pale as after a long illness, and her arms and legs were incredibly thin. Her little face expressed helpless suffering, and her sunken cheeks were wrinkled like a grown-up's who had been starved or had gone through some terrible experience. This exhausted, neglected child was a truly pitiful sight.

Abai and Gabitkhan rushed to her, but Kamshat did not recognise them and turned away in fright.

Gabitkhan was horrified, and could not control himself.

"Oh, my poor defenceless darling. How you have suffered, you innocent child," he exclaimed, in tears.

Abai's face was ashen, and he shook with rage.

The women hurried to offer absurd, irrelevant explanations.

"The others are well, but not this poor thing—her stomach ails her," began the baibishe in a sugary tone.

"'If your belly hurts then your mouth should be empty!' But does she understand this? No! The moment she's a little better, she snatches at everything! How can she ever get well! She makes herself ill," echoed the overripe maidens, anxious to display solicitude.

Abai would not speak. The very look of these heartless women had told him the worst as soon as he had crossed the threshold.

Bozhei's wife ordered the samovar, but Abai refused tea.

"We shall not drink," he said. "We are going."

How could one think of food with little Kamshat suffering in bondage! "Oh, my own, my very own!" That was the funeral cry for a kinsman. Of what avail was it to weep for a kinsman after death! He had to get out of the tent quickly or he would grab the child and carry her off. "My poor, defenceless darling!" he almost shouted.

It was best to keep quiet before these hard-hearted women. Stung by the lying words of Bozhei's daughters, he wanted to shout at them, to pour out all the anger and fury that was choking him. But it would only make Kamshat's plight worse, not better. He could do nothing.

The baibishe offered him a cup of kumiss, but how could he drink? He put the cup down on the floor untouched. Who was he angry with? Whom could he accuse or blame? Was Bozhei's family alone to blame? Of course not! These were Abai's thoughts as he left the yurta.

Never had he been so enraged. It was evening before he got back to his aul, but his anger had not subsided.

Tethered to the post between the Great Yurta and the Guest Yurta stood Kunanbai's long-backed bay, side by side with another animal, both of them saddled. It was clear that his father had just arrived. All the better! Abai was determined to have the piteous sorrowful moans of his baby daughter reach the father. He entered the yurta and sure enough, Kunanbai was there, having made the journey with old Zhumabai.

Aigiz entered the yurta on Abai's heels. The mother's heart had anticipated some fresh sorrow—some irresistible force had drawn her here. She knew that Abai went to visit Bozhei, and no sooner were they across the threshold than she pleaded:

"Abai-zhan! Have you learned anything of your poor little sister?"

Zereh and Ulzhan also turned, waiting for his answer.

Abai looked at his father. Kunanbai sat silent, regarding Aigiz coldly.

"I saw her with my own eyes," said the young man. "Kamshat is ill, a hair's breadth from death. She could not recognise us. She is surrounded by strangers, by enemies.... What can I say?"

Kunanbai gave him a baleful look, but said nothing. The women gasped, wept and lamented.

Aigiz grew pale.

"Light of my eyes! My little dove, my poor child, torn from its mother!" she cried. "Who has cursed the day you were born?"

Kunanbai flung out an arm to command silence, or perhaps to protect himself from the curse of a mother.

Aigiz, who always trembled before him, immediately grew quieter. She continued in whispers, scarcely breathing.

"Stop it or you'll be sorry!" he shouted at her. "To the devil with you and your spite!"

She dared not answer. Ulzhan, however, sitting next to Abai, managed to dry her tears and asked:

"What is all this? Would you have us die of sorrow with never a cry? Is that what you want?" Desperately she continued, "Do you think our grief began today? We have long been weeping for Kamshat. But to whom could we complain? Who would have understood?"

Kunanbai cut her short, but now Zereh was aroused.

"Do not try to put fear into my daugters-in-law!" she demanded authoritatively. She sat up angrily, her hands resting on the floor, and looked her son in the eye. Never had Abai seen his grandmother so formidable.

She continued to stare intently at Kunanbai. The determination in her look made him avert his eyes.

"To whom should they bring their grief and their hopes if not to you?" she persisted. "If you want to be cruel, then be so to your enemies! What is the good of your cruelty among friends, in your own family? You may think yourself a God on earth, but it was not from the heavens that you descended. You are the child of mortals and were born of a woman: it was I who gave you birth. They too are mothers and wish to share their grief with you. You have delivered up Kamshat to be rent and torn, and left us grief and despair. Cease your bellowing—find some means of consolation, some means of mending the evil! Rescue that orphaned child from its tormentors!"

Zereh spoke in an imperious tone.

All were still. Kunanbai himself was speechless with fury. Not for years had anyone dared to speak to him that way. But the voice of his mother was the voice of his conscience, of justice, and her words were scathing.

"What can I do? Such was the decree of the elders of the clans!" he made an attempt to justify himself.

Abai had long thought of that decree with abhorrence. "And what a heartless, cruel and inhuman decree it was!" he suddenly burst out. "Is that the way to reconcile people? Can such a decree bring peace to anyone? It can only stir up the dregs of bitterness in the hearts. What are these mothers to think and feel about the Zhigitek who took their child from them by force? What talk can there be of peace when the Zhigitek wanted cattle and instead received a child that requires care and attention? They may be inhuman and callous to value five mares above the life of Kamshat. But what about us who handed over a helpless child like a wretched puppy!"

His father was listening very attentively. This was something new. No one had expressed such ideas before. But one could not argue that way: Abai was not treading the beaten track of centuries, but some unknown path of his own.

"Eh, my son, my stripling! Your heart is right, but you ignore the customs of our people," he exclaimed.

His tone was different now, no longer commanding—he seemed to be willing to discuss the problem that was torturing them all. Though he had called Abai a "stripling", it was obvious that he was weighing up his son's words. His answer, too, showed that he was making a concession to Aigiz and Ulzhan.

"The customs of our forefathers teach otherwise," he said after a pause. "To reconcile those who have quarrelled it is customary to conclude a marriage between the hostile families. The girl is given away as an offering, as a slave and hostage. But we have given away Kamshat for Bozhei to raise as his daughter. Does this mean that we have delivered her to torture? That depends entirely on Bozhei. If he is capable of understanding anything at all, why did he not receive my child as one of his own? If he treats her as a stranger, then he is violating the terms of our agreement and has failed in his duty to us. He may hate me, but can he think that my child, whom I have taken from her swaddling clothes and handed over to him, is in any way guilty? If he could not impress such a very simple idea on his family, then he is good for nothing."

With these words Kunanbai annihilated Bozhei.

After his visit to Bozhei's Abai had for the first time felt deeply incensed with the Zhigitek leader, in whom he no longer had confidence. "If his wife is so inhuman, then why does he not show her where her duty lies?" he had asked Gabitkhan on the way back.

Kunanbai came to a decision, and on the following day old Zhumabai presented Kunanbai's salem in Bozhei's aul. Aigiz too had sent an aged neighbour to Bozhei's baibishe:

"Tell her she is killing my child. What woman, if she is in her right mind and has a conscience, would do such a thing?"

Zhumabai returned from Bozhei, gloomy and depressed. He reported that he had found Bozhei in the company of Baidaly and Tusip. Informed of Aigiz's complaint by his baibishe, Bozhei had conferred with his friends and family, and had sent Kunanbai the following grim reply, "Kunanbai once threw my honour to the flames. Does he think I have recovered from this? That the wound has healed? Has it occurred to him what I had to suffer? He doesn't care if we all burn to ashes as long as his smallest twig is spared! What has Kunanbai lost? Only one little grain that has fallen from his granary. Let him leave me alone—let him not try my patience!"

That was all that Bozhei had had to say to Zhumabai, his words throbbing with the old hatred. It seemed that strife and revenge had again raised their heads, once again crying, "Beware, we are still raging!" His last hope destroyed by Bozhei's reply, Abai was deeply troubled.

Where was their pity? The baibishe and her daughters obviously had none—they were stupid and ignorant. But what about Bozhei himself? How could he have sentenced an innocent babe to a lingering death? Such cruelty—and without remorse! Was it only on the surface that Bozhei appeared to be humane, gentle and merciful, as he had seemed when he had endured blows without attempting to retaliate? Was he any better than Kunanbai, whom he accused of cruelty? Kunanbai heard Bozhei's reply without looking up. His face turned grey and his breath came with difficulty. But his habitual morose taciturnity did not leave him. Only to Abai he said bitterly:

"To him my daughter is not a human being, but a wolf-cub. His hatred will die only in the grave. If one of my sons fell into his hands, he would put out his eyes or tear him apart! That's clear beyond doubt. Very well, then. I accept the position. I shall wait before striking."

Within a few days came the terrible news that Kamshat was dead.

She had died in the morning and was hastily buried in the afternoon of the same day. No one had been informed of her death—neither the aul of Kunanbai nor even her own mother Aigiz. Someone in Ulzhan's aul had heard the news from a passing herdsman.

Everyone was appalled by such bestial senseless cruelty. Kamshat had been just a small child, sacrificed on the altar of discord and hostility.

Bozhei had apparently realised something of this—when Kamshat died he ordered his wife to send word to Aigiz, but Baidaly made him revoke the order, and they buried the child without troubling to summon her kinsfolk.

Ever since Kunanbai had taken the summer pastures from the Zhigitek and given them to the Bokenshi, the two clans,

which had always dwelt in peace, had been living in mutual
suspicion and constant resentment. The grazing lands, the
pastures by the rivers — everything now gave rise to bitter
discord.

Baidaly and Tusip could see this well and were constantly
troubled by the thought that the discord sown by Kunanbai
might in time lead to a complete breach with the Bokenshi,
which would deprive the Zhigitek of their last ally in their
struggle against the Irgizbai. It was his hatred for Kunanbai
that had prompted Baidaly to advise Bozhei to bury
Kamshat without the formality of summoning her kinsmen.
Bozhei was fully aware of the enormity of this insult to
Kunanbai, but had agreed, although he quite foresaw the
consequences. His hatred of Kunanbai was too strong for
him to miss so convenient an opportunity for revenge.

Kunanbai was mad with anger when he learned that
Kamshat had been buried in such a way. Unhesitatingly, but
secretly, he summoned the elders of the Irgizbai, Topai and
Zhuantayak, told them of Bozhei's action and left the matter
to their judgement. A messenger was sent to Bozhei.

This time it was not Zhumabai who was sent to speak to
the Zhigitek. Instead, Kunanbai sent Izgutty and Zhakip, his
foster brother and his brother, who had always shared his
joys and sorrows.

They wasted no time on pleasantries with Bozhei.

"What have you done?" demanded Izgutty. "Was the
child a mere slave captured as plunder? Was she not the
child of Kunanbai himself? Could you not have told her
mother and let her at least throw a handful of earth upon
the grave? What senseless, stupid revenge!"

In the presence of Baidaly and Tusip Bozhei retorted:

"Of course, Kunanbai is looking for another pretext to
kindle hostilities! Did you expect me to proclaim the news
far and wide and hold a funeral feast for an infant no bigger
than my thumb? And would it have prevented him from
hurling himself on me! If I am guilty, let him exact
vengeance in blood. Let us see whether he is strong
enough!"

The quarrel over the grazing lands had apparently
reached its climax. Bozhei's challenge showed that he was
ready for anything.

Baidaly and Tusip firmly supported him and no sooner
had Izgutty departed than they summoned their kinsmen.
Their differences with the Bokenshi were forgotten: in this
moment of danger all rallied round the Zhigitek.

And on the very evening that Kunanbai addressed his
allies and gave his blessing for a renewal of hostilities, Baisal,
Karatai, Suyundik and others in Bozhei's aul likewise firmly
resolved to fight and sealed their decision with an oath to
the Zhigitek leader.

It was early summer and many auls which had just
crossed the Chinghis were beginning to set up their yurtas.
Both sides now hastened their preparations for the migration in order to reach the summer pastures on the banks of
the Bakanas and Baikoshkar rivers as soon as possible. The
season promised to be a stormy one. Both Irgizbai and
Zhigitek were preparing for a clash.

The large auls of the Tobikty moved quickly. The djiguits
held their soeels and shokpars constantly at the ready, and
the horses chosen for riding in the summer were kept
without food after dark so that they remained in good form.

The flames of anger and of enmity spread wider and
wider. Anxiety and fear stalked from aul to aul. There were
vague rumours of sudden attacks and looting, and the
people—both Irgizbai and Zhigitek—slept warily, ever
tense and alert.

In that troubled time of tension Zereh's aul travelled
night and day until it reached the Bakanas River. Within a
day it was surrounded not by ten but by forty auls. From
early morning until late at night the yurtas of Ulzhan and
Aigiz were crowded with armed men.

Kunanbai travelled constantly with the Great Aul, summoning the elders, issuing orders and instructions. Having
arrived at Bakanas, he gathered together all the biys, elders
and messengers. In the thirty or forty auls in his immediate
vicinity there were extraordinary assemblies which met not
to choose new officials and elders, to honour the memory of
the dead, hold races, or to celebrate weddings, but for no
apparent reason at all. Finally these vast gatherings came to
be a daily occurrence.

Abai knew nothing of his father's plans. Kunanbai was
constantly in the company of the old men and was virtually
unapproachable. Abai spent his days with his mothers,
sharing their grief.

The Zhigitek, Bokenshi and Kotibak had been expected
to settle on their summer grounds, which lay near the
Bakanas. For some reason, however, they failed to appear,
and it turned out that they had remained behind, somewhere near the pass. It was usual for warring sides to
overtake or harass one another on the way, and at the outset

it had seemed that the Zhigitek meant to repeat these traditional manoeuvres. What had happened to them? Why had they fallen behind? What were they up to? No one could find a satisfactory answer.

Three Bokenshi arrivals brought the news that Bozhei had been gravely ill for the past five days, and that his illness had taken a turn for the worse the day before. Perhaps feeling that the end was near, or for some other reason, he had gathered his kinsmen about him on the evening before and taken leave of them. The latest arrivals at Bakanas related that they had heard this with their own ears.

The auls of the Irgizbai and their allies along the Bakanas, which had been living in daily expectation of stormy events, of sudden attacks and violence, could now talk of nothing but Bozhei's illness.

On the next day there came the chilling news of Bozhei's death. He had breathed his last in the night.

It was Zhumabai who brought the news, as Ulzhan, Kunanbai and Zereh were sitting over their morning tea with Abai, Ospan and Takezhan.

Kunanbai sat pale and pensive, his one eye peering through the door at the distant green hills. Silently he moved his lips in prayer.

Zereh was bowed down with sorrow, and a heavy sigh escaped her as the tears gathered in her eyes.

Abai's heart cringed with pain.

The auls of the Irgizbai waited patiently for the messenger who must appear to inform them of the death of the Zhigitek leader. According to custom a fast rider should have dashed to their auls to invite them to the funeral.

No matter how bitter the enmities of daily life there was a saying which could not be denied: "All must recede before a splendid feast or a fresh grave." No matter what had happened when Bozhei was alive, not a single kinsman must be missing from his funeral or fail to lament his passing with the others.

Large quantities of kumiss were accordingly prepared; fattened horses were set aside for slaughter; the yurtas were folded away and there was talk of starting without waiting for an invitation. The messenger was awaited all day, but no one came.

It was incredible: Kunanbai had not been invited to the funeral, a deliberate slight to him and his aul.

Whether Bozhei himself had so decreed before his death or whether his kinsmen Baidaly, Baisal and Tusip had thus decided was a matter of conjecture. To Kunanbai it was more than a personal insult. Fratricidal hatred, suppressed for a while but not extinguished, had raised its head again and now menaced him across the body of a dead man. Not only had Bozhei's nearest kin been invited, but even the most distant auls of the numerous Tobikty people. None had been forgotten but Kunanbai.

Kunanbai felt depressed. But not for long. Irrepressible, consuming anger welled up in him. It was impossible to seek revenge upon a dead man, but he was determined to make Baidaly and Baisal pay for his humiliation, which was unprecedented among the Tobikty.

He knew that there could be no question of open hostilities for the time and issued fresh instructions to all the auls along the Bakanas as well as to the aul of Ulzhan: "See to your household affairs and fear nothing!" Accompanied by Zhumabai he then left for the aul of Kunkeh.

The auls which from day to day had been expecting an armed clash relaxed their tension and life took its normal course. Who would dare to mount a horse to attack his neighbours on days overshadowed by death?

ALONG THE FOOTHILLS

1

It was long before the hour of noon, but the stifling heat was already unbearable. In the skies there was not so much as a scrap of cloud. Nor had there been a drop of rain throughout that scorching, paralysing summer and the earth lay gaping in parched fissures. But the Bakanas was a copious river and its banks were richly clothed in shrubbery, wild acacias, feather-grass and wormwood, and for that reason the auls were anxious to spend the summer here. If not for that oppressive heat, there were no better pastures anywhere!

His face streaming with perspiration, Abai emerged from the yurta, but saw little to cheer him.

Where find relief? For a long time he stood dazed, then yawned and ambled towards the river. Drops of sweat trickled down his face, his head ached, and in his heart he cursed the Bakanas and its sweltering heat.

The boys had invaded the river and the noisiest of them were Ospan and Smagul. Abai plunged in some distance away. After swimming twice across the wide Bakanas he felt cool and cheerful, and he began to dive like a porpoise. Ospan came closer, watching with envious admiration.

Looking up, Abai saw Takezhan at the water's edge. He was mounted and ornately dressed, a real djiguit, with a falcon on his wrist. His black-maned bay was prancing about and straining at the bit.

Two wild ducks hung from his saddle. At the sight of the game, the children ran to him, each trying to outshriek the other:

"Oh, agatai,* give them to me!"

"No! To me! To me!"

Takezhan usually gave his game to the children, but first liked to have them plead and humble themselves in every way. The youngsters were used to this and continued to wheedle.

* Affectionate term for elder brother.— *Ed.*

Suddenly there was a strange rumbling sound from the other side of the hill, as of steppes afire or a great army on the march. The boys stood still, glancing questioningly at Takezhan and Abai.

A huge herd of horses appeared on the crest of the hill and began to descend into the valley. Snorting and neighing the white and grey animals moved steadily on. Foals and colts whinnied, and breaking away from the herd, the colts raced playfully about over the grass. The horses on which the children had arrived grew restive. They pricked up their ears and, hobbled as they were, made clumsy attempts to join the oncoming herd. The children flew to head them off.

In this deserted spot a herd this size could only mean the approach of a wandering aul, and when the children had remounted they were not surprised to see the first of the nomads silhouetted against the sky.

Fifteen camels strode at the head of the procession, followed by a lengthy winding chain of groups of eight, ten or fifteen camels. Then came riders armed with soeels and shokpars. Here and there a djiguit carried a hooded eagle.

But the caravan that emerged behind the riders astonished them all.

It was surrounded by numerous women on horseback, girls and women of all ages, richly attired and mounted on superb mounts whose saddles, reins and breast ornaments blazed with silver. An even row of girls on horseback led a saddled dark grey horse with crooped mane and tail. Then followed an elderly woman with a drawn, pale face, and dressed in black. The packs of all the fifteen camels of this group were covered with black rugs, dark embroidered cloths and felts patterned in black.

The boys dared not cross the path of this magnificently solemn and mournful procession, and had no alternative but to sit still on their horses, burning with curiosity.

As the girls of the front row approached they seemed to confer with one another and then altered their formation—two of them moved forward, leading the saddled dark grey by the reins.

Ospan came closer to Abai.

"Who are they? What does it all mean?" He fidgeted in his saddle and prodded his elder brother in the side with his whip. Suddenly he began to laugh. "My goodness! Look at their hats. Abai! Look at them!"

Abai turned on him angrily:

"Be quiet!"

The sight that had set Ospan off was equally strange to Abai.

Both he and Takezhan had realised that this was Bozhei's funeral train. Obviously the saddle and the red cloak carried by the cropped horse had belonged to its dead master. Bozhei's riding-whip was fastened upright to the front pommel of the saddle, and upon it hung his fox-fur hat. But most extraordinary of all was the appearance of the two girls who rode in front. Each of them wore a man's hat of fine black lambskin and dark velvet. The most curious thing, however, was not that they were wearing such hats, but that they were wearing them back to front, so that their faces were completely covered by the flaps which were made to protect the neck.

When they noticed that a company was waiting to let them pass, the two girls raised the funeral lament. The five behind aligned their rank and joined in the singing. It was customary for the girls of a wandering aul in mourning to sing these laments whenever they passed a settlement or some unknown travellers.

But what did Ospan care about old customs? As far as he could remember no one had died at home and it would have been quite useless to explain the meaning of such a procession to him. He would not even have understood. Everything seemed absurd to him and he could not help laughing. Afraid of Abai, he did not raise his head, but his shoulders shook with suppressed laughter.

Abai glanced at the girls and froze, his left hand thrust through the thong of his riding-whip and raised high, as though he were about to cry, "Stay, if only for a moment!" But not a sound escaped his lips. Pale and barely able to breathe, he let his hand sink again on to the mane of his horse.

The central one of the five girls riding by was Togzhan, whom Abai had not seen since their first meeting in the spring. She rode a white pacer with a silken mane.

The folds of her black satin cape rustled softly with every movement. Her head was graced with a new cap of home-spun silk, and a filmy shawl around her neck fluttered like gossamer. Large golden earrings swayed lazily from the lobes of her ears. Surrounded by girls of her own age, she shone like the morning star in the dimly lit heavens. Her hands resting on the yellow sash girdling the black satin, she rode slowly on, looking straight ahead and singing the lament, the song of death. Her clear, open brow, the soft line of her white neck and the waves of black hair cascading down her back merged in his sight to produce a vision of pure, unearthly and touching loveliness.

Abai watched her unblinkingly, no longer breathing. He listened to the lament—to the high, soaring voice. Was it Togzhan or one of the other girls singing? But such a voice, he felt, could come from no other.

For an instant he could see nothing. The lowering skies seemed to have suddenly parted to reveal the moonbeam, dazzling in its still beauty. For an instant he lost his senses. He bowed his head to this glorious vision, the like of which he had never before seen or heard of.

But it was only for an instant. Then this scene which set his mind in a whirl gave rise to a new and painful emotion.

The lament of Togzhan, the weeping of Bozhei's daughters, the funeral procession, the mourning colours, the riderless horse with the cropped mane and tail, all expressed the sorrow of an entire clan. They had not invited Kunanbai to the funeral, had not forgiven him, had not let him share their grief, their sorrow. This procession in which his Togzhan was the most brilliant gem had passed him coldly by, as though to say, "Away with you and your cruel father. It is not for you to look upon us!"

The lament sung by his beloved, the mourning for Bozhei, a close kinsman taken by death, was like a reproach to him as well. "Am I to blame?" He would have liked to vindicate himself, but his sadness overwhelmed him. Downcast, he saw nothing and heard nothing but the mournful melody of death.

Someone prodded him in the back, "Let us go!" Abai turned swiftly, startled from his trance. It was Takezhan frowning and jeering:

"What are you snivelling for?"

Abai shivered and passed the back of his hand over his cheek. He was surprised to find his face wet with tears.

The mourning train had moved on.

Takezhan and Abai fell behind. Takezhan continued to play the grown-up as usual.

"What's the matter with you? Do you call yourself a man? What were you snivelling about?"

Abai grew angry:

"You're quite the grown-up, aren't you? But you've no more sense than a child! Was Bozhei a stranger? You should have been weeping with the rest."

"We? Why should we weep?... They did not even invite us to the funeral!"

"It was the living who did not invite you, not the dead. Why blame the dead?"

"Why blame him? Of course I blame him. He was on bad terms with father."

"And who is to blame for that?" Abai asked. "You seem to know everything—just who is right and who is wrong?"

"Whether I do or whether I don't, I side with father! His friends are my friends, and his enemies my enemies."

"Do you really think it takes much wisdom for the cub to run with the wolf?"

"Oh, shut up," Takezhan snapped, lashed his horse and galloped ahead.

Glad to be rid of him, Abai rode at a walking pace.

"It doesn't take much wisdom for the cub to run with the wolf." He had uttered these words in the heat of the moment, but only now did he grasp their full import. Anyone could follow the beaten track, the path mapped out by their fathers! If one were only strong, and could find one's own way....

Lost in thought, Abai reached the Bakanas before he knew it.

No sooner did Zereh and Ulzhan learn from Abai that Bozhei's aul had come to its summer grounds than they hastily dispatched a messenger to Kunanbai. "The aul of mourning is quite near," said their message. "If we do not go there now, then how shall we afterwards look people in the face? Let Kunanbai decide what to do quickly."

And Kunanbai made his decision. Accompanied by Kunkeh, ten elders and djiguits he arrived in Bakanas on the same evening. The twenty neighbouring auls then prepared supplies of kumiss and slaughtered the fattened animals.

They set off at noon the next day, some fifty men, about forty women and a small group of boys, among them Abai, Takezhan and Ospan. Only Zereh and Ulzhan rode in the carriage with one other old woman known to everyone as Sary-apa. On Kunanbai's instructions the carriage had set off ahead of the riders.

Approaching the mourning aul the riders dashed down the slope with cries and shrieks that rang over the steppes.

According to custom, those who came to an aul or settlement during a funeral had to arrive at a gallop, crying,

"Oh, my own, my very own!" The elders had to begin, and
those behind watched for the signal. Kunanbai and the men
with him started off, howling and weeping, and the others,
followed.

Abai rode in the central group. Next to him galloped his
eldest brother Kudaiberdy, son of Kunkeh, the messenger
Zhumagul and old Zhumabai. Behind them rode Takezhan,
Ospan and others.

"Oi-bai, my own, my very own! My brother! My rock of
hope, my only support," they cried.

Zhumagul and Takezhan rocked to and fro in their
saddles as though they would fall off at any moment. To
look at them they were dying of grief, but Abai was not
deceived.

He too uttered the sorrowful cry, but with him there was
no need to simulate grief, and Kudaiberdy at his side was as
sincere as himself. Abai had always been fond of this
brother though they met but rarely, and now he decided to
stay near him throughout the ceremony.

Zereh's carriage had already arrived at the Great Yurta of
Bozhei, which towered over the other tents in the heart of
the aul. The white funeral yurta stood apart, the black-and-
white banner fluttering from a tall staff.

As they topped the hill before the aul, Kunanbai and his
party discerned the flag of mourning and swept towards it
like the flood waters of spring. On they came, shouting and
lamenting. Abai could see some thirty men before the white
yurta, weeping as they leaned on their white staffs. These
were Bozhei's kinsmen, preparing to meet the guests.

The riders dismounted. The group before the tent was
headed by Baidaly, Baisal, Tusip and Karasha. Other
relatives behind them also leaned on their white staffs,
sobbing.

Swift, agile djiguits swarmed forward to meet the guests,
helped them to dismout, tethered their horses, and then led
them to the elders. Instead of the usual greetings the guests
embraced their hosts and wept with them. When he saw how
Baidaly, Baisal and the other elders were weeping, Abai
could no longer restrain himself, and as he dismounted, he
began sobbing. And thus lamenting and weeping, all were
led into the Great Yurta where the sorrowful moaning went
on incessantly.

The Great Yurta was crowded with women. Sitting in
rows from the front door to the places of honour, they
rocked to and fro with their hands on their hips as they

chanted the funeral cry. The very loudest and most desperate of the mourners was Bozhei's baibishe in the centre. A black shawl covered her head, and the tears flowed from her eyes in an unending stream. Five girls sitting near lamented as bitterly as she, and it seemed that the great dome of the yurta was filled to bursting point with moans and wails.

As they entered the yurta, the men knelt before the women, embraced them and wept.

Abai followed closely behind Kudaiberdy and embraced all who were near him, finding it impossible to do these honours to everyone. Kudaiberdy, the tears streaming down his face, first embraced the baibishe of Bozhei, sobbing violently.

"Aga-ekem, my very own," he moaned.

Abai, too, approached her first and then turned to the girls who sat a little further away.

At last the lengthy general lamenting was over. Only the baibishe carried on while the five girls sobbed over her words. The baibishe bemoaned her irretrievable loss, bewailing the cruelty of fate, moving the heart of everyone in the yurta. Gradually, she too grew quiet.

But the two daughters of Bozhei would not cease. Their lament had now become a dirge, the two of them singing as one. Pronouncing every word very distinctly they broke off now and then to sigh or moan in unison, but always resuming:

"Oh, father!... Had you but waited until we were grown! You have left us as orphans and alone.... To whose care?... Why have you left us to bitter tears?" And the listeners could not help sobbing again.

To Abai these moments were the hardest.

The girls' lament gradually changed to a song about their father's life, becoming a song of his bravery, honour and good deeds. Their voices grew more and more plaintive.

But it was not only of Bozhei that they sang; they recalled all who had surrounded him, mentioned all his contemporaries, and suddenly mentioned Kunanbai.

The Great Yurta grew very still.

Kunanbai sat silent, his hat pushed down over his brow, his head bowed. The girls' lament was like a blow in the face.

But according to custom no one dared interrupt a lament: it was as sacred as the Holy Writ itself. No one could silence or curb it, for it stood above the law. And the words grew ever sharper:

> *Our foe he became, Kunanbai.*
> *For wrongs done he gave us his child,*
> *The name of our foe— Kunanbai,*
> *Fiercer he is than a kulan* wild,*
> *A serpent could not be so sly...*

The merciless voices scourged Kunanbai cruelly—as if striking him squarely in his single eye.

The old men who sat about him began to fidget, fearing an outburst. They coughed, blew their noses and stirred uneasily. But Kunanbai gritted his teeth and kept quiet.

Abai hung his head, dying from shame. Long before, when the baibishe had just begun her lament, he had noticed Togzhan among the girls. Her face was covered and he had only a side view of her. "If only the earth would swallow us," he thought, "it would be better than having to endure such a disgrace."

Someone nearby suddenly clicked a tongue. Abai raised his head; it was Sary-apa. Frowning, she got up, walked to the centre of the yurta, squatted on the floor, pulled the black cloak over her head and began a song of her own.

At first she sang only of Bozhei, lamented his death, but finally added:

> *Oh madens, have you lost all shame?*
> *Good men are fewer than the wicked,*
> *Was there so little honour to Bozhei's good name*
> *That he should have been buried in such secret?*

She sang these words loudly and clearly and was then silent.

Nothing could have expressed the feelings of the warring camps better than these two laments from the women. There was nothing more to say. Gabitkhan, who had been sitting at Zereh's side, began to chant the Koran in the sing-song Bokhara manner. All sat very still, listening.

Thus Kunanbai paid his last respects to Bozhei.

When the chanting was over, the women were left to themselves as the men retired to another tent for the repast. Everyone, including the elders of the aul, Baidaly and Tusip, waited on the guests. But the tea, the kumiss and the meat failed to break the ice between Bozhei's kinsmen and the guests. Baidaly himself offered tea to Kunanbai and showed him every attention; but the moment they tried to speak, the same frigid politeness stole between them, and there was nothing to say to each other.

---

* Kulan—wild ass.— *Ed.*

A few remarks were exchanged about the condition of the cattle and the fodder that year, about the skirmishes between the Kerei and Naiman and how they had pillaged one another. But nothing more. The guests departed on the same evening—quiet and subdued.

But Kunanbai felt as though a great burden had fallen from him.

Once at home, at Kunkeh's, he sat still for a time, and finally said emphatically:

"Sary-apa shall be respected and honoured by all!"

2

Autumn came. It had been drizzling for three days. The auls had returned across the Chinghis from their summer grounds, stored hay for the winter and without wasting time made straight for the autumn pastures.

Many auls had gathered in the meadows of Zhidebai and nearby places. They had flooded the wide Chinghis valleys, the foothills and the ravines.

The big summer tents had already been dismantled and packed away. The auls had smaller but warmer yurtas, and each tried to make his home as warm as possible, fires being kindled in the tents and the walls lined with felt. A small yurta made of one piece of felt, which was not harmed by smoke, was the best in this season.

The sheep were no longer milked—the surest sign that the summer grounds had been left behind and that the auls had moved to the autumn pastures. The lambs grew big and grazed with the sheep.

The men, mostly riding about from aul to aul to gossip or wrangle, looked quite different now. The cold nights and the mud had compelled them to put on high boots, with felt legs and lambskin coats. Their horses too were different. Those which had been used in the summer had grown lean and were turned out to graze with the herds.

The men rode the horses that had rested all summer—going at a walk to spare their fattened mounts, and often left them to rest overnight without food.

Autumn was a busy season, a time when horses were bought, exchanged or borrowed. If the season promised to be one of worries and restless activity or of difficult journeying and much riding, the demand for strong, dependable horses was even greater, and they were begged,

wangled and even extorted by constant harassing of their
owners.

It was on a business such as this that one evening Maibasar
and Kudaiberdy, hunched over their horses in the rain,
were riding to the aul of Kulinshak, the elder of the Torgai
people. They were accompanied by Zhumabai and
Zhumagul. All four rode quickly, anxious to reach their
destination as soon as possible.

In Kulinshak's aul they were obviously expecting someone from Kunanbai. No sooner did the four of them appear
in the meadows of the aul than Kulinshak rose from where
he sat on the hillside.

"Here they come," he said to his "bes-kaska".

"They're riding fast," added Tursinbai, his eldest
son.

"We're in for it, Manas. Ride to Pusharbai. We must let
him know. There won't be time to warn everybody. Let
Pusharbai pass the word to the other Kotibak," ordered
Kulinshak.

"And the others can tell the Zhigitek and Bokenshi,"
suggested Tursinbai.

"Tell them that if they really intend to help me get away,
they must come at once!"

"Let them come tonight if they intend to keep their
word," urged the other sons of Kulinshak.

Manas heard the instructions of his father and elder
brothers in silence. He was to leave at once, but he stood for
a while yet watching the approaching riders.

When Maibasar and his companions reached Kulinshak's
yurta, the latter had already descended from the hillside.
He greeted them curtly and ushered the unwelcome
company into the Great Yurta.

Manas immediately sprang upon his horse and rode off to
Karaul. When he saw Maibasar, he understood that there
was no time to lose.

Maibasar's demeanour as he entered the yurta was plainly
ominous. He removed neither belt nor hat. Pale, his nostrils
twitching, he stood, arms akimbo, without releasing his
riding-whip, and glared at Kulinshak and his sons with
loathing and contempt.

"What's this I hear, kinsmen? You beat up my messenger?
If he did wrong, why didn't you complain to the Mirza? Or
were you anxious to show how strong you are? Wasn't it only
yesterday that you stood with us? What do you want? Speak
up! The Mirza has sent me so that you could lodge your

complaint. He has sent his son Kudaiberdy too, as you see."

Maibasar spat into the smouldering embers and turned to Kulinshak.

Kulinshak sat on a bed made up on the floor. Kulinshak's sons had lowered their heads as though they had heard nothing. Only Kadirbai, sitting near his father, did not avert his gaze but boldly returned Maibasar's stare.

For some moments Kulinshak sat still, his eyes closed.

"You say that we have beaten up your messenger," he began. "But why, noble Maibasar, do you say nothing of your own actions? If the Mirza is so attentive, then why does he not turn his attention upon those who come to plunder? Why doesn't he attend to you?"

"Don't waste words, aksakal! I have come here to determine just who is to blame and to see that such things are not repeated."

"In other words, you suggest that I'd better keep quiet? But what if I've decided to break away from you and join those who need me?"

"But who will agree to that, eh? Who will let you go? The Mirza asks you to stay. He promises to look into everything himself."

"God be with him! But let him not be offended with me or rebuke me, if I go the way I choose."

"But why? What has happened, aksakal?" interjected Kudaiberdy. "This is what father says, 'If he wanders off, he'll set the entire Torgai people against me. We'd better talk things over together and find out who's to blame. Let him name a place where we can discuss it. Let him say what he needs, let him receive compensation. But tell him not to break away from us and join my enemies!' This is what father asks of you!"

Before Kulinshak could answer Maibasar broke in:

"Just what do you accuse me of? It was you who beat up my messenger," he persisted.

"My sons who stand before you have only one good pacer. When you demanded the animal I explained that I could not give it up. Was that so difficult to understand? And yet you sent your messenger, a cur more vicious than a wolf, to take the horse by force. You've tried to rob the aul. Where is the justice of that, Maibasar?"

"It wasn't I who demanded the horse, but the Mirza. Kudaiberdy here took a fancy to the animal and I thought: 'This is the first time the boy has reached for the mane of a horse — I'll have to help him. Kulinshak won't be angry over a little prank.' That is why I sent the messenger."

"A prank! What sort of a prank was that?" exclaimed Tursinbai, the eldest of Kulinshak's mighty sons.

"Are you trying to pull the wool over our eyes? That was no prank, but plain violence, the sort of thing one does to strangers, slaves and those who cannot defend themselves," spoke Kadirbai, the third son of Kulinshak.

It was impossible to come to terms. A glum silence ensued. Then Maibasar again began to reproach Kulinshak for his intended desertion to the Zhigitek.

The message which Kunanbai had sent with Maibasar and Kudaiberdy had concerned this matter alone. All the talk about the pacer and the beating up of the messenger had been added as an afterthought: Maibasar had meant to bluff Kulinshak, but the latter was not at all inclined to admit himself at fault.

Enraged by Maibasar's attempt to seize the horse, Kulinshak had thrashed the messenger and firmly resolved to break with Kunanbai. He had sent a rider to the Zhigitek, begging them to accept him into their clan and help him make the move. Rumours of this had reached Kunanbai only that morning. To let so close a clan as the Torgai slip away seemed to him a disgrace and a severe loss.

There had been no open clashes throughout the summer after Bozhei's death, but both sides had done all they could to enlist friends and allies. Though concealed and repressed, hostility was growing more and more intense. Hatred and anger on both sides had reached the point when an outburst was imminent.

The fight at Tokpambet, which had ended in the scandalous whipping of Bozhei, had been the last major clash. Since then the Zhigitek, Kotibak and Bokenshi had been preparing to fight back, determined to settle scores with Kunanbai. On the face of it there had been peace since the death of Bozhei, but it was an illusory calm. Actually, far from healing, the wounds had deepened. Bozhei's death had rallied the ranks of Kunanbai's opponents and strengthened their determination. And the most implacable were Bozhei's closest friends: Baidaly, Baisal, Karatai, Tusip and Suyundik.

Kunanbai had coveted that ill-starred horse at the wrong moment. At any other time Kulinshak would have yielded the animal, not having the temerity to refuse. But now he had allies — Baisal and Pusharbai had more than once

promised the protection of the Kotibak. Kulinshak saw his chance and refused to give in.

Maibasar had failed to grasp the new situation. "He won't let me have that horse," he had thought. "What's this nonsense! What are we worth if we cannot take what we like even from the Torgai? And what can he do?"

Kulinshak's refusal to give him the animal had infuriated Maibasar and he had resorted to force, thereby precipitating the Torgai's decision to break with the Irgizbai and join the Zhigitek and Kotibak.

Maibasar now did his best to dissuade Kulinshak, but his arguments were ignored. Finally Maibasar lost his temper and by sheer force of habit attempted to resort to threats.

"Now, Kulinshak-aksakal, I have brought you the Mirza's request not to leave. And I too ask you to stay. I have said everything and do not intend to go on talking. Give me your word that you will stay. Otherwise you'll rue this day!"

Kulinshak looked at Maibasar with anger.

"I shall, shall I? Very well then, I'll say nothing more either. I have seen and endured enough. Here is my answer: I will leave!" His tone was final.

Maibasar's companions grew uneasy and exchanged puzzled glances.

Explosively Maibasar brought his whip down on Kulinshak's bed. He was choking with rage.

"I know to whom you intend to go! I know who it is. No doubt they made promises to you: 'We'll protect you! Don't be afraid!' Let them try to take you out of my control. Baidaly and Baisal throw out their chests and think they are big and strong! Very well, we shall see! I shall stick a spear in the backsides of those mirzas!" Maibasar was shaking from head to foot, and his eyes gleamed evilly. "They shall pay for this. They shall pay with their naked backs! They'll remember Tokpambet!"

Kadirbai, the most excitable and bellicose of the five sons, could not control himself.

"Enough of that, honourable volost chief, enough! Such shameful happenings as at Tokpambet are better not remembered." He too was breathing heavily.

Suddenly Pusharbai entered with two djiguits, the same Pusharbai who in Tokpambet the year before had tried to shield Bozhei and had tasted Kunanbai's whip. He was a bearded man, huge and bold. He had not forgotten the injury, and it was thanks to him that Baisal and the Kotibak had left Kunanbai to join the Zhigitek.

The moment he entered, Kulinshak's sons stirred and grew tense as though expecting something to happen. More footsteps were heard outside. "Who can that be?" thought Zhumabai. "What is afoot?" He looked at Maibasar inquiringly.

"Is anyone at home?" someone asked beyond the door.

"I'm here," Pusharbai called back.

Ten djiguits burst into the tent, headed by Manas. His brothers, who had been waiting impatiently for them, jumped on Maibasar and his three companions.

"Get away," roared the volost chief, trying to strike out with his whip before he could rise to his feet. Kadirbai grappled with him, threw him flat and sat on his chest. The other three were similarly treated.

What happened then was far worse than the beating received by Maibasar's messenger.

Pusharbai, Kadirbai and Manas hit and punched Maibasar until they were exhausted. The same treatment was meted out to the others, but not to Kudaiberdy, who had been protected by Kulinshak. He had dragged the youth aside and covered him with the folds of his garment. Suddenly the djiguits, who had been silently beating Maibasar shouted together, "Take him out of the yurta! Let's drag him out!"

"He was threatening us, saying he'd tear our clothes off!" Kadirbai gloated as they dragged Maibasar out. "He can only talk, but we'll show him how it's done. Strip him bare, strip everything off!" Seizing Maibasar, he dragged off his cape, boots and trousers. His fist described a great arc as it crashed upon the naked back. He fell upon Maibasar and kicked him savagely. "What didn't you do to us!" gasped Kadirbai at every kick. "Cocksure, weren't you? I'll disgrace you even more!"

He rolled Maibasar over.

"Did you say you'd stick a spear in our backsides? Did you, now? Well, then here is your spear!" He yelled, and with the toe of his boot jammed some camel dung that lay near the yurta into Maibasar's backside. "If you've a grain of honour left, you'll die of shame," and he gave him another kick.

Having humiliated Kunanbai's brother and his son, the aul of Kulinshak set off to join its new allies that very night. No sooner was the aul in motion than it was surrounded by a convoy of honour made up of Zhigitek and Kotibak, summoned by Manas. Many of the Torgai auls went over to the Zhigitek that night.

Only when the Torgai were far on the way did Maibasar and his companions get free. It was sunrise by the time they found their horses, and noon before they came to Kunanbai. As it happened, all Kunanbai's supporters were then gathered in Zhidebai, and the auls of the Irgizbai, Topai, Zhuantayak and Karabatir packed the steppes closely for ten miles around.

"The Zhigitek have thrashed and dishonoured Maibasar and Kudaiberdy! They have carried off Kulinshak's aul by force!" So the news flew from aul to aul.

Kunanbai gave urgent orders and one hundred and fifty djiguits were on horseback in a twinkling. They were led by Kunanbai, his foster brother Izgutty and his nephew Akberdy.

At noon Kunanbai, who had not once lost sight of the moving Zhigitek, gave a fresh order:

"They're fond of raids and plunder. Let them have a taste of it themselves. Attack them and hold that Zhigitek caravan over there!"

Unhesitating, he led his men against a large caravan passing through the Musakul Valley. The riders descended upon the travellers suddenly and savagely, without caring whom they were assaulting, Kunanbai was too enraged to think things out clearly. "It is a Zhigitek caravan, and that's enough!"

It was indeed a Zhigitek caravan, but it was the caravan which carried Bozhei's funeral yurta.

Kunanbai's force struck at the herds in the vanguard, quickly scattered the men and made off with the horses and cattle. The Irgizbai had intended to capture the caravan as well, but Zhakip and Izgutty, who rode in advance, recognised the caravan as Bozhei's, and held the riders back. The two daughters of Bozhei continued their dismal chant, leading the riderless cropped pacer as though oblivious to their surroundings. It was only Bozhei's baibishe who reined her horse, stopped the camels and addressed the attackers:

"You! Have you no shame? You have attacked a funeral caravan! May you howl in your graves, you godless dogs!"

When he learned that this was Bozhei's caravan, Kunanbai at once changed his orders:

"Leave that caravan alone! Just let them stop and set up their yurtas where they stand."

Bozhei's caravan huddled together and began to set up its tents in the valley as Kunanbai's force withdrew.

The news quickly reached the auls of the Zhigitek: "Kunanbai has attacked the funeral caravan of Bozhei! He has desecrated the memory of Bozhei!"

The Zhigitek were busy with their weapons and other equipment all night. Every man of them took to horse and came to Bozhei's aul. At last Baisal decided that the time had come to strike, and rallied the forces of the Kotibak. Suyundik mustered the Bokenshi.

That same night, Kunanbai's supporters poured into Zhidebai. Musakul, a valley which lay less than three miles away, was to be the scene of battle. Kunanbai not only collected his supporters from the neighbouring clans, but dispatched his messengers with spare horses to the most distant branches of the Tobikty.

Baidaly and Baisal did the same, sending their messengers to the auls of Karatai of the Kokshe and the numerous branches of the Mirza and Mamai tribes.

As a precaution, Baidaly took yet another step. Grievances and petitions were drawn up against Kunanbai, and sealed by the various clans, complaining that Kunanbai, the Aga-Sultan and ruler, had pillaged the auls and attacked a mourning caravan, that he had embroiled the people of the Tobikty in fratricide. All this was done with dispatch. Baidaly then entrusted the petitions to Tusip's care, gave him five djiguits and stuffed his pockets with money. Leading several spare horses, the group set off for Karkaralinsk.

Baidaly could now calmly await the battle.

At the grey of dawn Kunanbai's forces swept forward with battle-cries and a roll of drums.

Baidaly, Baisal and Suyundik mounted at once and summoned their men. The horses of the Zhigitek stood saddled and ready; soeels and shokpars were quickly seized and within a few moments Kunanbai's riders met their opponents head on with soeels raised and lances at the ready. Great clouds of dust arose as the Irgizbai and the Zhigitek clashed in battle.

This fray, which was later known as the Battle of Musakul, was to be remembered by the Tobikty for a long time. More than a thousand riders fought on each side. Kunanbai had no superiority of numbers, and his attacks were inevitably repelled. Ten or fifteen men were wounded at every onslaught, and were immediately removed from the field.

The first day of hard fighting was indecisive, the tide of fortune turning first this way and then that, and after dark both Zhigitek and Irgizbai withdrew their forces.

On the second day there was again bitter fighting, but again neither side could gain the upper hand.

On the third day, Kunanbai ordered one hundred and fifty of his best djiguits to be mounted on picked horses and armed with pole-axes and sharp spears instead of soeels. Infuriated by the grim resistance and courage of the Zhigitek, Kunanbai was determined to crush them, by fair means or foul.

He set a trap for the enemy. Having thrown in several detachments armed only with soeels, he began to withdraw them at the height of the fighting, to simulate a retreat, hoping that this would bring forward the best djiguits of his opponents.

The stratagem worked. Valiant groups of Zhigitek and Kotibak horsemen soon emerged to pursue their retreating enemies, among them all five of Kulinshak's mighty sons and Pusharbai. Hot on the heels of the Irgizbai, they steadily pushed forward to the hill where Kunanbai stood watching. This was what he had been waiting for. Suddenly bringing forward the contingent of djiguits armed with pole-axes and spears, he plunged into the thick of the fight with them.

Led by Izgutty, they cut through the enemy ranks, put them to flight and began pursuit. Ten djiguits who tried to hold their ground were cut down on the spot.

The battle had reached the point generally designated by the words: "The enemy was fleeing."

Kunanbai was tearing ahead in hot pursuit when a great cloud of dust arose behind the positions of the Zhigitek. The broad shoulder of the hill seemed to be teeming with fresh riders.

The Irgizbai scouts had earlier reported: "The Zhigitek have sent a messenger to the Konir people. Mamai fighting men are expected." To Kunanbai it was clear that the arrival of the Mamai would give the Zhigitek the upper hand. This had indeed been the greatest danger. And now, at the very moment when he had put the enemy to flight, the Mamai had come. Izgutty and his detachment wavered and reined their horses. Judging by that cloud of dust there were no less than five hundred fresh riders coming over the ridge.

Kunanbai's forces rolled back, but the Zhigitek, curiously enough, showed no inclination to pursue them. The embattled clans separated at the very moment when one would have expected the fighting to develop to its highest pitch.

It did not occur to Kunanbai that he, too, could be fooled. But Baidaly had also resorted to cunning: having spread the rumour of approaching Konir and Mamai reinforcements, he ordered the nearest of the auls to gather their camels and drive them over the hillside, raising as much dust as they could. The formidable horde which had daunted Kunanbai's warriors had been nothing but a drove of camels.

Never suspecting this, Kunanbai had fallen back, and Baidaly, for his part, had not cared to risk pursuit.

Such was the outcome of the three-day battle of Musakul. Kunanbai had failed to defeat his opponents, while the Zhigitek had proved their ability to repel the Aga-Sultan and defend their rights with arms in hand.

The battle was over, but endless rumours, half-truths, differing accounts, heated arguments and stories without number filled the air, spreading like the smoke from a huge fire to envelop the whole area.

As for Baidaly and his friends, their voices now rang with confidence; they seemed to have grown taller in stature and become more impressive. Kunanbai's supporters, on the other hand, were reserved and silent, their brooding fury showing that they had suffered defeat.

What was to be done? How was Kunanbai to exact obedience from those who would dare to oppose him arms in hand and measure their strength against his? The thought gave Kunanbai no rest.

Then followed ten days of quiet and calm. Kunanbai's enemies were jubilant. "The fort of Kunanbai has fallen; his strength has been shaken," they kept repeating over and over. Feast followed upon feast and neither horses nor sheep were spared. Prayers of thanks were offered up. New friendships sprang up and amid the general rejoicing new marriages and betrothals were celebrated.

The Zhigitek had another cause for rejoicing. No more than ten days after Tusip's departure, fifteen armed Cossacks arrived from Karkaralinsk. By that time, too, Tusip had returned, and it was generally supposed that the chief administrator had arrived with an armed force to cross-examine Kunanbai.

Chernov, an official who had been sent by the Corps, arrived with the detachment. Ten yurtas were set up for them. Chernov conducted the investigation for three days and at once adopted a very stern attitude in his dealings with Kunanbai. Although he did not say so, it was evident that he regarded Kunanbai's removal from the post of Aga-Sultan as a foregone conclusion. Everyone could see that he was not treating the Irgizbai leader with any special deference. The Zhigitek, Bokenshi, Borsak and Kotibak hastened to make the best of this and inundated the official with grievances.

Kunanbai's supporters were not to be outdone, however, and retaliated in kind: "They have been killing people, pillaging the auls and burning the pastures!" The wildest complaints were lodged against the elders of the Zhigitek and their allies. Elaborate statements were written to prove that Kunanbai had been fighting for justice and that the real culprits were now seeking revenge in slander.

The official reserved his conclusions. Having heard both sides, he told Kunanbai on the third evening:

"You will come to Karkaralinsk with us. We leave early in the morning. See that you are ready."

This augured no good.

When he left the official's tent, Kunanbai urgently summoned ten of his closest friends and kinsmen. Among the elder men were Izgutty, Zhakip and Maibasar, and among the younger Kudaiberdy and Abai.

Kunanbai himself presided over the council and spoke of the impending danger. Some of the men went to pieces and seemed to be on the verge of tears, but Kunanbai had no patience with them.

"There's nothing to cry about! If you can, give me your advice. Help me."

Eloquence was of no avail at a time when practical action was needed. No useful advice was forthcoming, however, and Kunanbai realised the helplessness of his friends.

"The matter is to come up before the authorities and the evil now lies in the papers," he said. "Papers, as you know, have never respected a man's honour, good name or high rank. You must try to stop those complaints trickling in, prevent them from dogging my heels. Spare nothing, just stop the flow!"

But precisely what was to be done was more than any of these indecisive and unimaginative kinsmen of his could say. There was no one capable of offering a solution. Abai was astonished at the dumb helplessness of these men who surrounded his father. Never before had he ventured to say anything or offer advice, but now he decided to speak his mind.

"To stop the complaints you must gain the favour of those with whom you've quarrelled."

His father glanced at him austerely: .

"Do you suggest that I should prostrate myself at their feet?"

"No, why? But you could return what you've taken from them and make good their losses. Nothing else will silence them."

Kunanbai understood this very well, but eager to hear the opinions of the others, he made no answer.

Abai's suggestion found general approval. But although when it came to the point they were forced to the same conclusion, they were afraid to open their mouths. Only Izgutty was bold enough to say:

"All of them, the Zhigitek, Bokenshi and Kotibak think only of pastures and winter grounds. Let us try to share the land with them. What else can we do?"

This was tantamount to admitting one's guilt to the Zhigitek, and was a bitter blow to Kunanbai's pride. His helplessness infuriated him, but outwardly he was cool and composed. There was no other way. "If land and livestock are what they need, let them have it and be quiet!" he thought. "What can one do? Fate is merciless and imposes cruel humiliations."

Dismissing the others, he kept back Zhakip, Maibasar and Izgutty to decide on the best way of opening negotiations with the Zhigitek.

To placate the enemy was no easy matter. He could not go to Baidaly himself; that would have been more than humiliating—a disgrace not to be wiped out. On the other hand, those stupid kinsmen of his were good for nothing. Kunanbai foresaw their helplessness and himself named the men who should serve as mediators.

One of the first was Baigulak, the most respected of the younger men. The second was Karatai of the Kokshe. He, it is true, had quarrelled with Kunanbai, but had refused to join the Zhigitek. Kunanbai, therefore, desired his salem to be conveyed to Karatai: "We shall meet again if we live. All things may happen in life—enmity as well as friendship. May the day of our meeting be a happy one! That is all I desire!"

On the next day Kunanbai quietly took leave of his friends, children and wives and set off on his journey to

Karkaralinsk. He was accompanied only by five djiguits, the most dependable of whom was Mirzakhan, who had served Kunanbai from boyhood and had grown so attached to the Irgizbai leader that he would have readily given his life for him. He was the only man upon whom Kunanbai could fully rely in a crisis.

Just what awaited the proud Mirza no one knew. Would he be removed from his post or would he continue as Aga-Sultan? One thing was certain, however: the despotic ruler who had terrorised and looted the auls was now compelled to journey to the district town against his will.

Great rejoicing broke out anew among the Zhigitek, Bokenshi and Kotibak, who celebrated riotously for days on end as though this were a long awaited holiday. Both old and young took part in the festivities and games. For the time being their successful struggle against Kunanbai seemed to have welded the three clans into one, and they felt themselves kinsmen whose hearts beat in unison.

Fresh grievances and complaints were drawn up and Tusip was again to be sent to the district centre.

At the height of these preparations Baigulak and Karatai appeared, and after prolonged negotiations and discussions they were at last able to stem the flow of complaints. Baidaly spoke for the Zhigitek and at him, therefore, Karatai directed his eloquence.

"If you intend to stop at nothing, we shall not approve," he declared. "We are neutral in this matter. Kunanbai has now to pay for his obstinacy, and here's your chance to recover everything. Take land from him in exchange for the losses suffered by your people!"

The talks continued for three days. Karatai's proposal was hotly discussed and finally accepted.

Baidaly laid down his conditions. He demanded the return of fifteen winter places which Kunanbai had taken from his neighbours one by one in the past, either by cunning or by force. Each of the four clans—the Zhigitek, Bokenshi, Kotibak and Torgai—was to receive several pastures and winter grounds.

As it turned out, the land went only to the most prominent of the elders and the rich auls. They had talked about "making good the losses sustained by the entire people", but the result was that the pastures and the winter grounds went only to Baidaly, Baitas, Suyundik and their friends. The other auls were placated by presents of fattened sheep, the temporary use of horses, or smaller gifts of calves. The burden of this debt, on the other hand, was not borne by Kunanbai and his rich elders alone, but by the whole of the Irgizbai people.

The clans made peace ten days after Kunanbai's departure. Complaints were no longer sent in. Having received much land and cattle, the heads of the clans exulted in their victory and during the celebrations distributed gifts of cattle to their nearest kinsmen. Innumerable lambs were slaughtered as sacrifices to the Almighty and to the spirits of ancestors who had aided the clans so well in their grim struggle. Large gatherings, celebrations with races, games and songs went on for a long time. The general rejoicing expressed a new confidence — good times had come to stay.

3

When hostilities had ceased and life had returned to normal, the auls left Zhidebai and Musakul and moved down the slopes towards the autumn pastures.

It was unusually cold for the season. There were icy winds, drizzling rains and lowering skies. And when the breath of winter came so early, it was best to be near the winter homes. Ulzhan was worried about her aged mother-in-law and the children, and decided to reach Osembai in three laps, to shear the sheep there and to move on at once to her winter home.

Abai had visited no one since his father's departure, but he had heard of the celebrations and rejoicing among the Zhigitek. He also knew that the fifteen winter places given up by his clan had passed into the possession of a few of the elders. Soon there was more news: these same elders had failed to divide the newly gained land peacefully. There had been arguments and finally quarrels. This did not surprise him — he had seen a good deal that year.

"The people are suffering. They are groaning under an unbearable burden. They need land!" Such had been the talk of the elders previously. Why then had they not shared the land with the people? They had fought for the honour of Bozhei, but what was it worth if it could be traded for land and winter places? Abai had seen for himself that the quarrelling continued only until the leaders of the clans had managed to fill their bellies. The moment their avarice was gratified everything else was forgotten.

That autumn Abai at last understood the truth about the biys and the aksakals, a truth they took such pains to conceal. "Kunanbai is robbing the poor; he has seized their land and left them in tears," had been their plaint in the past. But now that power was in their hands they were robbing the people even more, instead of restoring to them what Kunanbai had taken. Kunanbai's booty had merely been divided between five smaller Kunanbais. They had fought Kunanbai for Bozhei's honour, and having defeated Kunanbai had traded it for winter places.

Abai now realised that the people had been deceived and he with them. "A raven will never peck out the eyes of a raven" — ran the saying. No, a real defender of the people would never spring from among those elders who one day were against Kunanbai and the next day with him. He would come from men of quite another sort.

After returning from riding one evening, he visited his mothers as usual and in the presence of Gabitkhan, Takezhan, Ospan and several of the herdsmen took up his dombra. He played with especial spirit and finally sang a song bristling with sly allusions to Baidaly and Baisal, who had at last recovered the land and immediately fallen out over it.

The song evoked praise and laughter.

"Whose song is it?" asked Ulzhan.

"Baikokshe's," answered Abai calmly. The akyn Baikok-she had once visited them in the company of Barlas.

All autumn, and especially after they had settled in their winter homes, Abai more and more frequently sought to express his feelings and thoughts in the melodies and songs he played on the dombra, always ascribing the humorous and satirical verses to Baikokshe.

In the winter home Abai again pored over his books for many hours. His imagination fired by the verses of Babur, Navoi and Allayar, he reached for paper and pencil and wrote verses in an attempt to emulate them.

Love and lovers was the theme that fascinated him now. The thought of Togzhan, the beautiful and only one, scorched his heart, which belonged to her forever. Togzhan.... So far away, separated from him by gory battle and feuds. What mountains and chasms lay between them now! How often Abai thought of her! All those timid, tender songs, everything he composed that winter were devoted to her. In the course of the winter he wrote a small collection of songs which he called *First Melodies — to Your Radiant Image*. And at last he found the words to complete the verse he had composed so long ago: "Thy dawn is in my heart, my love." At times he sang these songs to Takezhan and Gabitkhan as he plucked at his dombra.

They waited a long time for Kunanbai to return. The autumn had passed and half the winter was gone, but still Kunanbai had not returned. Every month he sent a djiguit for more mutton, and through him sent his instructions to the family and informed them of the state of his health and his affairs.

From all his messages only one thing was clear: he had been deposed from the Aga-Sultanship the moment he had arrived in Karkaralinsk. Would he manage to settle his affairs soon? Who could say? The investigation was officially underway and he was not permitted to go home. Such was the brief substance of his messages.

In Karkaralinsk a new Aga-Sultan had been chosen — Kusbek, he had once been Aga-Sultan before, but had been compelled to relinquish the post. Back in authority, he was unfriendly to Kunanbai from the first, intent on avenging himself for his defeat at the last elections. Through Baimurin he energetically supported those who had sided with Bozhei.

Quick to size up the situation, Kunanbai secured the assistance of the most influential of his sympathisers, first and foremost, Alshinbai.

No sooner did Alshinbai intercede than Kusbek began to withdraw, making the course of the investigation easier.

Kunanbai was interrogated briefly, and acquitted.

When the first grass sprouted after the thaw, Kunanbai at last left Karkaralinsk. He was appointed volost chief in place of Maibasar.

He had barely left the town before the news reached his auls.

4

A strange mood had taken possession of Abai that spring. He had grown indifferent to the bustle and noise about him, to the joys and sorrows of his kinsmen and friends. His thoughts and feelings were lost in a world all his own. Both dombra and paper served faithfully to record his passionate songs and verses — the frank confessions of a deeply stirred youth. Yet how much was left unsaid, how many songs were unsung! The mysteries within him had not all found expression. And what he had said and sung seemed so poor and flat.... If he could find a true friend, he would pour out to him all his longings, all the inexpressible anguish that filled his soul.

"What shall I do?" he thought sadly. "Words are so poor and language so futile." He was tortured by his helplessness.

All the poems he had written so far lived within himself alone. Not one of them had reached her to whom they were dedicated. Hope? What hope could there be? Only sad and lonely dreams were left to him.

At times, from far, far away he seemed to hear the familiar silvery tinkle — now more distinct, now dying away.... These feeble echoes of his hope were agonising. Its golden rays shone far away, beyond the range of his vision where there was dawn and morning, the brightest of morning. The image never for a moment left his mind.

When the first breath of warmth and sunshine caressed the earth, Abai felt that he could no longer stay at home. He would saddle his horse and ride off at random. And the pretext for this aimless riding was his fawn-coloured, black-faced hound.

Out of sight of the aul Abai would give rein to his horse. Let the dog find the hares by himself. Soon, in fact, he would forget all about the dog, not missing him for long hours, and then suddenly remembering and calling him. At times the hound would come upon a hare in the thickets and chase it across the plain, but Abai would watch him with an absent-minded air, as indifferent as before.

Occasionally the hound would catch a hare and with his paw upon the game proudly wait for his master to spring from the saddle and take the game. But Abai merely rode on. Watching him blankly for an instant, the dog would begin to run about and bark. But for some extraordinary reason his master failed to notice even this. The dog would dash frantically between Abai and the hare, obviously annoyed at receiving no attention for his labours. When his patience ran out, the dog would settle the matter in his own way: much of leaving his master to shift for himself, he would devour as much of the hare as he could, and with his nose and jowls dripping blood would then overtake Abai. It was only after this that the queer hunter would notice his oversight.

Even this, however, failed to break his train of thought and he would begin to sing a long and moving song, an offering to Togzhan.

When the cool breezes bowed the grass before him, Abai would bare his head and take deep breaths of the fragrant air. He liked to think that it came from the Chinghis, from

Camel Humps and the Karaul, warm breezes that seemed
to bring the gentle breath of his beloved. He could have
sworn that this was so. Reality and dreams, life and hope
overran their eternal boundaries and merged into one
indivisible and wonderful whole, filling him with inexpressible emotion.

One day, however, there was a sudden intrusion upon his
solitude. A rider seemed to appear from nowhere in the
midst of those vast and lonely steppes. Abai was startled and
his enchanting dream gone.

The two riders came face to face, the wide plains
stretching into the distance on all sides of them. Glancing at
the stranger with irritation, Abai was about to turn away,
when the other smiled gaily and called him by name like an
old acquaintance. Then Abai recognised him and flushed
with joy.

It was Yerbol, the djiguit whom he had met when
returning from Suyundik's aul the year before. For an
instant Abai feared that his too excited welcome had
betrayed his secret, but Yerbol seemed to have noticed
nothing.

"Hunting?" he asked. "Where is your dog?"

"Somewhere in the bushes," said Abai looking about.

The hound emerged from the undergrowth, and Yerbol
shouted with laughter.

"You're a fine hunter! Can't you see that the hound's
stuffed himself! Now what could he have eaten? Why, you
didn't even know that there was game. And now the hound's
eaten it!"

Abai did his best to change the subject. They rode on
together, and not wanting to part from his friend he invited
Yerbol to come to his aul.

For five days Abai kept Yerbol at the aul; the two
exchanged stories, and in the evenings sang and joked
together, Abai singing Yerbol some of his own songs. In
those few days Yerbol grew to be his closest friend, and
finally Abai confided to him the secret of his heart.

"Sing these songs to Togzhan," he begged.

Yerbol had learned all the songs by heart and having
promised to sing them to Togzhan set off for his aul.

Abai was obsessed with one idea: to see Togzhan alone
and speak with her, if only for a brief moment. Yerbol kept
his promise, and after three days, which had seemed like
eternity to Abai, he returned and took his friend away from
Zhidebai, over the Chinghis, direct to Camel Humps!

Yerbol had first confided in Karashash, the wife of Asilbek and sister-in-law of Togzhan, reciting to her all the songs which Abai had sent his beloved as a salem and begging her to arrange a tryst. Moved by Abai's songs and Yerbol's persistent eloquence she at last agreed and persuaded Togzhan to meet Abai.

Feverish with impatience, Abai scarcely noticed how they got to Camel Humps. At dusk the two reached Yerbol's aul perched amid the mountains.

This small and poor winter home consisted of the one hut of Yerbol. Suyundik's aul lay across the river, less than a mile away, and could be plainly seen. It had an air of prosperity about it. Dense black smoke rose lazily from the chimneys, and the fat dogs waddling among the huts barked with a smug dignity.

But access to the aul was barred for Abai. He was the son of Kunanbai, the enemy. If anybody over there were to learn why he had come, it would go ill with him. Both Adilbek and Asilbek were proud and vengeful djiguits, and had they known of his intention they would have been enraged. The two friends, therefore, decided not to cross the river until nightfall.

At the appointed time, when it was quite dark, Abai and Yerbol left their horses and crossed the ice to the other bank. The aul of Suyundik was peacefully asleep. Not a dog stirred.

Yerbol quietly opened the gates of the animal yard, led Abai into the camel stables and disappeared. Left in the dark, Abai scarcely dared to breathe; he could clearly hear the beating of his heart.

Yerbol soon returned, took his friend by the hand and whispered:

"Allah himself is with us.... Asilbek is not home. Come along!"

When Abai with a polite salem crossed the threshold of the richly furnished room, he found Karashash standing by the bedside and Togzhan sitting on a blanket spread on the floor. Rugs covered all the floor space; the walls were hung with felt rugs of vivid designs and silken draperies; and a curtain of white silk half concealed the tall bed with its bone ornaments.

Greetings were exchanged and Karashash came forward to remove Abai's hat and help him to loosen his sash.

Togzhan was overcome with confusion. She scarcely replied to Abai's greeting and flushed and paled by turn.

Her blood raced too hotly to conceal the secrets of her heart, her embarrassment, her fears and her hopes.

Yerbol did not want to disconcert his friends with his presence.

"I'll see to the horses across the river," he said.

Abai nodded.

Karashash went off to prepare tea, but did not return.

Left alone with his beloved, Abai was at first quite at a loss, and could see that Togzhan too was as bashful as a child. He leant towards her and just gazed at her, long and earnestly.

"Togzhan.... Did you hear my salem?" he asked at last. "Those words came to me from my longing for you, from my thoughts of you.... Did you listen to them?"

Togzhan's whole attitude seemed to answer: "Why then am I here? Was it not your voice which brought me?" Modestly she smiled and said:

"I heard them, Abai. Your songs are very fine."

"I am no akyn. But from the time I saw you I have been out of my senses. I have not been able to forget you even for a moment."

"Why did you not come to see me then?"

"How could I? You know what has been happening. It was only in our thoughts that we could meet!"

"True," said Togzhan and blushed. "But I saw you once.... During the wandering.... Whether you noticed me or not, I do not know."

Abai was thrilled by her words.

"Oh, Togzhan, how wonderful that you should say this! I nearly shouted at the time, 'Stop but a moment!' I could hardly control myself! I was certain you did not notice me. But if you did, then I must have been worthy of your attention. Could I ever forget you, Togzhan?" Abai took her slender white hand.

Trembling, Togzhan withdrew her hand.

The hours of that long evening bound the two young hearts with strong ties. They demanded nothing—only to see and talk to one another. It was their first meeting. There was no end to the flow of their talk, as though they were seeking to quench a long and burning thirst.

Karashash returned only at dawn, she prepared tea and departed again. Abai then took Togzhan into his arms and kissed her. Togzhan pressed her delicate hands to his face and gently pushed him away. But this was hardly resistance, rather modesty, charming and embarrassed. Abai drew her passionately to him again and pressed his lips to her eyes.

For an instant Togzhan's warm face caressed his, but then she slipped away once more.

"Light of my eyes," exclaimed Abai, when Karashash suddenly rushed in.

"May God have mercy on us, Abai, my dear! The ice on the river has broken up! The ice is moving! Where is your horse?"

Abai heard her tumbled words but could not take them in—he was so consumed with emotion. But Togzhan was worried and frightened.

"What are you saying? How will he get across the river? You must go!" she pleaded, fearing for his safety.

Abai at last understood. His horse was on the other bank and that meant there was no escape. It was impossible to stay in the aul, for he would soon be discovered. Even if they did not seize him at once, they would find him in the morning and there was none who wished him well on this side of the river. Above all, he must leave the house so as not to bring trouble on Togzhan and her sister-in-law, who had received him so kindly.

Slipping into his coat, he pressed Togzhan's hand reassuringly:

"Never fear, Togzhan, I'll cross somehow. And Yerbol will bring messages from me."

Togzhan touched Abai's breast with her white fingers and clung to him.

"Good-bye! Don't forget!"

Kind, understanding Karashash then led Abai through a dark passage into the open.

"Well, my dear," she said. "You've not been with us long, but you can see that you've friends among us who feel for you with every breath. Do not forget us! Be careful when crossing the river! Farewell!"

Abai took her hands in his.

"I shall never forget you, zheneshetai!* To the end of my days, I shall not forget what you have done for me," he said, and turned to go.

The roar of the drifting ice reached his ears, but he scarcely noticed it. His thoughts were still with those wonderful people he had just left. The joy within him caught at his breath, their beauty and radiance filled his entire being, and all he could think of was Karashash's sensitive sympathy and Togzhan's tender charm.

---

* Zheneshetai—an affectionate term for a sister-in-law.—Ed.

He came to the water's edge. The mountain torrent had burst its banks. Boulders thundered, and the shattered ice crackled and roared as the stream swept everything swiftly past.

Abai stood very still, not knowing what to do next. It would be madness to attempt to cross. But morning was near and something had to be done. He wandered along the bank until he saw a small grove. He walked faster, then rushed back, but there was no escape. He was merely losing time and it was getting lighter — he could already make out everything around him. The moment the aul was awake, people would come here to watch the moving ice. The first to appear would be the anxious old men. And here was he, the son of Kunanbai, near Suyundik's aul, alone and without his horse. Their suspicions alone might prove dangerous to him.

And yet Abai was not afraid. The happiness within him did not ebb, and there was no room for fear. Faced with danger he did not lose his head or run about aimlessly. He was cool and self-controlled, no longer a youth, but a man, mature and sure of himself.

Hiding somehow in the sparse bushes, he kept a sharp watch on Yerbol's winter hut. Soon he perceived a man rapidly approaching the river somewhat above his hiding place.

"Yerbol! Yerbol!" he shouted.

It was indeed Yerbol, who quickly turned at Abai's voice and sharply motioned him to crouch down out of sight. But Abai continued to stand, waiting.

The Karaul is a narrow stream, but its current is swift. Yerbol ran to a spot right opposite Abai's hiding place. He was very pale and almost beside himself with anxiety, as though he himself were in danger. Trembling for Abai, he thought that his friend was standing still from sheer helplessness and horror.

But Abai walked down the bank and shouted with a big white-toothed grin.

"Help me out, Yerbol! The Karaul's decided to betray me."

Yerbol leaped from the high bank to the edge of the water and shouted back:

"Keep low in the bushes. Stay where you are! I'll be back! Don't be afraid."

He disappeared, but soon returned riding a huge red bull. Abai was amazed. Why had his comrade not saddled a horse? Yerbol descended to the water and prodded the bull into the current. The animal was afraid to enter the icy stream and kept stubbornly turning round and round. But Yerbol finally got his way with it. Once in the water the bull no longer held back and moved steadily across. The stream at this point was not deep, but the current was strong and the ice bulky. The bull made slow but steady progress, and now Yerbol hurled the end of the long reins ashore. Abai caught them in mid-air and pulled hard. Lashed by the man on his back the bull finally scrambled up the bank.

Yerbol had proved himself a true friend. He had come to the rescue at the risk of his life. Abai flung himself on his neck.

"Where is my horse? Where did you find that bull? Why didn't you come on your own horse?"

"If I'd run back to the aul for the horse, they'd have caught you long ago," laughed the other. "We'll do without the horses."

The two climbed on to the back of the bull and turned his head towards the stream; but try as they would, they could not urge him into the water. Cursing the animal and all its ancestors to the seventy-seventh generation, Yerbol got off in disgust, and began to scan the scenery behind the sparse shrubbery. The eastern skies were reddening and all was as plainly visible as in broad daylight. Fortunately, the aul was still peacefully asleep.

Suddenly Yerbol rushed off.

Abai had not long to wait. Yerbol soon appeared on a strong grey mare.

"Where did you get it?" asked Abai.

"It was grazing over there. It belongs to the shepherd of Suyundik's aul."

"He's certain to need it."

"What do you care?"

"How will he herd the sheep? He can't do it on foot."

"To the devil with him! Let him go on foot, him and the protecting spirit of his flock! How can I leave you here? Get on! Quickly!" And he helped his friend to mount the unsaddled mare.

Abai was moved.

"Yerbol, my friend! You're very good to me! You're my best friend! I'll never forget it!"

Yerbol had mounted the bull.

"Stop chattering! Move on!" he said, handing him the reins.

Her hoofs seeking the treacherous bottom of the stream, the snorting mare kept her balance in the icy current and plunged ahead. The bull waded on behind, and the friends were soon safely across.

On the other bank the djiguits left both mare and bull and ran through the undergrowth bent over double to keep out of sight. They risked the open only when they were far downstream.

Abai did not enter Yerbol's hut, but asked that his horse be saddled as quickly as possible. Touched by the loyalty of his companion, he parted from him as from a life-long friend, and rode homewards down the river.

5

By the time Kunanbai had returned from Karkaralinsk, some of the auls had already moved from their winter houses to the yurtas, and the green of the steppes about the winter place was dotted with their white and grey crowns. Though the families in which there were old men and women still dwelt in the houses, the young folk had all moved to the spacious yurtas, so fresh in the spring. In their bright plumage of the new season the auls indeed seemed young, boisterous and intensely alive. Spotted lambs and kids gambolled about in the sunshine, filling the air with their bleating. Young shaggy camels strode about, rolling their large hazel eyes. The herds of horses were alive with innumerable woolly, long-eared foals. The calves too had grown and, lashing their tails right and left, they scampered and raced over the green. The whole of nature joined in an irrepressible riot of living and sang in exultant chorus: "We are the joy of this earth, sprung from non-existence to create beauty and good." It was spring indeed — shining, flowering and bubbling with life.

Both of Kunanbai's auls had settled at Zhidebai. The mares which had grazed with their foals throughout the year were being milked, and every morning and evening the kumiss was noisily stirred about in shiny black skins.

Kunanbai was received with special honours not only in his own aul, but in all the auls of the Irgizbai, Topai and Zhuantayak. His kinsmen and friends who had been riding with the happy news from aul to aul poured into Zhidebai, presented their salem to Kunanbai, and were feasted in his tents. In their turn they escorted him to their own auls, where feasting continued from morning till night.

The more prosperous of his kinsmen invited not merely Kunanbai, but his entire family as well—his mother, wives, children and nearest relations.

Zereh slaughtered the best ram which she had long promised as an offering for the safe return of her son. In Kunkeh's aul Kunanbai, too, slaughtered a horse that he had promised as an offering on the happy conclusion of his case. These celebrations were also a necessary piece of business to Kunanbai—such a gathering of his kinsmen enabled him to find out where they stood, to see who was on his side and who was not, to note how each received him after the difficult time he had been through.

All the aksakals and karasakals* were present in the crowded gatherings.

Karatai, the chief of the Kokshe, who had maintained so cautious and ambiguous a position in the autumn, gave Kunanbai a big, noisy welcome, and never left his side.

Only a few days previously the auls had been full of rumours. Kunanbai, it was said, had been broken, exiled, stripped of office and power. But here he was, fully acquitted and vested with the authority of volost chief, and the ill-wishers were silenced.

The auls had already left the winter places and were streaming down the hills towards the various spring pastures. Kunanbai's guests grew fewer, and he was able to spend more time with his wives and children. During his father's three-day visit to Ulzhan's aul in the valley Abai noticed that he had grown much greyer and that more wrinkles had appeared on his face.

When Kunkeh, Kudaiberdy and Aigiz had gathered to dine with Ulzhan one day, Kunanbai, though addressing Zereh, made a few remarks intended for the entire family. His words were full of a bitterness born of his recent harrowing experiences. Never before had he felt so alone, he said. Neither among the elder nor the younger kinsmen had he found a single man upon whom he could rely. He expressed his regrets that he had so long delayed the marriages of his grown sons and had missed the joy of bringing up his grandchildren and watching their games and frolics.

All the mothers including Zereh could only approve and welcome his words. This meant the marriage of the grown sons, the birth of grandchildren—the long-awaited answer to the womenfolk's prayers.

* Karasakal (black beard)—a middle-aged man.— *Ed.*

Kunanbai also said that Allah had been his mainstay in his hours of trial, but that his supporters among men had been the two prospective fathers-in-law of his children. In them, he said, he had found true friendship and sympathy. They were Alshinbai and Tinibai, a big Semipalatinsk merchant. On his way to Omsk, moreover, he had been received with friendly concern by Baitas, the elder of the Tasbolat clan.

Then Kunanbai spoke of a decision he had reached during the trip. Baitas had a little daughter named Yerkezhan, and Kunanbai had decided to seek her in marriage for Ospan. The matter was settled—she was the bride-to-be of this mischievous son of his. This was joyfully received by all, and especially by the mothers, who laughingly argued about how best to break the news to the imp who was to be hobbled at last.

Kunanbai now came to the two remaining sons of Ulzhan. Takezhan had called upon his betrothed the year before, and his future father-in-law had already received the whole of the bride money. Why delay any longer? Let Takezhan set up his Young Yurta. The second decision was the most important and deserved the concern and assistance of all present. Abai had to be made ready for a visit to his betrothed. Kunanbai had already discussed this with Alshinbai and they had decided to arrange the wedding in the spring.

Among the prospective in-laws Kunanbai attributed the greatest importance to Alshinbai, by far the most influential man in the region. To send a suitor to his daughter for the first time was no simple matter and required serious preparations. The outlay of livestock and other property would be considerable.

The mothers approved, though Zereh said thoughtfully:

"Would it not be better if we sent him when we'd arrived at our summer quarters and the troubles of wandering were over and done with?"

"Alshinbai's zhailyau is too far from our summer grounds and will be difficult to reach," Kunanbai explained. "The cattle and sheep will tire and grow lean on the way. Abai, moreover, will be accompanied by kinsmen of advanced age and the journey will be difficult for them. In short, he'll have to set off within the next five or six days."

He turned to Ulzhan. "You too will go. Take your son to his new family."

Kunanbai hated delay and then and there named those who were to accompany Abai and specified the number of animals and the quantities of cloth, money, jewels, bullion, silver ingots and other gifts to be sent. The gifts for Alshinbai also included two droves of picked bays.

The trip gave rise to endless discussion.

Izgutty and Kudaiberdy were sent to make the necessary purchases in Semipalatinsk that very night. They were instructed to consult with Tinibai in the town, to buy all they could find and to return quickly—within four days at most.

Each of Kunanbai's sons reacted to the decision in his own way. When Aigiz and Izgutty turned smilingly to Ospan, saying, "You have been betrothed and shall have a bride", the boy could not understand at first.

"A bride? What for?"

Izgutty then explained and demanded his opinion.

"I'll take her. Why not! A wife may be useful!" came the prompt reply, evoking general laughter.

Ulzhan herself told Abai of his father's decision. His look worried her. "He's bashful, perhaps," she consoled herself.

Abai received the news in cool silence. Inwardly he shuddered, as though an icy finger had touched his heart. The thought of Togzhan flashed across his mind; he felt he was committing a crime against her.

For days he brooded, withdrawing into himself. He now had a bride. And Togzhan, too, had a betrothed to whom she had long been promised. He could not refuse to go, refuse to marry—the will of one's parents was law. And what pretext could he find not to go? With all his heart he craved for Togzhan, but to extricate himself from the net in which he was so hopelessly enmeshed was impossible.

He set off to call upon his betrothed in gloomy silence.

THE ASCENT

1

The bridegroom's train at length reached the aul of his future father-in-law.

Alshinbai had but recently arrived in this broad valley of abundant springs and pastures. His aul stood surrounded by some forty others belonging to the Boshan clan. Everyone was eagerly awaiting the guests, yurtas had been prepared for them and food and drink were ready. On the day of the bridegroom's arrival the mares had been tethered for milking earlier than usual.

In accordance with time-honoured custom, Ulzhan and the elders, attended by thirty djiguits and a bevy of women, had arrived a half day earlier. The chief negotiator for the bridegroom was to be Kunanbai's foster-brother Izgutty, who was following with aksakals, singers, djiguits and herdsmen to see to the horses. Abai had a suite of twelve djiguits of the younger generation of Irgizbai, as well as Mirzakhan, the messenger Zhumagul, and Takezhan, his nearest kinsman. Abai had also invited Yerbol and throughout the long journey of more than a week the two friends were inseparable.

Ulzhan had brought valuable gifts: herds of horses and camels, fabrics for the women, and jewelry. Two camels were laden with gifts for the bride: bales of bright silks, velvet and other materials, and many shawls. Two other camels carried huge bundles of capes, shirts, kerchiefs, kaftans, all kinds of materials, footwear and other gifts as prescribed by custom.

The most valuable of the gifts were ingots of silver for Alshinbai himself.

Ten years before, when Kunanbai had come to obtain the promise of Dilda's hand, the bride's parents had presented him with a heavy tai-tuyak.* And now, Ulzhan had brought nothing less than a besik-zhamba ** of even more astonishing proportions. Kunanbai's gift had thus outshone Alshin-

---

* Tai-tuyak (foal's hoof)—silver ingot of specified size.—*Ed.*
** Besik-zhamba—cradle-ingot.—*Ed.*

bai's, and no sooner had the bridegroom arrived than the generosity and precious gifts of Abai's father became the talk of all the auls. It was soon learned, however, that Alshinbai was going to pay in kind.

Three enormous snow-white yurtas stood magnificently furnished for the bridegroom and his kinsmen. One-year-old foals just weaned from the mares, three-year-old rams and the largest of the lambs had been picked for slaughter. A fattened foal was especially set aside for the yurta occupied by Ulzhan.

Abai's train came to a halt as they drew near the aul, while a part of the djiguits, including Takezhan, Mirzakhan and others, rode on to announce his arrival. Abai and Yerbol dismounted to meet the girls and young women who were to come out of the aul to receive them. That would mark the beginning of endless and complex ceremonies, and Abai detained Zhumagul, who in his time had endured all the torments of the ritual and might be useful.

"A wedding is supposed to be a joyous occasion for the bridegroom and his parents," Abai remarked to Yerbol. "Why then do they torture people with those endless ceremonies?"

Zhumagul laughed:

"You are going to be tortured—and very soon! There are no feathers in your hat to begin with. And you'd better put on that red cape before you get your cheeks slapped!"

The bridegroom's traditional fur hat, pulled well over his eyes, had to be tufted with the feathers of an eagle-owl. In addition, he had to wear a cape of red cloth and high-heeled boots to distinguish him from the rest of his company. The attire had been prepared for Abai before the journey on Zereh's orders, and though the old woman had always let her pet grandchild have his own way, she had tolerated no objections on this occasion.

"It is the custom of your forefathers," she had repeated firmly. "It's not you whom they will blame, but us! 'Were their fathers never bridegrooms?' they will ask. Put it on at once!" She had helped him to dress with her own hands.

In this curious array, Abai felt much like a witch doctor or an itinerant magician. As soon as they had left the aul, he edged his horse towards Ulzhan and pleaded:

"For the love of Allah, why should I proclaim that I am a bridegroom throughout the journey? Please let me wear my usual clothes. I'll put on this bridegroom's dress when we arrive."

Very reluctantly Ulzhan had consented. And thus Abai had not yet once donned his "sorcerer's" apparel. The tufted fur hat and the red cape were still stowed away in a saddle-bag. It was of these that Zhumagul reminded him.

"As you know, Barak-Batir once said, 'My heart never quailed when I had to call upon the parents of my betrothed.'" Seeing that Abai was really nervous, he hastened to add: "Yes, there are horrors in store for you, but be firm of spirit, all will end well, I know it from experience."

The friends laughed and Yerbol once again begged Zhumagul:

"Please prompt him—when and how to bow, when to sit down or get up and when to push his hat back at last and be comfortable."

Yerbol's painstaking attention touched Abai—his friend was worrying over details that would never have occurred to himself. Could there be a truer, more devoted friend?

Until then Abai had believed that the finest moments of their friendship had been those when Yerbol had crossed the flood waters of the wild mountain stream on the back of a bull. But now he seemed quite another man. Where was the Yerbol he had known before? That old friend and this one were two different people. Which was nearer to him—more dear?

On the day the journey began Yerbol had brought Abai news which had distressed him deeply. When Togzhan had learned that Yerbol was to accompany Abai to his betrothed, she had begged him to convey to her beloved the following message: "He came as a brief flash of moonlight, and vanished. I am left in darkness. But may his way be a happy one, may he be cheerful and happy—such is my salem to him!" And as Yerbol had spurred his horse to go, she had covered her eyes with her kerchief and wept.

The vision had tormented Abai all the way. How acutely he felt the crushing burden of compulsion, the yoke of an alien will which had forced him to make this journey. Morosely he now awaited his first meeting with Dilda.

The ringing laughter of girls and women suddenly reached him, followed by the tinkle of the sholpy. It was a bevy of women in snow-white haddresses and girls in caps of homespun silk coming to receive the bridegroom. A crowd of children was milling about them.

As they came nearer to Abai and his djiguits some of them exclaimed:

"Now which is Abai?"

"Which is the bridegroom?"

"Why, they are all alike! He's not dressed as a bridegroom should be!"

Abai was embarrassed, but forced a smile.

"Pick whom you like best and let him be Abai," he said.

The girls laughed and quickly identified the groom. One of them, however, rebuked him:

"No, this won't do! You may wear the Tobikty hat in your own aul! In ours you'll have to wear the wedding dress!"

She began to question the djiguits and to search for Abai's hidden wedding clothes. Zhumagul finally yielded and took off the saddle-bag.

"Didn't I tell him, 'Put them on!' But no — he won't listen! Teach him a lesson now! I have his clothes right here!" He handed the bag to the girls.

While Abai was dressing, the children scrambled on to the horses' backs in twos and threes and galloped away towards the aul. A bunch of boys stood around Abai's white-maned golden ambler and looked at it admiringly.

"It's an ambler!"

"Oi-bai, how good!"

Three youngsters scrambled on to the saddle and drove the horse off. The welcoming party and the bridegroom's men had to walk to the aul on foot.

Against the other tents the yurta set aside for the bridegroom was a dazzling white. Inside, it had been decided not to decorate the tent excessively and to preserve an impression of spaciousness. The framework, however, was concealed by rich silken draperies and ornate carpets, and the vivid colours of many fabrics lent the dwelling a festive elegance. Wool and elaborately patterned felt rugs extended from the entrance to the places of honour, heaped with silk quilts and cushions. A couch of carved bone to the right was covered with fifteen silk quilts and pillows of immaculate white. At the head of the bed hung a satin curtain with designs in red and blue.

Seated in front of the bed, Abai was surrounded by his future sisters-in-law. Yerbol, Zhumagul and the other djiguits took places amid the girls a short distance away.

No sooner had all been seated than three young women ran into the tent calling:

"The curtain! Lower the curtain!"

The girl at Abai's side sprang up and lowered the satin curtain, to conceal him from the entrance. Only then did they fold back the door flaps.

"Come in, come in," they said, glancing meanwhile in the direction of the bridegroom. "Welcome the mothers-in-law!"

Abai and all the others leapt to their feet.

The curtain was not raised, however, when three elderly women entered. The first was the eldest mother-in-law—the stout, swarthy baibishe of Alshinbai. At her side stood the real mother-in-law, the mother of the bride.

"Well, mothers, the ransom! Where is the ransom? Or else we shall not show you your son," the young women said jestingly, holding the hem of the curtain in their hands.

"Raise the curtain! Here's your ransom," replied the baibishe, indicating the sweetmeats she had brought.

The satin curtain was raised high to reveal the bridegroom, standing with an air of dumb obedience, his head modestly bowed.

"May you live a long and happy life! May Allah grant you a happy future, light of my eyes," said the baibishe as she threw the sweets to the girls.

There was a shower of dried apricots, raisins and sweets, caught in mid-air or retrieved from the carpet by the laughing young women.

"May God give you joy from the first," chimed in the mother of the bride. "May you have lasting joy and happiness, my dear Abai!"

No answer was expected from the bridegroom. He had merely to stand still, submissively silent. Alshinbai's wives kissed him upon the cheek one by one and, without more ado, departed from the yurta.

Abai was uncomfortable throughout the evening, unable to accustom himself to his new position. The huge bridegroom's hat hung over his eyes, made him sweat and irritated him. But the worst to endure was the staring. From all sides they were staring unashamedly at him. "Is he handsome? Is he a fit spouse for our daughter? How is he behaving?" said every curious pair of eyes. Having arrayed the young man in clothing which turned him into a stuffed dummy, they seemed to be mocking him now: "Just look at him! See what he is like!"

Tea was soon served, but conversation flagged. Zhumagul and Yerbol, whose jokes had always evoked laughter, also felt awkward and sat stiffly, exchanging polite remarks with the girls near them. Abai was particularly struck by the appearance of three of the girls, who were elaborately dressed and had unnaturally white faces and flaming cheeks. He did not know that it was customary for the grown-up girls of the Boshan people to paint their faces.

The elder djiguits—Mirzakhan, Takezhan and their friends—gathered in the yurta after tea. With them they brought the singers and jesters of the Boshan clan. The company brightened up, there was a cheerful hubbub of talk and jokes. A merry noisy cluster of girls and women surrounded the bridegroom. All were there but his betrothed. Dilda had not yet appeared.

The first visit of the groom was known as "the ceremonial visit", or sometimes "the visit with gifts" or "the crossing of the threshold", or "the visit of the pressure of the hand". This being a first visit, it was hardly likely that he would see much of his bride.

The parents had to hold a toi * to celebrate the first visit and the finalising of the marriage contract. A toi was no light matter, and had to be arranged thoroughly and without haste. After this would come "the pressure of the hand" between bride and groom. So Abai did not see his bride on the first day. Nor did he see her on the second day, and he continued to stay in her aul without the faintest idea of what she looked like. Only Yerbol was able to pay his respects to Dilda on the day after their arrival. Pleased with her appearance he was glad for Abai's sake and returned to share his impressions with him. But Abai cut him short and changed the subject.

The toi, which the young people had been awaiting so impatiently, was held on the third day after the bridegroom's arrival. From morning till night Abai's yurta was thronged with innumerable women—the mothers-in-law, girls, young wives and his exacting and noisy sisters-in-law. Zhumagul and Yerbol received them with a most courteous and dignified air, and it was as much as they could do to greet each of the countless women who came. Abai was sorely harassed by both of them.

"Now get up! And now sit down!" They urged incessantly. "More have arrived! Oi-bai, many more!" And they would make him go through the ceremony all over again.

The singing did not cease in the bridegroom's yurta. The merry-making was in full swing, and sweetmeats were steadily consumed. A constant flow of servants kept the

* Toi—feast.— *Ed.*

guests supplied with kumiss and tea, and the table-cloths
were never removed.

"The toi has begun, the toi!" cries were heard outside.

"To your horses! Mount the horses!"

Abai and all the men of his company came out of the
yurta. The horses of the bridegroom's suite stood tethered
and saddled. Like other men, the groom was permitted to
mount and watch the feast on horseback. The girls and
young women stayed in the aul, while Abai and his suite of
fifteen rode off and took up a vantage point somewhat apart
from the others.

The numerous auls in that flourishing valley were
observing the occasion with extraordinary generosity,
regaling all whom they could gather. Alshinbai was
determined to dazzle everybody with the splendour and
magnificence of his toi, and the guests he had invited were
so many that their riding horses formed whole herds.

There were as many as five or six dozen yurtas set up for
the guests, extending in a double row for no less than a mile.
The kitchen yurtas had been placed at the other end of the
aul.

Abai and his suite had come out in time to see a long line
of servants charging from the kitchen to the guest yurtas,
every one of them on horseback. Some twenty masters of
the feast, easily distinguished by the white cloths wrapped
around their heads, stood waiting outside the kitchen
tents.

The djiguits detailed to serve the guests were mounted on
the fastest pacers—this to stress the magnificence of the toi.
The slender, well-groomed horses were dashing to and fro,
covered with lather. Twenty djiguits holding the reins in
their teeth then flew towards the guest yurtas with a deep
dish in each hand. Others followed at their heels. These
riding waiters galloped jauntily to their respective yurtas at
top speed and came smartly to a stop without spilling so
much as a drop of the gravy. The aksakals and karasakals
deftly took the hot dishes from them and handed them to
others inside the tents.

As usual the guests ate heartily and the waiters were kept
galloping between kitchen and guest yurtas. The feasting
had begun when Abai was still in his yurta. By now he had
ridden far into the steppes with his djiguits, but the eating
and drinking went on. The guests mounted their horses
only after they had drained an enormous number of skins
of kumiss and consumed innumerable dishes of meat.

ABAI   205

Then followed the games: races, wrestling, a game in which the riders struggled to capture the carcass of a goat, combat on horseback and horsemanship contests. The old men who came out to watch could not cease marvelling.

"This is a great toi," they said.

"The bridal gifts were very fine, but Alshinbai too has grudged nothing!"

It was on that evening that Abai first saw his bride.

The groom's yurta was bursting with guests. All the relatives of bride and groom had come, headed by Alshinbai himself, Ulzhan and Izgutty. Abai and his suite sat separated from them by a curtain, and it was only the elders who spoke and laughed freely. The young people behind the curtain spoke in whispers—only the girls dared laugh quietly, since they were more at ease in their own aul. Finally, there was a movement behind the door, and the young women at the entrance drew back the door flaps to admit several girls.

One of them was Dilda. Her face was hidden behind a red hood so that Abai and his friends could see only her figure as she removed her outdoor shoes. The bride seemed to be slim, tall and well-proportioned.

She was led to her place at Abai's side, and there she sat, without raising the hood. Abai would have liked to say a few words in greeting, but Dilda did not turn to him and he held his tongue.

Immediately the bride arrived, the meat dishes were served. Both the guests of honour and the young people behind the curtain applied themselves to the food, but the bride and the groom scarcely touched it. When the meal was over, a mullah, whom Abai could not see from behind the curtain, read the marriage prayer. A chalice of cold water was then brought and passed round, first of all to the guests of honour, until it finally reached Abai, who took a sip and proffered it to Dilda.

Two of the bridesmaids then smilingly seated themselves before the bride and groom, wrapped Dilda's right hand in a light silk fabric and placed Abai's right hand upon it. He could feel her slender fingers. One of the bridesmaids who sat facing him humorously observed:

"Oh, he's sharper than he looks! Has your hand stuck to hers? Now, give your hand to me! Stroke her hair," she commanded.

The girls beside her laughed loudly. The bridesmaid took Abai's hand and made him stroke the bride's braid with the palm. The silk used for the pressure of the hand was here used again. Abai had to stroke the braid twice.

The wedding thus concluded with this ritual, long known as "the pressure of the hand" and "the stroking of the hair". After this final ceremony it was customary to reward the bridesmaids.

The elders then raised their hands in a final prayer:

"May happiness accompany them! May they live long! May Allah grant them abundance!" they chanted in unison.

These wishes of their kinsmen reached Abai and Dilda behind the curtain. The elders then rose and left the yurta. The young people did not stay long either. They all went their ways to leave the groom with his bride.

Abai had not yet spoken a word to Dilda. They had not even seen each other properly. From the corner of her eyes she had only managed to steal a glance at his face when, herself concealed by the screen and the hood, she was taking her place at his side.

There seemed to be more room in the yurta now. One of the bridesmaids who had been rewarded for her part in "the stroking of the hair" now turned to Abai:

"We shall prepare the bed! You'd better go into the open for a while. Refresh yourself a little!"

Abai was shocked by her frankness. Quickly he rose and left the yurta. There was not a soul about, and even Yerbol had vanished. He was alone. The night seemed blacker, for the clouds had gathered in the evening. Abai walked far from the tent.

The girls too left Dilda. Only two bridesmaids remained, the two from whom she had been inseparable the entire evening. One of them now led her out of the tent while the other lowered the curtain and prepared the festive spreads of the couch for the night.

The bridesmaid embraced Dilda and laughingly asked:

"How did you like him?"

Her reply was calm:

"How can I tell—he's fat and dark, isn't he?"

There was a note of disappointment in her words.

"Nonsense! You did not have a good look at him! He's dark and handsome," the bridesmaid reassured her.

The bridegroom's heart was heavy.

All that abundance and glitter and his suite of friends and kinsmen truly belonged to the celebration of a happy occasion. Merriment, good food, crowds of guests, splendour and magnificence had followed his every step. The prayers and good wishes were meant to stress the happiness awaiting the two young people. But were they really? Had not the elders arranged it all merely to observe the courtesies and demonstrate their mutual regard—for the sake of upholding the age-old traditions.

Abai and Dilda had not even seen each other, but the elders were not concerned about that. The first real meeting of bride and groom was to take place on the nuptial bed now being prepared.

Abai had read many books. "My beloved and chosen one"—how he had worshipped those words! They had blossomed in his heart pure and bright. Togzhan's radiant beauty tormented him. He could not forget her for a moment. But Togzhan was far away—why did she not appear before him now, a winged vision?

A sudden silvery tinkle—Abai wheeled. It was only one of the bridesmaids.

"Do you really think you're such a prize?" she said jestingly. "Why do you make her wait so long?" With this, she led him to the yurta.

The curtain was down and the bed stood ready. Dilda and the second bridesmaid were nowhere to be seen. Abai removed his coat, which was promptly put away by the bridesmaid, who then removed his boots and reminded him that he was to give her a last gift for the last ritual—"the removal of the boots". The gift usual on such an occasion was considerable. But Abai's pockets contained sufficient money provided by his thoughtful mother. He flung the money to the girl almost with revulsion.

The moment he had undressed, he threw himself upon the bed and rolled under the silken cover. Dilda had not yet come, although he could hear the tinkle of her sholpy from time to time. Was that too a part of the custom? If she would only enter while the lamp still burned! But having seen Abai safely to bed, the bridesmaid took the lamp and opened the door to admit Dilda.

His bride was approaching in the dark. He had been indignant all day but now he suddenly grew numb and indifferent. As he lay quite still, he could clearly hear her every movement, every rustle of her approach. She was removing her beshmet; then she threw off her little boots and in an instant stood over the bed. Not at all bashful, she began to feel for her place. Abai had not noticed that he lay near the very edge. Suddenly he heard her say somewhat roughly:

"Move over!"

Such was the first meeting of the young pair whose union had been celebrated for days with magnificent festivities with all the attendant feasting and other lavish spending. So indifferent, commonplace, ordinary. Abai edged away towards the wall.

He could not overcome his coldness and reserve. In Dilda too there was no warmth. She had suffered herself to be led to the groom as prescribed by tradition, but he was alien to her heart. Her pride haughtily reminded her that while her spouse was the son of Kunanbai, she herself was the granddaughter of the esteemed and respected Alshinbai. Embarrassment and shyness was the lot of the common people. And so, very calmly she did all she had been advised to do by her sister-in-law.

Abai stayed in Alshinbai's aul for two weeks more. Ulzhan left five days before her son, but the djiguits stayed behind with the bridegroom.

In the time the young couple had grown somewhat used to one another. At times they had even joked and laughed together. To Abai Dilda seemed attractive and quite pretty. She, too, had grown used to his ways. But they were not drawn to one another and their hearts were cold.

The elders were wont to regard the first visit of a bridegroom as his initiation into a new life. Abai had left it behind him, but not a spark had been kindled within him. On the contrary, when he returned home something seemed to have snapped inside him, and he appeared to have aged suddenly by several years.

2

At home the auls had moved to their summer grounds beyond the Chinghis.

All the local Tobikty auls lived in anticipation of the forthcoming great event. Abai had heard something about it, but now learned the details. The children, the young people, the elderly folk and even the old aksakals were preoccupied with one thing, and one thing only: the grand funeral feast to be held in memory of Bozhei within the next few days.

Bozhei's kinsmen had been preparing for the feast since the winter. Invitations had been extended to everyone in the spring, and the day and place had already been designated for the ceremonies. The Zhigitek, Kotibak, Bokenshi and

Torgai peoples, united for a year now, had set up their
yurtas on the broad and verdant summer grounds of
Kazbala. An important feature of the ceremonies was
to be the grand baiga,* and nothing could have been
more convenient for the races than the vast spaces about
Kazbala.

Abai and Yerbol were glad to be back—they were
homesick. Yerbol was eager to return to his own aul which,
he learned, was also to take part in the memorial feast.

On the day after his return Abai had a long talk with his
mother, eager to hear all the family news.

Kunanbai, she told him, had been holding big councils
since the beginning of spring and seemed to be making
intensive preparations for something unknown to them. As
a result of endless feasts, Kunanbai had managed to draw
several of the clans to his side. Some had been won over
with gifts, some with promises, and some had been cowed
by his ominously cold salems. In barely a month he had
gained many new supporters, among them such important
and influential figures as Karatai. Kunanbai had at last
succeeded in drawing to his side those whose equal kinship
with his enemies had served them as an excuse to keep out of
hostilities one way or another. The Irgizbai chief was now
opposed only by three or four clans: the Kotibak, Zhigitek
and others.

These, however, had been preoccupied with preparations
for their funeral feast since the winter. Kunanbai was aware
of this, and before moving from the winter grounds had
demanded the return of the fifteen winter places they had
recently received from him. Their belongings had to be
removed by autumn and no people could be left behind,
since these lands would again pass into Kunanbai's possession.

Each of the auls had been informed separately. No
reasons were given — merely orders. In this manner
Kunanbai had recovered fourteen of the winter places. It
was only at the fifteenth that he met with resistance.

This was the winter home of Baisal.

When Kunanbai's message was conveyed to him by
Karatai and Zhumabai, Baisal replied:

"Carry my salem to the volost chief. Tell him we've known
each other from childhood and that none knows better than
he that I have no land. Kuneken is not short of land. He has

---

* Baiga—races; also the prize.— *Ed.*

already retrieved fourteen of the fifteen winter places. Let him leave me my share. I've invested money there and arranged things to my liking."

Kunanbai had been enraged by such a reply and on the same night sent Karatai and Zhumabai once more to Baisal; they were to tell him to stop wrangling and leave the winter grounds at once.

Now Baisal was enraged by Kunanbai's stubborn despotism, and he replied that he was ready for any encounter.

"I've reasoned with him, but he refuses to understand," he said. "The biggest affront is not that he is seizing the land, but that in his eyes I am nothing. When I sat peacefully still he kept picking at me until I was forced to rise. It was over land that he bored into Bozhci like a worm and finally drove him to the grave. Am I better than Bozhei? I have nothing to lose. I won't give up what is mine! I won't budge from these winter grounds!"

Fearing a fresh conflagration, Karatai decided to take the sting out of Baisal's reply when reporting to Kunanbai, but the Irgizbai chief was not easily deceived. "That is not the way that Baisal speaks," he said firmly, and demanded a word-for-word account. Karatai was thus compelled to repeat exactly what Baisal had said.

From that day Kunanbai's anger against Baisal and Baidaly flared up anew. The forthcoming memorial feast alone prevented him from taking decisive steps right there and then. Ulzhan knew that as soon as the clans had set off for their summer grounds, there had been endless quarrels and skirmishes between the auls of Kunanbai and Baisal. Kunanbai had set up his auls in the immediate vicinity of a Kotibak aul and was constantly harrying his enemies and driving their cattle from the pastures. Baisal was retaliating, and the djiguits of the Kotibak stood guard over his aul day and night.

The Kotibak were now located very near Kunkeh's aul, and the slightest thing might serve as a spark to kindle general hostilities. Kunanbai was constantly resorting to violence and deliberately provoking a clash. Guessing his plans, Zereh had left before the others and had placed her aul next to that of Baisal. She was determined to restrain the herdsmen and the more fiery of the djiguits and to prevent such injustices as might be wrought by Kunkeh's aul.

Ulzhan was deeply pained by these incursions and by Kunanbai's hostility to the memory of Bozhei. Not once had he visited the Zhigitek leader's grave. Surely he would not persist even now, a year after Bozhei's death? Ulzhan spoke of these things, sighing deeply.

Abai frowned, and began turning things over in his mind. He was silent all that day, and at night could not sleep, tossing restlessly. This was the first time his mother had laid before him all the details of his father's quarrels and litigations, and shared with him her long pent-up bitterness. Perhaps she thought that it was time for him to take part in the affairs of his elders. She had spoken frankly and with some heat.

Yerbol returned in time for dinner the next day, and the friends at once went to the Great Yurta for kumiss. Suddenly Kunanbai's loud voice broke into their conversation. He had arrived alone and, obviously annoyed, was upbraiding someone as he dismounted.

"Hey, Zhumagul and Mirzakhan! Come here!" he called as he entered the yurta.

The two djiguits obediently approached, while Kunanbai strode to the place of honour.

"It is not by accident that Baisal has set up his aul next to mine," he said without sitting down. "He is driving his herds in our direction. Very well, we shall see who'll get the upper hand! Take your shokpars and soeels and chase his droves away, to the farthest of the pastures!"

The djiguits left at once and within a few minutes one could hear the clatter of weapons and the sound of horses being led out. Abai went into the open.

"Wait!" he shouted, going to them.

The djiguits had already mounted and were fastening their hats.

"What are you going to do?" Abai demanded.

"We'll do what has to be done when there's a raid. What's unusual about that?" replied Zhumagul with irritation.

"You'll do nothing of the kind! Listen!" began Abai.

"Are you suggesting that we disobey the Mirza?" Zhumagul cut in.

Abai grew angry and came closer.

"Don't be mad. Wait a minute," he cried, his eyes blazing, and his pale features darkening. His fists were clenched, and the djiguits paused in spite of themselves.

"You're not to touch the horses, not to beat them or drive them anywhere! Just tell the herdsmen to move them away and then come back!"

"What about our orders?"

"I've given you your orders! Just try to do otherwise and you'll regret it!" threatened Abai.

So unusual were his voice and look that both Mirzakhan and Zhumagul were filled with misgivings as they rode away. Abai returned to the yurta.

"Father," he said firmly, "there's more than enough fodder on our vast summer grounds. Why be so miserly and anger our kinsmen?"

Kunanbai turned to him coldly.

"You seem to think that Baisal has no one to defend him?" he observed acidly. "Or should he, perhaps, not return my winter place?"

"That was a winter place, but these are summer grounds," Abai persisted.

"Do we not settle the scores of winter in the summer—on zhailyau? Do you think it was fair of him to make capital out of my misfortunes and seize my land?"

Abai was silent for an instant, but then went on as quietly as he could:

"To tell the truth, it was not Baisal who began this violence, but we. Did he not plead for a piece of winter land for years? Was it not for winter land that he followed you to take part in the thrashing of Bozhei? It is unjust to take his only scrap of land from him. It is from such things that...."

"Enough of your chatter!" Kunanbai snapped harshly, trying his best to keep his anger in check. "It is not for you to argue with me!"

Abai paused again, but then went on:

"It is unworthy to quarrel over a mere pasture with such vast summer grounds as ours."

When the affairs of his tribe were discussed, Abai had always been afraid to speak his mind openly and had made cautious and timid remarks, as though his tongue would not obey him. The new ring in his voice now compelled Kunanbai's attention.

Zereh and Ulzhan were listening. Did they too, perhaps, think like his son, but were afraid to say so? Kunanbai sat brooding. For some moments he was still, then lay down, turning on his side with his head on his palm. Abai at once offered him a pillow. Kunanbai tucked it under his elbow, turned his back upon his son and lay there meditating.

Meeting with no rebuff, Abai decided to go on to yet another matter.

"The children, all the members of the family must share their troubles with you. Is it right that they are afraid to speak, that they must conceal everything? You should hear them and know their views."

When addressing a pious father it was best to speak the language of the Holy Book and recall the first and second commandments. Abai had not miscalculated. Kunanbai was obviously prepared to listen, and the young man spoke more freely:

"Permit me to mention another matter: the funeral feast in memory of Bozhei. Upon us, his kinsmen, rest many duties which we have as yet not fulfilled. It is too late to speak of the past, but they are now preparing for the final funeral feast, and this will not only be a test of the Zhigitek but of humaneness itself, of kinship and of conscience. When Bozhei died, we were left out. But now we must do our part at his memorial feast!"

The humiliations of the past year rose in Kunanbai's memory.

"What am I to do? Force myself upon them uninvited? Shall I go there to be kicked in the chest as last year?" he bristled at once.

"You need not go yourself—you can send us. We'll take part in the ceremonies and that'll be enough. If you permit, I shall take care of this myself. Let me have only Izgutty and allow us the necessary cattle and everything else," urged Abai.

Kunanbai raised his head, put on his hat and got up. All eyes were turned upon him, expectant and pleading.

"Do as you like!" he growled reluctantly. "You may lick the feet of Baidaly and Baisal for all I care!" With this he left the tent.

And yet he had consented; whether he had felt compelled to do it, or whether he had said what he had in a fit of anger, Abai did not stop to think. It was sufficient that his father would put no obstacles in his path. He at once conferred with his mothers, explaining his plans, having thought things out carefully and well.

The next day Abai was heading for the Kazbal Ridge in company with Zhumabai and Mirzakhan. The numerous auls of the Zhigitek and Kotibak had been left behind and he reached Bozhei's tents.

The auls were preparing for the memorial feast, and a string of yurtas had sprung up on the hillside near Bozhei's aul. The great event was only a few days off and all were in a hurry. Every single man was on horseback. Long trains of camels laden with tents were converging upon the hillside from all sides.

Abai and his companions first stopped at the yurta of mourning for prayers. The Great Yurta had not changed. There was the same black-and-white pennant to the right, and inside were the same elaborate decorations. Solemn and sad, the yurta stood waiting for the first anniversary of the death of its master whose clothing hung emptily upon a richly designed felt rug.

Those who had come to arrange the details of the event had gathered outside the aul. Refreshed with kumiss in Bozhei's yurta, Abai and his companions mounted the low hill where the council was being held. From there riders were constantly being dispatched with the most varied assignments. Prominent figures amid the gathering were the elders—Baidaly, Baisal and Suyundik.

Baidaly had aged noticeably in the past year, and the grey of his beard and hair had turned to silver. When Abai approached to present his salem, the aksakals received him in a friendly manner without a shade of their former austerity. Baidaly and Suyundik asked about the health of Zereh and Ulzhan and invited the young man to seat himself at their side. Among the djiguits attentively awaiting orders from the elders stood Zhirenshe, with whom Abai had long been acquainted. This, however, was the first time he had seen him since Baisal's quarrel with Kunanbai, and Zhirenshe received him as warmly as the others.

With Abai's arrival the elders broke off their conversation. There was silence for a while, and then Abai turned to Baidaly:

"Baidash-aga," he began.

In well-chosen words he explained his mission.

His mothers, headed by Zereh, had wished him to convey their salem to those gathered here and to assure them that they, too, wished to partake in the commemoration of Bozhei as best they could. On the previous occasion they had been too late, but this time they had decided not to delay matters and had sent Abai with the sincerest of intentions.

Baidaly listened attentively.

"Your kinsmen are satisfied with you, my son," he said. "May Allah grant you success! Please tell us how you intend to begin?"

Abai repeated all that he had discussed the day before with his mothers.

He wanted a site in the valley for yurtas to receive guests. He promised that ten large tents would be set up not later than the same evening, sufficiently spacious to accommodate three hundred people. He would supply the food and furnish the crockery and other utensils. Let the aksakals trust him and give further instructions. He knew that each of the surrounding auls was to entertain the guests of one clan or another, and so he, too, would like the elders to say whom he should receive; he wished, moreover, that they should entrust him with the care of some honoured guests.

Baidaly, Baisal and Suyundik then discussed further details with Abai.

The feast was to be attended by envoys from the largest clans living in the most distant places—from Karkaraly, Semirechye, the lower reaches of the Irtish and the shores of Lake Balkhash. Among these there would be especially important guests: Bozhei's maternal kinsmen of the Naiman tribe. Once there was a famous Naiman leader by the name of Bozhei. Kengirbai had become his friend and arranged a match between his son Yeraly and the Naiman leader's daughter. These two were the parents of the late Bozhei who had been named after his famous grandfather. In the winter Baidaly had informed the Naiman people of the forthcoming commemoration, and recently it had become known that these kinsmen of Bozhei were coming.

"If he wishes to have guests, then why not entrust to him the care of Bozhei's kinsmen," suggested someone.

Abai gladly caught it up. He had, apparently, won the confidence of the council since the entertainment of such guests would require great tact and care.

"An excellent idea, Baidash-aga," he said. "We shall look after Bozheken's kinsmen of the Naiman. Entrust them to us."

The council offered no objections. The Naiman people had heard only of quarrels and clashes between Kunanbai and Bozhei; let them see, therefore, how everyone honoured the memory of the departed Zhigitek leader. Though unspoken, this thought was as clear to everyone in the council as to Abai himself.

The young man then asked for two djiguits well acquainted with the preparations in the other auls. Baidaly named Yerbol and Zhirenshe.

Not another moment was to be lost and Abai jumped to his feet. Suyundik regarded him with satisfaction.

"Is there anything more contagious than a bad example?"

he asked. "Those who seek evil do not do so out of excessive wisdom, and evil shall neither benefit them nor bring abundance. All the more, therefore, should we honour him who seeks what is good. I can see, my son, that your intentions are sincere and your path a true one. May God give you success," he concluded.

Abai was pleased with the council. He had been received as one of themselves. In good spirits he mounted, and accompanied by Zhirenshe and Yerbol surveyed the plain where the yurtas were being set up. After conferring with his djiguits, he indicated the place for his own tents and cauldrons. Yerbol and Mirzakhan marked the sites and stayed to meet those whom Abai would send later that day with the requisite cattle, yurtas and utensils.

Abai took his decisions quickly, gave instructions quietly and surely. When he left Zhirenshe remarked, "Abai has become a man! God grant that he keeps his word."

"He'll keep his word. He'll do all that he has promised! You'll see!" Yerbol assured him.

Before he had left Ulzhan's aul, Abai had ordered that the preparations should be begun in his absence, and the work was now well underway there. All instructions came from Ulzhan, Izgutty and Kudaiberdy. Before his departure Abai had made the rounds of all the Irgizbai auls on his bay to choose the yurtas he would need for the guests. Two which had worn felt had been rejected and replaced.

No sooner had he returned than all the ten yurtas were dismantled and packed. By evening a long caravan was on its way to Kazbala with swaying stacks of folded yurtas and huge bundles of ornate rugs, draperies, quilts and pillows. Ulzhan herself had picked the snow-white towels and elaborately embroidered table-cloths, and had arranged for the crockery and kitchen utensils to be packed separately. The caravan was accompanied by the djiguits who had been chosen to set up and decorate the yurtas and to wait upon the guests.

The first steps had been taken. When the caravan had set off, everyone gathered about the Great Yurta to discuss further details: the number of cattle for slaughter and how to transport the kumiss. Ulzhan saw to the arrangement of the kitchen and the preparation of the food, giving warning that this would require great skill. At last she declared that she, Aigiz and Sary-apa would go to Kazbala on the morrow.

"You have made your decision," Zereh declared to the assembled kinsmen. "Now do things in such a way that my children shall not be disgraced before their guests from afar. If each of you wishes to act with honour, then forget the old quarrels! If we were not able to preserve Bozhei's friendship when he was alive, let us not bring down upon ourselves the curse of his ashes! My sons and daughters, be courteous and attentive to your guests! A real man shows his worth not only in war and strife, but in his dealings with other men as well. Even if you die of weariness, let it not be seen! Wait on your guests cheerfully and happily but do not be noisy and never overdo things! Be calm, sparing of words and modest! If you fail, then I here declare — I would rather be buried alive!"

The Great Aul kept hard at work all night and by morning yet another caravan had set off for the site of the memorial feast with the kitchen yurtas. At daybreak Ulzhan, Aigiz and Sary-apa were on their way. Abai and Izgutty were the last to leave.

The yurtas sent with the previous caravan had already been set up in the Kazbala plain and furnished and decorated within. The djiguits took up their posts near the doors, and at every entrance stood a huge vessel filled with kumiss.

Ulzhan then threw herself into the work. She was determined to have Abai's yurtas outshine all the others and to see that the meals for the honoured guests were choice and lavish. The fattened animals were slaughtered on the river-bank, and there they were singed and carved for the cauldrons.

Even now Abai's yurtas were the finest of all. Splendid within and without, they were fit to receive the most distinguished of guests. Suyundik and Baidaly inspected the yurtas and dismounted near the kitchens to exchange greetings with Ulzhan. They were impressed and pleased with her diligent preparations.

"The food for the guests and their proper care are plainly necessary matters," she said drawing Baidaly aside. "But tomorrow there will be the horse races and wrestling matches and prizes for the winners, and you have already put up the Nine * with a camel as the chief prize. My son

* The prize to the owner of the winning horse comprised a camel, an eagle, a horse, a cow, a foal, a sheep, a goat, a rug and a cloak or any other nine valuable items. — *Ed.*

would like to give his share and has asked me to bring this."
Ulzhan produced a parcel bound with a silk cord. "Let it
be the chief gift of one of the Nines."

It was a large ingot of silver—the tai-tuyak.

The repasts were ready by sunset when the first of the
guests swept into the Kazbala Valley.

Upon a hill outside the aul Baidaly, Suyundik and Izgutty
had long been greeting the visitors, who converged upon
them from all sides in groups of forty and fifty. As they
approached, they were intercepted by a mounted djiguit
who asked whence they had come and then led them to the
elders, who stood on a rise. Custom demanded that the
newcomers should first greet the hosts of the memorial
feast, express their best wishes and only then retire to the
yurtas assigned to them.

Abai and his forty djiguits stood near the guest yurtas
ready to receive the most distinguished of the guests from
Semirechye.

By sunset several thousands had arrived. Most of the
yurtas set up by the Zhigitek, Kotibak and Bokenshi were
soon filled, but Abai's guests arrived only at dusk.

Bozhei's uncle on his mother's side, an impressive-looking
aksakal, arrived in the company of numerous relatives.
Dismounting on the hill, he embraced his hosts one by one
and then stood aside, surrounded by the closest of Bozhei's
maternal kinsmen, some sixty in all. Behind them gathered
a great throng in the lambskin hats of the Naiman tribe.

Izgutty and Suyundik led the guests of honour to their
respective yurtas, and the rest of the company followed
close behind. They were heartily welcomed and helped
from their horses by Abai and his djiguits. Suyundik then
presented Abai to the aksakal as the son of Kunanbai, and
the young man gave a low bow of welcome.

Even before they had dismounted, Bozhei's kinsmen were
struck by the splendour of the ten yurtas assigned to them.
Those who had been received in other tents had not been
able to refrain from asking, "Whose yurtas are those? For
whom are they intended?"

Bozhei's aged uncle and several other aksakals were led by
Abai to the central and most magnificent of the yurtas. The
other guests were also warmly received by the djiguits, who
cheerfully showed the way to the other yurtas. Bozhei's
kinsmen of the Naiman people had brought with them a
black and two greys for the morrow's races, with carefully
braided manes and tails and forelocks tufted with feathers.

Three agile boys were riding them, and Abai entrusted both riders and horses to the care of his djiguits.

The guests kept pouring in and it grew difficult to distinguish their dress or to tell the clans apart in the gathering gloom. Some were mounted on blacks, others on greys, and only when a ray of light fell did their saddles flash silver. By nightfall six of the ten yurtas were filled.

The hubbub at last subsided and, thinking that the last of his guests would arrive in the morning, Abai ordered the dinner to be served. He was interrupted by Yerbol:

"Many more have just arrived!"

Abai and his djiguits at once went out to meet them. There was a crowd of new guests from nearby Siban. Abai ushered them to their places and with his men went to see to the food. The kumiss was followed by tea and then by hot meat dishes carried to the tents on horseback.

Weary after their long journey, Bozhei's kinsmen soon retired, and Abai was then able to give his attention to the guests from Siban. Their eldest was the akyn Kadirbai. Many of his songs were well known, and Abai, who knew most of them by heart, was delighted to find him among his guests.

The old man was told that the yurtas in which he and his companions were to stay were those of Kunanbai, and he guessed as much when he saw the choice food, the expensive service and the abundance of sweetmeats. But now he learned that it had all been arranged by a youth, Kunanbai's son. When Abai appeared, the old akyn received him with sincere warmth.

Beckoning the young man to his side, he offered him a cup of kumiss with his own hands. Abai was greatly impressed by this white-bearded old man, with an open friendly face. Kadirbai inquired after the health of his parents and thanked him for his attention and hospitality.

Abai asked no questions, merely answering those of Kadirbai briefly and to the point. His guest of honour was obviously pleased and tried to draw him out.

"Barlas-akyn," he began, "once told me that Kuneken had a son just returned from school. If I remember correctly, he said that this youth, the son of Ulzhan, was brought up by Zereh and was a great lover of songs. Could that youth be you?"

Abai smiled bashfully.

"Barlas-akyn once visited us," he answered, returning Kadirbai's gaze.

"Your father is not distinguished for his love of songs," the old man continued, "but do not be offended; I am a man of his age and may freely speak my mind. Tell me, how did you come to be fond of songs?"

Abai was about to answer—the words were on the tip of his tongue, but it was not seemly for a host to speak overmuch and then, too, the guests might find a wordy reply to the old and revered aksakal impolite. He hesitated.

That did not escape Kadirbai.

"I can see you want to say something! Speak up," he encouraged.

"Be it as you wish, Kadekeh," said Abai finally. "Forgive me if my words seem irrelevant, but is there a man alive, unless deaf of ear and mind, who does not love songs? I am sure there are songs of which my father is fond too."

In this yurta the conversation did not flag, and no one cared to go to sleep for a long time. When Abai and his djiguits at last arranged the beds for the guests and drew the door flaps of the yurta behind them, the East was greying and the slumbering ridges south of Kazbal were growing lighter. The stars had faded and the feeble light of dawn had thrown into sharp relief the lonely peak sleeplessly watching over the rugged boulders and the still indiscernible gullies and ravines below.

On their way to the kitchen yurtas Abai, Yerbol and Izgutty spoke in undertones:

"It's morning! We shan't get any sleep now."

"Yes, we have other things to do!"

They decided to get down to preparing for the coming day, which would, undoubtedly, prove the most difficult.

Abai's guests stayed in their yurtas until the midday meal, when Abai devised a novelty which pleased everyone—guests, onlookers and those employed in the kitchen yurtas. The djiguits chosen to bring up the food were mounted on fast pacers with saddles inlaid with silver. A white silk kerchief was wound about the head of every man and when they darted from the kitchens towards the guest yurtas swinging their steaming meat dishes, the blaze of their silver seemed to shine over the steppes. The kinsmen of Bozhei could find no fault with their hosts; the feast had surpassed all expectations.

When the meal was over, Baisal, accompanied by fifteen of his djiguits, rode to the top of the hill with a banner held aloft. This was the signal for every man to saddle his horse and follow. The grand baiga was to begin: horse races, the chief attraction of the feast, followed by the wrestling matches. The animals chosen for the races, their manes and tails carefully plaited, headed smoothly and gracefully for the rallying grounds. There was an eager hubbub in the crowds.

Abai had no opportunity to see how many were going to the races. He could not go out with the rest because his guests from afar were not expected to leave that day and he had to see to their evening meal. Both he and Izgutty were hard at work, assisted by their djiguits, who had not been permitted to ride off to the baiga. Yerbol alone could not withstand the temptation.

"I'll tell you the news, anyway! I'll let you know what is happening!" he cried, as he galloped away. From time to time he came back to report the latest news. Although no one could yet say how many had arrived altogether, he was sure there were at least several thousand.

Abai's guests were on their horses in anticipation of the signal. At last Baisal gave the rallying cry, raised the banner and galloped off towards Karashoky, where the broad plains were admirably suited for the races. No sooner had the signal been given than all the riders swept forward. Abai could see that their number was enormous. From vantage points outside the yurtas Ulzhan, Aigiz and their servants watched the endless stream of horsemen with wonder.

But it was only one wing of this great body of riders that they could see—there were so many that the other was out of sight. Wave after wave of them swept by like clouds driven before the wind. Almost anyone who could ride a horse had come out for the races.

Yerbol reported that one hundred and fifty horses were to compete. The chief prize of the first day was to be a camel, and of the second, the silver ingot contributed by Ulzhan. The wrestlers, too, were to receive the ninefold baiga.

At noon Ulzhan summoned Abai and told him that they would run out of food if the guests stayed another day. Abai could not, therefore, attend the races, and he sent Mirzakhan and Izgutty home to ask Kudaiberdy to dispatch five fattened two-year-olds immediately and to remind him that more kumiss might be needed the next day. Most of the guests were to leave in the evening, but Abai's were to stay for another day.

The guests returned at sunset tired and thirsty. As on the evening before they were met by friendly and helpful

djiguits. After the guests had slaked their thirst with cool
kumiss, tea was served. In pairs the djiguits brought in huge
steaming samovars, and the yurtas at once grew cheerful
and cosy. The food was even more choice and abundant
than on the day before. Baidaly, Baisal and Suyundik joined
his guests after dark, having been especially invited by
Ulzhan and Abai to see for themselves how generous and
varied was the food and how warm the hospitality of the
Irgizbai.

Abai could not snatch a wink of sleep that night
either—the third night was as full of excitement and
worries.

On the following day Abai ordered dinner to be served
earlier than usual. When the meal was over, Bozhei's uncle
summoned Abai, thanked him warmly and gave him his
sincerest blessings.

It worried Ulzhan, Izgutty and Yerbol to see how Abai
had changed in the past days. He was pale and haggard and
his eyes red from lack of sleep.

Izgutty and Yerbol, too, were utterly exhausted, and the
three of them fell to joking over their appearance.

"We look like Karashi's old nag that was sent into the race
at the peak of the noon heat," laughed Yerbol.

"I could fall down and sleep where I stand. It's all I
want," admitted Abai.

But at that moment they were called by Baidaly to
Bozhei's yurta. The rituals were not yet finished: the
mourning horses still had to be slaughtered and the
ornaments from Bozhei's yurta distributed.

The closest kinsmen of the deceased could not refuse to
take part in this. All the Tobikty, headed by Bozhei's uncle,
therefore, made ready for the final rites. As Baidaly,
surrounded by numerous kinsmen, approached Bozhei's
tent, the women who had been in mourning all the year
came out to meet them. Baidaly then removed the
black-and-white pennant and handed it to Baisal who,
in accordance with custom, hurled it to the ground
and broke the staff. This signified the end of the year's
mourning.

At a signal from Baidaly the crowd headed by Suyundik
entered the yurta to remove the ornaments of mourning.
This was a second sign that the mourning was over. Bozhei's
baibishe and daughters turned their backs upon the
company and began the funeral lament. Their listeners sat
silently weeping. This was to be the last lament over Bozhei's

departure. The last reading of the Koran was followed by the final prayers. Then all arose and left the yurta.

The two mourning horses, grown fat and wild, were brought before the tent. With tears in their eyes a number of kinsmen brought them down, and then the horses were slaughtered by Baidaly himself.

All three—Baisal, who had broken the staff of the pennant of mourning, Suyundik, who had removed the ornaments, and Baidaly, who had slaughtered the horses—had been Bozhei's oldest and closest friends. The consummation of the final rites had, therefore, rested with them.

One was not allowed to leave without partaking of the final funeral repast, the meat of the slaughtered horses, and Abai found waiting very difficult.

When the last meal was over in the yurta of mourning, he took leave of the elders and was about to set off for his own aul when Baisal called him and briefly pressed his cheek to the young man's forehead.

"My son, I have not yet been able to speak to you and express what I feel, but I have remembered that Bozheken was once moved by your action in Karkaralinsk and gave you his blessing. Do you remember his words? He expected much of you and blessed you for that reason. I treated you with coldness then. But I have since heard more than once how you have spoken up for justice, and in these past few days, too, you have shown yourself the true brother of Bozheken. Try to justify the hopes of your eldest kinsmen! I am sure you will, light of my eyes! If only this cursed life of ours does not cause you to blunder. The future lies before you and your path is the right one. God give you success!" And Baisal blessed Abai.

Baidaly, Suyundik and Kulinshak heartily supported Baisal and added their blessings to his. Abai thanked the aksakals for their friendly wishes and took his leave.

He rode off with Yerbol.

In his aul, Abai entered the Great Yurta, greeted his grandmother and cried:

"Sleep, sleep!... I must sleep!"

He slept on and off for two whole days.

Abai did not suspect that common talk and rumour had brought him the glory of a famous and highly respected djiguit.

1

Several years passed. Akilbai, the first son of Abai and Dilda, was born a year after their marriage. Then came their daughter Gulbadan, now a year old, and Dilda was expecting a third child.

Abai could not get used to the thought that he was the head of a family, and it was this which had prompted Ulzhan to take Akilbai and raise him as a son. The child had learned to speak, but did not recognise Abai as its father; he was a stranger who came to the Great Yurta only to eat, after which he would vanish again. Nor did Abai, for his part, feel either affection or attachment for the child. The boy had come too soon and seemed to signify the end of Abai's youth.

Abai was only seventeen when his first child was born. He looked upon marriage as a kind of inevitable trial that had to be endured. Fatherhood, following in its train, seemed like a hideous jest of fate, almost an act of physical violence on his person. On the day Akilbai was born he could barely endure the congratulations and exclamations.

"You have a child. You are a father! Allah be praised!" Abai's kinsmen gushed.

He rushed out, leapt into the saddle and vanished in the steppes. He was away for five days, until the first ecstasies of his family had abated.

Nor was Abai moved by little Gulbadan. She, too, was constantly in the Great Yurta, doted on by the mothers. She looked like Dilda, was always crying, and did not resemble Abai in the least. This noisy infant was delivered to the Young Yurta only at dusk and then spent the nights wailing, as though hoping in this way to attract her father's attention. But Abai would only sigh.

"Her screaming makes you jump up in the night as if a scorpion has bitten you," he complained. And so he began to call the little girl the "yellow scorpion".

The "yellow scorpion" was screaming lustily one evening after being put to bed by Dilda. Though the sun had set and the room was nearly dark, Dilda had not lit the lamp or arranged the beds, but lay resting on a rug beside the child's couch. Gulbadan, just brought from the Great Yurta of the elder mothers, would not go to sleep and voiced her disinclination in a dismal wail.

Abai entered the room with some friends. A blizzard was raging and the djiguits' clothes were powdered with snow. Entering one behind the other, they brought the cold into the house. Dilda raised her head: she had heard the footsteps and felt the draft.

"Make the light, Dilda," Abai said as he shook the snow from his cloak at the door. "And either quieten that nuisance of a child or take her to the Great Yurta."

Dilda lit the oil-lamp, laid rugs for the guests and picked up Gulbadan. The servant woman came in, exchanged whispers with her mistress and began to prepare the food.

Abai's companions were old friends—Yerbol, Zhirenshe and Togzhan's brother Asilbek who had become friendly with Abai during the past few years. Another guest was Bazaraly, Kaumen's son. Though he belonged to the Zhigitek, the enemies of Kunanbai, and had defended Bozhei against the Irgizbai with arms in hand on the fateful day that the Zhigitek leader had been whipped, he was on friendly terms with Abai, who was attracted by Bazaraly's daring, by his wisdom and because he had the courage of his convictions. A man of thirty, Bazaraly was the oldest of Abai's friends.

Bazaraly stepped in, removed his cloak, settled on the rug laid for him on the floor and gloomily observed:

"What these frosts are doing to us! Another blizzard today! Blizzards all the time. The djut will spare no one. It will ruin the auls of the poor!"

He was silent, his hand clutching at his long black beard.

Dilda had set up a low round table, around which the djiguits took their places.

Abai had changed greatly with the years. His shoulders were broad and powerful. His sharply defined features went well with his tall, well-knit figure. The straight thin nose seemed larger now, and the bold brow had widened at the temples. His elongated eyes shone as clearly as ever, and the fires burning within them lent the young man that expression which so distinguished him from the others. On his swarthy face, now reddened by the cold, there was the suggestion of a moustache.

Abai was hardly handsome, but anyone who came into contact with him took to him immediately.

The djiguits might have spent a cheerful evening in the Young Yurta, but Bazaraly's anxious words set them thinking.

Except for Bazaraly, the young men had spent three days together. Bazaraly had arrived that day from the mountain auls where there were many winter places, and Abai wanted more news of them:

"Is the djut very bad there? Has it hit all the auls or only certain of them? Is there much distress among the people?"

Asilbek, Zhirenshe and Yerbol turned to Bazaraly. There was a note of despair in his answer:

"Does the djut ever pick and choose whom it strikes? There is suffering everywhere. The djut is terrible and is laying low the livestock. When we say the people, we mean the greater part and I can tell you that the people are suffering now. This blizzard has lasted for three days. The people were waiting for the spring hoping that it would bring warmer weather, but the storms and the frost have brought back the worst of the winter. Not many will come through this...."

"But surely it's only the sheep that are perishing. What about the cattle?" asked Zhirenshe hopefully.

Bazaraly shrugged his shoulders.

"The Tobikty herds consist mainly of sheep and horses. And the cows have proved to be even weaker than the sheep. The camels too are easily mown down by the djut. How can anyone emerge unscathed?"

They spoke of the calamity all evening. The animals were perishing, but that was not all. The people, too, were beginning to starve. In the Chinghis, Bazaraly had seen the poor roving the auls for food. Some had even turned up here, in Zhidebai. Old men and women had been received in the home of Abai's mothers. They had been given meat and enough grain and millet for two meals.

"Will the djut ruin everyone?" sighed Zhirenshe. "Won't anyone come through unharmed?"

Bazaraly looked at him thoughtfully:

"There'll be some, of course. A white spot may be found even on the blackest horse.... Among the Irgizbai, the Kotibak and the Zhigitek there are auls with good pastures and plenty of land. These have nothing to fear."

To this Yerbol agreed: the Irgizbai would feel the effects least of all. They had plenty of good winter places and much hay had been laid in store in the autumn.

"What good will it be to the others? Who will be the happier for it?" Abai asked.

"Those who are the strongest are the stoutest," smiled Bazaraly. "The lands seized by Kuneken are now saving the Irgizbai."

"Land!" Abai retorted. "Land taken by force! Do you call that land? It's not land but the tears of those who were robbed!"

There was repressed anger in his words, and Asilbek and Zhirenshe smiled approvingly.

"That's true, Abai-zhan! You've expressed what every man feels but is afraid to say."

Even Bazaraly, oppressed by his dark thoughts, seemed to brighten.

Abai was speaking from the heart. He regarded these djiguits as his friends and had long shared his innermost thoughts with them. This, of course, was not at all to the liking of Kunanbai. "He deliberately finds himself wolf-cubs from the auls which have so recently been our enemies. Fine friends!" he would say of his son, frowning with annoyance.

Since he had begun to analyse his father's actions, Abai found himself drawn to the best men of the auls against which Kunanbai had transgressed. Thanks to them he got to know more about the lives, hopes and aspirations of the people. Zhirenshe and Asilbek were five years older than he, but they frankly told him all that they had heard from the old men and boldly discussed all their anxieties with him.

Only Bazaraly had not taken part in these friendly talks until this evening. He was convinced that it was Kunanbai who was mostly to blame for the distress of the people. The auls supported by Kunanbai had driven their herds to the pastures of the Irgizbai and would unquestionably preserve them. But the small and landless clans were waging a hopeless struggle. Their herds were roaming hungry in the lifeless steppes. Hitherto he had kept his angry thoughts to himself, but now as he heard Abai's words he could restrain himself no longer. He tried to seek out the causes of the general calamity.

"The people? What are the people? A force to be used when fighting one's rivals, but mere trash when they are needy themselves. It is the people's hands that win victory, but once it is achieved they may only clutch at the dust of the captured herds as they are driven by. And so the people perish, nameless and unknown. Now, too, they are covering the steppes with their bones. Can their plight move the

hearts of even one of those whom they yesterday called 'our
best sons', 'our support and mainstay'? Where is the man
who will sorrow for them and take their side?"

Abai was moved by the sincerity of Bazaraly's words. He
was amazed by their profound truth, so warmly and
eloquently expressed. Bazaraly was a handsome powerfully
built man, daring and sharp of tongue. He was a good
singer too, but the elders regarded him as a trouble-maker.
"A runaway horse," they called him. "His words are empty,
though stinging and spiteful," they said. Abai realised now
that it was not true.

The djiguits sat listening grimly. Bazaraly's words were a
reproach to them.

"A real man, a man of honour and determination, would
defend those who are now driven by the storm," he said,
"Kuneken would give up nothing for the people when days
were good. But in this time of general distress he should
share at least those things he has in abundance. Let him give
the people pastures for their cattle, shelter in his winter
homes. Let him share his stocks of food with them. If Baisal,
Baidaly and Suyundik alone pull through, apart from the
Irgizbai, they will find no peace. The people, left with
nothing but the tethers of their cattle, won't move on
elsewhere without settling scores. They'll go, of course, but
they'll go like the whirlwind, smashing all the yurtas in their
way. And if they did otherwise, they would be hares and not
men."

The djiguits again grew thoughtful, but to Asilbek it
seemed that Bazaraly was exaggerating.

"There have always been djuts," he objected. "They are
a natural calamity. You can hardly blame ordinary mortals
for them. You put all the blame on one man alone, and that
is unjust."

Asilbek's words filled Bazaraly with disgust. "As slippery
as his father Suyundik," he thought. Instead of arguing he
merely raised his eyebrows, looked at Asilbek, and contemptuously shook his head.

Three men suddenly staggered into the room, barely able
to keep on their feet. Their clothes were covered with snow,
their moustaches and beards glittered with hoarfrost. Even
the eyebrows of the first, a tall elderly man in a lambskin
coat, were crusted with ice.

It was Darkembai and his two Bokenshi neighbours, the
selfsame Darkembai who had tried to shoot Kunanbai at
Tokpambet when Bozhei was whipped. This had come to be

known among all the Tobikty, and the Irgizbai had never ceased to harass and molest him wherever and whenever possible.

Darkembai did not remove his coat. He had come on an urgent matter.

"Abai, my son," he began, "I have heard that you are good to your kinsmen and that is why I have come. If you were Takezhan, I would not be here. Misfortune has brought me. I have some sheep, and these men," he gestured to his companions, "have twenty and maybe thirty head, but even with these small flocks we cannot find shelter anywhere. We are being driven on, hardly able to walk. On our pastures there is not a blade of grass. The sheep are dropping with hunger, and five have died on the way here."

"Why don't you move on towards the Chinghis?" interjected Asilbek. "You would at least be shielded from the blizzard there."

"But the wind is blowing from the Chinghis and you can't drive weary flocks in the teeth of a blizzard. And how far off are the Chinghis! But Musakul and Zhidebai are near and down the wind. If they let us, we'd find enough fodder on the Musakul and Zhidebai pastures to feed several flocks! I'd dig away the snow and let the sheep graze, and the cattle wouldn't perish there. It's a quiet place and it would save the sheep.... It's our last hope—perhaps they'll let me take the animals there?"

Abai fully understood the hopelessness of the man's plight.

"You're right, bring your flocks there!" he declared immediately.

"That is easily said, my son, but what am I to do? No sooner did I get to Musakul than Takezhan came out to drive us back, and that cutthroat Zhumagul with him. They threatened us with their whips and ordered us off. That's why I've come to you. If I'm to lose all, I thought, let Abai at least know that his helpless kinsmen are doomed."

Without waiting to hear any more Abai briefly instructed Yerbol:

"Dress warmly, Yerbol, and get on your horse. And you," he turned to Darkembai, "will go back to your flocks! Dilda, tell them to give these men food for the way!"

Dilda at once left the room.

Abai then told Yerbol to convey his salem to Takezhan: let him not interfere with Darkembai. Let him allot a pasture for the small flock and restrain Zhumagul. Yerbol dressed quickly and set off with Darkembai.

Takezhan was wintering in Musakul. Married earlier than Abai, he had set up an independent yurta in the same year. He had proved himself to be close-fisted, a man who watched jealously over his land. The herdsmen said that he had even driven the cattle of his mothers from his pastures when no one could see. That year Abai had heard a good deal about Takezhan's misdeeds and was furious with his elder brother.

Yerbol came back late at night. He was covered with snow, his short thick beard was white and his broad nose red from the cold. The flash of his dark eyes spoke of humiliation and anger. Without removing his hat, he sank on one knee to shake the snow from his beard.

"The devil himself is more likely to help a man than Takezhan," he said. "He kept shouting that no strange flocks would set a hoof in Musakul or Zhidebai. And he ordered Zhumagul to whip Darkembai and drive his flocks away! Zhumagul, of course, was more than willing. He came riding up, may he be damned, and is chasing the sheep away right now."

"What about Darkembai? What is he going to do?"

"What can he do? Where can he go on a night like this—in the blizzard?"

"Better die under the whip of Zhumagul than perish as a tramp!" exclaimed Zhirenshe and Bazaraly, unable to withhold their wrath any longer.

"Another such dog as Zhumagul is not to be found anywhere," continued Yerbol. "Try to understand, I begged him, wait until the morning, but he only swore at me."

Abai knew his friend well and asked no questions. He understood that there was more behind that brief account, more of Takezhan's and Zhumagul's cruelty and viciousness. Ominously pale, he stood staring at Yerbol, thinking hard, and then suddenly sprang to his feet.

The other djiguits looked up inquiringly. What was he going to do?

Scarcely able to breathe, Abai snapped:

"Get up, Yerbol! Come with me!" Hurriedly he began to dress. Donning a light cloak, he drew the sash tight, seized his whip, threw back the door and was gone from the room. Yerbol followed.

Two greys stood pressed to the wall, their heads turned away from the wind. Both were saddled and ready. Abai untethered the first, sprang lightly into the saddle and galloped into the raging blizzard, with Yerbol on his heels.

Zhumagul had succeeded in gathering all the sheep belonging to Darkembai and his companions and was now lashing at them furiously to drive them from the pasture. But the frozen and hungry animals had bunched together and would not move. Enraged, Zhumagul heaped curses upon them and Darkembai. As to Darkembai's friends stumbling about in the snow-drifts, he paid no attention to them at all.

Exhausted with hunger and cold, several of the one-year-olds had collapsed and lay motionless, their heads buried in the snow. Darkembai tried to hurl himself at Zhumagul, but the latter, swift and agile on his well-fed animal, darted like the wind itself among the sheep, lashing mercilessly right and left until they fell. If the meek animals could pray to Allah, they would have prayed in that icy wind under the relentless blows of their enemy only for the deliverance of death.

When Maibasar had ceased to be the volost chief, Zhumagul, too, had been deposed from his position of messenger and was suddenly bereft of his strength, like a gelding. "Zhumagul is going out of his mind," old Zhumabai had observed jokingly. "He has even promised a sheep to Allah if only he could pick a quarrel with somebody but he's still out of luck." In the past two years Zhumagul had nonetheless found a place to his liking. Takezhan had employed him as his noker! True enough, Takezhan did not wield such authority as before, but in the autumn and winter he watched over the land like a dog on a chain. The cruelty shown by this pair against the defenceless auls was as bestial as that of any volost chief and messenger. They whipped the herdsmen, drove off the animals and roped horses from the herds of others. Takezhan's kinsmen trembled before him, often pleading for mercy.

Darkembai was a real find for Zhumagul and Takezhan, who were always spoiling for a fight. This was the very man they wanted, the very same Darkembai they had been after for so long. Charging Zhumagul with the task, Takezhan had gloated, "God himself has placed my old enemy Darkembai in my hands".

And so Zhumagul had attacked the sheep, cursing Darkembai and all his ancestors. But just as he knocked down another sheep, two riders pounced on him from out of the blizzard, almost as though they had lain in wait for him behind the white screen of the storm.

Not a word was spoken by either of the two. They had not come to ask questions, to fume or quarrel with Zhumagul. The first of them flew up and clutched the reins of Zhumagul's horse. Zhumagul roared a protest and raised his whip.

"What are you doing, you scoundrel!" Abai cried, choking with ungovernable rage.

Zhumagul at once recognised Abai, but found that this time friend was worse than foe. Abai's whip whistled through the air and crashed on his head. Zhumagul jerked at the reins to dart out of reach, but Abai had wound the thongs around his left wrist and would not let go. Silently he struck again and again with a heavy hand; the whip was as painfully effective as a club. Better death than such disgrace! Zhumagul raised his hand, but Yerbol, waiting for this, leapt forward and held him fast.

"May Allah bring you happiness," cried Darkembai behind them. "Not all men have become wolves. Let me get my hands on him, just once!" Seizing the hem of Zhumagul's cloak, he tugged so fiercely that Zhumagul toppled over and fell on the snow like a rotten tree-trunk.

Abai ordered the flock to be turned and driven once more towards Musakul. The sheep and their harassed masters at last reached a pasture so well sheltered that the snow-drifts hardly covered the grass.

A haystack stood near and Abai directed the flocks towards it. At the sight of the hay the sheep ran eagerly, but Darkembai was frightened; they would say that he had not only driven his sheep into these pastures unbidden, but had led them to Kunanbai's stacks.

"Drive them back! Don't let them get at the hay," he shouted to his herdsmen.

But Abai broke in gruffly:

"Let them—let them feed! Hey, drive them to the rick! What are you afraid of?"

The sheep buried their heads in the fodder, eating voraciously. They would not budge another step.

"Don't drive them anywhere until morning! Let them be until the blizzard's over. I am as much the owner of this hay as Takezhan," Abai assured him. "Let your two neighbours stay with the sheep. They'll keep the flock together. And you get on a horse—that one over there, one of Takezhan's horses, and ride as hard as you can. Tell the surrounding auls. Tell them that I've sent you. Let those whose sheep are too weak to reach the Chinghis, drive their flocks here, to my father's pastures. Let them bring shovels and rakes! The flocks can be saved where the wind does not blow. Let them dig up the snow and get at the fodder. Tell it to all such as you: to the Torgai, the Zhigitek, the Karabatir, the Bokenshi and all who are near. If we must suffer, we'll suffer together. Off with you! As fast as you can! And bring everybody!"

Darkembai sprang into the saddle, and Abai turned upon Zhumagul.

"Let this be the last time that you attack people like a vicious watch dog, you scoundrel! Understand? And tell Takezhan not to torture the hungry! If he doesn't know what to do with his strength, let him pit it against mine! Tell him just what I have said, even if it should make him burst with anger! Move on! You'll get there on foot," he commanded.

Zhumagul waded off through the drifts.

Abai and Yerbol then galloped off towards Zhidebai in the face of the wind. The blizzard raged as furiously as ever, lashing their faces and blinding them with snow.

By morning the wind had dropped, and the snow was falling more gently. As though emerging from some fearsome ordeal, the red sun rose from behind the pass, fiery ribbons streaming away on either side like trails of blood through the cold morning haze. Having swept relentlessly across the steppes for some days, the wind was reluctant to subside completely, and spasmodic gusts still whipped up the powdery snow. But at last there was a lull, a terrifying silence, when the very air seemed to crackle in the frost.

Darkembai rode hard all night. "Tell it to all such as you...." Those words of Abai had touched him to the heart. He dashed on with the message to all the poor of the clans of the Karabatir, the Torgai, the Borsak and the Zhuantayak. He visited all who owned few—no more than thirty or forty sheep, and did not forget the neediest near the rich lands of Musakul and Zhidebai.

In three days the blizzard had covered every pasture, and the people were sadly convinced that it would carry off all that remained of their sheep. The wind shrieked over the huts, rattling the windows and keeping every man awake. The poor were at the end of their tether and the old people prayed to God for mercy. No man, woman or child dared undress and none slept by day or at night. They were constantly watching the sheds where they kept their wretched sheep.

A sprig of acacia protruding from the snow would be cut
away and carefully brought home, as were the tops of the
bushes that still showed above the snow-drifts. Even the
rushes on the old barn roofs were taken off and dragged
home for the animals. But can thirst be quenched with a
drop of water brought on a lark's wing? Which should
receive this pitiful sop—a sheep that had lambed prematurely? Or the milch cows? Or the one and only camel?
Their poor gatherings could not save the livestock upon
which their lives depended.

The thought that aid might come from those who
possessed the wide pastures and abundant stocks of hay and
other fodder occurred to no one.

And on such a night of despair Darkembai descended
upon the auls like a whirlwind, resurrecting long-buried
hopes.

By sunrise flocks were on the move towards Kunanbai's
pastures from all directions. Abai and Yerbol were on their
horses, and rode to meet the people and their herds—in
each case a handful of sheep and three or four cows,
followed by weary men, women and children.

The sheep were a pitiful sight. The skin hung loosely
from their bones and their sides were caked with frozen
droppings. Tottering goats fell dead with a last feeble bleat.
Behind most of the auls stretched a sad trail from their
winter places to the Irgizbai pastures—the gleaming snow
was dotted with carcasses.

It is said that sheep can go without food for six days.
Judging by the number of carcasses these flocks had starved
longer—they were completely exhausted. Within two or
three days not one would have been left.

It was difficult for the sheep to push through the deep
snow and the herdsmen sent a horse, a camel or a cow ahead
for the smaller animals to follow. The sheep suffered such
pangs of hunger that those in the lead chewed at the tail of
the cow or horse before them.

The men and women who followed were scarcely in a
better state: pale and wan, they followed the lean herds
like bloodless spectres. The faces of the aged were deeply
lined, and their tatters flapped in the wind. Not only the
women but even the bearded men had wrapped their heads
in old rags, and most of them were shod in felt stockings,
without boots. But no sooner did they reach the pastures
than every man, woman and child fell to clearing away the
snow.

All three of Kunanbai's pastures were known for their wealth of rushes, sweet briar and other shrubs. The storm had deposited drifts only at the edges of the pastures. In the middle the snow was not deep and gave way underfoot like sand. Wherever it was raked aside, there was thick, luxuriant vegetation.

Reaching fodder at last, the animals fell upon it greedily. More than fifty auls had come, and by noon Abai and Yerbol had found room for most of the herds. Those pastures which Takezhan had so jealously guarded against even a single poor cow were now feeding more than a thousand head of sheep. Of cattle there were few.

Abai was filled with sadness at the sight of these shivering animals and worn-out people. On the wide zhailyau, they had appeared to be living in plenty and were strong and well, but the djut had revealed the full extent of their poverty and helplessness.

Most of the households owned only twenty or thirty sheep and three or four head of cattle. These animals had to support their owners all the year round. They were used for hauling, slaughtered for meat, sold to meet urgent needs and skinned for clothing. And such a life was termed "a prosperous life for the people"! How could one describe it now? Today there was dire need, general suffering, the djut — and Abai could see as never before what a wretched existence was eked out by his own people.

Once more he rode through the pastures, pausing before the old people and telling them:

"If you are cold then go to the nearest of the auls. You can warm yourselves there and have something to eat. There are kinsmen all around you! They won't drive you away. Don't be afraid."

The old men and women could not thank Abai enough — he made them feel as though all their troubles were over.

Instead of turning homewards, Abai made the rounds of all the Irgizbai auls near the pastures and everywhere summoned the elders or the old women in charge of the cooking.

"Help your kinsmen. They are in distress," he said. "Prepare hot food for them in all the cauldrons and feed them once a day."

The hungry were looked after, each aul taking care of those who were nearest.

Abai and Yerbol finally reached Takezhan's aul, which

was wintering in Musakul, but found that he was not at
home. Having learned of all that had happened from
Zhumagul, he had not stayed to argue with Abai but on the
same night had galloped to Karashoky to complain to their
father about Abai's arbitrary actions.

Abai did not dismount at Takezhan's house but sent
Yerbol in to summon Takezhan's wife. Karazhan soon
emerged, her jaw set firmly, her face pale and furious. She
was a tall woman with an enormous nose, shrewish and
given to making caustic remarks. Not even her husband was
spared, who was kept well under her thumb. Though
young, she was callous, heartless and a tight-fisted house-
keeper. Takezhan indeed could not have found a more
suitable mate and after his marriage he quickly amassed
wealth. It was Karazhan, moreover, who had disapproved of
Ulzhan's generosity and insisted that Takezhan separate
from the Great Yurta. The renown and popularity gained
by Abai, who had so completely outshone his elder brother
Takezhan, was another of her sorest grievances: her hatred
for this younger brother-in-law was almost an obsession.

Abai knew it, and without greeting his sister-in-law came
straight to the point.

"I hear that your husband has gone to complain about
me. If I am guilty of any crime, I shall answer for it myself.
But now I have come to charge you with an important
matter — and you'll do exactly as I say."

"What matter?"

"The surrounding auls are perishing in the djut. These
kinsmen have always mown and stacked your hay, dug your
wells, herded your cattle and done all your chares for you.
They are in distress and you must help them. We have
given them the pastures — their own winter places are far
away and the cold is severe. We are also feeding them. Your
job is to provide twenty people from four auls with hot food
once a day!"

"How can we, Abai? We ourselves have nothing to eat."

"It's a lie! Only recently the caravan brought you three
sacks of flour, and you have five more of wheat! Your stocks
of meat have not been touched. I warn you — I am not
joking, Karazhan! Share at least a little of your supplies with
the hungry! If you prove obstinate, there will be trouble."

"And so you think we should go hungry ourselves?"

Abai flared up:

"Go to the devil if you like, but just dare to refuse! I'll
come here to check every evening! If you refuse you'll have

only yourself to blame for the consequences. As long as I am here, I am strong enough to make you do as I say. I'll force you to your disgrace, but force you I will. Understand?"

He glared down at her, his hand clutching the whip. Karazhan noticed the gesture and said nothing more.

Abai had assigned Darkembai and his friends to Karazhan the evening before. Now he summoned them and again turned wrathfully to his sister-in-law.

"This is Darkembai! He'll bring those whom I choose to be fed in your aul. You're not only to prepare everything for them yourself, but to make the whole aul take care of them!

"And what are you standing there for like an orphan?" Abai turned on Darkembai. "Don't hem and haw, do you hear! When you come back from your work in the pastures, just ask for food! If they refuse or put you off, come to me at once! And if you try to shield them — then you're not Darkembai, but just an old woman! Understand?"

Abai spurred his horse to a gallop.

Aided by Yerbol, he kept hard at work all day and returned to Zhidebai at sunset. In his mother's house he found Takezhan and old Zhumabai waiting for him, the former having returned with Kunanbai's instructions.

On his way to the Great Yurta, whence he had been summoned by Ulzhan, Abai noticed intensive preparations underway everywhere — around the houses, the storerooms and the kitchens. The great cauldrons were steaming, three wooden mortars had been set up and the women were pounding wheat in them. Ulzhan had obviously taken the care of the hungry upon herself.

The first group of twenty or so had already been served with hot food. Not wanting to embarrass them with his presence, Abai made for the Great Yurta.

He greeted Zhumabai and presented his salem to him. The meeting between the brothers was more than cold, Abai not so much as deigning to notice Takezhan. Zhumabai conveyed Kunanbai's salem to Abai.

Takezhan had apparently been so angry the night before that he had not even bothered to find out all that Abai had done, and had told Kunanbai only of the clash over Darkembai and Zhumagul. That the poor of all the surrounding auls had been invading his pastures from early morning was as yet unknown to Kunanbai. To Takezhan the mere appearance of Darkembai on his land had seemed incredible and the thought that many others might follow his example had not entered his head. It was simply out of the question! But now he knew the whole story and was virtually mad with rage.

Zhumabai told Abai that Kunanbai considered it wrong to shelter Darkembai. "A kindness shown to one who is unworthy will lead to no good," he had said. "Darkembai once aimed a rifle at me. Let him be content that I have left him alone. If Abai wishes to show kindness, then let him show it to friends and not to such scoundrels. Let him turn Darkembai away." Such were his father's orders.

Far from acquiescing, Abai did not even attempt to make excuses:

"My father says that as a true Moslem he wishes all men well. It is the first virtue of a true believer to help those who are in distress. I have already given my word to the people. I am feeding them. Let my father not regard this as a self-willed action but give me his blessing," he declared firmly.

Takezhan could barely contain himself.

"If you're so righteous, then put on the mullah's turban and collect kushir* for Darkembai!" he burst out.

"If need be I shall. The people are suffering, and I am ready to make the sacrifice."

"Go ahead then! Go begging for them!"

"Before I do, I'll give the people all that's mine, and all that's yours too."

"That's exactly what you've done already! You've put not only Darkembai but everyone else on our pastures! You're not satisfied with beggaring yourself — you want to drag us all down with you! You want to ruin us, don't you — to starve your mothers!"

"Don't you worry about my mothers!" Abai snapped. "My mothers are not marmots in their holes like that stingy hag of yours! They can share wholeheartedly and suffer with the people if need be! Everything I have done has been according to their wishes. Don't worry on their account!"

It was as though a father had spoken to his son: Abai's words sounded like a command. Takezhan would have continued to argue, but Ulzhan intervened.

"Now stop this! Enough squabbling," she broke in sharply and, turning to Zhumabai, added:

"You'd better go back. Before you came, Abai summoned all the hungry. We shall share what we have with them — so far we are not short of food. Tell Kuneken not to worry; we

* Kushir—the tithe collected by the clergy.— Ed.

shall give the people our share. Let him not disgrace his son by compelling him to break his word!"

Takezhan said nothing more, although his views had not changed in the least. He had put on his hat and was about to go when Ulzhan noticed the repressed fury within him and raised her voice:

"Just a moment! Tell Karazhan to check her temper and feed the hungry kinsmen as they should be fed! It is not her dowry she is giving away. Let her come to her senses and have a good look about her!"

Takezhan and old Zhumabai rode off. Having inspected the pastures and counted the auls that used them, they set off for Karashoky.

Kunanbai heard them attentively. He was indignant that Abai and his mothers were forgetting themselves. It was clear from Abai's wilful actions that he had lost all sense of proportion, that he reckoned with no one.

On the following day it was Zhakip who came to Zhidebai to convey Kunanbai's salem to Abai.

The fact that his father had entrusted this second command to his brother Zhakip, who was sent only on important missions, was significant. Kunanbai's kinsmen were wont to estimate the importance of Kunanbai's salems by the messengers they were entrusted to. When it was necessary to break a man and seize his property, he would send Karabas and Kamisbai. If the message was: "Tell him, let him know," he would send such as Zhumabai, though he had at times sent Abai or Kudaiberdy with such messages. If it was a matter of: "Intimidate them, frighten them, scold them severely," it was Maibasar who was chosen. "Explain and persuade!" was the message entrusted to Zhakip in highly important matters concerning entire clans unless indeed it was some really extraordinary question relating to controversies among the clans. In such cases Karatai was sent.

When Abai saw Zhakip, therefore, he realised that the orders from Karashoky were growing in scale and importance. He was prepared for this, however, and scarcely glancing at Zhakip sat listening, coldly silent.

Before conveying Kunanbai's instructions, Zhakip set forth several considerations of his own. He seemed to be speaking for himself, but Abai very well knew whence the words had come. He had learned to decipher the hidden meanings in his father's salems.

Zhakip explained that there were certain matters in which

the initiative must be left to the father and in which a son could only support him. This must be understood quite clearly. The father's good deeds did honour to the son, but wayward actions, disregard of the paternal will, a stubborn striving for independence would be no credit to the son.

Abai was unmoved. Surely there were fathers who supported their sons' actions and did all they could to win them honour and respect!

"There are fathers who do not oppress their sons with the weight of their· demands, plans and will," he uttered his thoughts aloud.

But Zhakip went on: If one must render aid and permit others to use one's lands, such aid should be rendered to well-to-do auls, to those with considerable herds, in the event of temporary difficulty. The time might come when their help would be needed too. But what were all those people worth with whom Abai had taken so much trouble? Lumped together they would not be able to spare a single horse or camel. Such was the opinion of his father, and his view was similar to that expressed by Zhumabai in the first salem.

This argument failed to convince Abai. What Zhakip was speaking of was not aid, but mutual assistance between friends or close relatives. Abai explained his own attitude and his objections — and did not yield an inch.

"Are you the master of the land and the cattle?" interjected Zhakip. "Was it by your labour that all this was amassed? Do you really intend to squander all that your father has gathered? Tomorrow it may be your own cattle or Takezhan's that will be stricken by the djut. There are your mothers — at least think of them!"

That, too, was nothing new. But it would have been impolite to repeat to Zhakip what he had answered Takezhan on this point.

"You're right, I must be squandering my mothers' bread," he admitted sarcastically, and glanced at Zereh. "But here sits one of my mothers. She is not only my mother, but yours and my father's too. It is she who is the real owner of our property. In other words — we must all obey her wishes. We'll listen to what she has to say, shall we?"

And Abai moved closer to his grandmother.

Old Zereh seemed to have withered in the past few years, and her face was deeply wrinkled. She saw that Abai was leaning towards her and turned her ear to him. Her grandson loudly explained everything, briefly but clearly, and concluded by saying that her word would be final.

Zereh frowned upon Zhakip.

"Convey my salem to my son," she said. "I have not long to live. Am I fated to witness the destruction of my kinsmen who are homeless and hungry? Am I yet to see an ocean of tears shed by orphans and widows? Will my son not feed those who gather at his mother's funeral when I die? Then let him not drive away those poor helpless people; let him consider that they are mourners at my funeral."

Zereh's words caught Zhakip unawares, and he was completely at a loss. But Abai was angry with Zhakip when he saw that his grandmother was so bitter.

"If you are really concerned for Mother Zereh, then don't make her talk of death," he said. "I shall let no one drive away those to whom I have given shelter," he declared firmly.

Zhakip did not dare to cross Zereh, but was resolved to put his nephew to shame.

"Do you realise what you are saying? Do you really mean to stick to this impudence? I hate to see where your words are leading."

"There's no need for further explanations," Abai said, still furious. "You have understood me well enough. We are not children! If those over there are enjoying their new-found happiness, then let them leave us in peace and let us live as we choose!"

In all his life Zhakip had not met a man among the Irgizbai who would have dared to condemn Kunanbai so sharply.

"Enough, my son! Say no more! How shall I convey your words to your father? Never shall I forget that the most awful words I have heard in my life, words that another would tremble to utter, came from you!" With this Zhakip sprang up.

There was a special meaning in Abai's words. He was hinting at the ill-advised action taken by Kunanbai that winter. It was actually because of this that the negotiations ended happily as they did.

Under different circumstances these negotiations might have indeed ended differently. The thing was that Kunanbai who was over sixty had married a young wife.

Ulzhan and all who surrounded her had fallen out with Kunanbai over this two months before. In Zhidebai there were Ulzhan and Aigiz, in Karashoky—his baibishe Kunkeh, but now he was taking another wife, the seventeen-year-old Nurganim.

She was the daughter of the Hadji Berdikhozha. They did not come from the Tobikty, and were recent arrivals from Turkestan. Kunanbai liked the hadji for his knowledge of the holy books, for his wise sayings and interpretations of the Koran, and often spent his evenings with him.

Nurganim had never been betrothed. She was a well-built girl with attractive features and luxuriant jet-black hair. Her face breathed a tender sweetness and her eyes shone with intelligence and vitality.

Ulzhan and Aigiz learned of the new tokal from a man sent by Kunkeh. Ulzhan did not feel jealous any more. She had four grown sons, grandchildren and was not the kind of person to flare up. She no longer looked upon Kunanbai as her husband, but merely as the father of her sons, a person grown close to her through the long years they had shared together. All other feelings for him had long since died within her.

And yet she was opposed to his new marriage. She summoned Zhumabai.

"If he would but once in his life take our advice," she said, "he would not marry; there will be endless wrangling. He might feel some shame before his children."

When Ulzhan told the news to Abai, he shuddered with disgust. "He wants us to stop respecting him as a father—to alienate us," he thought indignantly. "Why doesn't he consider those who are near and dear to him— Grandmother, for instance, or my mother who has been his life's companion? Doesn't he understand that we, the children, will be ashamed to receive a new mother who is younger than any of us?" To Ulzhan he said merely that he could not approve of his father's action and advised her to send Zhumabai to him with the following answer: "Since he has no regard for us, let him burn alone in the fire into which he has hurled himself, but let him know that he has abandoned us in sorrow caused by his action."

His talk with Zhakip had touched Abai on a raw spot. The old wound had been reopened at the sight of the general distress of the people, and both harrowing experiences had brought him into conflict with his father.

Only fifteen days had passed, but they seemed like many months. The beginning of April, a month which usually brought the first green shoots, was the hardest. The unusual frost and blizzards had caught the people unawares and brought an irreparable calamity that would always be remembered as "the djut of April" or "the djut of the last snow" — so great had the snowfall been in that brief interval.

The herds of the stricken auls had spent fifteen days on Kunanbai's pastures, but then came a change of weather and a warm southern breeze blew over the steppes. Had it come a month earlier, it would have been joyfully welcomed as the harbinger of spring. But now it merely signified the end of the last adversities of winter.

Ignoring Kunanbai's persistent orders, Abai and Ulzhan devoted themselves heart and soul to the hungry, to their comfort and the care of their flocks, Abai riding among them for days on end. He had grown thin, his face was weather-beaten and even swarthier than usual. But his efforts were not in vain; the livestock of the fifty auls survived the djut.

2

The first spring winds quickly thawed the land. Not only the hills but the valleys, too, discarded their mantle of snow. As though ashamed to have dallied so long, the snow seemed to be hurrying away before the advent of those days of which it is said, "the earth has unfolded its embrace". The sun began to shine, and the fleecy clouds of the new season sailed across the sky.

The auls sheltering at Zhidebai began to leave for their various winter places. No words could express the people's gratitude to Zereh and Ulzhan for helping them to survive. When they had gone, Ulzhan announced that her winter stores of meat were exhausted.

The disastrous force of a djut does not only affect the livestock grazing near the auls, but also the horses returning from the winter pastures at the first signs of warm weather. All the hardships of a hard winter affect these herds as well.

From the numerous herds of the Tobikty only those of Kunanbai and the Irgizbai in general, and those of Baidaly, Suyundik and Baisal had survived. And even these could scarcely reach the winter places. The living skeletons were strung out across the steppes like a vision of the end of the world.

Many had lost their herds to the very last animal. Among the Torgai, Zhuantayak, Topai, Zhigitek and Bokenshi only seventy to eighty horses returned out of every thousand that

had been herded to the winter pastures in the autumn.
They had suffered even more than the other animals from
the djut.

The auls were oppressed. People ceased to visit one
another and lived as though they had been left amidst the
wreckage remaining after a hurricane. They were all
concerned with one thing only — to save what remained of
the herds from the killing winds of the early spring.

Only one aul had no need to worry about its horses:
Zereh's aul in Zhidebai. Kunanbai had ordered all the
horses that had returned from the winter pastures to be
driven to the Chinghis and took their care upon himself.

Then came the warm weather, and luxuriant grass sprang
up. The decaying carcasses about Zhidebai began to poison
the air and were a constant threat of infection and disease.
Ulzhan, therefore, decided to abandon the winter houses
for the yurtas.

The evening before they were to have moved, Zereh was
suddenly taken ill. Moaning pitifully, the old woman was
scarcely able to breathe and by the morning was so weak that
she could not stir. Abai and Ulzhan were frightened and
never left her bedside. They nursed her themselves and
were reluctant to admit anyone into the house, for fear of
tiring her. On the next evening Ulzhan began to lose hope.
Saying nothing to Abai, she sent a messenger to Karashoky.
Daughter-in-law and grandson sat by their old mother all
night, and in the morning Zereh's failing eyes sought them
for the last time. For an instant Abai's heart warmed with
hope, and he stood looking expectantly at his grandmother,
who was trying to say something. Abai could not understand, but Ulzhan was able to read her every movement.
They both leaned over the dying woman, who began to
whisper indistinctly.

Her mind was clear, but her strength was gone, and her
voice had become almost inaudible.

"Was I ... was I able ... to set a good example ... to you ... in
life? Was I ... until my hearing failed ... able to ... set you on
the right path? ... What can I do ... now? What do you expect
.. from me now ... when my remaining strength ... is going?
... You have ... bent over me.... What do you expect ... of
me?"

Each word cost her a great effort.

It was better not to weary her with replies. Abai pressed
his hands to his breast as he bowed low before her. "All that
best, all that is purest in my heart, belongs to you, my sacred

mother," his silent gesture declared. He clasped the hands of the frail old woman, then placed her small withered fingers against his cheek and covered them with kisses. Hot tears fell upon them.

"Light of my eyes.... Apple of my eye."

Turning her eyes towards Ulzhan, she added:

"Take care of your mother.... And obey her."

Life was ebbing from her. Silent for an instant, she spoke again:

"After all ... he's my only son.... Let him throw a handful of earth ... upon my grave...."

These words were clearly pronounced. Zereh said no more, and Abai understood that this was her last wish concerning Kunanbai. Ulzhan quietly nodded. "All shall be done...."

The life that was so dear to them ended before the first rays of dawn.

Not a word was uttered by Ulzhan or Abai until well into the morning. They could not take their eyes away from the wise old face of Zereh.

This was the first bereavement in Abai's life. The features of his grandmother had now taken on a deathly hue and yet she seemed as bright and serene as ever, as though death had not laid its hand upon her, as if Zereh had at last achieved a cherished desire and had become the embodiment of tranquillity.

By sunrise everyone, from the oldest to the youngest, had gathered at the house. The grandchildren and daughters-in-law wept silently. The people of the house and the neighbours sighed deeply. During the morning all the kinsmen dwelling in Karashoky and the Chinghis came to the house, the first arrivals being Kunanbai and Kunkeh. By noon the entire clan of the Irgizbai was present.

Zereh's death was a loss to all, yet there was none of the usual violent sobbing, but rather a silence of special respect for the departed. The poor of all the fifty auls which had received shelter and food from Zereh and Ulzhan during the djut came to the funeral on the following day. The senior mother of the clan was buried with great ceremony.

Kunanbai and Kunkeh remained in Zhidebai until the seventh memorial day.

Abai had decided not to entrust the reading of the Koran to a mullah and instead read the holy book himself. In the course of the week he read it through twice.

Alone with her son one day that week, Ulzhan began to

speak of Zereh. Abai listened avidly, drinking in her words.

"Our mother," she said, her eyes filling with tears, "set an example of true honour. If not for her, I, too, should have grown heartless and deaf to the needs of the people. We are indebted to her for everything and must treasure her memory always."

It was only now, quite suddenly, that Abai noticed how Ulzhan had aged. It seemed that life had stamped her face with the pain of her hidden thoughts. Silently he nodded his head in agreement.

A week later, after the final readings of the Koran, Kunanbai and his family departed for Karashoky.

Soon afterwards, all the auls set out as usual for the zhailyau. But Abai would not lay aside the Koran until the fortieth day. Keeping aloof from the wandering caravans, he sang mournful songs and sad hymns to her, that splendid soul who had departed. When they reached the mountains, he climbed to the peaks, glanced across the steppes and continued to sing.

The sorrow of those songs shrouded him like the mists of autumn.

When the auls at last crossed the ranges, the people lay exposed before Abai in all their wretched poverty, and he was seized with a fresh spasm of pity when he saw what was left of the once prosperous auls. How they had dwindled! Where the herds had barely found sufficient room on the pastures, there were only small clusters of animals here and there, lost in the vast expanses. The herds had grown so small that the auls had been able to merge together. Most of the pastures and verdant mountain slopes, as well as the broad summer grounds beyond the Chinghis, remained unpopulated. Many beggars appeared, men and women hopelessly floundering in the quagmire of poverty. To Abai it seemed that after old mother Zereh's passing another great mother lay ill and wasting away — the people.

3

It was rumoured that the district officials were coming to hold elections, and Kunanbai summoned Abai.

The young man had spent the autumn in solitude with his dombra and his music. Whether he played *The Yellow Saimaka River*, *The Tears of Two Girls*, or *The Song of the Lark*, every note was fraught with meaning.

He gave up the usual pastimes of the young men, and actually shunned their company. When Yerbol visited him, he invited Abai to join in the games and other fun, tempted him with the names of new beautiful girls. But Abai was indifferent. He composed a new song: *Be Quiet, Heart! Be Quiet!* in answer to his friend. But when Yerbol heard it, he began to reason with him.

"Are you really saying good-bye to youth forever? You're not even twenty-five! What strange notions fill your head? I just don't understand you," he said.

But Abai laughed quietly. As always when alone with his friend, he played the dombra and sang song after song, pouring out his thoughts and feelings. *Be Quiet...* was a song he could repeat day after day.

Yerbol could not agree with the meaning, but liked the words and sometimes joined Abai in *Be Quiet...* For ten days the two djiguits seemed to be taking final leave of their youth.

Yerbol had to go home.

"It is not old age that I crave, Yerbol," Abai confided to him as they separated. "Don't you think I value my youth? What can be better than youth? You know it yourself. But to take the place of fleeting childhood and restive youth, I should like to find the youth that is wise and fruitful. There are new loves waiting for me too. If I were to tell you about them, you would see that my heart is bursting with dreams.... You'll learn about it some day!"

This sounded like a self-revelation.

On that day Abai was summoned by his father, and as Yerbol set off for home, Abai headed his horse towards Karashoky.

It was growing dark when he approached his father's aul. In a ravine overgrown with willows he saw another rider advancing towards him, a tall, broad-shouldered djiguit, who turned out to be his younger brother Ospan. In the growing dusk Abai recognised him only when they came face to face, and was astonished. Although he had seen Ospan day after day he had not noticed how he had grown. At eighteen Ospan was even taller and broader than himself.

In Karashoky, Abai did not go at once to his father, but first visited Kunkeh's house. Kudaiberdy, his favourite brother, had been ill for a long time, and Abai decided first to see how he was getting on.

Kudaiberdy lay on a high bed, tormented by a wracking cough. He had grown a black beard, long and straggling; he was thin, his bones were protruding and his veins swollen in

evil dark knots. At the sight of his brother his wan features
brightened perceptibly.

Abai was pained by his brother's pitiful appearance.
Removing his cloak, he approached and seated himself near
the bed.

The malady which had been sapping his brother's
strength had now taken possession of him completely. Abai
had seen him only fifteen days before and since then his
brother had visibly declined. Reaching for Abai's hand,
Kudaiberdy pressed and then stroked it with his weak
fingers.

"Good of you to come," he said.

Abai took his brother's hand in both of his and pressed it
to his breast. Both were silent, but they understood each
other without words. At last Kudaiberdy asked quietly:

"Have you seen father?"

"Not yet. I came here first," Abai answered.

Three boys ran in from the neighbouring room to salem
Abai. These were the sons of Kudaiberdy — Shakke, Shubar
and Amir.

Embracing the youngsters, Abai kissed them warmly.
Shakke and Shubar already had a tutor, and whenever Abai
came he would ask them about their studies. The children
were fond of him and not at all bashful in his presence.

Kudaiberdy watched his children as they surrounded
Abai and, overcome with emotion, turned his head to the
wall. This did not escape Abai. He spoke to the boys for a
while, then sent them off to play and again took his place at
the bedside.

Kudaiberdy looked sadly after the children as they went
off.

"What's to become of them? What will happen if.... They
are your brothers. * What sort of life awaits each of them? I
shall remain their debtor," he said, as though taking leave of
his boys.

Hot tears welled up in Abai's eyes, and his voice shook as
he said:

"I shall take that debt upon myself, Bakke! I'll carry them
through life on my shoulders as best I can!"

"Don't weep.... There's no need to weep," Kudaiberdy
repeated to comfort him.

Both were silent for some moments. Kudaiberdy turned
on his side to face Abai, but the movement brought on

* According to the family traditions of the Kazakhs, no distinction is
made between a nephew and a younger brother. — Ed.

another fit of coughing. Abai pulled his blanket over his shoulders and tucked him in.

"Do you know why father has called you?" Kudaiberdy changed the subject.

"No, Bakke, I know nothing yet."

"Well then, I'll tell you. The officials arrived today; they're going to hold elections. Father has put them up in Zhakip's aul. They say there will be new volosts and new authorities — 'rulers'. Father intends to propose you. What do you think of it?"

"And you? What do you advise?"

"If you want to know my advice," said Kudaiberdy, reflectively, "I'd refuse. The worth of a man does not at all depend on whether or not he is a ruler. We've seen that for ourselves. Power spoils a man and instead of bringing anything good earns him only curses. Don't sacrifice your youth for nothing!"

"Yes, Bakke. All that is true," agreed Abai readily.

"Takezhan is trying to get himself elected. Let him have the post of volost chief for his pleasure!" concluded Kudaiberdy.

Abai did not leave his brother until nightfall. At Kudaiberdy's request, a dombra was brought and Abai played one melody after another.

The official who arrived to conduct the elections had a long talk with Kunanbai. He was obviously ready to be guided by Kunanbai's opinion in the selection of candidates for the post of volost chief.

From the day of the new law on volost administration Kunanbai had been firmly determined to refuse such a post. Kunanbai loved the idea of power and craved the title of Aga-Sultan, when this institute existed. Later he had been deposed and had become the elder of the Tobikty, but even then the entire tribe had lain on the palm of his hand or in the grasp of his fist as he chose.

But the authorities were reaching their hands ever farther and deeper. There was no longer to be a single Tobikty tribe. The Tobikty were to be split into three volosts. To be the ruler of but a third of the tribe was no great honour, while by refusing the post and keeping aloof, he would, undoubtedly, preserve his influence over the whole. Such was his first consideration.

But there was a second as well: it was growing increasingly difficult to rule the tribe. There were men who would not obey. If he were to punish them himself, hostilities would flare up as of old.

They needed a young ruler with a firm grasp.

Let young men fight among themselves. The younger generation had grown up. It was best to hand over authority to them and exercise his will through others.

And, finally, there was a third consideration. He was nearing seventy, and it was time to choose a successor from among his sons.

Considering the matter well, his choice fell on Abai. Here, too, his calculations were shrewd.

Abai had grown up beyond the reach of his influence. His behaviour and speech had shown that a stern judge had arisen behind Kunanbai's shoulders in the person of his son. This had been particularly evident in the past few years, and Abai had indeed completely estranged himself from his father when the latter had married Nurganim. Kunanbai was inclined to blame Ulzhan most of all. "You've brought him up to be such a cold-hearted fellow," he had rebuked her last summer.

But Kunanbai knew that Abai was intelligent and energetic. He must win over this son who was drifting away from him. Were he to assume the heavy burden of authority, Abai would find himself in his father's hands whether he liked it or not. If Kunanbai could have his way—if his son would but agree, there were many matters beyond the powers of most young men which Abai would be able to handle very well. His father had faith in him and this, indeed, had prompted his decision.

Abai arrived when his father had already finished tea. The cloth had been removed and the rugs on the floor had been freshly swept. Takezhan had forestalled him and already stood resting on one knee beside his father like a pious pupil of the madrasah. Kunanbai then dismissed everyone from the room but his sons. Though he spoke to both, it was evident that his words were meant for Abai alone. He was growing old, he said. All his life, the humble days and the years of glory had been filled with anxiety and struggle. What had he been striving for? For the future of his sons, his children. They were now grown men and it was time they disposed of their own lives. Whomsoever they might acquire in future—friend or foe—would be sure to spring from among their contemporaries. The mysteries of the present age were more accessible to them than to the old men. They would more quickly find the best way forward.

Their interests should be safeguarded by both of his sons here in turn, the one today and the other tomorrow. Let them not envy each other and dispute the gains. For the present he, their father, had fixed his choice upon Abai. He believed that Abai would do right to accept the volost.

It was indeed long since Kunanbai had addressed himself so lengthily to Abai.

Abai was silent for a moment, as though in deep contemplation. Then he cleared his throat and said:

"I am grateful to you, father, for your confidence. You are right to shift the burdens of life to us. It is time that you should be relieved, and you have every right to demand peace at last. But if it is me you have chosen, then I must say that I do not want to be the volost chief. I have no heart for it. Takezhan is older than I am and more resourceful. He is more suited for the post. Let him accept the volost!"

With the last words Abai turned to Takezhan who had flushed with pleasure but kept his pose of the submissive pupil, much resembling the mock-pious mullah anticipating rich remuneration at a funeral.

Kunanbai fastened his one eye fiercely upon Abai and twice demanded to know the reason.

Abai's first reply had been: "I am not fit for it." But when his father persisted, he answered in greater detail.

The ruler must be a really mature man, and he, Abai, did not feel himself up to the task. Power in inexperienced hands was like a razor in the hands of a child: the poor thing would either cut itself or injure others. It was not for himself that he feared, but he could not help pitying the people who would find themselves dependent on him, and thus he was obliged to refuse. When his knowledge had sufficiently grown to benefit the people and he truly felt fit for the task, he would not wait for his father to speak, but would come forward and say so himself—he gave his word. But for the time being he begged his father not to insist.

Kunanbai abruptly turned and offered the post to Takezhan, who needed no coaxing and agreed then and there.

4

Kunanbai sent Abai to Semipalatinsk to arrange certain business matters with Tinibai, a big merchant. Kunanbai had promised his and Ulzhan's youngest daughter Makish in marriage to Tinibai's son.

In town Abai made the acquaintance of a Russian lawyer Andreyev, whom the Kazakhs called Akbas* Andreyevich.

He was a tall man, solidly built, impressive-looking, and had a large handsome face. His sharp eyes, peering earnestly through his spectacles, gave him a meditative, engrossed air. His hair was prematurely white, and his beard was also turning grey.

Andreyev was a man of great erudition and enormous experience, but had only recently come among the Kazakhs and did not yet know this people. In his youth he had lived in St. Petersburg, where he became connected with men who had fought against the tyranny of the tsarist authorities and was compelled to flee from the capital in consequence. He found that he was free to practise law again in the provinces, and settled down there peacefully. For a long time he had lived in Volga towns and later in the Urals. The last few years he had spent in Siberia. A highly educated man, an earnest champion of enlightenment, he had begun to collect material on the life and customs of the Kirghiz.** His influence in the town was considerable, although he held no official post of importance.

Abai and Andreyev met frequently, and held long conversations about the life of the Kazakhs and their destinies.

It was time for Abai to think of going home, and he went to say good-bye to Andreyev.

"You are deeply concerned for the people," remarked the lawyer. "That's a splendid quality in one so young. But if you really want to help the people and yourself, you should strive for enlightenment. You should study."

Andreyev had divined Abai's fondest hope.

"I've wanted to study," said Abai sadly, "but where? I can't go to school—at my age. Tell me, can one study without going to school?"

The lawyer hastened to reassure Abai: one's age had nothing to do with studying. There were people who had taken up studies when they were forty; though self-taught, they had won renown scholars. He mentioned their names and explained how one could study without going to

* Akbas—white-haired.—Ed.
** Before Soviet times, both of these large peoples—the Kirghiz and the Kazakhs—were often lumped together even by progressive Russians. —Ed.

school. And the lawyer promised to find a teacher for him. Abai must first make quite sure that he wanted to get down to the books and work hard. If Abai were ready to do this the doors of knowledge would be open to him.

Abai's joy knew no bounds. It seemed to him that the bonds which had held him so tightly were at last to be loosened. He returned to his aul to receive the blessing of his family, to get what he needed, and to set off again as soon as possible. He was full of youthful enthusiasm.

In Zhidebai he was not long detained. Dilda and his mother were quick to agree and the opinions of the others did not matter. Mirzakhan was sent to Semipalatinsk with a horse which was to be butchered in the town. The next problem was that of money. This was solved by sending a bale of skins and several head of cattle to town. Abai then himself prepared for the journey.

Dilda had been delivered of a third child that summer. Tiny Abdrakhman was the first child to stir Abai's paternal feelings.

Dilda's children took after their mother, and did not resemble Abai in the least. All of them had their mother's pale complexion. Abdrakhman did, too, but the delicate features on his oval face, the wonderfully large eyes and clearly etched eyebrows were different, Abai's own.

He took leave of Dilda when they were alone. There was little to say. Each had a sincere affection for the other. Dilda, reserved and sparing of words as always, expressed but a single wish:

"Your mother and the little children are left at home. Don't forget them. I ask nothing for myself. But don't let us wait too long. Come home when you can!" She smiled at him.

Dilda was not one to express her feelings with tears or sighs. But when there was something on her mind, she always spoke up frankly, without subterfuge. Abai looked at her warmly and caressed her shoulder.

"I'm not going off to amuse myself, but to become a worthier man. Just remember that."

He dressed little Abdrakhman, took the child in his arms and went to visit his mother.

Ulzhan had visibly aged in the past years. She stood looking at her son with unwavering eyes for a moment and took the infant from him. Then she pressed her face to the child's head for an instant and handed him on to Dilda. With a light sigh, she drew Abai to her and kissed him.

All the emotion in her heart was expressed in her pallid face.

"Light of my eyes! Your deceased grandmother once called you 'her only one'. All the others were one to her, but you were special. Do you remember how she prayed to God when you were ill: 'Oh Allah, preserve this light of my soul from the cruel and the heartless....' She departed from us with those words on her lips."

Abai remembered Zereh's last words; his mother had somewhat changed them.

"Your time has come," continued Ulzhan pensively, "and your field of battle lies before you. Be brave! Just how you are to gain the victory is something you can see better than we. It is not for us to be shackles on your feet. God grant you happiness!"

As he had done as a little boy, Abai embraced his mother fondly and took leave of her. The entire aul had come out to see him off, and when Abai had mounted and said his good-byes to everyone his mother called to him again.

"Abai-zhan, you should stop at the aul of Toiguly! Your father and his friends have gone there to celebrate a betrothal. He asked us to follow him with the whole of the aul, but it is too difficult for me. If you don't go there either, he'll be hurt. Stay with them a while before you go on," she begged.

Abai promised to do as she asked, waved his hand and spurred his horse.

Toiguly's aul lay somewhat out of his way, on the slopes of Orda Mountain, but was nearer to Semipalatinsk than Zhidebai.

Toiguly was a prominent biy of the Mamai people, and Kunanbai had this winter decided to form an alliance with him through marriage. The winter had been a good one and the cattle well fed. Toiguly had, therefore, been able to fix a date for Kunanbai's visit. The latter had now arrived with a crowd of his kinsmen to celebrate the betrothal.

Abai went there with Yerbol. Kunanbai was accompanied by Karatai, Zhumabai, Zhakip and other old men. All the three houses of Toiguly were filled with guests, and everywhere there was noise and laughter. Abai and Yerbol entered one of the houses and sat down, listening to the general conversation. As always, Karatai had the most to say.

Discussing various matters, the old men compared the old days with the present. Karatai spoke of his youth, of his

father and grandfathers and, finally, came to the present;
the people had grown puny just like cattle in the djut and
poor in virtue.

To this Abai said with smiling sarcasm:

"Those were good old times when neighbouring clans
were constantly raiding and pillaging one another! Then
the old people, the women and the children could not sleep
or even eat in peace. And the lone traveller was in constant
danger on his way from the Siban to the Tobikty or from the
Tobikty to Semipalatinsk. He constantly had to keep watch,
for fear of being robbed or killed! Yes, those were grand
times!"

But the old men would not listen. The past seemed so
wonderful to them; they spoke of the untrammelled life and
abundance of bygone days.

"And the people were taller then, and more impressive,"
they said.

Kunanbai fully agreed with this and clinched their
arguments with a weighty observation:

"Every new generation is nearer to the end of the world
than the last, and humanity is withering away. Our times, on
the other hand, were nearer to the days of the Prophet than
these. And the nearer to the Prophet, the better the
people!"

But Abai responded at once. He was curiously elated, like
an akyn about to engage in a contest of verse and song. The
powers within him craved for open combat.

"Goodness and happiness are measured neither by time
nor space," he objected. "The pinnacle of Ala-Tau is nearer
the sun, yet it is covered with eternal ice, while its foothills
are wreathed in verdure and flowers and abound in fruit
and are blessed by all living things. Abu Talib, the father of
the Prophet, was even closer to him, than you, and yet died a
gyaur."*

There was general laughter. The old men felt the force of
the blow and silently watched Kunanbai, who wrathfully
shouted at Abai:

"That's enough!"

Abai raised his hands in surprise, but said nothing more.

The laughter ceased instantly and silence hung heavily
over the room.

But Karatai was secretly delighted and, nudging Zhakip,
whispered to him:

* Gyaur—an unbeliever.—*Ed.*

17—168

"Just see, he won't let us have our way; he's got us in a stranglehold!"

Soon the refreshments were served. Abai and Yerbol arose to put on their cloaks in order to set off again. Kunanbai followed them as they left the house.

Calling to Abai, he led him aside to a rocky hillock. It had been a long time since the two had been alone together.

Kunanbai looked at his son coldly.

"You were sent to study, to acquire knowledge, and were brought up by a tutor, whereas we grew up in ignorance. But why has your knowledge failed to teach you to respect your father in the presence of others? What merit is there in tripping up your father and worsting him in front of strangers?" he asked reproachfully.

So his father admitted that he had been worsted.

Abai regarded him intently; the stony, commanding features seemed to have withered and shrunk. He was bent and shrivelled, and in his reproaches, too, there was something childishly petulant, almost helpless. But it was the duty of young people to respect their elders, and of a son to respect his father.

"You speak justly. I am to blame, of course. Please forgive me!" he replied, to end the conversation, but his father had not yet finished.

"I have been meaning to talk to you for some time," he said after a moment's reflection. "I can see three failings in you. Listen to what I have to say."

"Speak, father." Abai looked at Kunanbai expectantly.

"First, you do not know how to tell the grain from the chaff. You do not value what you have and squander your treasures senselessly. You are too open and accessible—like a lake with flat shores, whose waters are lapped by dogs and muddied by the hoofs of cattle. Second, you are unable to distinguish between friends and foes and to treat foes as foes and friends as friends. You conceal nothing within yourself. A man leading the people cannot afford to act in such a way. He will not be able to keep them in hand. Third, you are beginning to lean towards the Russians. Your soul is fleeing to them and you do not care that every Moslem will come to regard you as a stranger," spoke Kunanbai.

Abai at once understood where his father was aiming—at his dearest hopes. Having chosen his own path, Abai looked for support in the very things that his father now condemned.

Kunanbai had indeed correctly estimated the qualities of

his son. Abai would bend his will to no one and nothing. Again he was strangely agitated, as he had been in the house. He could not keep quiet—not even out of pity for his father.

"I cannot accept a single one of your reproaches, father. I am convinced that I am right. You say that I am a lake with flat shores. Would it be better to be like the waters of a deep well, accessible only to him who has a rope, a pail and strong arms? I prefer to be accessible to the old men and the children, to all whose arms are weak. Secondly, you have spoken of keeping the people in hand and of the sort of man needed for such a task. In my opinion the people were once like a flock of sheep: if the shepherd shouted, 'Ait!' they would all jump up, and if 'Shait!' they would all lie down. Then the people came to be like a drove of camels: if you threw a stone before them and shouted, 'Shok!' they would first look round, think—and only then turn from their path. But now the people, who have overcome their former meekness and boldly opened their eyes, are like a herd of horses obeying only riders who share all their hardships—the frosts and the blizzards—who can forget their own homes for the sake of the herd, who can use a lump of ice for a pillow and a drift of snow for a bed. Thirdly, you spoke of the Russians. The most precious things for the people and for me are knowledge and light. These things are in the hands of the Russians, and if they will give me the treasures I have sought all my life how can they be alien to me? Were I to reject this, I would remain ignorant and I cannot see much honour in that."

Kunanbai, who had been listening attentively, heaved a sigh. An unusual look of frustration darkened his features, but he spoke no more.

Abai took leave of him and set off.

Kunanbai remained on the hill alone, pensive and despondent. And so he had been defeated again—and not by his son alone, but by life, swift and all-conquering. "Your strength is exhausted, your time is past and you must go," life had coldly told him in the voice of his own son; and its relentless currents were sweeping him aside.

Abai was riding through the same plains over which he had come when returning from the madrasah as a boy, so homesick for his family and his native aul. The steppes that were green then now lay covered with snow as far as the eye could see. The mounds and the hills loomed white on all sides and seemed to be listlessly brooding over faint visions of the past. There was a time when the sight of these steppes had filled his boyish heart with joy, when he had sought happiness here in its vast spaces, in his native aul. But now he was leaving them for the town, hopeful of finding that which he had sought even then....

He was now twenty-five. A long vista of days receded into the past in an endless chain. He could plainly see how the trail of his life had led him now into the thickets and now over the mountain passes. And once again it was leading him upwards over a winding course—that tortuous path of his life.

Yes, he had emerged on the heights.

The seedling which had once struggled to break through the stony ground had eventually sprouted a slender shoot—a lone living thing on the rugged cliff. It had struck deep roots and had risen to be a strong, upstanding tree that feared neither the winter frosts, nor the wild blizzards of the mountains.

PART TWO

1

He did not sleep that night. It was only at dawn that Abai lay down, but feeling wide awake he soon went back to his desk, heaped with open books. There were volumes in old Uzbek, a language he could freely read, books in Persian and Arabic, which he found more difficult, and some in Russian—the hardest of all.

These multilingual friends had not got together on his table fortuitously. Life itself demanded of him the knowledge secreted in these books. Lately Abai had been reading day and night like an obsessed scholar or a devout recluse. Glancing up from the pages from time to time, he would look about, momentarily awaking to reality.

The Uzbek works carried Abai to the flowering gardens of Shiraz; he saw the ancient tombs of Samarkand, strolled through the orchards fringing the limpid waters of Merv and Mash-had, wandered through the magnificent palaces, the madrasahs and the libraries of Herat, Ghazni and Baghdad, the land of the immortal poets. The books in Arabic and Persian conjured up the fierce clashes where, with their flashing scimitars, the Arabs, Persians, Turks and Mongols settled their centuries-old scores. The Russian books disclosed the mysteries of the seas and sandy wastes of Central Asia, Persia, Arabia and the life of the great trading cities.

Abai wanted to know how these countries lived today. He made careful notes of the caravan routes and waterways, of great cities and rich bazaars.

All such information was essential to a traveller about to set off on a long voyage. "What a pity it's not I who is going," Abai exclaimed again and again as he thought of all those distant lands that had filled his imagination since childhood.

His table stood by the window. A breath of cool air came through, billowing out the white curtain, which played with the books like a mischievous child, now covering a page, now wiping it as though to erase the writing on it. Abai looked up—the door was opening for the first time that morning.

It was Ulzhan shuffling in, grown heavy with the years and short of breath. She was supported by two women. Abai sprang up and quickly spread a soft corpeh * on the floor. An elegant, fair-faced young woman who had entered with Ulzhan arranged the cushions. Her resemblance to Abai was striking—this was his sister Makish, who was married to the son of Tinibai, the wealthy owner of this house in Semipalatinsk where Abai was staying. Ulzhan's other companion, her life-long friend Kalikha, who had accompanied her all the way from the aul, now set a shining brass basin before her and proceeded to pour water over her hands from a long-necked Kashgar pitcher covered with delicate chasing.

Makish unfolded a low table in the middle of the spacious room.

"You may set the table! Bring in the food," she called through the door.

Another of Tinibai's daughters-in-law entered. She was about the same age as Makish, a tall, fine-looking woman with shining ebony hair brushed back from the temples, and wearing a black velvet jacket with an embroidered border. She spread the cloth and arranged the table for the morning tea.

Abai removed his beshmet and began to wash. It was only now that he realised how heavy his head was. Makish poured the water over his hands.

"The water feels so good today. Pour some over my head," he begged, bending his neck. "I must freshen up."

Having dried her face and hands, Ulzhan looked at her son's desk and then at her son, at his pale face and red-rimmed eyes.

"You've been up all night again, Abai-zhan?" she reproached him.

"No, I had a bit of sleep."

"Don't you get your thoughts muddled, sitting there without sleep?"

"I do, Apa, but time is pressing. Father will be leaving today."

Ulzhan asked whether one could really learn the routes from the books.

"Some footpaths, leading to the highroad if not the road

* Corpeh—a quilt.— Ed.

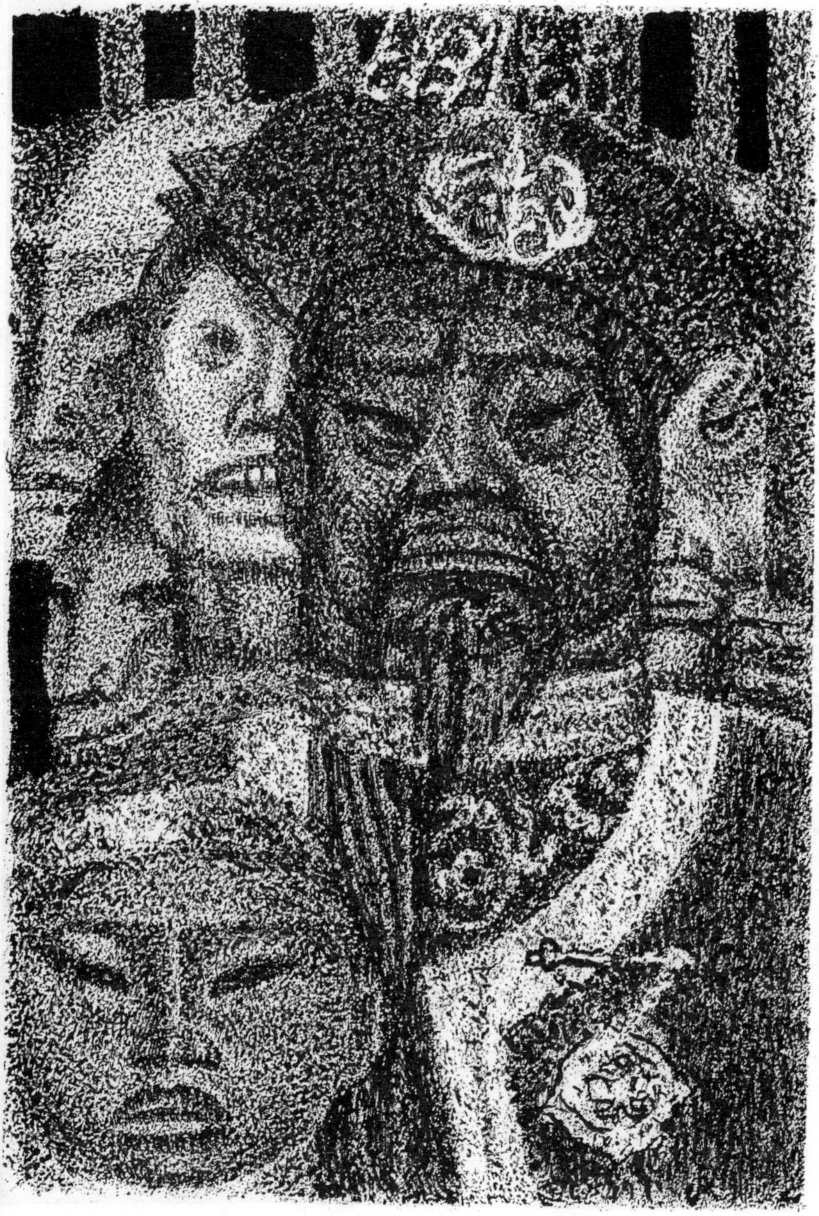

itself, I can already see," answered Abai and told his mother what he had memorised in the past few days. "I feel as if I'd been there myself—the books have told me so much about those places."

He spoke like a man who had found a buried treasure.

Ulzhan knew that the journey would be long, and over tea continued to question her son about the hardships of the way. Abai had never withheld anything from his mother, but his sister Makish was present.

"Yes, please tell us about it, Abai dear," she asked. Her worried look and slight pallor betrayed her anxiety, and Abai hesitated to answer.

She was the spoiled darling of a rich house, but had never ceased to love her own family and native aul and was always deeply concerned about their welfare.

Only a girl who had also been given in marriage very young to live in a strange land, only a girl who saw life with Makish's eyes, could know that her deeply hidden homesickness was a lingering and painful ailment that time alone could cure.

Abai sensed all this and would not speak, but Makish was insistent.

"They say that nobody from our parts has ever been there. Will he ever get back?"

She said what Abai dared not say.

After a sip or two of tea, he pushed the piala * aside, ignoring the steaming pies baked in the lower kitchen by a skilful cook. Reaching for the notes he had made during the night, he answered the questions one by one.

"Father's journey will be far from easy," he concluded, "but there is hope...." He hesitated as he saw the effect his words were having on Makish. Ulzhan came to his rescue, exhorting Makish with the words:

"Don't let your father think that his child is faint-hearted, now that he is about to leave."

Someone looked in at the door to announce the arrival of Kunanbai. Everyone but Ulzhan sprang up and busied themselves with spreading the floor around the table with rugs and rearranging the cushions.

Kunanbai came with a large company, but the retinue stayed in the next room, which was equally large and festive, and had its own table laden with food. Only Izgutty and Tinibai, the host, Makish's father-in-law and Kunanbai's old

* Piala—a small bowl.— Ed.

crony, followed him into the room. Tinibai, wearing rich clothes, ignored the place of honour and settled on the corpeh beside his daughter-in-law. Nor did he lean back on the cushions comfortably as might have been expected from the master of the house. He squatted like a pupil before his teacher at the madrasah, in a position to serve Kunanbai and offer him tea with his own hands. This had always astonished Ulzhan, though the townsfolk saw nothing unusual about it. That was how they received the imams and khazrets, with this elaborate courtesy and deference.

Kunanbai seated himself beside Ulzhan and looked with his single eye at Abai and Makish; it was a penetrating stare which at once caught all the subtle shades of feeling among those around him. His eye was more watchful than ever, and he could see from Makish's reddened eyes and pallor that she had just been weeping.

The chill of old age had at last laid its hand on Kunanbai. He had turned grey late in life, and until seventy his hair and beard had been but lightly threaded with silver. Now, however, the grey had spread and whitened, and the furrows on his brow had deepened. But he still looked big and solid, and bore himself as upright as ever.

His stern face showed not a trace of doubt or hesitation.

The resolution to make a pilgrimage to Mecca came to him a year ago, and that very spring he began to sell his livestock to procure the means. He was not worried about money, but was more troubled by the thought of his approaching senility and ebbing strength. After prolonged deliberation, he decided to take a trusty companion with him, and his choice fell upon Izgutty, his constant and loyal friend. Makish had therefore sewn all Izgutty's travelling things with her own hands and Izgutty was now sitting there beside Kunanbai.

Izgutty was over forty but he still looked like a djiguit of twenty-five and was gay and quick as ever.

Near relations and friends entered one by one: Takezhan, Ospan, Zhakip, Maibasar and Mullah Gabitkhan. Kunanbai quietly sipped his tea, and had some of the pies and cold meat. Those of his relations who had had no chance to sit at his table during the meal were pressing in to hear his last words before departure. Kunanbai had intended to speak his final words of farewell to his nearest kin alone, but soon realised that within a short time there would be an entire crowd there. He looked at Makish again, his face becoming even sterner.

"My children, friends and kinsmen," he began, sweeping and silencing the company with a cold look. Kunanbai drew himself up, and staring stonily before him said: "You seem to be worried by my departure and in your anxious eyes I can read: 'How can he, an old man, hazard such a thing? Shall we ever see him again? Will he come back?' I am not sure if it is me you want to keep safe from the road or the road from me. What is the good of my living on into peevish senility, grumbling at my grandchildren at the fireside, at my daughters-in-law by the cauldrons and the workmen around the yurta? My journey is the final aim of my last days. And this is what I beg of you all: if you learn that natural death has overtaken me during my journey, let none of you exclaim, 'Poor soul, he died in sorrow without attaining his goal.' There would be no genuine compassion in such words. I am past the time of youth which yet lies ahead of you. I have tasted the honey and gall you have yet to taste. The days we have been destined to live together were spent in friendship and mutual respect—whether they were many or not. I am satisfied. And though our lives have been as one, death will come to each in his own way and will remove each from his family in turn. If that is so, what does it matter where it overtakes me? What remains of my days is now as short as the trail of an old arkhar,* too weak to follow the herd—from the water hole to his last lair in the gully. So do not detain me. See me off without wailing and tears. That is all I wanted to say. Now let us get down to the preparations for the journey."

Kunanbai looked at Izgutty, who at once got up. He was quickly followed by the others, and Abai was about to join them when he was checked by Kunanbai's restraining hand on his knee.

"Now, my son, tell us what you have learned."

Abai produced a bulky packet of papers covered with writing and handed it to Izgutty.

"All that I have found is in this roll, Izgutty-aga. Keep it safe."

Kunanbai wanted him once again to name the cities they would pass through on their way.

When the bright spring sun indicated that midday had come, the crowd poured out of Tinibai's hospitable house. Most of them had come from the auls and were dressed like people of the steppes, but there was a sprinkling of

* Arkhar—a mountain ram.— *Ed.*

townsfolk among them: merchants, shakirds,* khalfes **
and khazrets. They emerged in order of precedence,
smiling happily, replete and with full pockets — Kunanbai
and Tinibai had been generous, asking them to pray for the
pilgrims.

The large coach drawn by three bays stood ready in
Tinibai's courtyard. The big, deep-chested animals, fed on
oats during the winter and thoroughly rested, stood
snorting and champing at the bit. Whenever the middle
horse shook its mane, the little bell in the shaft-bow over its
head gave a clear, cheerful tinkle. The provisions,
the bedding and spare clothing had all been stowed
away.

Kunanbai had not yet reached the coach when two
figures rose to meet him. One of them presented his salem
as he approached from afar. It was Darkembai, his beard
perceptibly whitened with age. The other was a boy of
about eleven, pale and thin. His chapan*** was in
rags; his chapped bare feet were covered with dust and
mud.

As he approached Kunanbai, Darkembai wished him a
pleasant journey and at once got to the point.

"You are setting off on a holy journey, Kunekeh," he
began. "You have chosen the path of humility. Listen, then,
to the plea of another humble creature — this boy. In the
name of Allah, he begged me to bring his matter before
you."

Kunanbai stiffened. Frowning, he checked his stride.

"I have renounced all earthly matters," he answered. "It
is to others and not to me that people should talk of their
needs."

"No, Kunekeh, it is to you that we must speak."

"What have I to do with that boy?"

"A great deal, I'm afraid. That's why we have come."

Kunanbai looked at the crowd out of the corner of his eye,
obviously embarrassed by the presence of the merchants
and the mullahs in the courtyard. Maibasar realised that the
old man had to be driven away at once.

"Look here, this is no time for pleas," he said, stepping
nearer. "Don't get in the way of a man who is just leaving.
Be off!"

* Shakird—a pupil of the madrasah.—*Ed.*
** Khalfe—an instructor of the madrasah.—*Ed.*
*** Chapan—a kind of robe.—*Ed.*

He spoke in an undertone that held a threatening note, but Darkembai was not daunted. He noticed that Kunanbai was ill at ease and raised his voice.

"The plea of this boy is such that you can't refuse to hear him. Of a thousand beggars and orphans, this one alone you must hear, especially now that you are setting off on a holy pilgrimage."

"Who is this boy? What does he want? Speak up." Kunanbai, scowling and obviously irritated, paused to listen.

"The boy is a nephew of that same Kodar of the Borsak," explained Darkembai. "When Kodar was killed, his only brother Kogedai was a hired hand in the distant Siban. He was a sickly man all his life and died six years ago. This boy Kiyaspai is Kogedai's son, Kodar's only heir."

On Kiyaspai's wan features the down, which generally lends softness to a boy's face, gave the impression of a sickly mildew. The skin was stretched tautly over the bones, and the throb of his pulse could be seen in the blue veins at his temples; his right eye was bound with a dirty rag. His chin trembling, the boy raised his face fearfully to Kunanbai and met a glare of cold hatred.

"Well, what does he want from me?" Kunanbai demanded.

"What could he want from you?" echoed Darkembai looking Kunanbai fully in the face.

"Tell me what's it all about then. Here, let us move away."

To let the old man speak in the presence of the crowd would have been tantamount to meekly allowing someone to hit him squarely in the face, and so Kunanbai from the outset had been imperceptibly pushing the two away until finally he squatted down with them in a corner of the yard.

The Irgizbai, both old and young, were well dressed to a man. The townsfolk—the merchants, imams and khalfes—were especially vain of the cut and costliness of their finery. Their dazzlingly white turbans, chapans and beaver-trimmed hats proclaimed their prosperity. Against the background of this festive throng, Darkembai and the boy, haggard and frightful in their poverty, seemed all the more wretched. Their rags were in such a pitiful state that the man and boy looked like a couple of prisoners who had endured much beating and abuse.

Maibasar and Takezhan followed Kunanbai out of the crowd and squatted down nearby. Abai, too, joined the group.

"Kodar was innocent," Darkembai was saying. "But nobody dared to say anything about kun * then. Who could have raised his voice at such a time? It was-your day—a grim day."

The words struck home.

"What sort of nonsense are you talking, Darkembai?" snarled Kunanbai. "If any of the Bokenshi or Borsak have sent you to demand a kun, then name them!"

The pious demeanour Kunanbai had maintained all day was gone, and now all the old hatred and enmity were seething within him. His face livid and ominous, he looked like some predatory beast about to seize its prey and tear it limb from limb.

But Darkembai was still not intimidated.

"There is no Borsak living who would dare to demand retribution from you. The time has not yet come. I am not concerned with kun, but with the Karashoky pastures. That land is Kodar's heritage. It belongs to this boy, but on it the aul of your eldest wife Kunkeh multiplies its droves and lives in abundance. It is to a holy place that you are going. Do you want to carry the burden of sin with you—your unpaid debt to a poor orphan?"

"Hold your tongue!" snapped Kunanbai.

"I have said all I had to say."

"A more vicious enemy I've never known. Stalking me all my life! Your very eyes are bloodshot, like a wild beast's."

"No, Kunekeh, I was never one to stir up evil. All my life I have been protecting myself from evil."

"And who aimed a gun at me? Wasn't it you?"

"I aimed, but I did not fire. Remember, too, that the man who roped and strung me up is still at large!"

Pale with fury, Darkembai stared fixedly at Kunanbai. His words went home, and Kunanbai trembled.

"You did not fire then but you have done it now. You have fired a shot into my coffin! He wants to be my undoing," he said, turning to Maibasar as if asking him to do something.

Breathing heavily, Maibasar advanced on Darkembai. Screening the old man from the crowd as best he could, he swore viciously and punched him in the chest.

"Shut your dirty mouth!" he hissed. "Another word and I'll take you by the beard and slaughter you like a goat!"

Kunanbai rose to his feet, Takezhan and Maibasar

* Kun—compensation for a murder.—*Ed.*

meanwhile stepping on the ends of Darkembai's rags to
prevent him from following. Kiyaspai burst into tears.

"The debt is on your conscience, your debt to me,"
Darkembai repeated.

"Yesterday, you lorded it over us as Aga-Sultan and today
you are trying to crush us as a holy hadji," Darkembai flung
after the departing Kunanbai, though he was firmly held by
the two djiguits. "It's not the trail of Allah you're going to
pave but, as always, your own! Go on, set those wolf-cubs of
yours upon us!"

"Hold your tongue, you dog!" snarled Maibasar and
Takezhan at his sides. They would have gladly killed the old
man on the spot.

Abai quickly sat down before them with his back to the
crowd. With a sudden movement, he tore the hands of the
two from the old man's collar.

"Have you no shame, damn you? Leave him alone," he
cried, "What can you understand when your hearts are
blind and deaf to honour. Isn't Father going to Mecca to
account to God for the very things this old man has spoken
about?"

"I see that you could keep silent no longer, Darkembai,"
he said, eyeing the old man as sternly. "I cannot blame you.
If a plea is just, then let it be made even in such an hour as
this. I'll be your debtor instead. Go in peace and don't curse
us any more. Your words have reached my heart, they have
burnt into the marrow of my bones. But now you must go."

Assisting Darkembai to his feet, Abai took a hundred-
ruble note from his pocket, gave it to the boy and
accompanied the two to the gate.

Kunanbai was speechless for a long time, his lips moving
silently in a repentant prayer, until he was recalled to reality
by Ulzhan and Izgutty, who reminded him that the hour of
departure had come. After a few words of leave-taking to
the townsfolk, he took his place in the coach.

Ulzhan sat between him and Izgutty; she had resolved to
accompany her husband part of the way with the other
kinsmen. The smart coach, drawn by three bays, rumbled
through the wide gate, its bells tinkling. Behind it came two
brand new carriages, one carrying Makish and Abai, and the
other Tinibai and his baibishe, followed by carts and riders.
As the noisy train strung out along the street it raised clouds
of dust. Old and young wanted to see the party on its way,
some standing at the gateways, others leaning from the
windows.

Kunanbai's coach soon reached the edge of the town
and emerged on the westward highway. The horsemen rode
on the flanks or bunched together ahead.

Kunanbai did not once look back, knowing that his
kinsmen would be with him on the first lap of the journey.
His ill-humour persisted. "He's spoilt it all," he kept
muttering. "Stirred up all the dregs." He visualised deep,
still waters suddenly troubled and clouded by the fall of a
stone. Everything had been going so well. All his words and
actions until the very moment of his departure had been so
carefully planned. Had he not kept scrupulously to his
decision? His humble talk and pious conduct were designed
to evoke the sincerest wishes for his happy journey. And
now, Darkembai had swept it all away like a hurricane
shattering the serene mood of his leave-taking and separating him from the people. Kunanbai was bitter, but kept
silent, trying to master his anger. At last he decided to take
his leave of Ulzhan, hoping that this would quell the storm
raging in his soul.

Without ordering Mirzakhan to rein the horses, he
turned to Ulzhan.

"You've always been more than the mistress of my
hearth," he said. "You've been my life-long companion, my
baibishe. It's a long way we've travelled together. No matter
what mountains lay between us, I have always felt your
support. I may have wronged you in certain things, but for
my part I can find nothing to complain of where you are
concerned. May fate reward your children for your honest
heart and your sincere attachment to me."

Ulzhan was deeply moved. She said nothing for a time,
overwhelmed by her feelings.

"I too have nothing to complain of, Mirza — not even the
slightest reproach will go with you." She seemed to be lost in
thought.

"When one is young, the bed is too small, the house and
even the world seem cramped." She spoke her mind wisely,
as to an equal. Something of her majestic beauty returned to
her, her face glowing with an inner light. "But as one grows
older, the world seems greater and oneself smaller. One
feels a vast emptiness around, and one must give way to
others, curtail one's activities, cool one's ardour, and become
resigned. This I have felt for a long time."

Kunanbai was following her words carefully, as though
probing the depths of her thoughts with his look.

"A man protects a woman like a mare her foal,"

continued Ulzhan, half closing her eyes. "The wife takes both the good and the bad from her husband. If there is something good in me, then there must be something good in you, too. Both my faults and merits have come from you. Because you are taking leave of me with gratitude I am content."

Not a word would she say of the humiliations she had suffered at his hands in the long years of their married life.

Kunanbai now turned the conversation to everyday matters, and Izgutty joined in. They spoke of the Khalfe Ondirbai; he had always enjoyed the respect of the Mirza and by accompanying him to Mecca had now become his most intimate friend, bound to him by ties stronger than any blood relationship.

Ondirbai had once expressed the desire to establish family relations with Kunanbai through the marriage of their children. Kunanbai was inclined to consent, if Ulzhan did not object. Ondirbai had a daughter, who might make a good wife for Ospan who, though married for three years, had not yet sown his wild oats. The childlessness of the couple was a source of anxiety to both Kunanbai and Ulzhan, though not at all to Ospan. This was sufficient reason to find him a second wife. Let Ulzhan be prepared for this; if Ondirbai should mention the matter again on the journey, he would let her know.

The second vehicle, drawn by three dun-coloured horses, was occupied by Abai and Makish, each deep in thought.

Abai could not dismiss Darkembai's boldness from his mind. The old man had upset the chalice of honour prepared for Kunanbai with a single kick. Kodar, Kodar! The innocent victim had come alive in that wretched orphan. Abai could not forget him: the emaciated boy with the dirty bandage hugging his head like the grip of penury. His glaring need and Darkembai's just and vehement words were like a sentence passed on Kunanbai by life itself. No prayers or namazes, fasts or pilgrimages could wipe them away. How different it would have been if his father had gone off after repenting his sins and crimes. But there was no repentance in him, nothing but his old harshness and anger. Then why the pilgrimage? Could Darkembai be right in this too? Was it not the way of Allah, but his own way that he was seeking? Abai smiled bitterly.

The carriage rolled swiftly along the verge of the highway, on a carpet of young grass.

It was a long time since Abai had been in the country. Out here in the steppes one was more alive to the fact that it was spring. Semei Mountain looming over the horizon far to the left was veiled in a blue mist.

A cool, refreshing breeze blew from the mountain although it had already shed its covering of snow, and Abai sighed with relief and joy. The beauty of the land came fully home to him and lightened his heart. The new grass, the spring sun and the cool breeze invigorated him; fresh melodies and fresh verses sprang from his heart, and he burst into song. As Makish listened she guessed that it was his own song he was singing.

"Why, you're a real akyn," she said, smiling.

Abai was startled and stopped singing. He had completely forgotten that his sister was there.

"Why do you say that?" he asked after a pause.

"Can't I hear it? Or is it a secret? But all your friends talk about it, Yerbol and the others. They say you're a real akyn, though you've never sung at the aitises. It is true then?"

"Yes," Abai replied with a smile.

"What was the song about?"

"Ah, Makish, my songs are carried away by the wind."

"What do you mean?"

"I sing about love and sorrow. My sorrow is constant and near — my love far and unattainable. What does it matter then, if the wind carries it away? To sing about these things is like singing to the winds."

"What sorrow are you talking about?" demanded Makish reproachfully. Abai frowned and turned pale.

Under his sister's searching gaze Abai's face seemed to radiate a soft light. The thin line of moustache, and the short black beard made his perfectly smooth, roundish face look somewhat longer. Abai was twenty-nine years old, a man in his prime. His eyes were bright, blazing with inner fire, his gaze so clear and penetrating that it attracted general attention. His long, slender eyebrows seemed to stress the beauty of his youth.

Makish regarded him with silent admiration. It seemed unbelievable that he was nursing a secret sorrow, and she decided to draw him out.

"What was that sad song about?"

The remote dream of his youth, the beloved vision that had never left him rose before him with renewed force. The spring day evoked in him a fierce longing for Togzhan. He sang *Topai-kok* in an undertone, and Makish had to listen hard to catch the sad, tender words.

The sun and moon shine brightly in the sky,
But darkness floods my heart and mind.
She may well find a lover worthier than I,
While I another love will never find...

Let my beloved all my words of love forget,
Let my devotion and my anguish leave her cold,
And let her hurt and humble me without regret,
My love will stay alive, I shall endure it all!

Makish had never heard the words before.

"I don't quite understand whom you call your beloved," she said in bewilderment.

"Beloved? She's the one who makes me sad. Don't you know what beloved means?" Abai answered evasively.

"A wife, I should think."

"You mean Dilda?" frowned Abai.

"Of course! Who else?"

Abai turned away from her in annoyance.

"Makish, Makish, my dear! Why bring Dilda into this?" There was a dull bitterness in his voice.

Makish was embarrassed when she saw how her words had affected him.

"Oh, I said something very wrong, Abai!" she forced a smile. "But why blame poor Dilda?"

"Of course, she's not to blame. But nor am I to blame if my song of desire was not meant for her. Why talk about Dilda surrounded by her four children?"

"What's wrong with her giving you four children?"

"Nothing, of course. They're fine children. She's the mother of my children, a wife given me by my parents and nothing more. But what about the heart? Love? Desire? That flame has died out long ago in her. It never burned very brightly. Yes, her heart cooled long ago...." Abai broke off.

They soon neared the end of the stage and it was time to take leave of Kunanbai.

The front vehicles ahead had stopped and the travellers alighted. The riders dismounted. A black skin filled with kumiss was unfastened from the rear of Tinibai's carriage, and all the members of the party took their places around Kunanbai and Izgutty to drink a final cup. The latter urged

them to hurry, Kunanbai wanted no delay. He soon stood
up, everyone else following suit.

"Well, my friends, you've accompanied me far enough.
Give my greetings to my land and people. Farewell, my
kinsmen. If I'm destined to taste food on my own land
again, let our meeting be a blessed and happy one!"

"Inshalla, inshalla, amen, amen," the elders intoned, led
by Tinibai.

Kunanbai embraced each one in turn, starting with
Ulzhan and ending with Abai.

The strong, well-fed horses dashed ahead, as fresh as if
they had just begun the journey. The coach soon
vanished in a cloud of dust, but the merry peal of the bells
could be heard for a long time. The horses had begun to
climb a hill overgrown with tall grass, and soon the coach
was lost to view behind it.

There was a stir as all turned for home.

Abai and Makish led Ulzhan to her carriage. There was
no room for three and so Abai mounted and rode slowly at
Yerbol's side, lagging behind the other riders.

2

The numerous guests who came to Tinibai's house after
seeing Kunanbai off soon left. Ulzhan stayed on for a while.
She came to town but rarely, and Makish, who was so
homesick, was loath to let her go. Tinibai too urged Ulzhan
to remain:

"Stay with us a little longer! Your daughter will miss you.
She's quite alone now, with her husband away trading.
You'll go when she has recovered a little."

Only a few guests remained, but these received especial
attention from the host. They were Ulzhan, Abai, Takezhan
and the three or four djiguits who accompanied them. All
the rooms in the spacious two-storey house were hung with
carpets, striped home-made rugs, and embroidered and
patterned felts.

Ulzhan tried to remember what else she had to buy before
their departure. She was the mother of a large aul of many
families and everybody would be expecting presents from
her. Furthermore, the aul was soon to move to summer
pastures, far from the town. Many things were needed:
summer clothes for the children and daughters-in-law, and
tea and sugar for the whole aul and also to be kept for
guests.

Abai more and more often brought home piles of books along with his purchases. He had spent the entire winter in town, busy with the preparations for his father's journey, and had been studying Russian since the day of his arrival. He had been interested in the language for a long time and though he had never learned it properly he took every opportunity to draw what knowledge he could from this fresh source. But the better he knew Russian, the more he despaired of learning it to perfection. "What a pity I missed the chance to learn it as a child," he kept saying. "That was a real loss."

But the long winter nights had not been wasted. Abai could now read pages of prose without much difficulty. Poetry was harder. Still, the Russian books had become his inseparable friends and he collected them diligently in order to continue his studies in the aul. He crammed a long coffer with books to be sent home with his mother.

Ulzhan asked Abai to come home with her, but he had not yet finished with certain matters entrusted to him by Kunanbai. He and Yerbol would catch up with his aul on its way to the summer pastures.

Though Ulzhan was in no hurry to go, the day finally came when she was to leave with Takezhan, Gabitkhan, and Zhumagul.

"You haven't seen your native aul for half a year. You'll be just like a wanderer returned from a far country," said Ulzhan to Abai as she took her place in the carriage. "Your wife misses you, my son. The children are waiting for you like motherless chicks. 'Ata, ata, won't ata ever come?' that's all I heard from them. Not even once have you asked me about them—about Abish and Magash, my little lambs! Whenever I think about them at night, my sleep fades away like mist in the sun. How can you bear the separation?"

"I miss them too, Apa. Especially the youngest, the first that made me feel like a father. But you know why I can't come."

"Do I really? I rather think you're looking for excuses to go on living here. You've grown used to the dust of the town. If you go on that way, I'm afraid you won't care whether you are at home or not. You're like a young kulan who has stranded from the herd. Oi, Abai-zhan, please come home soon, my dear!"

Ulzhan's words sounded simple and tender, but they implied more than they said. She felt that this was not the time to speak frankly. Nor did Abai say anything, although he understood his mother's doubts, and evaded further talk with affectionate words of farewell.

"God willing, we'll overtake you as you cross the Chinghis. Give my love to the children. Happy journey! May you get home in good health and spirits."

About three weeks later Abai and Yerbol set off after them. Starting at sunrise, they covered a good distance on that long spring day. Both were men of endurance and used to fast riding. No matter how hard the going, or whether it were winter or summer, neither ever complained. On the contrary, they always tried to conceal their exhaustion from one another after a hard day's jolting, just as though they were undergoing an endurance test.

They were travelling over a rarely frequented route, Abai having chosen the way across Orda Mountain in order to reach the Bakanas River along which his aul was then wandering.

By sunset the djiguits reached the part of Orda Mountain known as Chiliktinsk Hill. Most of the auls had wandered off and they found nowhere to spend the night. Chiliktinsk Hill seemed to be the most likely place, since a few of the poorer Baishor auls of the Mamai tribe usually set off later than the others.

In the foothills, the travellers were caught in a sudden downpour. But the wind soon dropped and the rain dwindled to a warm drizzle. The slopes of Orda were alive with the undulating green of feather-grass and worm-wood. The spring shower came down with a cheerful rustle and on all sides rose the pungent smell of worm-wood. The travellers rode along a stony road, through a veil of rain which suddenly grew heavier. The sky darkened once more, blotting out the sun except for a yellow haze far away on the horizon.

The horses thundered up a small hill. Dogs could be heard baying in the distance and a few lights flickered in the thickening dusk. Seven or eight yurtas of a small aul stood dimly silhouetted on the bank of a river. A small flock of sheep, a few cows and camels were trying to find shelter from the rain, while the finicky goats huddled close to the yurtas. About a dozen horses were grazing near the settlement, some of them hobbled and others tethered with long ropes. Approaching the aul, the riders checked their pace, trying to choose the best yurta to spend the night in. The dogs grew so frantic that the mountains rang with their barking. The nearer the djiguits approached, the more dogs joined in and the more desperate their baying became.

Of the eight tents, it was the central, pentagonal yurta which seemed the largest and the sturdiest. Yerbol urged his horse towards it, and as Abai rode up as well, the bearded owner of the tent, a beshmet thrown loosely over his shoulders, came out to meet them. He seemed to be limping slightly. Yerbol exchanged greetings with him, introduced himself and asked for shelter.

"You're welcome, djiguits! We'll share what we have with you," the man said genially, as he tethered the horses.

"You must have heard about the two brothers of the Baishor who live near the Orda — Bekei and Shekei?" whispered Yerbol to Abai as they entered the yurta. "It's Bekei who lives here."

The djiguits had never been in this aul before.

A fire was burning brightly inside. The guests looked round and greeted each member of the small family in turn. On their right an old woman sat on a rug dandling a baby. A thin woman of about forty was busy over the fire. Tall, fair-haired and hazel-eyed, she must have been a beauty in her youth.

Abai now had a good look at the host: grey eyes, a straight, prominent nose, a reddish wavy beard, a healthy ruddy face and a confident, impressive manner. In a deep, manly voice Bekei asked whence they had come, whither they were going and to which tribe they belonged.

The dancing flames of the kizyak* made the yurta seem cosy and hospitable. A large blackened pot hung from a tall tripod over the fire.

Satisfied with the answers he received, Bekei turned to the old mother, and said something to her in an undertone.

"Don't waste the kizyak. There's very little dry fuel," he admonished his wife as he arose. "Is there enough water for the pot? I'll take the boy with me and we'll see about a lamb."

The wife tacitly agreed.

Just as the tea was served to Abai and Yerbol, the felt door flap was drawn back to admit Bekei and his son who carried a slaughtered lamb. The fair-haired hostess tucked up her calico skirt, set a smaller tripod over the fire with a round rim and put a pot of water on it. Seating himself beside his guests, Bekei handed round the tea.

* Kizyak — horse dung dried for fuel. — *Ed.*

"Where is Shukiman?" Bekei asked his wife from time to time. "She should help you."

"What for? She's in the other yurta with her brother-in-law. I'll manage! Let them have some fun," she answered.

At the mention of Shukiman, Yerbol thought to himself, "There must be a grown daughter in the family," and he looked about. In addition to Bekei's wooden bed, there was another bed heaped with brightly coloured quilts and cushions — no doubt a girl's — on the left side of the yurta.

Bekei's wife was putting the meat into the pot, her husband handing her choice pieces and saying: "Put this in too. Let there be plenty." She glanced at him questioningly, as if to say, "Isn't that too much? Won't this be enough?" But Bekei was not satisfied.

"Let's have more of it. We haven't fed the brother-in-law and his friends. Shukiman has already hinted that they could do with it. There are not many guests, most of them of her age. Let them have supper with us."

Fuel was now ungrudgingly added and the yurta quickly warmed up. The rain had abated and the night grew windless and warm under lowering clouds.

Yerbol fell asleep, while Abai sat thinking. The stuffy tent made him sleepy and he too decided to have a nap before the evening meal.

He did not know whether he had slept long or not when he started up. He must have been talking in his sleep, for the words were still on his lips. Yes, he had just said, "Come here, my darling." Had he spoken aloud? Had anyone heard him in the yurta? What was the matter with him?

Yerbol had also raised his head, and stared at Abai who was listening intently. He too could hear a woman singing in the neighbouring yurta.

Abai was trembling all over. Yerbol feared that his friend was in a delirium, about to run off somewhere. His face was deathly pale, tears filled his wide-open eyes, his shoulders twitched and he breathed in gasps. He stared upward, lost to the world. Suddenly he caught Yerbol by the hand.

"Get up, Yerbol!"

"What's the matter with you, Abai?" his friend exclaimed.

Abai seized his timak,* threw his chapan over his shoulders and rushed to the door.

"Come, follow me!"

* Timak—a fur hat—*Ed.*

The hosts seemed to have noticed nothing. The old woman was asleep, and Bekei sat drowsing at the fire, his back to the guests.

Abai still could not control his agitation, and not only his ears but his entire being strained towards the sound of this one and only voice in the world. He reached the door in a daze. Once across the threshold, he pulled on his hat and stood still, as if waiting for the singer to appear at his side.

The song floating over the yurtas was *Topai-kok*. The moment it was over, Abai rushed to Yerbol.

"Togzhan! My God, that was Togzhan! That's her voice, her singing, that's her! How can it be, Yerbol? Where am I? That's Togzhan, I tell you. She's calling me from that yurta!"

A fresh wave of emotion swept over him.

Yerbol, too, was bewildered. The voice seemed familiar to him, and he racked his brains to remember where he had heard it before. Suddenly he realised why Abai had made for the door, dragging him along like an impatient child.

He well knew that Abai's love for Togzhan was a deep, unhealing wound, but he had never seen his friend in such a state. Abai seemed to be desperate, ready to say and do something rash.

"Hold on, Abai!" he interjected. "What's the matter with you? Shall we jump headlong into the fire? Pull yourself together!" He tried to draw Abai back into the tent.

"Let me be! Togzhan is in that yurta! It is she! It must be! I want to make sure! Or will you go and find out?"

Yerbol hesitated, but as Abai continued to plead, he said: "Very well. Only be patient. I'll go alone."

"Go quickly then! Take a look and come back. I'm sure it's Togzhan."

Yerbol returned very soon and he was no less staggered than Abai.

"My God! It wasn't a dream after all, it's she and none other." His voice was shaking.

"Is it true? Can it really be Togzhan? Of course! I knew it all along!" Abai rushed to the yurta.

"Just a minute — it's not Togzhan at all."

Abai turned on him angrily. "What are you talking about?"

"It's not Togzhan. It must be her double. My God, the very image of Togzhan and just as young, she hasn't changed at all. I came in and there was this girl — a second Togzhan!"

"What do you mean? Is it a miracle? Who sang that song?"

"I don't know. I didn't ask — I didn't know what to say, I was struck speechless when I saw her."

"But if she was so like her and sang like her... If it was someone else the voice would have been different too...."

"That's it. I didn't ask because it was enough to look at her face. But what about you? How could you have known? You were fast asleep! You are not a seer by any chance? Was it an omen or a dream? Or perhaps both of us are asleep and raving?" Yerbol was utterly perplexed.

Again and again Abai repeated his friend's words "her very image". His heart jumped like a wild colt, but then came doubt: what if she were not like Togzhan at all? What if it were only a dream, a vision that would dissolve like mist at sunrise? He was determined to see for himself. What matter if he burnt in the fire? He was ready to plunge headlong into its fiery embrace.

At that point the door of the Young Yurta flew open and with a shaft of light came the hubbub of voices.

"Here they are, they are going to Bekei for supper."

Yerbol took Abai by the hand and drew him quickly on ahead of the company. They entered the master's yurta and seated themselves at the place of honour as before. Yerbol began to rake the smouldering kizyak. "Perhaps it will burn brighter in my hands," he said jokingly.

Abai was impatient. The young people were laughing and joking, apparently in no hurry to enter.

The door opened, admitting the guests. The first to enter were two djiguits dressed in simple robes, timaks, and knee-high boots. Respectfully they presented their salems without raising their eyes. Next came several youngsters and two young women. Abai did not take his eyes off the door. Another young woman with a silver-embroidered robe thrown over her head and concealing half of her dusky face appeared at the door. This was probably Bekei's married daughter.

The last to enter was a girl bearing an astonishing resemblance to Togzhan. Silver sholpy tinkled in her braids and the rosy tint of her cheeks emphasised the fairness of her skin. She came in with a smile, a reserved yet slightly mischievous smile, revealing her beautiful white teeth. She greeted the guests and her flush of embarrassment was to Abai like a long-awaited dawn. Unable to return her greetings, he only muttered a few words and sat stock-still, his eyes fixed upon her. She reddened still more.

Like Togzhan the girl was of medium height. Yes, Yerbol was right, she was the very image of Togzhan — the same features, the same fair complexion, the same rosy apple of a chin, the same black silky hair — all that had haunted him in his dreams. There was the same nose, slightly upturned in a provocative and charming way. Red lips, clearly outlined and somewhat childish.... Dark eyebrows, long, and rising to the temples like the wings of a swallow. And that light smile of unclouded serenity. Yes, it was another Togzhan, Abai's one and only love. She was like a rising young moon — ever new, yet ever the same. She, the only and incomparable one, was now ascending the sky of his life.

The girl seated herself beside him. Abai was lost in a dream, oblivious to everything, aware only of the beating of his heart. He was caught in a whirl of emotion — his dream, it seemed, had become reality. Had she not whispered, "I am coming"? And here she was. It was no delusion, she had come indeed — in the pure bloom of youth.

Abai was still looking at her with unwavering eyes, his face bloodless and his pupils dilated. He was like a man watching a falling star and whispering a wish on which his very life depended.

Yerbol made conversation to distract their hosts' attention from Abai's unnaturally tense look. The bridegroom and his friends belonged to the Yeleman clan of the Mamai tribe — Yerbol knew the aul and was acquainted with their elders. He plied them with customary questions — where was the aul now, was it wandering and to which summer pasture.

From their conversation Abai understood only one thing — that Shukiman was the host's daughter.

"Will you help your mother, Shukiman, my dear? Give the towel to the guests and lay the cloth," Bekei said to her when the guests were seated.

The girl moved about the yurta, a gentle supple figure, her jacket and white dress emphasising her slenderness. But the beaver hat, rusty with age, spoiled everything. "I wish she would take it off!" thought Abai. He did not like her name either.

Yerbol and a dark-faced, narrow-bearded djiguit, one of the suitor's friends, continued their conversation at supper as well.

Shukiman had heard something about Abai. A year before there had been rumours that Kunonbai's son, a young djiguit, had become the ruler of Konir-Kokcha Volost. But then people had said that he had resigned the post last winter. There was nothing in this talk that did Abai credit or discredit; nor did it interest her.

When she heard that Abai was her father's guest, she did not hasten to see him. But when he ignored her salem, her pride was wounded; she decided that the haughty Mirza of the rich aul thought it beneath his dignity to speak to her.

After supper the huge smoky pot once more made its appearance over the tripod and the fire burnt cheerfully again.

"Enjoy yourselves, my children," said Bekei to the djiguits good-naturedly. "You were singing in that other yurta, so why not sing here?"

Abai had taken to Bekei from the first and liked him all the more for this.

"Yes, why should we interrupt your singing?" Abai agreed. "We've just heard a beautiful song. Don't mind us, please!"

"Yes, it was a wonderful song," agreed Yerbol, looking meaningly at Shukiman.

Shukiman smiled shyly.

"Do we alone sing songs!" she said in her beautifully clear, soft voice and laughed. "You've heard and seen more than we — and so you must know more songs." She laughed again and, glancing at Abai, slyly added," It's the guests who must pay the first penalty, you know!"

Her laughter, clear and true to her voice, was more remarkable even than Togzhan's. It was a song in itself and unforgettable.

Abai was not disconcerted.

"Well, if I must pay, I'll pay with a song, a poor one perhaps, but still a song."

Everybody smiled. He took the dombra and ran his fingers over the strings.

He sang in an undertone. It was the same sad and gentle tune which Shukiman had sung before; only the words were different, full of passion and longing.

> The sun and moon shine brightly in the sky,
> But darkness floods my heart and mind.
> She may well find a lover worthier than I,
> While I another love will never find.

The note of sadness faded as he sang. Hope flamed anew. The song seemed to be addressed to someone for whom he had been looking in vain, but had at last found. Both the voice of the dombra and that of the singer reached out towards the shores of fresh hope.

Abai had to repeat it three times, at the request of his delighted listeners.

"Debts have to be paid," he said. "Yerbol and I heard someone singing *Topai-kok* in the next yurta. The song is still with us! There is no need to ask who was singing. Please sing it again." His eyes pleaded with Shukiman.

"That was my aunt singing. She's still there, shall we call her?" The others laughed with Shukiman.

"But that's not true," Abai and Yerbol continued to insist. "We know it was you who was singing."

Shukiman had to give in.

Her voice, so pleasant in conversation, was bewitchingly lovely when she sang, the sound stretched like a fine and even silk thread. Abai had never been so stirred by anyone's singing before. Never had the meaning of the song been brought out so clearly. He listened as to a prayer and only once dared to raise his eyes. All her shyness was gone. Oblivious to everything, she sang in complete absorption, her eyebrows rising and falling with the melody. Her young, generous soul was revealed in its entirety. One vision came after another; her voice was now the crest of a transparent wave heading for happiness, now a murmuring brook sparkling with moonbeams.

Everyone listened enraptured. When Shukiman had finished, Abai sighed deeply, his heart overflowing. He looked at Shukiman and silently bowed his head.

"What a song! No one else could have sung it like that," Yerbol exclaimed.

Abai thought so too, but said nothing. His heart was filled with a light strong enough to flood the world. What was there to say? Any words would have been a mockery of his feelings. But this much he knew: a new sun had arisen in his heart, his lost joy had returned, happiness itself had sought him out, taking pity on him....

A firm and inflexible decision matured within him. Once, when he was young and unsure of himself, he had had to renounce his happiness. This time he would not let his fortune out of his hands. Let all the world come tumbling down, let his father and mother disown him, his kith and kin condemn and drive him away! Come what might, he would not and could not give up this girl or yield her to anyone. Without her life would not be worth living.

When the young people moved to go, Abai could only say, "Thank you" to Shukiman again and again. No other words occurred to him, but his pallor and shaking voice told her what he could not express. Blushing gently, she gave him a warm smile. He was no longer the overbearing Mirza she had seen when entering the yurta earlier that evening. This was a man to whom one might be drawn, one who felt deeply. He could indeed arouse affection, abandoning himself so completely to his feelings as he did. Shukiman caught a glimpse of something she had never encountered before. Abai suddenly seemed very dear to her. Her eyes unwavering, she took leave of him with especial warmth.

Everybody was retiring for the night. Shukiman, who was to stay with her sister-in-law, went off with her brother-in-law and the others and did not return to the yurta.

Abai and Yerbol were scarcely over the Chiliktinsk Hill the next morning when their talk turned upon Shukiman.

"She's a real korim," * Abai said again and again.

"Ai, a korim, ai, a real korim!" Yerbol enthusiastically agreed.

"What's that you say?" Abai looked up, then laughed and added, "Do you know what I think, Yerbol? Shukiman is such an ugly name and doesn't suit her at all. Let's give her a name of our own. You've just found the name; we'll call her Aikorim.... Or still better—Aigerim!"

They recollected Abai's dream, marvelling at the way it had come true. They were lost in conjectures until Abai expressed his view:

"An old idea has just occurred to me. Magicians and witch-doctors can tell the future by dreams, or as the books say it is a gift of the sage or a saint. But I'm none of these, I don't tell fortunes or make magic. Still, there are people who differ from others by the sharp way they feel things, by their sensitivity and keen perception—the akyns. Perhaps I'm one of them?"

To Yerbol, Abai had long been an akyn. Unable to understand his friend fully, however, he kept silent. But Abai was elated with his discovery and filled with fresh inspiration.

With warmth and passion, Abai explained his thoughts to Yerbol, telling him that he had made up his mind that night. This seemed a sudden decision, but it was justified by all

* Korim—a beauty.—*Ed.*

that he had felt the day before. He told his friend about the hopes that had filled him since the morning.

"Do not condemn me, Yerbol, try to understand how I feel," he pleaded.

These were familiar words, words that Yerbol always heard when his friend had decided upon something sudden and wished to win his approval. He smiled, his eyes crinkling up at the corners, for he well understood Abai's feelings.

"I crave this unknown, untried and even, perhaps, forbidden future," Abai went on without noticing his friend's amusement. "All my thoughts, all my being belong to it. I am in love with Aigerim and want to marry her."

His friend's passion did not surprise Yerbol. But this talk of marriage was like a bolt from the blue, and he looked at Abai in astonishment. For the rest of the journey the two of them could talk of nothing else. They halted on the Chinghis and did not begin their descent to Shalkar where Ulzhan's aul stood until they had talked everything over.

These broad and even pastures in the foothills, where the waters of the river were clear and the springs were blessedly cold, were famous for their lush grasses. Their vast expanses, known as Shalkar, that is, boundless, were one mass of green. A cool breeze, the constant, invigorating and fragrant guest of spring from Sary-Arka,* swept over the grass in soft green waves.

The aul welcomed Abai joyfully. Ulzhan was the first to embrace her son with a happy smile, pressing her face to his for a long tender moment. Then she brought her smallest grandson, three-year-old Magash, a thin fair child with delicately arched brows and dark shining eyes. Abai bent over his son and the child clasped his father's neck, his face pressed to Abai's cheek. He was not shy at all when Abai lifted and kissed him and called him by name, and obviously remembered his father, though the latter had been away the whole winter. Caressing Abai's face with his small hands, he laughed, revealing tiny white teeth.

"You've forgotten us, Aga. I am Abish, not Magash."

Who had put him up to it? The words of his pet touched Abai to the quick, but he could see that this was not Ulzhan's doing. She noticed the frown on her son's face and admonished the little boy:

---

* Sary-Arka (Yellow Back), the Kazakh name of the Aral-Irtish water-line. — Ed.

"What are you talking about, you silly! Daddy has come from afar and has missed you so all this time. Is that the way to greet him?"

But Abai's mind was not at rest. He greeted everybody kindly, but as he entered the yurta with his mother he said bitterly:

"What was that your grandson said, Apa? It was a stupid thing to teach him whoever did it."

A joyful crowd burst into the yurta after him and the place rang with talk and laughter.

Everybody asked about Kunanbai. What was the news from the road? Was he in good health? Abai told them what he knew; Kunanbai had only sent word that he had reached Karkaralinsk and there met Ondirbai.

Dilda had also entered the yurta with Abai. It was she who had prompted little Magash's rebuke, and seeing that Abai was hurt was not at all sorry; she even smiled spitefully as if to say, "Serves you right." How many times she had heaped curses on her absent husband that long winter! Could he not have come home once in half a year? There must be another woman there, she thought. He had quite lost his head. For whom had he deserted his home and his family? Suffocating with anger and wounded pride she wished him ill with all her heart, spitefully making sure that Ulzhan heard her.

Akilbai, Abai's eldest son, was twelve and had been brought up by Nurganim, the youngest wife of Kunanbai, while six-year-old Gulbadan, four-year-old Abish and little Magash were being reared by Dilda herself. Ulzhan and Aigiz, her two mothers-in-law, and the entire aul held Dilda in great esteem and her children were pampered by young and old. The daughter of a rich aul who bears many sons is apt to become spoilt, wilful and headstrong in speech and behaviour, and this was exactly what had happened to Dilda. Her husband's neglect had only intensified these traits; she had become cold, callous and inordinately touchy.

The lack of any love between Abai and Dilda became fully apparent at their first meeting. Their estrangement had long been coming, and the tenuous thread that had kept them together had evidently snapped at last. The two exchanged not a single warm word during the evening nor afterwards when the guests had gone.

But the more coldly he treated his wife, the more tender he was to his children, whom he had really missed. Nevertheless he had no intention of giving up the plans he had formed during his journey.

That evening he told Ulzhan and Aigiz of his decision, which astonished and terrified them. It was a matter in which he sought no advice and admitted no argument; his mind was made up that Abish and Gulbadan would study at a Russian school in town.

But Abish was so little and weak. Let him stay with her for a little longer, Ulzhan pleaded, and Abai did not insist — the matter could wait.

"I'll make real men of your grandchildren, Apa. I'll give them an education. Perhaps Abish is too little just now, but both of them shall have a city education. That's what our times demand and my mind is made up!"

The three children cuddled up to him.

"We're going to school. Take us to town soon."

He put off telling the family of his private plans for a long time. Could his desire be fulfilled? Where to begin, and how to go about the matter? Aigerim was said to be betrothed. To whom? What would she say? What would her aul and her parents say? He had to find out how the land lay first. He must look before leaping — rashness could spoil everything.

Yerbol alone had been trusted with the secret, but on his advice Abai decided to take another friend into his confidence. His choice fell on Zhirenshe, whom he had known intimately for years. He was quick-witted and a good talker.

In recent years, Abai had been inseparable from him on all his journeys. When he had become the Konir-Kokcha volost ruler, he had set him up as a biy, and when Abai had resigned from his post, Zhirenshe had continued to hold office as judge in the same volost.

Abai sent Yerbol for Zhirenshe, and when the latter arrived at Ulzhan's aul he told him about his problem in great detail. After much reflection Zhirenshe agreed to be his friend's mediator.

"Zhirenshe, I would like you to represent me in this matter," Abai said. "First become acquainted with her and see how the land lies. Find out what she thinks about it and then try to learn the opinion of her parents and kinsmen. There's just one thing you must be careful of: don't rub it in that I am Kunanbai's son and we are a famous and powerful aul. Let them not be afraid of reprisals should they refuse. As Allah is my witness, I shall not be offended if the girl does not want me. If I gain their consent only thanks to my father's name and my aul, I shall know no happiness, only disgrace. Try to understand and remember this. You'll

19*

tell me the truth when you come back, no matter what
it is."

Abai sent Yerbol with Zhirenshe to see that his instructions were carried out. Abai had not long to wait, for
in three days his friends were back from the Mamai
tribe.

Zhirenshe had spoken to Aigerim herself. He too had
been struck by her beauty, but even more so by her
intelligence and kindness. Aigerim, he said, was betrothed
to a djiguit of her tribe. The man had died, but according to
custom his rights were transferred to his elder brother, a
man who had long been married. A part of the kalim had
been paid, and when the girl had grown up the brother of
the deceased had refused to give her back her freedom,
declaring that he would marry her himself. Bekei's daughter was thus tied without a rope, as the saying goes. The
girl's family had more than once begged him to annul the
betrothal, but he would not agree, arguing that since the
bride had been promised to him by God, he was obliged to
marry her. While depriving the poor girl of her freedom, he
could not, however, pay the rest of the kalim and so he
never visited her. His wife, too, was opposed to the
marriage.

Zhirenshe had gathered all this from his conversations
with Bekei and Shekei. Aigerim told him that she longed to
be released, and did not at all want to marry that old man.

But there were other difficulties. Abai was also bound by
strong ties. Neither his parents nor his kinsmen knew of his
decision. Then there was Dilda — he had yet to see how she
would take the news.

Considering all this, the cautious Zhirenshe advised Bekei
and Aigerim to keep their conversation secret. He had the
friendliest feeling for Bekei's aul and he wanted them to
understand him well. He was more concerned for Aigerim
than for Abai. If the plan fell through, Aigerim's reputation
might suffer, and if the kinsmen of the man she had been
promised to got wind of the matter there would be no end
of bitter strife between the two clans.

He did not tell Bekei of what troubled him most: rumours
might get abroad that he, Zhirenshe, had tempted a bride of
the Mamai tribe into marriage with Abai. Fresh enmity
might spring up and dishonour Zhirenshe himself.

Nonetheless he had been a great help, cleverly conducting
the negotiations. Delighted with Zhirenshe's resourcefulness, Abai asked him to do yet another favour.

"I know I should have handled the matter myself. But since you have taken it up, I beg you to see it through to the end. Father is far away, but Mother does not deserve to be ignored. Speak to her and get her consent."

Ulzhan did not approve of Abai's decision. She listened to Zhirenshe's lengthy explanation with a deepening frown.

"If Abai is going to do what he wants to, let him do it openly. Why these roundabout methods? Why send you as a mediator? Let him come himself and we'll talk it over together."

When Abai came, she greeted him without her usual friendliness. Her voice was firm and inflexible.

"Abai-zhan, your decision is clear to me, my son. Zhirenshe has told me whom you have chosen and has asked for my advice. You want to know if I approve. I do not, and will tell you why. You know and have seen a great deal yourself. I was one of your father's wives — and weren't you one of the many sons of one of the many wives? You and I shared the same sad lot, the same hardships. Was it a pleasant life for me? Was it an easy life for you? I always had but one wish — that our children should not follow in our footsteps. I am afraid you will regret this step which you think will bring you so much joy. The step itself is not difficult to take, but the consequences will be bitter. You will be sorry, my child. Of course, it's for you to decide; both the joy and the gall will be yours, while we, that is your friends, Zhirenshe and myself, will remain mere onlookers. But I had to tell you my doubts. Think twice before you make up your mind, my son. That's all I wanted to say to you."

Abai left without replying. This was the first time they had ever failed to understand each other. There was a good deal he could have said to his mother but she would not have understood him — to do so she would have had to feel what he felt. Did he not know himself that his decision was unreasonable? She need not have told him this. But what of his feelings? He had spared her his thoughts — hadn't his parents done him harm enough by uniting him with Dilda against his will? They had not consulted his feelings and had cruelly separated him from Togzhan. But could he have said this to Ulzhan, his kind mother who had never suspected her guilt and had indeed been sure that she had always done the best for him? And so Abai went away without saying a word.

But he would not let the matter rest. Zhirenshe was again sent to the auls of Mamai; in two weeks he had obtained the family's consent and brought the negotiations to a successful conclusion. He had also visited the aul of Aigerim's fiancé and settled everything there.

The knot had been untied. Abai had only to send a large gift to Bekei and the former bridegroom in compensation.

Ospan, who was in charge of Kunanbai's property, grudged Abai nothing. He quickly reckoned everything up, and had a large herd driven off at once as part of the kalim. Zhirenshe, Zhakip, Ospan and Gabitkhan were dispatched to Bekci's aul as matchmakers and were generously rewarded for their services. More cattle was then sent as the last portion of the kalim and a wedding gift from the bridegroom's parents.

At last Abai went to call up his bride accompanied by Yerbol, Ospan, Gabitkhan and Zhirenshe, the latter, as at Dilda's wedding, playing the role of senior matchmaker. So Abai brought Aigerim to his home for ever.

THE FOOTHILLS

1

The door was wide open, the flap raised and the yurta was cooled by the breath of a fine spring morning. The smells of worm-wood and feather-grass rushed in together with the manifold sounds of spring. Abai was sitting by a high bone-carved bed, his elbows on a round table. Though he was reading, he was conscious of the stirrings of nature around him.

A cuckoo could be heard on the distant slopes of the Akshoky; this small insignificant bird was calling its mate, telling its insignificant secrets to the whole wide world. A lark was trilling high above the yurta. At times, Abai could hear the beating of wings — coveys of ducks were flying over the sprawling hills, towards the meadows flooded with spring waters. The lambs and kids skipped by, their strong little hoofs drubbing the ground. Something must have frightened them and they stamped as though to save their lives. From the neighbouring yurta came a hubbub of children's voices, mingling with the bleating of the lambs.

This joyous burgeoning of nature, re-awakened by the spring, burst upon Abai's solitude, and he was acutely aware of it. The sun-rays coming through the circle of the shanrak and falling on the decorated rugs were as soft and caressing as the spring itself, and the quiet of the ornate yurta was wonderfully soothing. Abai took deep breaths as he pored over the pages, re-reading them with fresh elation, as if he were just seeing them for the first time. It was as if book and reader had at last come to a complete understanding.

This was the first fairly large Russian book that Abai had read to the end almost as freely as if it had been written in his native language.

Entrenched in dictionaries and textbooks, he had been studying Russian all the winter. When the light of this new world seemed to be revealing itself to him, he turned to Pushkin. He began with prose, delighted to see that he understood everything. The book was *Dubrovsky*. Pushkin gave him the key to the great wealth of the Russian language and he could now appreciate the wealth of ideas stored in the book as well.

It was *Dubrovsky* which was responsible for his mood of deep satisfaction and keen awareness of all that was going on around him. The book seemed to him like a fellow-traveller who had unexpectedly come to be a friend. It was a long time since he had been so elated. His life of seclusion and escape from household cares was at last justified. He had found and crossed the ford he had sought so patiently for years.

Maibasar, Takezhan and Zhirenshe had been making fun of him for a long time. "He has not once left his yurta since he married Aigerim. He can't see his fill of her. He used to be in the clouds, but now he's caught in her snares like a sparrow in the coils of a snake. He used to fly high, but has now hit the dust."

Abai had laughed on hearing this, and had continued to study his books as industriously as a pupil of the madrasah. He shared his thoughts with no one and sought nobody's advice. It was clear to him that in his day and age a man must not shut himself away in his small steppeland world. Thinking of the town, of Akbas Andreyevich, the library and the education of his children, he came to another decision: to build a comfortable house in Akshoky, forty versts nearer to Semipalatinsk, where he could live as he liked. The snow was hardly gone when he moved to Akshoky, though no auls had left their winter places as yet, and the yurtas of his mother, Ospan and Dilda were still in Zhidebai. Abai took with him only Aigerim and his children by Dilda — Akilbai, Abish, Gulbadan and little Magash. Also their tutor, who was known as the Kishkeneh Mullah, that is the junior mullah, to distinguish him from Gabitkhan. Several neighbours who served the Great Aul, handi-craftsmen and workers, came with their yurtas, and so the building of the house began at once. The work was supervised by Yerbol and Aigerim, while Abai never left his yurta, devoting all his time to his studies.

He was reading when Aigerim, Yerbol and the Kishkeneh Mullah entered.

"Merciful Allah," the mullah said to Aigerim in astonish-ment as he crossed the threshold, evidently continuing an unfinished conversation, "is it possible that even today, when the foundation stone of the new house is to be laid, Abai will not leave his books. Is he ill and bedridden, perhaps?"

Aigerim laughed softly.

"He's quite well. The truth is that he has no time. He has more important work than building a house."

Abai asked Aigerim and Yerbol how the work was progressing, wished them good luck, and then gaily confirmed the words of his wife.

"Aigerim is right. You will laugh if I say that my work is harder than that of a mason. What a mason does is evident to all, of course, but I have accomplished something with my labour too."

He suddenly wanted to share the elation he had felt on finishing the book with his wife and his friends. He turned the pages before him, and spoke between sips of the thick, cold kumiss:

"To build a house, to prepare a threshing-floor or knead the clay for the bricks requires much labour, of course, but to attain the understanding of a wise book which for years would not speak to you takes no little effort either. Aigerim and Yerbol know and you, Mullah, must also guess that all this year my life was dedicated to a single purpose. And now I am happy because I see my wish materialise in a finished edifice before me."

He fell silent afraid that his words were not clear to the others. But then, an apt simile occurred to him:

"The Kishkeneh Mullah will explain it," he went on, looking at Yerbol. "An industrious shakird may study at the madrasah for many a year and then one day the truth dawns on him and he is able to see what has been concealed from him for many years. When this happens, the mullahs say that he has found the key to knowledge. You know how long I have been studying. I was a pupil without a teacher, but today I, too, have found the key. And on the very same day when you, Aigerim and Yerbol, laid the foundation stone of our new house! My labours have been justified, my friends."

Abai's words held a world of meaning. He was pleased and excited. Aigerim, who was always quick to understand Abai, smiled at him, and tears rose to her eyes.

"And so it turns out that it is you who have greater reason to celebrate today than we. It is we who should congratulate you and wish you well." With these words she filled a piala with kumiss and handed it to him.

Yerbol made no remark, but smiled happily, too. Only the mullah was not in accord.

"The key to knowledge? I would agree that you had

gained the key to knowledge if you had been studying *Mantik* and *Gakaid* without a spiritual teacher, without a khalfe or khazret, or if you had penetrated the meaning of *Kafiya* or *Sharh Gabdullah*, but if it is a matter of studying some Russian nonsense, the expression is not appropriate. You are under a misapprehension, Abai," he added sententiously.

Abai frowned, but said nothing, trying to keep himself in hand.

"Our spiritual teachers, the khalfes, khazrets and ishans, have always been narrow-minded," he said calmly, after taking a sip from his piala. "I can see that you are not free of this vice either."

"I would not object if it were a question of Islam, but why bother to talk about such books as yours?" the Kishkeneh Mullah persisted. "The infidels of ancient times also had a science of their own, but it was not recognised by a single Moslem scholar. It is inadequate for true knowledge."

Abai saw that the debate might go on for ever. He was not in the mood to bandy words with the Kishkeneh Mullah and though he had many arguments to put forward, he chose only one in order to stop the mullah's flow of talk.

"You say that no Moslem ever recognised the science of the infidels. Just remember what the Prophet said in the Hadith—let alone what others have said—'The ink of a scientist is more precious than the blood of a shahid*.' You assert that the science of the infidels is inadequate for knowledge. But can you regard as science the story of the origin of the world as given in the history of the prophets *Kissasul Anbiya*. And what knowledge of mankind and of the nations can one gain from *Krik-Hadith*, from *Lauhunameh* and *Fikhkaidani?***"

"If these are not enough for you, then read other books by Moslem scholars," said the Kishkeneh Mullah, little put out. "You'll find more than enough wisdom there to last you a lifetime."

Abai smiled.

"I would understand if you said what the real scholars say: 'Borrow knowledge where you find it. Take it from whoever has it.' But what advice have you given me? Those pastures you have mentioned I have travelled far and wide a long time ago. I have trodden many a path to master the

---

* Shahid—one who falls on the battlefield of a religious war.—*Ed.*
** Ritual books.—*Ed.*

knowledge gained by mankind through the centuries. I am
really surprised at you, Mullah. If you were an ignorant
man it would be one thing, but you are a teacher. How can
you say that knowledge should be sought along one narrow
path alone? Isn't science a boundless world? Haven't the
wisest of the Moslem scholars availed themselves of the
wisdom of Socrates, Plato and Aristotle? Which of these was
a Moslem? You see before you a man who has spent years in
quest of knowledge and you tell him, 'Do not strive, give up
the quest.' No, we shall never understand each other.
Everyone has his own goal, a summit he strives to attain. My
goal lies far ahead and I shall strive on until I reach my
summit. Let us finish with this."

He frowned again, and drawing out his ornamented
shaksha,* he tapped it with his finger and took a pinch of
nasibai.

The Kishkeneh Mullah, however, thought the remark
rude and uncalled for. He left in a temper, and the moment
he entered the yurta next door, the hubbub of the children's
voices there, so much like the bleating of the lambs at dusk,
stopped abruptly.

Aigerim who had followed the mullah out of the yurta
now paused at the threshold. She had noticed two riders
approaching the aul.

"There is someone coming," she said turning to the
others. "I can't make out who they are. Perhaps they're
from the Great Aul. No. They're strangers. One of them is
such a giant." She looked intently and began to laugh.
"Oi-boi! It must be Kenzhem. Of course it's Kenzhem!"

That was Aigerim's name for Ospan.** Yerbol sprang up
and went out. Abai followed. They had all been a little
homesick for the noisy and crowded aul from which they
had separated more than a month before. Kunanbai's aul
usually remained at the winter places in the Chinghis and at
Zhidebai until late in spring.

As the riders drew nearer, Abai was no less astonished
than Aigerim to perceive how tremendously his brother had
grown and broadened since he had last seen him. He was
mounted on a well-fed, long-tailed bay. His massive body
looked enormous because he was still wearing his heavy
winter coat and a huge hat of long-haired lambskin. His

* Shaksha—a snuff box.— Ed.
** Kenzhem—the youngest son. According to custom, a new
daughter-in-law gives her own names to all the members of the family.—
Ed.

enormous legs were clad in warm boots. Abai always gasped
when he saw his brother after an interval.

Ospan lashed his horse and soon flew into the little aul
with his friend. The two were joyously received. Aigerim
went to meet them, took the reins of Ospan's horse and
greeted them heartily.

"You're wrapped up as though you've been riding all
night," she observed good-humouredly.

But Ospan was in no mood for joking. His large eyes were
red and puffy as though he had spent a sleepless night. He
was sullen and taciturn, quite unlike the happy-go-lucky
Ospan of old. On their way to the yurta, Abai plied him with
questions—where were the auls, and were Kunanbai and
Ulzhan in good health? Ospan briefly replied that the auls
had that day left one of the slopes of Akshoky and were
bound for Korik. Plucking his moustache and sparse beard,
he said nothing more. It was a curious beard for such a
giant. Every hair of it grew apart, as stiff and wiry as horse
hair.

Aigerim busied herself with the tea and refreshments,
giving instructions to Zlikha in a low voice. Ospan told her
gruffly that he would not eat. No sooner had he sat down,
without even troubling to remove his belt, than he
announced that twelve-year-old Makulbai, Kunanbai's
favourite and oldest grandson and the son of Takezhan and
Karazhan, had died the day before from an illness he had
had since the winter.

So that was why Ospan was behaving so strangely, Abai
thought all the more highly of Ospan since he knew that his
younger brother had not been on friendly terms with
Takezhan. He stopped questioning Ospan, and left him
alone.

Abai was silent until the guests, having finished their
kumiss, began to ask him about the progress of the new
house.

Ospan knew very well that Abai had always been inept in
household matters. He, himself, on the other hand, had
always been a far more thrifty and capable aul master, one
who knew how to look after his livestock and other
property. When Abai had set off for Akshoky to build his
house, it was Ospan who had picked the most capable
handicraftsmen and workers for him. He had also seen to
the tools and food supplies.

Now that the conversation had turned upon their affairs
it seemed that not Abai, but Ospan was the elder brother.

His questions were brief and to the point; how much clay
had they kneaded, how many thousands of bricks had they
prepared, and how many were made by the best workman
in a day? Abai could not answer and looked to Aigerim and
Yerbol for help. It was clear that he had not followed the
progress of the work at all. At any other time, Ospan would
have made sport of him, but now he merely smiled and
turned to Aigerim and Yerbol.

Aigerim was still weeping over Makulbai, but Ospan
ignored this. He put many questions to her and demanded
detailed answers. Finally he decided to inspect the work
himself. As Aigerim and Yerbol walked out in front of him,
he paused at the door.

"Tell them to saddle your horse. We'll have to go to
Korik. You must visit the Great Yurta and make your salem
to Father. You should read some prayers in Takezhan's
yurta too. We'll have a talk on the way. There's something I
must ask you about." Looking at him intently, Abai guessed
that this "something" troubled his brother deeply, and was
the main reason for his glumness.

"Has it anything to do with the tribe?" he asked casually.

"You'll see for yourself whether it's the tribe or just some
bad kinsmen," said Ospan evasively. "I must talk to you.
Have your horse saddled at once."

As things turned out, the two brothers were accompanied
by the Kishkeneh Mullah, who had been summoned by
Ulzhan to read the funeral service from the Koran. As
Ospan was unwilling to speak of intimate matters before a
stranger, the talk revolved round the building of the house,
the haymaking and the storing of fodder for the winter.
Since the winter was severe here with much more snow than
in Zhidebai and on the Chinghis, they had to store up a
great deal of fodder in case there was a djut. Ospan advised
Abai to cut as much hay as possible on the neighbouring
meadows, remarking that the auls which had gone to Korik
were situated too near Akshoky and that this was a
disadvantage.

"The auls have returned to their old grounds. That's
something I'd overlooked," he said ruefully. "I was too busy
with the funeral or else I would have chosen another place
farther on."

Abai had also overlooked this, and was now touched by
his brother's concern for him.

"You're right," he said, "but I'm not an Anet or Kotibak.
I can't go about shouting, 'Keep your cattle off. This hay is

mine!' Will you talk to our mothers and brothers about my winter place?"

But it appeared that Ospan had already seen to this.

"Let the auls stay here to the seventh day and accept first mention in the prayers of the kinsmen. I'll take our auls farther on after that. The flood waters have spread far, so there is plenty of water this year. The grass will grow quickly here and you'll have all the hay you need."

As they had left Akshoky, Abai had seen huge herds in the meadows, but no auls. Now that they had reached the valley, at a distance of a two-year-old's run,* he could count at least fifteen auls huddled together. Around each of them the herds and the flocks were grazing on the meadows abundantly watered and richly covered with grass.

An occasional yurta could be seen among the herds. It was obvious that the wandering auls had been travelling in even rows and had halted simultaneously; each aul had already set up its keregeh and was now shaping the domes from the long uiks, painted a vivid red and easily seen from afar. They had begun to cover them with felt, and the green expanses were now flecked here and there with white. Ulzhan's octagonal Great Yurta had quickly risen in the very middle, and when it was finished, Great Yurtas likewise sprang up in the other auls.

By the time Ospan and his companions reached Ulzhan's aul, the yurtas were completed everywhere. The fifteen auls filled the once deserted valley with noise, movement and life.

Without pausing at the Great Yurta, the brothers made directly for Takezhan's mourning tent, near Ulzhan's aul. Takezhan had separated from his kinsmen and wandered independently, but when Makulbai died, Ulzhan had decided to keep her auls closer to those of her son for the last lap of the wandering. She and the elder kinsmen spent much of their time in Takezhan's yurta. The death of their first-born evoked everyone's sympathy and concern for Takezhan and Karazhan, and it was not only Ulzhan who mourned the loss of the child, consoled the parents and arranged the prayers: Kunanbai also kept close to his son and daughter-in-law, in these days of grief.

* Distances in the steppes were sometimes measured by the lengths covered by the horses in the baiga (races): Run of a foal—5 kilometres, run of a two-year-old—8 to 10 kilometres, of a horse—20-35 kilometres.—*Ed.*

Abai approached the yurta of mourning slowly, neither setting his horse at a gallop nor chanting the lamentation, since the deceased was an adolescent. He embraced Takezhan at the entrance, and began the prescribed mourning chant—"My child, my poor little foal"—only when he had entered the tent where Karazhan and the other women sat wailing.

The yurta was full of kinsmen and both the men and the women were weeping. Still chanting, Abai and the Kishke-neh Mullah embraced the elder women in turn, beginning with Karazhan, Aigiz and Ulzhan, and then seated themselves in the places of honour lower than Kunanbai and Karatai. Soon the general lamentation abated and only Karazhan was left voicing her grief.

Sad though the occasion was, Abai could not bring himself to feel fully for Karazhan. Her voice was deep and unpleasant, it warbled irritatingly, and the words sounded cold and formal. She was weeping over her son, yet her voice held no warmth.

The Kishkeneh Mullah read the Koran in the sonorous, sing-song Bokhara fashion. At the first words, Kunanbai lowered his head, closed his single eye and motioned to his wailing daughter-in-law. Aigiz and Kalikha, who sat next to Karazhan, understood his gesture.

"Enough, Kelin. Let him read the Koran!" they said to her.

Abai and Ospan stayed on until almost everyone had left except Kunanbai, Karatai and Ulzhan, who had been there all day.

It was only at the end of the winter that Kunanbai had returned from his pilgrimage to Mecca, which had kept him away for four years. His hair was white and he looked very old. His large body had preserved something of its regal bearing, but his face was furrowed with countless lines. Once a hale and hearty man, he now seemed weary and limp. He wore the white skull-cap he had brought from Mecca and a white silk chapan with a quilted collar, likewise an unusual garment among the Tobikty. The low thunder of his voice was gone, and he spoke in soft undertones. To his kinsmen he seemed to have come from another world. His whole manner bespoke the piety and humility of a repenting sinner.

On his return from Mecca, he had settled in Nurganim's yurta and separated himself from the others with a curtain, converting his abode into something between a monastery

cell and a mihrab.* Only the death of his grandson had
drawn him temporarily from his seclusion. He spoke to no
one but his old friend Karatai, and that only on rare
occasions.

Abai knew there was nothing he could discuss with his
father and kept silent the whole day. It was only Kunanbai
and Karatai who talked. Old Karatai could draw anyone into
the conversation. To get Kunanbai to talk he turned to
topics appropriate to a yurta in mourning and asked him
about the tombs of the saints which Hadji Kunanbai had
visited in Mecca and Medina. No pious Moslem could help
answering.

"In Medina I visited the tombs of Rasul Allah, Khazret
Abu Bakh, Omar and Fatima," Kunanbai replied in a soft
voice, fingering his beads. "I was also privileged to visit the
tombs of the worthy khazrets Gabbas, Khamza and
Gusman."

"And did you see the tombs of the Sahabs?"** Karatai
went on in an awestruck tone.

"Sagdi-bin-Wakas, Gabdrakhman-bin-Gauf and Khazret
Gaisha lay buried there," Kunanbai answered willingly.
"Their resting places are called 'the places of repose of the
Prophet's friends'."

Kunanbai then began the tale of his journey from Mecca
to Medina. He had travelled over the Arabian Desert by
camel for thirteen days after leaving Sham with the caravan.
He named the place where he had donned his ikhram, the
robes put on by every pilgrim before entering Mecca. He
told how he had ascended the hill of Arafa and how many
namazes he had chanted in the sacred Mosque of Kaaba. He
had left Mecca on foot and now described his return
journey in great detail. Kunanbai seemed to enjoy this talk
with Karatai — a change from his life as a recluse. He had
shown Karatai much attention at tea and dinner and when
his friend left, he commented on the conversation to Ulzhan
in these words:

"There are few among our illiterate Kazakhs as well
informed as Karatai. He knows all the things I have seen
so well that he seems to have seen them with his own
eyes."

"May all his wishes come true," said Ulzhan. "He has
done us much good today. He made you tell us what we

---

* Mihrab—the place in the mosque corresponding to an altar.—*Ed.*
** Sahabs—Mohammed's associates.—*Ed.*

never heard before. You have seen and come to know so much and yet have kept it from us."

Ulzhan's observations were rare, but always to the point. Both Kunanbai and Abai understood that through praising Karatai she was reproaching her husband. Kunanbai, however, considered the remark flippant and frowned, as though to say, "Women will be women, and sacred things should be kept in the heart when they are about." He told his beads with quick fingers, then turned away from her and passed his palms over his face as he whispered a prayer.

Abai smiled faintly to his mother. Kunanbai's talk with Karatai, his mother's just reproach and his father's annoyance exposed the vanity and emptiness of the old man's existence. The four years of pilgrimage had yielded him nothing but the names of a few tombstones. What was the idea of turning away from his family, friends and kinsmen and withdrawing from the world? He had gained little, and lost so much! Was there any sense in his present life?

The sun was setting when Abai and Ospan left Takezhan's aul. They mounted and started along the river-bank away from the auls and the droves going down to the waterside. Ospan had chosen the road and Abai had followed in silence, expecting his brother to start the conversation which had been postponed in the morning. They were interrupted again, however, this time by their nephew Shakke, the son of the late Kudaiberdy. They were descending to the river when the young man overtook them at full gallop on a splendid light-grey mare. His light chapan billowed out behind him while his gold-topped timak of black lambskin had slipped down over one ear. Coming abreast of them as smoothly as a sailboat, he presented his salem.

"I've caught up with you to tell you about my falcon," he said excitedly, exhibiting the grey falcon perched on his arm. "Abai-aga, please ride on along the river and my name is not Shakke if I don't get a duck apiece for you!"

The steel-grey feathers of the bird shone like molten gold in the setting sun. Its dark-brown eyes had a blood-thirsty glitter in them, their fire a challenge to the rays from the west. Fascinated, Abai took the falcon from Shakke, perched it on his wrist, and stroked its head and feathers, feeling for its muscles with knowing fingers. He could tell how well the bird had been trained by its impatient movements.

"There's a falcon for you," he said. "He'll pounce on any bird in the air. Who trained him, Shakke?"

"I trained him myself. I've learned how to do it."

Abai was pleased.

"Good for you. It's quite an art, and takes a lot of skill and patience. Now let's see what he can do."

Abai returned the falcon and lashed his bay to a gallop. Shakke's grey dashed after, followed by Ospan's horse.

Before them the river widened. Flocks of pintails, pochards and mallards circled over it, some all but skimming the water, others flying high up in the sky. The hunters were still riding swiftly when the falcon sensed its prey and beat its breast against the restraining hand of its master. Shakke looked about, but could see no birds nearby.

"Let him go. He has sensed his prey," Abai said, as he overtook his nephew.

The falcon slipped from Shakke's arm as if to drop to the earth, then dived under the very nose of the mare and flew over the ground almost touching the grass. He shot across the river and, flashing behind the reeds for an instant, vanished from view. The riders thought the bird would strike from ambush, but the falcon suddenly appeared again. They could just glimpse his breast, glowing red in the sun's rays, as he shot upwards and then swooped. The birds whirled away in a panic with shrill cries. The riders galloped to the spot where the falcon had disappeared.

In the reeds, a pair of motley-coloured ducks were struggling with the enemy that had dropped from the blue. The duck was quacking and thrashing about in the water trying to shake off the falcon, whose claws were sunk into her feathers, while the drake was hovering above to strike at the attacker as though he were a bird of prey himself. The wings of the drake fluttered like yellow and crimson tongues of flame, and the solid blue-grey body of the falcon looked like an iron bar as it is cast into a glowing furnace. Abai reached the birds when the fight was at its height. The colourful scene compelled him to pause. Shakke, however, got ahead of Abai, leapt from his horse and waded out to the reeds.

By the time he got there, the falcon had killed the birds. The beating of the drake's wings and his pecking had enraged the falcon, and with the talons of one foot still clawing the duck, he had struck at the drake with the other and brought him down. Shakke shouted in high delight.

With his kamcha he hit at the duck which was shedding her feathers in a desperate attempt to fight free, and tore the drake from the falcon's clutches.

This happened once in a lifetime — the falcon had got two birds at a go. Shakke beamed with pride. Severing the head of the duck, he scooped out the brain, sprinkled it with sugar and fed it to the still excited falcon. He then tied the game to the saddles of Abai and Ospan, and remounted.

Though frightened, the other birds had not flown far, and the riders soon came upon another big covey of ducks on the water. Feeling the pressure of the falcon's breast on his wrist, Shakke lashed his mare to a gallop with his arm extended. When the ducks sensed the approach of the riders and took wing, he flung the falcon into the air after them. At first compressed like a ball bounding in space, the bird then spread its wings and darted forward.

"Now that was fast," Abai cried in delight.

Shakke was racing after him, beating the dabil* at his saddle with the handle of his whip. Frightened by the drumming, the ducks rose in a body. The falcon shot upwards like a lance hurled skywards and pounced upon the green and yellow drake flying above the others. It happened so quickly that Abai, speeding along with his chapan fluttering behind him, and shouting something, thought that the drake had dropped into the falcon's talons of its own accord. Clutching its prey by the breast, the falcon made several circles and descended to the grass in front of Shakke. Abai was overwhelmed. This had been even better than the fight with the two ducks.

"What a falcon! And some training! You're a real hunter, Shakke, as every djiguit should be," he said to the young man.

Ospan, who had remained preoccupied and glum during the exciting hunt, could not help laughing at Abai's boyish enthusiasm. The flattery left Shakke quite unruffled. His self-control, whether inborn or cultivated, was remarkable. And Abai looked upon his nephew's conduct with almost paternal pride.

The brothers were about to take leave of the young hunter when they saw Akilbai, Abai's elder son by Dilda, galloping towards them from the neighbouring aul. The boy resembled his father, though the whiteness of his skin

* Dabil—a small hunting drum.— Ed.

came from his mother. He presented his salem to Ospan
and gestured at the game, his face beaming.

"I was sent by Ani-apa,"* he began. "She saw you
hunting and asked you to send the game to our aul." He
brought his horse across the path of Shakke. "Will you
fasten those birds to my saddle, Shakke-aga?"

Shakke was raising the game to do as he was asked when
Ospan stopped him, saying:

"Hold on! I wouldn't give a feather to Nurganim, let
alone a fowl."

Abai was struck by the malice in his brother's voice.
Shakke was embarrassed.

"I didn't know you were so mean, Ospan-aga," Akilbai
blurted out on the verge of tears, and started his horse.

"Just a minute," Abai said. "What brought you here?"

"Mother sent the carriage to bring us to Akshoky, and so
we're all here—Abish, Magash and I," the boy retorted,
and set off for the aul at a gallop.

The head of his horse was graced with a plume of owl
feathers, the harness ornamented with silver. He wore a
sable hat, a cape of blue cloth with silver buttons and a
gilded belt studded with semi-precious stones. He was as
prettily dressed as a girl, a habit he had formed under
Nurganim's care. It was she who had reared Akilbai, as
though he were Kunanbai's youngest son. The boy had been
born when Abai was only seventeen, and he could not look
upon him as his father. Abai, for his part, regarded the boy
as a favourite younger brother rather than a son. And so the
incident, which made the youngster dash off in a huff, was
more like a quarrel between brothers. Abai felt upset by
Ospan's unexpected rudeness. The excitement of the hunt
was gone. With a brief farewell to Shakke, who was feeding
his falcon, Abai wheeled his horse and rode for Akshoky.
Ospan soon caught up with him.

"Why did you pounce on the boy?" Abai demanded.
"Losing your temper in front of children! Can you be
envious? Are you a man or not?"

Ospan had borne himself as his elder brother's equal all
day, but now he had been put in his place.

"You're right, I suppose," he mumbled contritely. "I just
lost my temper. Children should be kept out of this affair,
of course. But I've reason to be angry; I've been trying

---

* Ani-mother in Tartar, apa—the same in Kazakh. The combination
means elder mother.—*Ed.*

to tell you about it all day. My heart's been bleeding all these days. To think that we've lived to be disgraced like this!"

"Who is disgraced? What are you talking about?" Abai reined in his horse, fastening his eyes upon his younger brother. He was chilled with foreboding.

Ospan returned his gaze squarely, with lowering brows and an angry glint of red in his pupils.

"Nurganim is disgracing us," he snapped. "This tokal's dear guest, Bazaraly, has been living in Father's home for three days. They are defiling the bed of our father! I knew about it long ago, but I shall keep quiet no longer." Silent for an instant, he flared up again, "I'll have the two of them hanged from her own shanrak this very night, while Father's in the mourning yurta."

"Stop it!" Abai cried, gasping for breath. He felt as though he had been stabbed in the chest. His feet shook in the stirrups, anger choked him. "Is that the way to protect the honour of the family? That's ignorance, stupidity! How could you think of such a thing? I'll have *you* hanged from that shanrak. Father is nearer the grave than a walk to the hearth in a yurta. Are you trying to push him into his coffin stripped of all honour? Do you want to make his disgrace known to all the world, to throw his name to the dogs? Listen to me: let your tongue and your hands be tied!"

Giving his horse the full measure of his whip, he flew on towards Akshoky. The sun was setting and the edge of the sky was scarlet. Abai would not spare his horse, for a storm raged in his heart.

He was furious with Nurganim who had lost all shame, with Ospan who was so ready to expose his father's disgrace, and with Bazaraly. "Ah, Bazaraly, you were the only man whom I held in such high regard, but now you've become a stranger." It was long since Abai had been so shaken. Resentment, pity, rage, shame and bitterness raced over the steppes with him, each more painful than the lash of a whip. He did not know what to think, what to do....

He suddenly remembered the Russian book he had finished this morning.... *Dubrovsky*! The feuds handed on from father to son, the generations stricken with blood and strife. He remembered Bazaraly's relatives who had always suffered at the hands of Kunanbai's kinsmen. The image of the old and dying Dubrovsky, crushed by Troyekurov, flashed into his mind. And Vladimir? He too was engaged in the feud, but had found salvation in his love for Masha. Was

Bazaraly really to blame? The truth of art merged with the
cruel truth of life.

He had to find the way out, he had to act as a man of
honour. Spurring his horse, he seemed to be spurring his
thoughts as well. In his mind Kunanbai, Nurganim and
Bazaraly were identified with Troyekurov, Vladimir and
Masha. He saw no way out!

Abai reached his aul at dusk. Everything was quiet and no
one came out to meet him. There were no children about
and the workmen too were gone, having ridden off to visit
their relatives in Korik. Abai rode up to his yurta at a
walking pace, dismounted, and was about to enter when he
heard someone singing softly, a song that floated on the
evening air like a silk thread. Afraid that it would break off
at his intrusion, Abai sat down on the grass near the door.
Only Zlikha, who was sitting outside by the fire, noticed him
and, getting up quickly, come over to him.

"Sh.... Aigerim is singing a good song," he whispered to
her. "Don't go in now. Let's listen."

"But I was going to light the lamps," she answered.

"Never mind the lamps. You'll interrupt the song."

Zlikha smiled understandingly and returned to the fire.

Abai removed his timak, unbuttoned the shirt under his
chapan and exposed his chest to the evening breeze as he sat
listening. Aigerim, left unexpectedly alone, was singing by
the bedside of her first-born, Turash.

She sang the sad *Karagoz* (*Dark Eyes*), one of Birzhan's
songs. The high, pure voice vibrated over the stillness of the
evening. She was singing in an undertone and this made the
melody even more moving and tender.

> *My dark-eyed beauty, when I leave*
> *Her far, so very far behind,*
> *I am disconsolate, and she?*
> *Does she our parting also mind?*

This refrain was especially moving. She was improvis-
ing and singing some of the lines in her own way. In this
evening hour, the time of prayers and supplication, she
merged her own sadness and Abai's grief in one melody.

Abai had not heard her sing for a long time. When
Kunanbai returned from Mecca, they had to conceal the fact
that one of his daughters-in-law was a singer, for worldly
enjoyments were obnoxious to him. To make matters worse,
Dilda had been doing her best to turn the kinsmen against
Aigerim, and Abai was frequently rebuked by his relatives

for his wife's singing. Even when she sang softly to him alone, in response to his pleadings, it somehow became known in Kunanbai's aul and caused fresh trouble. Singing was no longer a pleasure to her, but a torment. Aigerim, therefore, often begged Abai not to make her sing, and he could not but agree, though he felt that in this he was helping his family to stifle her rare talent.

Every time he played a tune on his dombra, Aigerim paled, her beautiful eyes filling with tears. Abai tried not to show that he had noticed, and would go on playing, hoping to comfort her without words.

But one evening this winter, when Abai had been playing longer than usual, Aigerim's deep sigh made him lay his instrument aside.

"What troubles you, Aigerim?"

A hot tear fell on his hand as he embraced her.

"You were my nightingale," he said sadly. "Your free voice soaring freely could enchant anyone, touch every heart. I have turned out to be a bird-catcher. I caught a nightingale and locked it in a gilded cage. It is not the aul alone that has stifled your song and buried your talent, I too am to blame."

And now, today, he sat listening to the voice of his caged nightingale who was afraid to sing too loudly. Aigerim imparted many new undertones to the melody of *Karagoz*, each of them vibrant with a meaning of its own. Now it was a mother's tenderness, now anxiety, now happiness, and now a deep love for Abai. It was the sorrowful confession of a grief-laden heart, sad as a mother's lament, and Abai grew oblivious to the world.

Aigerim sang for a long time, as if unable to part with this song, her only companion in the cage that kept her prisoner. Abai entered the yurta only when the darkness was complete and the song was over. Aigerim was startled and embarrassed.

"When did you come?" she asked, rising quickly.

"While Turash was still awake, and the dark-eyed beauty was in the yurta," he laughed.

Zlikha came in and lit the lamps. Abai seated himself beside his wife.

"This is what I thought of while I was listening," he said. "You'll go to Takezhan's aul tomorrow for the mourning. I have heard Karazhan's lament today and I must say that though she is Makulbai's mother, she cannot sing her grief. Listening to your song, I thought of some words, I'll write

them down for you to learn. You've been singing *Karagoz* in
your own way and I think it will suit my new, mournful
words as well." He reached for pen and paper.

Abai reflected, searching for the words, now and then
glancing at Aigerim's delicate features. He had been moved
by her song and was now convinced that she was more than
a singer; she herself could give birth to new melodies.
Watching his hand on the paper, she was full of awe,
realising that a new song was coming into being. A smile
hovered about her lips. It was an evening of inspiration, an
evening of melody. When the lament was ready, Abai read it
to her.

> *The finest of the falcon's young*
> *A wicked hunter has shot down;*
> *The tallest tree that reached the sun*
> *Was struck by lightning, gone its crown;*
> *The proudest horse that had no twin*
> *Was maimed — of tail and mane completely shorn.*
> *You were the joy of all your kin,*
> *And yet you left them, never to return.*
> *Your light, before it fully glowed, went out.*
> *How sore the wound of early death!*
> *The sunrays warm the soil, but then the sprouts*
> *Are killed by winter's angry breath.*
> *Death knows no pity in its greed,*
> *All living things it will devour.*
> *We are bereft, our hearts with sorrow bleed,*
> *Our tears we cannot stem, oh cruel hour!*
> *With all the gifts you were endowed,*
> *You were so gentle and so wise,*
> *And here you lie beneath the shroud,*
> *In sleep eternal closed your eyes....*

Full of maternal love herself, Aigerim had felt poignant
sorrow over Makulbai's death and Abai's words now
brought tears to her eyes.

She had a good memory and quickly learned the words
her husband read out to her.

On the very next day, Abai, Aigerim and Zlikha took a
remembrance gift with them and went to Takezhan's aul.
Aigerim began the lament in a high voice as they
approached the yurta of mourning. The tent was as
crowded as on the day before. Aigerim seated herself in a
place lower than that of Karazhan and continued her song
with her hands on her knees. The elders, including

Kunanbai, listened attentively. The bitter words on the death of a child and the melancholy tune composed by Aigerim touched every heart. The sobbing that had subsided after the general lamentation broke forth afresh.

"My little lamb, light of my eyes," Ulzhan chanted, overcome.

Even the men could not hold back their tears and wept with the rest, singing the melancholy words under their breath. Aigerim's voice not only stirred up the grief that Abai felt over the death of Makulbai, but all the past sorrows that lay dormant within him, and he too wept with the others. The general grief seemed to have found expression in Aigerim's voice, and the sobbing continued even when the Koran was being read.

"Let this daughter-in-law mourn over my boy until the fortieth day," said Kunanbai to Ulzhan when the mourners had somewhat composed themselves. "Let her stay here as long as mourners shall come."

He had anticipated Ulzhan's silent wish. Aigerim did not return to Akshoky. Sitting beside Karazhan, she poured forth the lamentations of a mother.

2

Kunanbai stayed in Takezhan's aul until the end of the memorial week. Bazaraly was still Nurganim's guest, and though it had aroused no talk, Ospan grew increasingly restless. His hatred for Nurganim mounted until it burst into flame.

Bazaraly had come to the aul just before Makulbai's death to salem Kunanbai on the occasion of his return from Mecca. In conversation with Nurganim, Kunanbai had often said it was a pity that so intelligent and strong-willed a man should have been born in a poor family, and had he been the son of a stronger man, he could have been the pride of his clan.

Since her husband treated Bazaraly with such distinction, Nurganim felt she did not have to conceal her sympathy for the djiguit. Her manner was unconstrained, though rumours about Ospan's irritation had reached her more than once. She received Bazaraly as her most honoured guest, rather pointedly so.

On his way to the well on the day after the falcon hunt, Ospan passed Kunanbai's yurta and overheard Nurganim and Bazaraly laughing. This was the last straw.

"Clear out of here," he pounced on the servant woman who was drawing the water. "There's no water for Nurganim here. I won't have my well befouled. Go back to her and tell her this: I'll break the head of anyone who comes to fetch water for her."

He kept returning to the well on his horse to see if his orders were obeyed, and Nurganim's aul was unable to get water for an entire day. Towards evening, however, Ospan noticed two women leading a camel carrying a barrel of water obviously brought from the river. He promptly fell upon the camel and overturned the barrel.

"Tell your mistress there shall be no water while Bazaraly is her guest," he shouted. "Let her remember who she is before she comes to some harm!"

Ospan continued to guard the river and the well even at night. Wild with anger, he completely overlooked the fact that his conduct would in itself give rise to gossip.

Nurganim's aul faced a second day without water. Ospan's hostility had come into the open and a clash was imminent. Nurganim was no less angry than Ospan and far from sending Bazaraly away, she did not even tell him about Ospan's behaviour. She went about the aul with an angry scoul on her preoccupied face, but the moment she re-entered the yurta she assumed a carefree attitude and put on a radiant smile. She redoubled her attentions to the guest and there was no end to her cheerful and winning words for him. Bazaraly was perfectly aware of what was happening outside, but pretended to notice nothing. He admired Nurganim's poise and was secretly amused, wondering what would happen next.

By the time of the midday meal, Nurganim had found a way out which no other woman would have taken. The aul stood in the midst of moist grass, a sure sign that a well could be sunk here. Summoning three djiguits to the Kitchen Yurta, she ordered her maid to clear a space in the middle of the yurta near the hearth.

"Dig a well right here," she commanded briefly.

The djiguits fell to with a will, while Nurganim watched smiling, her slightly protuberant brown eyes twinkling merrily.

"Ospan is too sure of himself. Won't he be angry when he finds he's been fooled! Dig as quickly as you can, and then get the tea prepared."

She went out, stalking through the aul, her stately figure erect, her sholpy tinkling in her heavy braids as if laughing

at Ospan. The women of both auls marvelled at her
audacity. This was a direct challenge to Ospan and all the
gossips.

But Ospan retaliated unexpectedly and cruelly by placing
Bazaraly in the hands of his enemies.

The election of the volost rulers was then being held on
the cool and spacious Yeraly, some fifteen versts from
Kunanbai's aul. More than a hundred auls had come to the
district: Bokenshi, Zhigitek, Irgizbai, Kotibak and the
numerous clans of the Mamai which had been wintering on
the Orda Mountain. It was indeed the most convenient time
and place for the election. An even row of thirty new tents
had been set up for the expected authorities and the elders
of the clans. The election this time was not to be supervised
by a mere local chief and his officials, but by Koshkin, the
chief of Semipalatinsk District. It was rumoured that he had
arrived not only for the elections, but also to investigate
some important case.

He came accompanied by the local chiefs of both volosts
and a large number of policemen and guards. There was a
long train of carriage with tinkling bells. Shabarmans * with
bags slung over their shoulders and guards with bared
sabres in their hands rode at the head and the sides of the
procession. While still on his way to the election, Koshkin
had ordered two volost elders of Kzil-Adir and Chinghis,
who had come to meet him, to be publicly whipped. The
news of this had travelled before him and those who were
gathered in Yeraly referred to Koshkin only as Tentek-
Oyaz.**

Abai was in Akshoky when a messenger arrived from
Zhirenshe and Asilbek asking him to come to Yeraly as
quickly as possible; evil days lay ahead. Another message
arrived from Abilgazy. The chiefs were there to investigate
the case of Oralbai, and Bazaraly had been seized in
Nurganim's aul and arrested.

Oralbai, the younger brother of Bazaraly, fell in love with
Sugir's beautiful daughter Korimbala, who had already
been promised in marriage to a man of the Karakesek clan.
After an unsuccessful attempt to elope with Korimbala,
Oralbai had vanished without a trace.

Abai mounted at once and asked Yerbol to come with
him.

---

 * Shabarman—messenger.— *Ed.*
 ** Oyaz—chief; tentek-oyaz—angry chief.— *Ed.*

On arrival in Yeraly, they went to the yurtas set up for the authorities, expecting to find Zhirenshe there. The Great Aul of zhataks, of no less than forty yurtas, stood nearby. This settlement differed sharply from the others as it lacked the usual large herds. Though it was the largest in the valley, this aul had no tethering posts for foals, nor were there any sheep droppings to be seen on the kotan. Only a few clusters of animals could be seen grazing here and there. The small yurtas covered with sooty and patched felt stood huddled together. Dire need was in evidence everywhere. Early in spring, Dandibai and Yerenai, two old men of this aul, aptly called Kop-zhatak,* had come to Akshoky to tell Abai of the poverty of their aul and to ask for help.

"Look at this wretchedness," Abai said to Yerbol when he saw the aul. He pointed to the shanties and tents, very small and more like piles of rubbish than human dwellings. The spaces between them were cluttered with old coffers, hearth tripods, shabby saddles and broken beds.

"Let's turn off the road here, to see what has happened," suggested Abai, and veered towards the afflicted aul.

An old man, in a ragged chekmen** that barely covered his naked body, came to meet them, leaning on a long staff. His face was deeply lined, and to his astonishment Abai saw that it was Darkembai.

"I didn't know you had come to live in Kop-zhatak, Darkembai," he said after greeting the old man.

Darkembai did not answer at once. It was only when the younger men had dismounted and followed him to the nearest shanty that the old man said sadly:

"You could not have known. I have not been here long, but here I shall probably stay until I die. Here are about forty beggars such as I. I have worked for Suyundik and Sugir all my life, but do you think either of them have ever said, 'When you were strong, you held my soeel, watched over my goods and guarded my herds in the winter. And now that you are old and weak, you'll be taken care of. You've earned an untroubled old age by your labours.' No, our ways have parted and I thought it better to live with others than to roam the steppes alone with a saddle on my back."

"Haven't you any relatives here?" asked Yerbol. "You know the old saying: 'Even if it's poison that your kin drink,

* Kop-zhatak—a host of zhataks.—Ed.
** Chekmen—a light coat closely fitting at the waist.—Ed.

drink it with them.' Why have you gone away from them and to whom have you come?"

There was a reproach in Yerbol's words. Both Darkembai and Yerbol belonged to the Bokenshi clan.

"My kin are right here, in these forty households," he answered, his eyes still on Abai. "We are not related by blood, perhaps, but we have been drawn together by our common sorrows and common troubles."

"What do you mean?" asked Yerbol, puzzled.

Darkembai smiled bitterly and pointed to the shanties with his staff, as he explained in a weary voice:

"These people here come from the Anet and Karabatir. All the year round they used to herd the cattle of the rich Irgizbais and also of your father, in Kunkeh's aul. Those over there used to toil for Bozhei, Baidaly, Baisal and Tusip. We've all had our share of misery, living with kinsmen. They too have been abandoned to their fate, and are beggars like me. They and their families did all the hard work around the yurtas of the bais, like their parents, grandparents and great-grandparents before them. That is why we are kinsmen all. Just look at us. Here am I, old Darkembai, and there is Dandibai, just as withered as I, and the aged Yerenai. We're all sick old men with not a single grown-up son between us to take care of us. Some are younger than us, but many are cripples, or their wives are, or else their children are sickly. And why? Because they never spared themselves in the frosts and the blizzards, because they lost their strength working for the bais. And what for? For an extra ladle of shurpa. Just come into these yurtas and take a look. Some are weak with old age and some have wasted away while still young; some have a pain in the chest and others an ache in the back; some are lame and others blind and many others bedridden. Our yurtas are bad and our lives are as bad. Everything here is poor, shabby and worn out. The bais have cast us out like so much rubbish. We could no longer follow the herds and flocks of Kunanbai, Bozhei, Baisal, Suyundik, Sugir and Karatai, and so they had no more need of us—no more than for an old saddle or leaky pail."

The old man smiled helplessly.

"You, Yerbol, have said that: 'Even if it's poison that your kin drink, drink it with them.' These people here are my kinsmen. We have the same life and the same thoughts.'

Abai listened with aching heart. He frowned, and fidgeted with his timak, unable to sit still.

"Our people have fallen on evil days," he said, when Darkembai had finished. "And you've become as sharp-sighted as a falcon. There are many glib-tongued windbags among us Kazakhs. Their tongues are oily and their speech is as smooth as a fast ambler, but what's the good of it? Words should be judged by the truth they contain. Those were bitter things you said just now, but true. What could Kunanbai and Suyundik say in reply? You've nailed them down properly and you've opened my eyes too."

They were joined by several others, among them Dandibai and Yerenai, old men whom Abai knew, some middle-aged men with haggard, grey faces, and glum young djiguits. Abilgazy, who had come to visit his friends, also approached, salemed Abai and took a place near him. Meanwhile, many more people came crawling out of the shanties and the heaps of sooty felt scraps.

"What has happened here? Was it a hurricane? Why were so many families left without shelter, old people and children?" Abai asked Darkembai, pointing to them.

"You've guessed right, my dear Abai," Dandibai answered. "It was a hurricane sent not by God but by the authorities, by the volost ruler." The old man smiled grimly. "Do you see those yurtas near the white yurtas of the chiefs?"

Until then Abai and Yerbol had not noticed the small, sooty yurtas near the festive white tents. They huddled so close together as though whispering secrets to each other.

"The white yurtas for the chiefs to live in and our yurtas to humiliate us with," Dandibai explained with an oath.

"What humiliations are you talking about?" Yerbol demanded.

There was a hubbub of voices:

"Our yurtas have been taken from us for the prisoners."

"And others have been taken as kitchens."

"Kitchens are not so bad. They've turned our yurtas into lavatories. The whole of Yeraly is not enough for them."

"The volost ruler and those scoundrel elders are to blame."

"The devil knows when we'll be rid of that pack of dogs."

"The old people, children and cripples sit about in rags with no place to lay their heads."

"But why did you give up your yurtas?" Abai looked at the crowd, puzzled. "Let them take the expenses upon themselves!"

All tried to answer at once.

"Oi-bai, oi-bai! What are you saying!"

"What could we do about it?"

"They don't let us say a word!"

"They are not shabarmans, but real sabarmans." *

Abai looked at the ravaged homes. Two babies wrapped in an old chekmen lay among the old coffers and bundles. Both looked very ill; their matted hair hung over their pale foreheads and dim eyes, and flies clung to their parched lips.

"Good God! Leaving those poor children to be eaten by the flies!" Abai gasped. "Where is your old courage, Darkembai? You should have kicked those shabarmans away!"

Darkembai smiled bitterly.

"My dear Abai. That's just what we did, and it only made things worse." He then related what had happened on the eve of the elections.

On his way to Kunanbai's aul, Bazaraly had stayed with him for a time ten days before. Despite the great difference in their ages, these two resembled each other in boldness and sharpness of opinions and were good friends.

"He's like the leader of a pack of wolves lost in the steppes," Darkembai said. "He's not like our djiguits nowadays. I couldn't help pouring out my heart to him."

During his three days' stay, Bazaraly visited every single yurta. He called on the sick, talked to the others and gave what advice he could. He would sing or tell funny stories to give them heart and cheer them up, and thus came to be a real friend of this paupers' aul.

He told them that such auls as theirs could be found everywhere. In other places, people who were cast out by their clans, were raising grain; they subsisted on this all year round, working for themselves and not for the bais.

"You, too, should learn to feed on the breast of mother earth," he urged. "Let two or three families get together, plough a plot of land, if only a desiatine, and in the spring sow grain. In the summertime you can turn to haymaking. Look at all those unused meadows and autumn pastures! Even if you have only one scythe between you, you'll make plenty of hay. The town is not far and you can sell it at the market and buy what you need with the money. Your own father could not find a better spot for you to live in!

"What else can you do? You've been deluding yourselves

* Sabarman—tormentor, robber.— *Ed.*

with empty hopes all your lives, using up all your strength. There were many of you who thought the kinsmen would never let you starve, that they would be sure to help. And yet they were cast out. Forget the tribal cries of the Zhigitek or the Bokenshi. You have but one cry now: 'Zhatak of Yeraly!' You are the closest kinsmen now, people sharing the same life, destiny and faith. The main thing is to hold together."

Now Darkembai continued his story. The shabarmans had come galloping to Yeraly on the day that Bazaraly was to leave. Caravans of white yurtas had arrived with many flocks of sheep for slaughter. The shabarmans had been sent by Takezhan and Maibasar with the following message: "Trouble coming! The district oyaz is on his way here. Set up the yurtas!"

Bazaraly and Abilgazy were sitting in Darkembai's yurta when the shabarmans fell upon their aul like an invading enemy.

"Where is Darkembai?" shouted three of them from their horses, as they flew to Darkembai's yurta.

Bazaraly gave Abilgazy a wink.

"Keep quiet," he said to Darkembai. "We'll see what happens."

"Come out at once. Who do you think you are!" the shabarmans yelled, maddened by the delay. "The volost rulers are pressing us and now you, too, are making trouble, you cursed beggar."

"Hei, djiguits, where are you from?" Bazaraly called calmly from the yurta. "Dismount and come in for a talk."

Lashing away, the shabarmans drove their horses against the yurta. "Come out at once, do you hear!" they shouted, swearing foully.

Their heavy whips descended on the yurta, setting the uiks groaning. Infuriated, Darkembai leapt from the tent, but found himself caught in a shower of blows. Bazaraly and Abilgazy bounded out of the yurta like a pair of tigers springing from the thickets. Bazaraly pulled two of the shabarmans to the ground, while Abilgazy unhorsed the third.

"Sitting on their heads, the two pulled up the shabarmans' chapans and flogged them with their own whips," Darkembai related gleefully. "All the zhataks were there to see and were greatly pleased, for here was someone at last, man enough to defend them. And Bazaraly kept whipping the cursed shabarmans until the handle of the whip came off."

"But how did they get the yurtas after all?" asked Yerbol.

Darkembai told it briefly: when the shabarmans went away, the zhataks thought their worries were over. Bazaraly stayed with them two more days, but when he left about thirty men came galloping to the aul—the shabarmans, headed by the volost ruler and the elders. They dismantled the yurtas in a trice and took them away.

"They're robbers, all right," concluded Darkembai. "The curs! They'd dig graves for their own fathers if their chiefs told them to. Ah, Abai, I'm not the Darkembai that I once was. Couldn't you put in a word for us, light of my eyes? Make them return our yurtas. Can't those swine set up their kitchens and lavatories some place else?"

"Make them, make them!" clamoured the zhataks. "Don't let them trample on us!"

Abai rose, brushed the dust off his coat, and stood for an instant with his whip doubled against his side.

"Let's go. You too, Abilgazy!"

Leading his horse by the reins, he set off at the head of the zhataks. It was about a verst to the white yurtas, and as they passed through the aul they were joined by more and more men who had crawled out of the heaps of rubbish and dirty shanties. Some were young and strong, others old and feeble, and all of them were grimly silent and determined.

On their way, Abilgazy whispered to Abai that the zhataks knew nothing of Bazaraly's arrest. The biys were afraid of general unrest. It was with Takezhan's help that he had been arrested. Takezhan had come to Yeraly a few days before and, frightened by the news of Koshkin's arbitrary punishments, had decided to hand in Bazaraly himself.

Three of the most ornate hexagonal yurtas had been put together in the centre of the election aul. The entrance to the big tent was flanked by ominously silent guards, while messengers were hurrying to and fro with a preoccupied air or tiptoeing in and out. It was evident that the great man in the triple tent was in bad humour.

As soon as Abai approached the white yurtas, he was met by Zhirenshe, Urazbai and Asilbek, who took him aside and told him all the news, interrupting one another and each adding his bit. This is what Abai gathered from their stories.

Koshkin had come to Yeraly with a group of Naiman plaintiffs. They claimed that horse-thieves of the Tobikty, headed by Oralbai, had driven some horses away from one of their richest auls.

After losing Korimbala, Oralbai had vanished and never came back to Tobikty again. For a long time nothing was heard of him. Now it had become known that the embittered djiguit had gathered a band of accomplices, armed them with rifles and organised the stealing of horses all that year not only from the Naiman and the neighbouring Kerei and Siban, but also from the Tobikty. The band was hiding among the crowded auls of the poor Kerei.

In all the complaints Oralbai was named as the head of the gang, which was apparently determined to ruin those who were rich, influential and held official positions, for the horses were taken only from the richest auls. The complaints had already gone through all the offices of both the Semipalatinsk and Dzhetisuisk districts— the gang operated on the border between them—until they had reached the office of the zhandaral, the general who ran the gubernia. But Oralbai was so vengeful and desperately brave that he was not even intimidated by the tsar's troops. Late that winter he had enticed a detachment sent from Semipalatinsk to catch him into the wildness of the steppe and there, at one of their bivouacs, made off with all their horses. The forty soldiers had had to wander on foot through the steppes for days without food or water. Then there was another charge against him, one which Zhirenshe and Urazbai were inclined to ridicule, whereas Asilbek anticipated grave consequences. On the high road, between Ayaguz and Shubaragash, a local chief from Semipalatinsk accompanied by two guardsmen had been waylaid and robbed. The Naiman put the blame for this on Oralbai too.

The claims were evidently developing into a serious, involved case seeing that Koshkin had arrived in person to investigate. The five Naiman with him were both plaintiffs and witnesses, and they refused to leave the Tentek-Oyaz's yurta and negotiate with the Tobikty in the Kazakh manner. Bazaraly's name must have figured in the complaints, for Tentek-Oyaz had ordered the three biys to arrest him and his brother. "That scoundrel Oralbai belongs to your tribe!" he had repeated again and again. "Are you trying to shield an offender against the tsar? All of you—the volost ruler, his deputy, you biys and you elders will stand trial for this."

"This is where we disagreed with Takezhan," Zhirenshe explained. "We wanted to answer like this: 'We know nothing about Oralbai. He is an outcast and a tramp, and neither the people nor Bazaraly have any idea where he is. Find him yourselves and do what you like with him. The

Tobikty won't support him.' We had agreed with Takezhan and Maibasar yesterday to give this answer, but towards evening Darkhan came galloping to the volost ruler. He had been sent by Ospan who must have quarrelled with Bazaraly, because this is what he advised Takezhan: 'Clear yourself as best you can and let them have Bazaraly. He's in my hands.' Takezhan sent the shabarman Zhumbagul with four guardsmen to Korik, where they seized Bazaraly and turned him over to the authorities. He's either being interrogated now or is already locked up somewhere. Takezhan accuses us of shielding him. That is why we wanted you. Tell us what to do. Shall we defend Bazaraly or denounce him?"

Abai knew better than did the others that the tangle would not be easy to unravel. The menace from outside seemed more ominous than the inner strife fanned by Ospan. It was Asilbek who spoke first.

"The oyaz has not yet begun the elections though the people have gathered long ago. He seems to have got his teeth into Oralbai's case, interrogating countless people. He takes to task all those who speak against the volost ruler, and simply beats up anyone who tells the truth to his face. Some of the witnesses have said that we are shielding Bazaraly. If Takezhan says so too, our troubles will really begin. If we try to help Bazaraly, who is innocent, and tell the truth, what will happen to us? Dare we stop the tongues of the malicious? We haven't been troubled so far, but what will happen if we side with Bazaraly? What do you think we ought to do?"

Abai still did not answer.

"We have told you how things stand," said Urazbai, "and will do whatever you say. How can we keep our honour and avoid trouble? The three of us will go with you. Just tell us what to do."

Just then several shabarmans shot out from the triple yurta, brandishing their whips and yelling:

"Zhirenshe Shokin! Asilbek Suyundikov! Urazbai Akkulov! You're wanted by the oyaz!"

"They've called our names," said Zhirenshe to Abai impatiently.

Abai glanced at the three and clenched his fist.

"Mind you don't lose your wits from fright," he told them. "Zhirenshe's way was the best. Keep Bazaraly out of this. Let the oyaz hunt for Oralbai himself. His halter is longer than ours. If the evidence you give differs from

Takezhan's, we'll find a way out. I do not know why he is so savage, but it is better to be buried alive than to bring trouble to the entire people. Remember that if you involve Bazaraly, you will be admitting the guilt of the entire tribe."

The three biys were led to the chief by the guards. Abai beckoned to the shabarman in the rear.

"Watch how the oyaz treats them, and let me know," he whispered to him. "I entrust this task to you alone, you understand."

The shabarman was a local djiguit who knew Abai very well. Though forbidding in the presence of his superiors, he nodded understandingly, proud of Abai's trust.

"Send messengers to the auls," Abai instructed Yerbol and Abilgazy. "I want all the men to come here right away, on horseback and on foot. And meanwhile go and call all the servants—old and young, men and women, stablemen, water-carriers, cooks, anyone you meet, and be quick about it."

Abai himself stayed to wait where Zhirenshe and his friends had left him.

People began to gather round the election yurtas. With whips and shouts the guards and shabarmans chased them off. They retreated only a little and stopped there. Bazaraly was innocent, of course, they were sorry for him, and they all hated Takezhan. Most of the onlookers were poorly dressed. Among them were the zhataks who had come with Abai. The news of Bazaraly's arrest had reached them at last and now they stood about murmuring and glancing furtively at Abai, who waited silently.

The shabarman to whom Abai had spoken returned and said a few words to him in an undertone. Abai then made his way to the edge of the crowd where Darkembai, Abilgazy and Yerbol stood.

"I'm going to the yurta of the oyaz," he said to them. "Zhirenshe and the other biys are being questioned. Bazaraly is also there. The chief, I hear, likes to whip and humiliate people. If he starts that now, it will be an insult to us. I will not have Bazaraly or Asilbek so much as touched with the end of a whip. Stay where you are. We cannot let them brand the innocent as a criminal. Yerbol and Abilgazy will come with me."

The three made for the entrance of the triple yurta.

Abai's words quickly spread through the crowd, bringing a look of determination into the faces of the djiguits, of the old men and the zhataks.

There were only armed guards, policemen and clerks, in
the first of the three united yurtas, and none of the local
people. Interrogations were conducted in the adjacent
section, where the chiefs sat facing the door at a table
covered with green silk. The chief interrogator was
Tentek-Oyaz Koshkin, a thin, slight man with a drooping,
colourless moustache, and a cold and sullen look. As Abai
entered, he was shouting at Urazbai and stamping his feet.
A fat cross-eyed interpreter stood at his side, his head
attentively inclined.

Either because his dignity was outraged by Koshkin's
rudeness or because he had seen Abai through the open
door, Urazbai assumed his usual superior air and addressed
the interpreter in a loud voice:

"Tell the oyaz this. I am not Oralbai. I am neither the
culprit nor the defendant. Zhirenshe and Asilbek have
spoken truly, and I can only say the same. Nobody here can
be held responsible for Oralbai. Not just the tribe, his own
father and mother cannot hold answer for a man who
disappeared more than a year ago. If anyone is answerable,
it is the authorities who have been unable to track him
down. Bazaraly has nothing to do with it either. If our volost
ruler Takezhan brings Bazaraly into this, we, the biys,
cannot support him. Bazaraly is innocent. Instead of
shouting at me, the oyaz would do better to consult the local
people and do his job. Tell him exactly what I have said."

"Good for him," Abai whispered to Yerbol and Abilgazy.
He stood at the entrance of the central yurta to hear how all
this would be translated. The guards barred his way.

"Who are you? Keep out!"

"Don't shout at me! I want to see the chief Koshkin," Abai
answered in Russian.

The guards refused to budge, but an official who
happened to be standing near was surprised to hear Russian
words from a steppe Kazakh and scrutinised Abai with
interest.

"What can we do for you?" he asked. "Who are you?"

Abai doffed his timak and bowed politely.

"I am Ibragim Kunanbayev, a man of the people," he said
and raised his eyes hopefully.

The other smiled and pushing the guards aside came
forward.

"So you are Ibragim Kunanbayev. I know quite a lot
about you," he said, extending his hand. "Your friend
Akbas Andreyevich, as you call him, had told me a great

deal about you. This is really a pleasure. Permit me to introduce myself: Counsellor Losovsky."

"What's happening in there?" Abai asked, shaking his hand. "It is an affront to us, the people."

"I quite understand you," Losovsky said with a fleeting grimace of distaste, as he bent over confidentially. "Not only do the people resent it, but it is quite useless too. Riding rough-shod over people will never get us anywhere. But what's to be done? Everyone acts in his own way." The man actually flushed with annoyance and as if to spite the other officials who were looking at them with a shade of scorn, he gestured to the guards to admit Abai into the central yurta.

The interpreter had just finished translating Urazbai's words and the Tentek-Oyaz was shouting, "I'll show you how innocent they are." He motioned to the two guards who at once flung Bazaraly to the ground and got busy with their whips.

"Stop it at once. How dare you!" shouted Abai rushing in. The guards lowered their whips in astonishment, and Koshkin sprang from his seat as though he had been stung.

"Who are you? Who has let you in?" He glared at Abai, his moustache trembling. Abai, who was taller than Koshkin, looked down on him accusingly, his face white with emotion.

"I'm just a man and you are behaving like a brute," he said in Russian. "Stop this outrage at once!"

"Whip him, don't stand there gaping!" Koshkin shrieked to the flabbergasted guards. "And as for you, I'll have you locked up," he hissed, nearly jabbing his finger into Abai's eye.

Heedless of Abai's shouts, the guards resumed the beating. This was not enough for the Tentek-Oyaz, however.

"Twenty-five lashes! Thirty! Fifty!" he yelled to the guards, pointing in turn to Zhirenshe, Asilbek and Urazbai.

Abai was livid with rage. He was no longer merely seething with indignation, he was thirsting for a fight, and was ready for anything, however desperate.

"Very well! Just remember you'll have no one to blame but yourself!" he shouted to Koshkin and rushed for the exit.

Losovsky, coming into the yurta, almost collided with him at the door. Abai's angry cries clearly showed him that the patience of the people was at an end.

"Enough of your outrages, Koshkin!" His fist thundered on the table. "This is a terrible mistake. Tell those men to stop."

Koshkin was at a loss for an answer and the raised whips froze in the air. Meanwhile, Bazaraly sprang to his feet.

"Look out, Takezhan, we're enemies now!" he shouted to Takezhan, who had backed away in fright against the Russian officials. "It's not me they were beating, but my honour! You'll pay for this if I live."

Abai's voice came to them from the outer section.

"Yerbol and Abilgazy, bring the people here. Break down the yurtas."

The crowd seemed to have been waiting for the signal. Short bludgeons and heavy whips appeared in a flash, and the words "Break them down" were hardly out of Darkembai's mouth when many hands, bludgeons and whips struck at the yurtas, raising clouds of dust. The wooden frames creaked as if lashed by a storm. One of the policemen fired into the air, the bullet striking the shanrak of the central yurta. The guards followed his example. But by now the Tentek-Oyaz had pulled himself together and ordered the shooting to be stopped. Some of the old men had shrunk back nervously. But Abai, the only Kazakh who understood the oyaz's words, called through the door, "Don't be afraid. They won't dare to shoot again!" His words were echoed by Yerbol, Darkembai and Abilgazy.

"Don't be afraid. Overturn the yurtas! Break them down!"

The crowd, with the zhataks in the lead, hurled themselves against the side of the outer yurta, breaking the keregehs and uiks. The yurta sank in and collapsed.

As the administrators retreated in a panic to the rear yurta, Abai sprang to Bazaraly's side and seized him by the sleeve.

"Go now!"

Bazaraly gained the ruins of the outer yurta with one leap, closely followed by Asilbek, Zhirenshe and Urazbai. All four quickly vanished in the crowd, while more and more people, led by Darkembai, Abilgazy and Yerbol, pushed their way into the central yurta. None of the three leaders had ever been a biy or an elder, but all spoke and acted with authority, for the wave of the people's wrath had swept them above the others. The Tentek-Oyaz winced at every shout—they were showering him and Takezhan with demands. Abai now kept aloof, leaving the crowd to exact justice by itself.

"We won't let you hold those elections!" the three shouted. "You haven't come here to hold elections, but to ruin us. Go away and be quick about it. Nobody here will obey you."

With this, they withdrew into the crowd, but loud voices could still be heard, now here, now there.

"Take your yurtas down and go home!"

"Let the Tentek-Oyaz stick here by himself!"

"And his lickspittles too!"

"Get out of the valley, every one of you!"

"Take your yurtas back, zhataks!"

"Go home with your things and to the devil with the chiefs!"

"Let them sit in the open if they like!"

Then things moved quickly. The yurtas set up for the elections disappeared except for the two where the administrators were huddled. People were dismantling their yurtas everywhere.

The zhataks were the first to leave, but that was not all. The herds too were driven from zhailyau.

The seat of power, which had commanded fear throughout the Yeraly a few hours before, was now empty steppeland again. The sumptuous aul had vanished. A heavy wave of popular anger had swept it away, leaving only the debris of keregehs and uiks and two crooked yurtas like bubbles on a pool after rain.

The Tentek-Oyaz and his suite were in an absurd position. Helpless and disgraced, they were left alone amid the steppes. Not a soul was to be seen anywhere. Losovsky came out of the yurta, shaking his head and laughing.

"There's not even a mongrel left about."

Koshkin thoughtfully paced to and fro outside the tent. He knew that he had gone too far, that he had himself alone to blame, but he was seething with impotent rage. Losovsky, for his part, was cool and unperturbed.

"I've known the Kirghiz steppes for many years, but have never seen the people here acting so unanimously," he dryly observed. "That will be a good lesson to you. Your methods are unpardonable. You savagely abused the men they've elected and punished them for nothing. Of course there had to be an outburst. You asked for it! I'm sorry, but I cannot keep quiet about the things I've seen. We'll talk about it in town."

The Tentek-Oyaz had nothing to say to this, only waved his hand and looked away.

Only Takezhan, his two messengers and two elders stayed with the Russian officials, but the erstwhile formidable volost ruler was now utterly helpless. He could not procure a pinch of tea, a handful of baursaks, a crumb of cheese, or even a sip of water.

The elections had been disrupted and it was useless to try to gather the people again. There was nothing to do but to return to Semipalatinsk. Koshkin ordered Takezhan to obtain horses. The volost chief could only harness his own horses to four abandoned carriages. At long last, the officials were ready for their return journey at dusk, while the guards had to follow on foot.

Before their departure, the Tentek-Oyaz had put several questions to Takezhan and the elders and drawn up something in the nature of a statement which he intended to submit to the authorities. The purport of this document was to justify his own actions.

The statement said that Oralbai had turned out to be a big steppe robber, while Bazaraly was his mainstay and a shrewd and clever leader of the population. The locally elected biys, Zhirenshe, Urazbai and others, had proved to be confederates of the bandits. Another accomplice was Ibragim, nicknamed Abai, the brother of Takezhan Kunanbayev, the ruler of the Chinghis Volost. Bazaraly and Abai had incited the mob of poor servants, beggars and the like and disrupted the elections. Furthermore, volost ruler Takezhan Kunanbayev had proved unequal to the office he held. Though he had not abetted Oralbai and Bazaraly, and was evidently hostile to them, he could not keep the population under control. He had failed to suppress the outburst against the administration. He had not been able to detain a single aul when they had deserted the election grounds, leaving the officials alone in the bare steppes. Nor had he attempted to resist when the mob had forcibly released Bazaraly. It was obvious that he had no prestige among the nomads and it was, therefore, advisable that he resign his office, which should be temporarily assumed by his deputy, Zhabai Bozheyev.

Such was the Tentek-Oyaz's decision. He announced it to the interpreter who was staying on in Yeraly, just before he got into his carriage, hoping thus to save his face, and then set off for the town.

3

It was the tenth day of Abai's detention in Semipala-tinsk.

This was not a real prison, just a detention room at the police station, but it was guarded with all the strictness of a regular jail; the windows were barred, the cells constantly under lock and key; only a small aperture enabled the prisoner to communicate with the outside world, that is with the turnkey. But the guards, elderly men with sleepy eyes and sallow faces, armed with sabres as a mark of authority, did not always respond to the pounding on the door from within.

All this was very different from the free life that Abai had led in the steppes, but he had already accustomed himself to his surroundings and spent most of his time reading. The days slipped by unnoticed.

The books were brought to him by his old acquaintance, the lawyer Andreyev, who visited Abai the day after he was arrested, pretending that he had come to obtain particulars of the case. Since then he had been to see Abai every other day, each time bringing new books.

"I've brought some new friends to your dungeon," he would say with a smile.

Abai was allowed to see his visitor in the guardroom, which hardly differed from the cell. It was just as dark and equally infested with flies. Andreyev had long talks with Abai, trying to keep his spirits up. He did not conceal, however, the fact that the situation was grave.

"To insult an official in the execution of his duties is no joking matter. I can understand that your anger was justified; it does you credit, in fact. But in the eyes of the law your actions are nothing less than incitement to rebellion and the consequences may be serious. We'll see what charge they prefer."

Before he visited Abai, Andreyev found out all the details from his old friend Losovsky. The lawyer thought that a great deal depended on Losovsky's evidence, and the latter was more than eager to testify, especially since he differed sharply with Koshkin on the methods of governing the people of the steppes. He could never mention Koshkin without a scornful smile and regarded him as a bureaucrat and a bully. He attributed the outburst to Koshkin's arbitrary actions, and Abai, in his opinion, had merely sought to preserve his dignity.

They had discussed the matter in the presence of their mutual friend, Mikhailov, a determined and intelligent-looking man in his thirties, with a broad dark beard and a prominent forehead which seemed still larger owing to the thinning hair above his temples. Though Mikhailov was living under police surveillance, his friends had secured him a post in the local administration. He laughed heartily when he heard of the absurd position in which one of the most prominent of the local officials had been placed, and asked Andreyev to introduce him to the bold man of the steppes who had put that petty tyrant in his place.

Abai was always heartened by the lawyer's visits. He felt quite safe in the knowledge that he had such a protector. Andreyev had immediately obtained permission to bring him books and so interesting did Abai find them that the days were too short, and he continued to read far into the evening and even at night, standing under the dim lamp suspended high above. When the wick began to flicker, he would pound on the door with his fist. Awakened from their sound sleep, the guards, mostly old men, shuffled up grumbling: "Look at that Kirghiz, he thinks himself a scholar! He's trying to make up for all the reading his grandpa and grandma didn't do. Isn't the day long enough?"

Abai laughed at their gibes, called them by their first names — Sergei and Nikolai — and they were impressed by his calmness and courtesy.

"You know the jail's full of bedbugs, Sergei. How can I sleep? The books are my only consolation. And remember, the jail pays for nothing but the oil. I don't even take the food."

The old man would argue stubbornly, but invariably brought the oil and refilled the lamp.

"A fine place you've found to study in!" he would grumble. "School is the place, not jail. Real people learn in school from childhood, and you left it till you were put in jail."

Abai was right when he said that his upkeep cost next to nothing; he did not take much food in the jail. Kumiss, shurpa and tea were daily brought by his friends Yerbol or Baimagambet, the latter having been taken on by Abai to attend to the horses.

A large cup of kumiss, boiled meat and biscuits wrapped in a cloth lay untouched on the table. It was not worry that put him off food, but simply the stuffiness and the heat.

He had slept little the previous night. In the morning, he took a few draughts of yesterday's kumiss and at once absorbed himself in reading. The title of the book was *Sokhaty*; it was a story of a band of Russian outlaws. The hero was the just avenger, the brave Sokhaty who lived in a dense forest with his friends and waylaid government officials. Abai recalled his impression of *Dubrovsky*, which he had read the spring before. He thought of Vladimir, who had set fire to his house full of corrupt officials, and was again thrilled with the idea of outraged honour being avenged. Yes, it was from such things that courage stemmed. Had he not been through an experience much like that described in the book? How well he remembered it all! The Tentek-Oyaz, the guards and policemen, huddled together in the rear yurta, terrified. The creaking of the tent props and the roaring of the crowd. It was just as the writers described it. It seemed that people who spoke different languages and lived in different countries still acted in the same way when they had to defend themselves against violence or had to avenge their wrongs. Different people, different nations were equally unable to take violence and injustice lying down. In other words, it was not the feeling of clan, tribe or race that motivated people's actions: it was their similar plight that roused them to anger. Abai fell into deep thought, the book lying open on his knee.

The creaking of the rusty door startled him. It was Khomutov, the warder, coming in. His appearance always announced the arrival of the lawyer or investigator. Abai was surprised, expecting neither the one nor the other that day. Was he to be set free? The thought flashed through his mind. He got up to receive the warder, who paused in the doorway.

"Kunanbayev to the guardroom," he said glumly. "Your father has come to see you from the aul."

Abai followed him, crestfallen and disappointed. "Why should father drag his old bones all this way," he thought as he entered the guardroom. There were several people waiting for him, in the foreground Yerbol and Baimagambet. Exchanging greetings, Abai looked about for his father. In the dark guardroom he discerned Darkembai, but not Kunanbai.

"Where is father?" asked Abai. "I was told...."

Yerbol nudged him warningly.

"Today Darkembai is your father," he muttered hurriedly, pretending to address Baimagambet. "They wouldn't
have let us in otherwise."

Abai smiled knowingly and extended his hand to
Darkembai, who solemnly embraced him.

"My son, the support in my old age," he exclaimed kissing
Abai.

Khomutov had received a handsome bribe from Yerbol
and was now convinced that the old man really was Abai's
father. He left them to talk in peace.

Abai now had a better look at the two other visitors whom
he had not previously recognised. Overjoyed, he embraced
the two tall djiguits, who had been standing by so quietly.
He was astonished—neither of them should have dared to
show himself in Semipalatinsk, not even in the auls of the
Irgizbai, let alone in Koshkin's police station.

The Irgizbai were convinced that the Zhigitek were at the
bottom of all the trouble. Everything had started with
Oralbai, and, they considered, had subsequently been
aggravated by Bazaraly and Abilgazy. It was about these two
that Takezhan and other Irgizbai leaders had complained to
the Tentek-Oyaz. They had stirred up the trouble in Yeraly;
it was they who had incited the zhataks to pull down the
yurtas. Abai had gathered that this was how their actions
were looked upon from the questions of the interrogator.
He had avoided mentioning their names even though he
saw that he was only prolonging the investigation and his
imprisonment.

After the events in Yeraly, Takezhan had been dismissed
from office. Abai had been summoned to town for
questioning and taken into custody, while Bazaraly and
Abilgazy managed to escape. And now, with the entire
administration against them, the two of them had risked
coming here to see him. Abai was dumbfounded; only true
kinsmen and friends could do such a thing.

"What made you enter the lion's den, my friends?" he
asked. "Is it because the Irgizbai have turned your water to
poison and your food to stone? Or did they lead you here by
the halter?"

"You're wrong this time, Abai," smiled Bazaraly. "If they
could, they would have brought the whole of the Zhigitek
here, but no one has forced us to come. Your old friend
Darkembai and the brave Abilgazy announced that they
wanted to be with you, and even prison would feel like a

palace. If Takezhan were in your place, we should never dream of coming here."

Darkembai and Abilgazy nodded in agreement.

"Why should you be locked up because of us?" began Darkembai. "We have neither the skill nor the wisdom to speak for you."

"We'll stay here in your place," Abilgazy cut in. "Of what use are we? The people need you to wipe their tears for them. If you want to help us you'll get us out, you're courageous and a good fighter. And so let us change places."

Except for their brief meeting during the tussle in the tent of the Tentck Oyaz, Abai had not seen Bazaraly since his talk with Ospan. Though Bazaraly was referring to the other two, it was evident that it was he who had brought them here. It was a plea for pardon. He had unhesitatingly sacrificed his pride and put his fate in Abai's hands.

After some moments of thought, Abai raised his clear bright eyes.

"The camel is tested in the journey and the brave man in time of trouble. You have made me very happy, my friends. There is Darkembai, a grey-haired old man, ready to sacrifice everything if I am in danger. And I see that you two batirs are no less determined than he. What fires then can frighten you? And why should I flee from danger?" He laughed and went on: "And there is no danger, really. The blanks fired by Tentek-Oyaz won't kill me. I've had no real troubles so far, and there's hope ahead. I have a friend among the Russians—I have told you about him. He has found several staunch men and one of them is a wise and honest counsellor. He saw the outrages of the Tentek-Oyaz with his own eyes and has promised to confirm it. That is how things stand. I'll have to meet the Tentek-Oyaz one of these days at a confrontation and I'm afraid that our good Darkembai here would be no match for him," he concluded jestingly.

"It is true, Bazekeh, that you're as eloquent as any Kazakh could be," he said to Bazaraly in the same jesting vein. "But allow me to demonstrate my skill as well this time. The more people there are to argue, the more difficult the argument, complaints and appeals will start pouring in, and the trial will drag on for ever. No, you're not wanted here, my friends. Please go back to your auls."

He embraced them in turn and took leave of them.

On Yerbol's advice, Darkembai and Bazaraly decided to

stay in Semipalatinsk and found shelter in the Tartar district rarely visited by the Kazakhs of the steppes. Meeting Yerbol after dark, they decided that if complications arose over Abai's case and he were threatened with serious punishment, Bazaraly would take the guilt for the Yeraly riot upon himself.

To save Abai, he was prepared to die. Bazaraly could not stifle his passion for Nurganim nor reject her fervent devotion. He did not care what anybody thought, except Abai. He felt that the very earth would swallow him for shame if ever Abai learned of it, never suspecting that Abai knew everything but had not permitted his personal feelings to interfere with his sense of social duty. After his talk with Abai in the guardroom, Bazaraly felt better.

"It's a true saying that 'the djiguit will perish unless he finds a worthy friend, and the people will perish unless they find a worthy leader'. I have found both a friend and a leader. It's all clear now: either Abai will be released and come home, or Bazaraly will never see his native aul again and will go into exile. And he'll go without flinching too, because he has learned from Abai that real honour lies in the hearts of men and not in vain pride."

"Abai says: 'Never bow to your enemies and spare nothing, not even life itself, for your friends'," Darkembai echoed. "What a clear mind!"

Abai's solitary confinement brought him esteem and fame, and the circle of his friends grew steadily. In telling him of this, Yerbol said nothing about the interest taken in him by Saltanat, the daughter of Aldekeh, Tinibai's brother-in-law and friend, a rich merchant who lived on the banks of the Irtish near the town.

The life in the auls along the river differed greatly from that in the steppes. The inhabitants tilled the land and sold the crop; they were no strangers to city life, since they often brought their produce to the markets and fairs. Unlike the Tobikty, they lived in log houses surrounded by barns and other structures.

Saltanat, who had been betrothed to the son of a rich aul, had come to town with her younger mother to make some purchases.

She was worried about Abai's imprisonment, and often asked his sister Makish what could be done and what was the worst that might happen.

Saltanat, her mother, Makish and Tinibai's baibishe were at tea one morning when Yerbol entered the room. "How is

Abai's case progressing? What does the lawyer say? Will they set him free?" they all demanded to be told. Yerbol hesitated to speak, his eyes on Saltanat, whom he did not know. The girl blushed, raised her shining eyes at him briefly, and strained forward, her whole attitude pleading: "Don't hide anything from me!"

Makish hastened to set him at ease: "You may speak freely. We're among our own people."

"Both Akbas Andreyevich and Abai hope that it will be over soon," he told them. "We don't know the details. Akbas Andreyevich says that Abai may be released on bail immediately after the investigation. We must find someone who is known to the authorities and who would be willing to put up the 1,000 rubles they demand. A house-owner or a merchant would be best. That's the sort of person I'm looking for."

Yerbol clearly meant Tinibai or one of his sons. Tinibai's old baibishe had been in such situations before, but now she could only spread out her hands helplessly.

"If there were only something I could do for you, my dear," she said regretfully, "but my husband is away, as you know, and my sons too. No one will pay any attention to me. Besides, I have no money of my own."

Yerbol and Makish were disappointed.

"Is there no way out?" asked Yerbol. "There's no time to fetch cattle. Our auls have gone to summer pastures, and are too far away. Could you talk to one of the local merchants, baibishe? I could go to such a man with your recommendation."

That was his only hope. The baibishe and Makish went over the names of the rich merchants whom they knew, but unfortunately they were all away on business.

"Why can't they stay home where they belong?" said Makish indignantly. "As soon as summer comes, they pile into their carriages and off they go — some to the mountains, some to the steppes."

What was one to do? It was at this point that Saltanat addressed Yerbol:

"Why look for friends to help Mirza Abai only in town? You know the old saying: 'Friendship is paid with friendship!' My father has often said that Abai and his father have befriended him more than once. Convey a salem to Abai from my mother and me. We shall take his cares upon ourselves. Let him name me, Aldekenova, for surety."

"Our beloved sister," Yerbol said, "you've done more

than most men would. What nobler thing can one do than restore a friend's freedom? It is too big for gratitude.... And what use is my gratitude when Abai will soon be here safe and sound to speak for himself."

Saltanat's fresh young face with its noble forehead, straight and dainty nose, and soft round chin was bright with animation and seemed to radiate a tender rosy glow. There was a hint of gold in her glossy hair. Though her eyes, limpid as a doe's, seemed grave and calm, an impish twinkle lurked deep within them. Her slender wrists and fingers were laden with bracelets and gold rings, and gold pendants hung trembling from the lobes of her ears. "Yes, she really is Saltanat in beauty and virtue," * thought Yerbol.

And so one of the chief worries of Abai's friends had been removed. And none too soon; the case was about to be heard in the office of the district administration, and not to be tried in court, but to be decided by the officials themselves.

Two guards brought Abai to the office, a large room on the first floor, and told him to sit at the foot of a long baize-covered table. The room was soon filled with officials in brass-buttoned uniforms. Andreyev came in with them, but Abai did not notice him at first among all these unfamiliar faces. He was followed by Counsellor Losovsky and a stranger, a broad-shouldered man, with a bald head and a long dark beard. Abai was struck by the man's serious yet energetic air. When Losovsky spoke to him, he smiled and looked curiously at Abai. Both of them took seats behind him.

The administrators sat around the table. Presiding over the proceedings was an old man with a greying beard, grey hair brushed smoothly back and piercing blue eyes. He opened the session by summoning the district chief Koshkin. The Tentek-Oyaz, trim in his uniform, and as cold and forbidding as ever, marched smartly to the table, glancing haughtily about him. Passing behind Abai, he took his place at the green table. The only other Kazakh in the room was the flat-faced interpreter, with a sparse moustache and sleek hair. He stood near the chiefs; his eyes blinking nervously, while the questions Abai had been asked during the investigation and the answers he had given were once more repeated.

* Saltanat—luxury, luxuriance, festiveness.—*Ed.*

22*

Abai gave a detailed account of the events at Yeraly, and described the unlawful and humiliating actions of the Tentek-Oyaz, who had ordered the flogging of the biys. He especially emphasised that it was the biys who were beaten, men chosen by the population and approved by the authorities. This was what had caused the general outcry, he explained. No one could respect such a chief. Still, no one had raised a finger against him. The people whose dignity had been insulted had simply refused to take part in the elections and gone home.

"Was it a crime to convey the words of the people to him?" he concluded.

Abai spoke in Russian. His speech was fluent as long as he confined himself to the words advised by Akbas Andreyevich and set down in his previous statements. But the moment he tried to emphasise some point of his own, he floundered—his vocabulary was not yet big enough. He then appealed to the interpreter, adding in Kazakh, "Tell them exactly what I say." But after a few sentences he turned to Russian again, secretly pleased that he was able to talk so long in that alien tongue. He was not afraid of making mistakes and tried accurately to convey his thoughts, translating Kazakh expressions as he went along.

The aged chairman seemed a fair-minded man. To everyone's surprise, he had determined that the two cases, that of a tsarist official and of a plain Kazakh, were to be heard simultaneously. This and the fact that he had permitted Abai to speak at such length was not as puzzling as it sounded to anyone who knew the inside story.

On return from Yeraly, Koshkin had done a lot of wire-pulling; he was the son-in-law of the president of the district court who was a friend of the governor. To clear Koshkin, the two had at first attempted to quash everything concerning the flogging of the men elected by the people. This had been prevented by the interference of Andreyev, whose authority and persistence were well known: he was quite likely to refer the matter to the offices of the governor-general of the steppes, which could give an ugly turn to Koshkin's case. Besides, the young Counsellor Losovsky had already submitted to the governor his report on the events in Yeraly, a document describing the unlawful action taken by the chief of the district. Hushing up the case would be rather awkward under such circumstances and a way had to be found of clearing Koshkin, sentencing Abai and settling the whole affair in Semipalatinsk.

For that reason the governor thought it best to avoid an open hearing with its inevitable publicity and to deal with the case in the privacy of his offices. The matter required cautious and expert handling and, therefore, was entrusted to the old and experienced official Khorkov.

From the outset, Khorkov realised that if Abai were to receive a heavy sentence, the lawyer would most certainly obtain a second hearing in the offices of the governor-general and reopen the case. In the circumstances he decided that a fine would be enough. Abai would be released and there the matter would end. This made it necessary to combine the two cases and hear them as quickly as possible.

Khorkov, who was an influence in the administration because his niece was married to the governor, never missed a chance of accepting a handsome bribe. This time, too, he decided to make the most of the situation. While pleasing the governor and the president of the district court, he would not forget himself either. Talking to Andreyev, he hinted that the lot of the defendant depended to a considerable degree on his generosity, since there were some who needed persuasion and it was not impossible that this would gain him a full acquittal. The hint was not lost on Akbas. "Our chairman seems a little indisposed," Andreyev said to Abai. "Five hundred rubles is just the dose he needs to heal him," and Yerbol promptly counted the money off from the funds brought from the auls.

All Khorkov had to do now was instruct Koshkin on his conduct during the hearing, but here he ran into difficulties. The Tentek-Oyaz, who knew Khorkov's weakness, at once jumped to the conclusion that the man was out to clear Abai at his, Koshkin's, expense. The fact that his case was to be heard together with that of one of those savages was a deep humiliation to him. He had accordingly demanded a separate hearing. Khorkov had tried to reason with him, but to no avail, and, in an attempt to frighten Koshkin and make him toe the line, he assured him that the floggings meted out to the biys might produce grave consequences.

On hearing this, Koshkin turned the tables on the old official. The threat had stung into action the same arbitrary bureaucrat as had ordered the floggings in Yeraly. He retorted that he was afraid of no publicity, since, except for the mishandling of the biys, he had nothing to conceal, which was more than could be said for some who went in for extortion and bribery. Moreover, he was ready to tell any court against whom and by what circumstances his actions had been prompted. In any event, he would demand to be judged by men who had no blot on their characters.

Getting the hint, the old official took matters into his own hands. When invited to tea at the governor's house, he described Koshkin's excessive pride in such a way that the ladies decided that this upstart should be put in his place. When the governor heard what had passed between the two of them, he concluded that Koshkin was a fool who did not even know on which side his bread was buttered, and fully agreed that Khorkov should get both hearings off at one session. But on the day set for the hearing of the case the president intervened. This was a man with whom the governor preferred not to quarrel, and eventually it was decided that Koshkin's case would be heard separately, though he was to be present at the first hearing as well. This was why Koshkin looked so haughty when he now appeared before the court and took his place at the green table.

And so the case in which so many personal interests were interwoven took a rather unusual course. The presiding officer's show of impartiality concealed his desire to wind up Abai's case, to gag his lawyer by pronouncing a mild sentence and only then to proceed to the hearing of Koshkin's case.

"The district chief deals only with official persons," he said after hearing Abai to the end. "Kaumenov, Shokin and Suyundikov are elected biys and your brother is a volost ruler, and they have the right to speak on behalf of the population. Where do you come in? You are neither a volost ruler, nor even an elder."

"The people made me intervene," Abai replied calmly. "When the chief Koshkin began to flog Urazbai Akkulov, the people told me to intercede for him."

The Tentek-Oyaz, incensed because Abai had been permitted to speak freely, could not control himself any longer. "And who are you, pray," he shouted. "What right have you to speak for the people? Who gave you the power?"

Abai glanced at Koshkin mockingly and turned to the presiding officer:

"It is true that neither I nor the people were as powerful as he and his guards, but there is a force even stronger than his power and his orders. That force is called justice and honour." Abai here turned to the interpreter, saying, "Tell them what I say word for word", and went on in Kazakh:

"They used to say in olden days, 'Believe not in power but in the truth. Do not obey injustice. Stand up for what is just even at the cost of your life'."

The essence of his evidence was clearly stated. Andreyev, Losovsky and Mikhailov exchanged glances.

The hearing then went quicker. It was actually a duel between Koshkin and Abai.

"You, Kunanbayev, have defended Bazaraly Kaumenov, though his brother is a bandit," Koshkin accused.

"It was only the elected biys whom you were beating up that I tried to help," Abai parried.

"That's not true. It was not of them you were thinking. You wanted to release Kaumenov and you provoked all that trouble because of him."

"I did nothing of the sort. But, for that matter, I do not consider Kaumenov guilty of anything."

"Ah, there you are. You'll soon be justifying his brother too." Koshkin turned to the presiding officer. "I want his answer to be put on record."

Abai gave his explanation to the presiding officer. Oralbai Kaumenov had been on the run for a year. Before that, there had been nothing against him. No one knew where he was, and somewhere he had committed a crime. He was lost to his family and the tribe. The presiding officer should know this himself: If a young peasant from Semipalatinsk District were to run away to Orenburg and commit a crime there, would Koshkin be allowed to go to the young man's village and flog the elder, the volost ruler and the scribe? Would such actions be approved? Would he continue in office after that? Or be promoted?

Koshkin brazenly denied that he had ordered the biys to be flogged. Abai looked at him with aversion.

"I have nothing more to say to you," he declared. "You are not only an official who abuses his power, but also a liar. When an ordinary man tells a lie, he is merely being shameless, but when a man lies in his official capacity, he is committing a crime. And since you are a criminal you have no right to be sitting there among my judges. Counsellor Losovsky can testify to the fact that Koshkin ordered the floggings."

Losovsky confirmed Abai's words.

But Koshkin did not lose his composure. "Oh well, I'm not denying it. They were all shielding the criminals. Their stubbornness was exasperating, and perhaps I was a bit rash." He added with a sneer: "When one's conscience is clear, one can afford to let fly. And I have never traded in my conscience or taken bribes, as some do."

Losovsky laughed and shrugged his shoulders, looking at the presiding officer.

The public part of the proceedings was over, and the officials did not wish to discuss the matter further in the presence of an ordinary Kazakh. Abai went back to spend another night in his cell. The next morning he was set free.

But not acquitted. The sentence ran: "Ibragim Kunan-bayev is fined 1,000 rubles for disturbing the peace and obstructing the district chief Koshkin in the execution of his duties." The sentence was calculated to maintain Koshkin's authority in the eyes of the nomads, and his own conduct was not even mentioned. The outrages perpetrated by the official in full view of the people went unpunished, while the man who had protested against these actions was ordered to pay a heavy fine.

On meeting Andreyev, Mikhailov could not hide his indignation.

"It's outrageous! The investigation itself was a crime, giving all the Koshkins a free hand to bludgeon the people as long as they endure it in silence."

Abai, as yet unaware of the details, was overjoyed at his liberation. But there was still another case to be heard: that of Oralbai and Bazaraly, the Kaumen brothers. Bazaraly, who had never been a fugitive from justice, was now to be placed under police surveillance. If any of the volost rulers were to complain of him or if Oralbai were caught by the authorities, he too would have to answer.

Three excellent bays stood waiting for Abai; Makish and Yerbol came forward to meet him and threw their arms about him. There was also a strange and smartly dressed young woman with them.

Yerbol had not told Abai anything about Saltanat and had cautioned Makish to say nothing either, afraid that Abai might refuse help and bail money from a girl. But when she saw that Abai stood staring at Saltanat, Makish smilingly explained:

"Her name is Saltanat. You must have heard about her from Aldekeh."

Abai inclined his head as Makish continued:

"She has been a real friend. You have known her only by name until now, but there you can see her, true friendship in person. It was Saltanat who put up the bail for you."

Such conflicting emotions as gratitude and indignation

left him speechless. He asked no questions, silently took Saltanat's hand in both of his, bowed and laid one of his palms reverently on his breast. Saltanat lowered her eyes in embarrassment, and waited for him to speak.

"Have you lost your wits in prison, Abai-zhan," Makish scolded her brother with her usual alacrity. "Can't you say anything? Aren't you ashamed of yourself?"

Abai showed his friends into the carriage.

"It is said that wit is the essence of charm, but reticence is always the companion of wit," he countered as he got into the carriage with them. "Now what could I say, Saltanat?"

"You're right," she replied with a smile. "Happiness should not be voluble."

With its bells jingling, the troika sped towards Tinibai's house on the other side of the river.

Although the case was closed, Abai stayed on in Semipalatinsk, sending his djiguits and Bazaraly back to the auls, and keeping Yerbol and Baimagambet with him.

In the evening Abai learned from Yerbol what Saltanat had done for him. Though she was the daughter of Aldekeh, well known to the authorities, she had been rejected as a surety. She had then persuaded Duisekeh, a well-known Semipalatinsk house-owner and felt manufacturer, to represent her, taking advantage of Duisekeh's friendship for her father and her kinship with him—she was his niece on her mother's side. Duisekeh was cautious and cowardly. He had no connections with the Tobikty; and actually shunned them. Only a girl with Saltanat's will power and courage could have made him represent her in this matter while she put up the money.

The more Abai learned about the trouble she had taken for him, the more awkward he felt. He felt that he ought to have a frank talk with Saltanat, no matter what it led to. He had to know just what had prompted her actions.

As it happened, Saltanat's mother had gone to the market on the other bank of the Irtish, accompanied by Makish and Yerbol, and Abai found himself alone with Saltanat in Tinibai's great house. The heavy dark silk curtains kept out the sun and the rooms in their quiet half-light were cool and comfortable. Abai and the girl sat on the soft corpeh by a low round table, their arms resting on cushions, talking quietly. Abai thanked Saltanat for what she had done for him, but she was too embarrassed to answer, waving his words of gratitude aside with a slight movement of her fingers. "Why remember?" her eyes seemed to say.

Baimagambet entered and set a silver bowl of cold kumiss before them. Abai stirred the kumiss, then poured some into a coloured piala and handed it to Saltanat.

"There are times when one djiguit helps another. I have found myself indebted to my friends more than once, but I never imagined that I would get help from a woman, not even from my own mother. I would never have thought that a woman could act so boldly without fearing for her good name. Straightforwardness is no vice, as you know. Please tell me what prompted you to help me?"

Saltanat seemed to have expected this question. Her face turned crimson and paled at once. The corners of her full-lipped mouth were trembling. She took the piala from his hand, sipped the liquid and only then raised her eyes.

"I suppose it was compassion for another young person. No one asked me to do it. I did it of my own accord. You owe me nothing. You did not ask me to help you, did you? I only hope you will not be angry with me and say that you would have done better to find other friends."

Abai was now convinced that she had truly acted on her own, unafraid of the consequences. Her strength of will and determination appealed to him enormously.

"Well spoken, Saltanat. I shall never forget your words," he began when a man entered the room. He was tall and sturdy, he wore high boots and a hat of black lambskin in the Tobikty fashion, and carried a whip in his hand. It was clear that he had just come from an aul in the steppes. Coming in from the bright light outside, he was momentarily dazed, but Abai recognised him at once and invited him to come nearer.

The man stepped warily through the dimly lit room, sat down, feeling for the cushion, and then saw Saltanat. His surprise was so great that the piala of kumiss that had been offered him remained untouched in his hand as he sat staring at them.

It was Manas, one of Kulinshak's "bes-kaska". Ulzhan had sent him. The auls had wandered to a distant zhailyau. The roads were deserted and a solitary traveller was far from safe; for that reason they had sent such a man as himself to learn the news. Abai's parents, wives, children and other kinsmen were distraught with anxiety over his fate.

"They do not sleep at night, thinking that you are languishing in the cage. But you're free and well, light of my eyes. They told me so at the gates. So my journey was lucky after all. Baimagambet tried to hold me, saying you were

busy, but I just couldn't wait. I can see that you're not
feeling lonely here. More power to you!"

He guffawed and took a long draught of his kumiss. This
home-spun witticism was quite refined for Manas, and Abai
quickly interjected to prevent him from saying more.

"It was only yesterday that I was set free and I have
hardly had time to meet my friends. The matter is not
finished yet. We are discussing what to do next. I'm still on
bail, you know, but we'll talk about that afterwards."

He called for Baimagambet.

"Take Manas-aga to the guest-room and see that he is
made comfortable for the night," he commanded briefly
when the young man appeared.

Abai resumed his conversation with Saltanat as soon as
they were gone.

"How could I be angry with you for setting me free?
Nothing is farther from my thoughts. There's only one
thing that troubles me: in what way can I serve you? All I ask
for is to be allowed to carry out one of your wishes. I shall
really be sorry if there's nothing I can do for you."

Saltanat listened without raising her eyes.

"Thank you, Abai," she answered. "But let my wishes go
unfulfilled for the time. Did you not say only yesterday that
reticence is the companion of wit? This is the first time I
have ever spoken to you, but I have heard a good deal from
Makish about your sense of justice and your clear mind. I
have always regarded you as a man upon whom one could
rely. And I can see that I have not been mistaken. Your
words have put me at ease. They have told me a lot." She
added with a faint smile: "Though this room is spacious, my
path within it is short. Allow me to go now."

Abai helped her to her feet.

"What real friendship can there be when there's a veil
between friends? Should not hearts be unveiled?"

"'In rending the veil from your heart, do not rend it from
your honour!' that is what Suffi Allahyar says, I think," she
said, as she crossed the threshold. "Let us be modest and
keep these veils in place." And she was gone after a last
glance at him.

He remained standing at the door, puzzled and enraptured. "In rending the veil from your heart, do not rend it
from your honour!" he said to himself. Those were good
words. "She has a rare self-possession and a keen mind.
Perhaps I have found a treasure." Recalling everything he
had said to her, he was annoyed with the way he had ex-

pressed himself. Who would have done what she had? That was no mere woman's caprice. It was genuine kindness. And she had been so reserved, courteous and dignified.

He realised that this meeting with her would be a test for him. Her feelings were so honest and sincere that they had to be answered as sincerely. He decided not to stay in Tinibai's house any longer, but to move to the other bank of the Irtish, to the house of the hospitable Kazakh Kerim, where he had usually stayed during his visits to town.

A few days passed. Abai was now living in Kerim's house, devoting all his time to reading. Every morning, accompanied by Baimagambet, he rode to the heart of the town and halted before the two-storey stone building in the narrow alley near the bank of the Irtish. Instructing Baimagambet to be back with the horses in the evening, he entered the white building of the public library.

On this day, however, he had decided to bring the books away with him and told Baimagambet to wait for him. The large reading room was crowded. There were two or three people at every table, most of them young students. "These are the best people of the town," thought Abai as he entered.

The librarian, a modest old man with a lined face and a goatee, greeted him like an old acquaintance. An official with a luxuriant growth of hair and rakish moustaches sat at the table near the entrance, ogling his pretty and smartly dressed neighbour whom he had obviously pursued into the austere premises of the library.

"Amazing! Since when have they been admitting camels to the Gogol Library?" he had remarked loudly as Abai appeared, intending his witticism for all within earshot. Some of the young readers looked up and sniggered when they saw a Kazakh in his wide chapan. The young woman frowned, however, and gave her neighbour a reproachful look. Abai turned his head sharply but repressed his anger.

"Why should a camel not enter here, when he has been preceded by an ass," he remarked calmly.

This time there was general laughter. The official turned white, but held his tongue when he saw his pretty neighbour rocking with mirth. Abai then turned to the aged librarian and asked for a copy of the *Russky Vestnik*.

A man of medium height, with a black beard and a prominent forehead, now turned to Abai. "I have it here. I've finished with it and can give it to you, if you like," he said. "But would you mind telling me please what interests you in that magazine?"

"This issue carries the first instalment of Lev Tolstoi's novel," said Abai. "I should like to read it."

"Oh, you've read Tolstoi, have you? Why does he interest you?"

The stranger's intelligent face and kindly tone appealed to Abai.

"I haven't yet read Tolstoi," he answered politely, "but I have heard that he is a real Russian sage, and so I should like to know what he teaches."

"An excellent idea!" said the stranger, handing him the magazine. "I've seen you before, under less pleasant circumstances. It was in the office of the district administration. But to be frank, I am even more impressed with our meeting today. I am very pleased to meet you. Yevgeny Petrovich Mikhailov is my name."

"Ibragim Kunanbayev," Abai introduced himself. "I have also heard a good deal about you from your friends. I, too, am pleased to meet you."

They left the library together and slowly walked along the bank of the Irtish, talking. Abai walked with his chapan open, his hands holding his whip clasped behind his back. Baimagambet followed slowly on horseback, surprised that Abai should have preferred to go on foot merely to talk with some Russian. When they reached a white stone house on the riverside near the mill, Mikhailov opened the door.

"Will you come in? I have more to say to you."

Mikhailov lived in a large, well-kept room. Abai was in no hurry to go home and stayed with him until late in the evening.

He had good reason to be interested in Mikhailov. Andreyev had often told him that Mikhailov was, probably, the most intelligent and erudite man in the town. According to the lawyer, he had devoted his life to social work and had been prosecuted by the tsarist authorities when still a young man. This had not broken his spirit, however. Rather the contrary. Living in prison and exile among the finest people in Russia he had broadened his outlook and his knowledge immensely. Akbas had said that Mikhailov was one of the advanced men of his people and would have been regarded as a great man in any other epoch. And now Abai was talking to the man himself.

Mikhailov first asked him what books he had read in Russian and warmly advocated self-education, explaining its

advantages and disadvantages. As he voiced his thoughts
and doubts, it seemed to Abai that he was listening to an
expert teacher. He said as much, telling Mikhailov that his
words were like the hands of a bone-setter, finding the
fracture at once.

Abai spoke in Russian, managing the sentences with
difficulty and pausing to find the words, but Mikhailov
quickly got his meaning, and the comparison with the
bone-setter set him laughing.

"Your comparisons are apt," he said. "If I understand
you right, they are always original and hit the nail on the
head. I noticed it during your argument with Koshkin."

Abai spoke indignantly about officials like Koshkin who
never troubled to think about the people they ruled and
preferred to get things done by shouting and wielding the
whip.

"You cannot imagine the harm done to Russia by these
officials," said Mikhailov. "We call them bureaucrats.
They're all the same — from Petersburg to Semipalatinsk.
You can't judge them properly from those you see here. To
study them the way you do — by colliding with all sorts of
Koshkins and spending a month and a half in jail in
consequence — is a long and painful method, to put it
mildly. There is a less bothersome way of studying that
breed. We have such writers, Saltykov-Shchedrin for one,
who ruthlessly show up the officials for what they are. Just
read some of his books and you'll get the right idea about
the people you came up against."

This sweeping generalisation surprised Abai. He had held
to quite another belief: "People are as different as the
fingers of a hand." When he tried to express this view,
Mikhailov laughed:

"Oh, how naive you are, my dear Kunanbayev. Officials
are all alike, big and small, young and old."

Seeing that Abai could not agree with him, Mikhailov also
resorted to a figure of speech. "They're as alike as the seeds
of the bur and they're sown by the same hand, by the tsarist
regime." He hesitated about going further.

Abai was beginning to understand what Mikhailov meant.
His new acquaintance attracted him more and more, and he
tried to get him to explain himself further.

"Your words sound convincing. But there are officials
like Losovsky," he objected. "You can't deny that he showed
a real sense of justice in that trouble I had with Koshkin."

But Mikhailov gave the conversation an unexpected tone.

"I see. You mean to say that Koshkin is bad and Losovsky is good, implying that things would be better and justice triumphant if there were less Koshkins and. more Losovskys?"

"Yes, I think so."

"It's true that Losovsky turned out to be better than others. If he hadn't given the evidence he did, things would have looked bad for you. And so you've decided that he is the ideal official, isn't that so?"

"Yes. He was fair...."

"And so he was, under the circumstances. He might be in the future too, in little things. Oh well, an official like that should not be scorned unless, of course, he begins to do harm like the rest. Since he has such liberal inclinations, you are quite right to make the best of them — but never forget the essence of the man."

"But how is one to judge a man if not by his deeds? What essence are you talking about?"

Mikhailov replied with an ironical smile: "Try to rely on Losovsky not in such trifling matters as yours, but in more serious issues affecting the welfare of the entire nation and then see what happens. Losovsky is simply a white crow among the officials, but a crow nonetheless."

Abai did not understand.

"Let me explain. It's a saying we Russians have about those who differ from their kind and are as rare as white crows. I wouldn't be deluded by its whiteness, if I were you. Don't mistake it for a nobler bird, because, black or white, it is still a carrion-crow; it lives by its trade."

It was only now that Abai caught Mikhailov's idea.

"Our people also say that one crow never pecks at the eye of another."

Mikhailov laughed, and then continued gravely:

"Remember that a carrion-eater will always remain one, and it's not for carrion-crows to decide the affairs of the people. Losovsky has no business to look like an innocent dove and take in such as you. I would rather deal with Koshkin. He, at least, appears in his true colours and the people can plainly see his ugliness, while such as Losovsky and their half-hearted justice and dubious virtues only beget futile hopes. It is thanks to him that you suffer under the illusion that it is not society that is to blame, but individuals. It's just such good officials as Losovsky who prevent the people from discerning the true nature of the crows known as tsarist officialdom."

Abai fully understood Mikhailov's meaning and marvelled at his great concern for the people. He was grateful to Mikhailov for his outspokenness

"You've opened a door to an unknown world," he confessed. "This talk of ours has been a useful lesson."

Mikhailov touched Abai's shoulder.

"It's not from me that you should learn," he said kindly. "There are wiser Russian thinkers than I. If you like, I can lend you some books. Please allow me to help you in your studies. It's an excellent idea. There are far too few educated men among you Kazakhs. Suppose something like your experience occurs again? You've got to know a lot to distinguish the truth from deception. It is only thus that you can be useful to your people. Russian books will be very helpful to you. They'll be your loyal friends, believe me!" he smiled. "And I'll be happy to be your adviser in your work of self-education, especially since I have had some experience in this field."

Abai was touched by his kindness.

"I can thank Allah that your path has crossed mine. I accept your offer as a precious token of your sympathy."

After that conversation, Abai called upon Mikhailov every few days. They often talked about the life of the nomads. Mikhailov was curious about the real story of the events in Yeraly. Who was Oralbai?

Abai told the story at length—about Oralbai's love for Korimbala and what the two had had to suffer. Unable to endure the humiliations Korimbala had died, while Oralbai had become an outlaw. Both had been gifted singers.

Oralbai had been goaded to vengeance by his best friends. It was a view Abai had kept to himself, but now he openly confessed his sympathy for Oralbai.

"He has been branded a thief and a bandit. Perhaps he is! But only in the eyes of the authorities! The people at large regard him as a bold and just avenger. You Russians, too, have had such men as he. Haven't they rebelled against tyranny? Are they not worthy of respect? I would certainly support such men if I could. And what do you think?"

Mikhailov had been listening intently.

"You have told me a remarkable story," he said thoughtfully. "There is something of an old legend in it. One could write a book about it. But in actual life, in public life especially, it is not an example to copy. Public opinion among your people is immature and almost helpless and I can well understand that in your eyes this djiguit is a rebel against tyranny. Still, the tragic love of a djiguit and a girl is not cause enough for a popular movement. The fugitive who plunders out of vengeance is not the man to lead a popular struggle."

Mikhailov tried to deepen Abai's outlook. In experience Abai was the equal of those around him, including Kunanbai. Such men as Andreyev, of course, were better informed than he, but hardly superior to him in his knowledge of life. But Mikhailov was a man of wider horizons, with greater social acumen. Abai wanted to know his opinion of his own conduct in Yeraly, admitting that it was he who had led the people.

"You've taught Koshkin a lesson and that's a good thing," Mikhailov answered without hesitation. "Do you know why you have succeeded? Because you correctly guessed what the people wanted. It was a striking example of their unanimity. Your case was more serious than Oralbai's. If there hadn't been so much evidence to support you, the matter would have been given a political angle. Your arguments struck home and that is why you got away with it."

He told Abai about the news in the district and regional offices: Koshkin had been transferred from his post in Semipalatinsk to a similar post in Ust-Kamenogorsk. Counsellor Losovsky was to assume Koshkin's former duties. The district office had instructed him to go into the steppes and arrange the elections of volost rulers which Koshkin had bungled. They were to be held in the Chinghis Volost to which the Irgizbai belonged and the neighbouring volosts of Konir-Koksha and Kzil-Moly.

Mikhailov advised Abai to accompany Losovsky and to help him to elect really useful people. Losovsky was well disposed to him and would be more than glad. It was the advice of a friend, which he would do well to follow. Abai was prompt to agree. Word was accordingly sent to Losovsky through Andreyev and the invitation to Abai was soon extended.

When Yerbol and Baimagambet learned why their departure was put off again they stopped bothering Abai with their homesickness and their complaints about the heat and dust of the town. They had been waiting to go for more than a month and had seen little of Abai in the time. He had spent most of his days at the library, with Mikhailov, or poring over books at home and meditating on the things he had read.

It was only on rare occasions that Yerbol could induce him to visit Tinibai's home on the other bank.

Saltanat and her mother were still there, and Abai had an opportunity of talking to the girl alone one day.

Perhaps it was Yerbol's doing or mere accident, but whatever it was, they arrived one evening to find that Makish and Saltanat's mother had gone to call on a neighbour and the girl was alone. Yerbol stayed in the front rooms, and kept the servants' minds off the tête-à-tête.

The two were sitting on a high coffer covered with rugs and a thick corpeh. The twilight was deepening and a soft breeze stirred the curtains. Both were loath to light the lamps. Since they were in the dark, invisible to the passers-by in the street, Abai parted the curtain, laying one side of it over the bed. The pale moonlight filtered into the room, lighting up Saltanat's flushed face. A moonray showed up the long arches of the girl's brows over her large eyes, and shone softly on her white forehead.

Saltanat had greeted Abai like an old friend. She asked him about his family in the aul and chided him for neglecting his kin. Didn't he miss them at all, she asked.

Abai admitted that he missed the children and added that his marriage with Aigerim was disapproved by his relatives. In his turn, he asked about her life and future.

She seemed to have lost her former reserve and spoke of herself, her long fingers playing with the tassels of her sholpy. The fire in her eyes seemed to be extinguished and came alight again only when they narrowed as though with pain. Abai was not like other djiguits she knew; she felt that she could trust him.

"My freedom is worth nothing. I, too, am a captive, though the fetters can't be seen. Many are amazed that I am allowed to enjoy such freedom. In truth, I'm like a falcon primed for hunting, but fastened to his master's wrist by an invisible thread. Soon I shall be the property of another man. He is to visit me in the autumn. You know how many unhappy girls there are among us Kazakhs. I have let my father know through my mothers that I do not love my fiancé and would prefer to be married to anyone but him. Still, father won't change his mind. I am his only and beloved daughter, and they call me Saltanat. My home has been like a nest in which I have always been petted by my parents. Even now they will deny me nothing but this. As I am doomed, my house is no better than a cage. When I think of the future I lose hope.... It seems to me, sometimes, that I desire nothing and care for nothing. At night I weep and pray God to take my life. Death is better than such humiliating captivity. A life like mine is nothing to regret."

She pressed her kerchief to her flushed face, trying to stem her tears. Abai did not speak, and his heart was heavy.

"You, I am sure, understand how a young heart reasons," Saltanat went on calmly, though her voice faltered. "In my place, others would say, 'Why think of the future? I'm free for the time being and shall make the best of it and throw all caution to the winds'. That's what usually happens. But I can't do that. Revulsion and fear deprive me of all desire. My affection wilts as soon as it appears. What for? I say to myself. If I'm to be pushed over the precipice just the same. I'm like a sparrow fascinated by a snake; no matter how the poor thing flutters, it will be drawn into the snake's mouth."

She fell silent. The room was very still. Abai had heard sad confessions of young people before, but had never been affected so deeply. Only in some Russian book he had read such a truthful admission. Indeed, it was a language spoken by the heart; and once the words are uttered the heart must die....

Abai leaned forward and took her hands into his. They were soft, warm and a little moist. When he kissed the tips of her fingers, she gently pulled her hands away.

"Saltanat, my dear, I have never heard a sadder story. Such sincerity deserves to be matched with sincerity, and it would be a sin were I to utter one word that might deceive you. Let me tell you about the grief that rends my heart."

Saltanat made a scarcely perceptible movement towards him.

"You are afraid of the future, tormented by the thought of one you do not love, while I am tormented by longing for a beloved, by sorrow for those moments which I shall not forget until I die.... It was the dawn of my life. And nothing can mar my memories. Now those brief moments of happiness are gone for ever, like the moon that has set. Her name was Togzhan. Many years have passed since I saw her last, but the memory of my beloved still lives within me—it is a song written with my blood. You have heard it—Makish told me you liked it."

Saltanat nodded, her head swaying as if she were humming the song to herself, the golden pendants trembling in time to the rhythm as though repeating: "We've known, we've heard, we've seen."

"I had to marry a woman I did not love," Abai went on.
"There were children and they gladdened my heart, but
anguish would not leave me. Then one evening when I was
dreaming of Togzhan I heard a voice very much like hers. I
was awakened by that voice and its owner, Togzhan's twin in
appearance, came to be my song, my joy and my support.
We have a beautiful child, a symbol of our love for each
other. People think that I live in town for pleasure, but they
do not know how much I miss Aigerim, my second
Togzhan."

Saltanat nodded, without speaking. There was no need to
say more.

Saltanat offered her love to Abai bravely, true to her
brave and straightforward character, in a manner that most
Kazakh girls could not dare to even contemplate: she herself
opened the doors of his prison and set him free. But she
did not want a love that was not free, nor could she share
it with another woman. Abai, who sorely missed Aigerim,
could not lie either, and tell Saltanat that he reciprocated
her love.

With this their heart-to-heart talk came to an end.
Saltanat reached for her dombra and handed it to Abai.

"Would you sing that song for me? Softly, only for me "

Abai needed no coaxing. He sang in an undertone, first
the song written to Togzhan, and then other words, gentle
and sincere, to the same tune. They sprang to his mind
spontaneously and he sang of Saltanat's face in the
moonlight and the new feeling born that day. It was
unforgettable. The akyn's dombra would long sing of this
bond, and their hearts would always cherish it. Their
parting was inevitable, the song went on, but his memory
would always preserve the image of his friend. Their secret
would be treasured by their hearts like a precious gem.

Meanwhile, Yerbol had been waiting in the next room
expecting some sign from his friend. When he heard the
singing, he ordered Baimagambet to light the lamps,
entered Makish's room with a lamp in his hand and looked
at the two with undisguised curiosity.

Abai and the girl were sitting exactly as he had left them
and Abai was singing softly. His face wore a peculiar
expression—not what Yerbol had expected. Frankly, Yerbol did not approve. He was displeased and even hurt.

Baimagambet and some servants also entered to lay the
table for tea. Makish and Saltanat's mother soon returned,
and Tinibai's baibishe arrived shortly after.

Abai and Yerbol sang all the evening, singly and together. At the baibishe's request they sang a variety of songs. Saltanat appeared withdrawn, listening to the tunes of the Tobikty, so unlike those of her own clan. It was only towards the end of the evening, when no one but Abai, Yerbol and Baimagambet were present, that she broke her silence.

"An unforgettable evening," she said to Abai. "How quickly it flew by! I am deeply grateful. I knew that you were not like others and I do not at all regret that which did not come to pass. I wish you happiness as long as you live."

Abai was once more impressed by her frankness. Without speaking, he inclined his head and put his hand to his heart. Saltanat realised that he did not wish to mar the evening with a single unnecessary word. She nodded and went to the window, and stood there watching him go, with tear-filled eyes.

At last came the day for departure. Abai had been visiting Mikhailov daily, and on one occasion Mikhailov received him with an open book in his hand. He greeted Abai, took him by the arm and led him to his room.

"I've prepared some books for you, Kunanbayev. Here they are." He pointed to the pile on the table. "Besides Russian fiction, I've picked some books on general knowledge as well."

"And what are they like, Yevgeny Petrovich?"

"There are some on world history, the history of Europe and geography. You should study them well this year. Some of them are mine and the others are kept for you in the Gogol Library. I've given the list to the librarian. You seem to have studied history before. Yes, history is the mother of all wisdom."

"I've read the history of Islam—the books required in the madrasah and others which I found myself. Since I have met you, however, they seem to have lost their importance. I am not even sure they were history at all. You've swept them away, as though they were but mist."

"Not all, I hope," Mikhailov laughed. "The history of Islam is a science, of course, a great science, but one should never forget by whom and how this history was written."

And Mikhailov began to outline a theory entirely new to Abai. The culture of the East had influenced world science for several centuries and had greatly contributed to human knowledge, he said. Between the ancient world and the Renaissance in Europe lay several centuries of mental darkness which would have been complete if not for the light from the East. The East thus became a link in the chain of intellectual development, imparting much of its own character to it.

This talk especially heartened Abai and he could not conceal his jubilation from Mikhailov. Hitherto he had believed that the East had stood apart, for all its culture and knowledge. But now his friend had gathered all these treasures, which Abai had thought were poles apart, into one whole. Of course, this was the right way to look at things! Were there few people in the world who thought about the common weal, justice, truth and conscience? Each era, each nation produced its own scholars and teachers, who though speaking different tongues were all deeply concerned for the future of mankind. Surely this was why he and Mikhailov understood each other so readily. It was, perhaps, this understanding that so quickly strengthened their friendship, in spite of the fact that one had inherited culture and the other had only just begun to draw on its riches.

Mikhailov's prominent brow, penetrating eyes and thick well-kept beard made him look like a scholar, a wise teacher even in appearance. Abai hung on his words; every sentence sounded like a maxim. Mikhailov spoke in a simple, easily understandable way, but brought out bold and far-reaching conclusions. He reiterated his opinion that the study of Islam was a serious science and put forward the idea that the Kazakh people had gathered a treasure of culture as yet unknown to science and not duly appreciated by Abai. It was still hidden in the people's midst like gold in the bowels of the earth.

The talk had brought the two even closer to each other. Mikhailov was like an elder brother, nearer to him than a kinsman by blood.

"I've learned more about you today than ever before," Abai told him at parting. "I can truly appreciate your qualities now. I thought you were concerned only with the Russian people, that I must seem like a man from a strange world to you, a creature of the steppes with outlandish thoughts. You have taken me to the top of a mountain and from there pointed out to me the settlements of all the peoples in all the times, explaining that all people are kin, even if distant. I am glad to hear that even my Tobikty have not been forgotten. I am both glad and proud."

Mikhailov responded with a friendly smile, placing his hand on Abai's shoulder.

"Let us hope that our friendship will be useful to both. Only keep your promise. Don't forget the library."

Before Losovsky's departure for the steppes, Mikhailov met him at Andreyev's house.

"Kunanbayev has a great thirst for knowledge," he said. "That is just how a young nation should strive for knowledge, with fervour, energy and even greed!"

Losovsky was not convinced.

"One man is not a nation, Yevgeny Petrovich. His people have a long way to go before they can appreciate the use of Russian culture and are actually in a state of hibernation. As to Kunanbayev, I think his urge is simply a property common to the young in general. As we grow up we all strive for knowledge."

Mikhailov did not argue, but hoped that Losovsky would get to know Abai better.

"Kunanbayev has an interesting feature. He likes to talk about justice, about people and serving the people. These ideas are deeply rooted in him and they're close to Russian culture, aren't they? He is the first such nomad I have ever met. I would like to know your opinion. You know the steppes and the relations of the people far better than I. I'm impressed by his humanistic leanings and wonder what will become of him in a few years."

Mikhailov had never said this to Abai himself, but now he spoke with conviction, and Andreyev was prompt to agree.

"You've always said that Kirghiz rulers are mostly obtuse and dishonest ignoramuses," he said to Losovsky. "Let Kunanbayev point out to you the men suitable for the job. There's no harm in trying. Put them through the elections and see what they're like."

Losovsky did not object, but expressed some doubts.

"The elders of the Kirghiz tribes are not only a mystery to us, the officials, but also to Kunanbayev himself. I'm not sure that his friends will prove much different from the others. They'll hardly be able to put the life of the steppes on the right lines. Unless the steppes have changed very much, we shall have a good deal of trouble. But as you say, there's no harm in trying." He smiled ironically and concluded: "Let's hope that in two years Kunanbayev and I will see the success of our experiments. I have my doubts."

A few days later Losovsky left for the elections. Abai and Yerbol followed him to Kzil-Moly, dispatching Baimagam-bet to the zhailyau with the news. A cartload of books selected by Mikhailov went with him.

Losovsky kept his promise. Consulting Abai during the elections in the Kzil-Moly, Konir-Koksha and Chinghis volosts, he did his best to strengthen the young man's authority everywhere. In all the auls they were received with great honours: yurtas were duly set up, cattle slaughtered and food cooked. Abai could be constantly seen in the company of the district chief, and the people were convinced that Abai had returned from the town more trusted and respected by the authorities than ever. Some, indeed, got the idea that he was a counsellor.

In every volost Abai first spoke to those he knew to be honest and just and then himself proposed one candidate or another. These men were invariably elected, and their eligibility was not disputed.

Though his experience in the town had taught him to mistrust the nomads Losovsky felt nothing but respect for Abai, and the two grew very friendly after a month together.

"Be very careful, Ibragim Kunanbayevich," he said jestingly. "It is you who are holding the elections and not I. I only listen to your recommendations and approve your candidates. What if they, too, turn out to be corrupt and arrogant; what if they draw up false statements and incite tribal warfare? How will you face your friends Mikhailov and Akbas then?"

There was no need for Losovsky's warning to make Abai conscious of his responsibilities not only to his friends, but to the people, whose life he was trying to improve. He succeeded in having three young men elected to volost rulers though no one had ever expected to see them in such a post, themselves least of all.

For the Chinghis Volost, Abai suggested Asilbek, Togzhan's brother, a friend he had respected from childhood for his good nature and his humaneness. Asilbek was elected to the office which Takezhan had hitherto regarded as his own domain—to the great chagrin of the Irgizbai and especially the older generation.

In Konir-Koksha, Abai prevented the election of the rich and ambitious Aban, who tried to obtain the office through bribery, and instead proposed the steady and intelligent djiguit Shimirbai.

For volost ruler of Kzil-Moly Volost, he proposed his younger brother Iskhak, a man of his own cast of mind. Iskhak was the son of Ulzhan, but had been brought up by

Kunkeh with Kudaiberdy. For a long time he had been under Takezhan's influence, but lately he had grown closer to Abai, recognising in him the just elder brother and true friend.

Such was the outcome of Abai's duel with the authorities which began in Yeraly. The people now believed that he was the victor and his fame spread ever wider over the steppes.

OVER THE RUTS

1

"Ah, Abai, Abai! May you never know happiness. Why have you deserted us in the desolate steppes, alone without kinsmen and friends? The house is without its master, the wife without her husband, the children without their father. What have we done to deserve this? Allah has punished us with blazing heat—the heavens must surely fall to earth. Is this a fitting place to camp, where the flies give us no rest? Each day it becomes hotter and hotter. And it is all your doing, Abai. No, there will be no happiness for you, never. For what sins am I so cruelly punished?"

Such were the words Dilda chanted in her shrill warble as she walked through the aul to Aigerim's yurta. Aigerim received her as one should an elder and rose to meet her respectfully.

Dilda now looked an old woman, thin, restless and cantankerous. Child-bearing had aged her prematurely; her face was wrinkled, and her cheek-bones protruded. Angular even when she was young, she now looked really scraggy.

Her visit to Aigerim and her vituperation against Abai in the younger wife's hearing were not in keeping with her usual scornful attitude to her rival. Dilda had her reasons for this.

Manas, who had arrived from town the night before, had brought a salem from Abai and a message to the effect that he would be away for the rest of the summer. Helping himself to refreshments, he had then discussed Abai in the presence of the neighbours and servants gathered in Dilda's yurta.

"His old mother sent me all that way with orders to keep galloping day and night. 'My son must be wasting away in jail. At least try to find out if he is in good health.' I galloped like mad. And what did I find? He turned out to be free and enjoying himself."

Manas chattered on—guardedly at first, fearful of arousing Dilda's jealousy, but then noticed to his surprise that she seemed even pleased.

"Don't hold back anything, my dear, and may Allah grant your wishes," she coaxed. "Tell us all you've seen and heard. God will surely punish you if you hide things from us."

Subtlety was unknown to the rough and stupid Manas. He had seen Abai and Saltanat in a half-darkened room and drawn his own conclusions. Rambling on, he was finally trapped in his own words.

"I don't blame Abai, though I gave him a piece of my mind right then and there before the girl. I couldn't help thinking about you, kelin, could I? Why shouldn't I talk to him as man to man? 'Your wife and children keep awake at night,' I said, 'pining for you. They can neither eat nor drink in peace, and here you are, embracing Aldekeh's daughter.' I didn't mince words. I was so angry."

Dilda extracted all she could from Manas and saw him ride off to zhailyau in the morning. She then went to Aigerim to cause what trouble she could with her talk.

At first Aigerim was completely bewildered. Dilda was excited, laughed and all but hugged her rival—something that had never happened before. But at last Dilda came to the point without concealing her glee, relishing the details and exaggerating a story already exaggerated by Manas.

The heat was intolerable, but Aigerim suddenly felt chilled to the marrow; it seemed to her that a vicious whip had struck at her heart. She seized Dilda's hand with icy fingers.

"What are you saying," she whispered, trembling. She peered into Dilda's face, unable to say more. It was only pride that restrained her tears, though large drops had frozen in her dilated eyes. Her colour changed, as though she were about to faint.

"Just listen to this, Aigerim," Dilda shrilled triumphantly, moving closer to her and pressing her knees to Aigerim's. "I haven't told you the main thing. That hussy Saltanat came rushing to town in a carriage with three bays to find a husband. 'Marry me,' she says to Abai. 'Don't you know the proverb: "You'll be cleansed with her with whom you've sinned." How can I look people in the face when everybody knows that it was I who dragged you out of prison. Even my fiancé will not have me now. I won't let you disgrace me before everyone.' 'But I have a wife and children,' Abai says. 'Your wife is no obstacle,' she says, 'that harpy of the steppes is no match for me. She'll do the chares for me. I am

your equal, not she. I'll have my way, I tell you, and you
shall marry me. Meanwhile you are to stay in the town all the
summer, I want to keep you for myself alone.' All this
means nothing to me, of course. I've given him up long ago.
But you.... Ah, the traitor! Leaving us here, like beggarly
zhataks, to build the winter place, while he....I have felt all
along that there was something keeping him in town and
there you are. May he never know happiness!"

Having unburdened herself, Dilda stalked out of the tent,
leaving a dark cloud over Aigerim's yurta. The days
dragged into weeks, but there was no sign of Abai.

Abai had gone to visit his mother at the Great Aul after
the elections and was there detained for two weeks, his
mothers, brothers and the relatives refusing to let him go.
He was anxious to go home and was worried about Aigerim,
but tried to show nothing of this. It was only when the
preparations for the final move to the Chinghis were
underway that Abai was able to set off, accompanied by
Baimagambet, Yerbol having decided to stay on until the
auls had left for their autumn pastures.

Setting off at dusk, they crossed the desolate range at
night. Despite the intense heat, they did not dismount until
midday, when they reached the winter place at Akshoky.
When Abai had left here in the spring, only the walls of his
future home could be seen; and now there was this large
building on one of the slopes. They dismounted and went
into the winter house. Baimagambet was impressed with the
height of the walls and the sturdiness of the roof. Abai
inspected the rooms carefully, beginning with the two
larders for winter storage and the special room with a
chimney for smoking meat. These premises were located on
the right of the building.

Aigerim and Ospan had supervised the work, but it was
Abai who had drafted the plan. He had done this very
carefully, indicating the length and breadth of the rooms
and the positions of the doors. Now he compared every wall
with the picture he had in his mind. Baimagambet grew
impatient and dashed ahead into the other rooms, to come
back bubbling with admiration.

"Abai-aga, come here. This is a fine house, a real city
house. And there's a ceiling of boards—and what a stove!"

The tour of inspection left Abai well pleased. The best
room was the bright and spacious corner room, which was
reached through a long hall and was next to another small
room, the last in this wing. Abai and Aigerim had intended

one of these rooms for Dilda and her children and the other
for the mullah.

Abai then inspected the rooms meant for himself and
Aigerim. According to his plan, the door to these premises
was to lead from an ante-room at the entrance. This had
been altered by Aigerim, however, who had ordered the
door to be built into another ante-room leading to an exit in
the other wing. Abai realised that this was in order to avoid a
meeting with Dilda. A separate entrance would give them
more privacy.

This cool and comfortable house was wonderfully restful.
Abai stopped in Aigerim's room and in his mind's eye
sought the place where the bed would stand. He could
visualise shimmering silk curtains, changing from red to
blue.

Baimagambet went all over the house, he had inspected
the rooms intended for himself and the other servants and
was greatly pleased. Abai followed him, peering into every
nook and corner.

Finished with the inspection, Abai sat down to rest in the
shadow of the high walls.

"Thank goodness that we've been spared all the fuss and
bother. Good for Aigerim, she coped with the job very
well." He rose to his feet. "Bring the horses and we'll ride
on—home!"

He was suddenly overwhelmed with longing for Aigerim
and the children.

Abai arrived at his aul just before sunset. The children
ran out to meet him and Baimagambet, while the grown-ups
stood waiting to greet them at the entrances of the yurtas.
Abai looked anxiously at Aigerim, who held the reins of his
horse. She seemed unwell, her face was drawn and strangely
pale, as though someone had snuffed out the
inner rosy glow that had made her so beautiful. Abai kissed
Abish and Gulbadan, hugged Magash and picked up little
Turash, who greatly resembled his mother, Aigerim. After
asking Dilda briefly about the affairs of the aul, he turned to
Aigerim.

The usual tenderness which had so gladdened him in the
past was gone and some great burden of grief appeared to
be weighing her down.

Abai could barely wait for the others to go, and when
Aigerim suddenly seemed to cringe, as from cold, hardly
able to control her tears longer, he said in a low voice:

"Look at me, Aigerim."

They had not spoken a word to each other yet, but in his tender tone Aigerim again felt her husband's usual, loving concern for her.

She smiled sadly, as if to say, "I am glad you have noticed how I feel at least", but the tears glistened on her lashes.

"What would you wish to say to me, Abai?"

Abai was startled and stared, surprised.

"Are you ill, Aigerim? What is the matter with you? You've not a drop of colour in your face. Has anything happened?"

Dilda's rasping voice cut in with the reply:

"Why such anxiety?" she asked with a malicious chuckle. "It's not illness that torments us but grief. And the cause of it must be well known to you." She chuckled again.

Dilda's tone to Abai was always resentful, but especially so now. Abai could feel that there was a serious accusation in her tone. Perhaps his family were displeased because he had not left the town as soon as the trial was over. He controlled himself, however, and continued to speak to the men, avoiding both Aigerim and Dilda.

He and Aigerim had never quarrelled. Her heart had been always constant and her love unchanged. Whatever was troubling her, he could not discuss it before the others, and he forced himself to talk to the children and the neighbours about the new house.

Neither Abai nor Aigerim slept during that long weary night of misery. Aigerim was obsessed with jealousy and a sense of injury, and as soon as they were left alone, she told him the story brought by Manas, and wept without restraint.

"How could you do it, Abai?" she asked again and again between her sobs. "Was it so long ago that our house was a place of happiness? But you have burned my heart out. My tears have put out the joyful light of this house. There is no remedy for my illness and there are no words to console me. My days are over."

She sat sobbing at Abai's feet all night.

Abai did his best to explain that Manas's words were merely a stupid conjecture, a downright lie. But nothing would console her, neither words nor caresses, and he suddenly realised with horror that all his efforts were in vain. The very earth seemed to heave beneath him and he saw himself amid the smouldering ruins of his happiness.

He lay awake, silent and crushed, till the pale dawn. Aigerim sighed, and bitter words burst from her deeply wounded, irreconcilable heart.

"May the lot of an unfortunate woman be cursed and its ashes scattered to the winds. What other consolation has she but scalding tears? But tears are nothing. Let them stream over my cheeks to the end of my days. The terrible thing is that they have washed everything from my heart, all my love for you with which it was filled. There is nothing to regret. Nothing matters any more. I have never concealed anything from you and this you must know too: I have no more heart, no more fire. There is only emptiness within me."

This was not his proud and beautiful wife. This was a woman mourning over a departed happiness.

Abai half rose, alarmed.

"What are you saying? Take back your words, cast aside such thoughts. Have pity on my past, which is clear of guilt. I believe we have a happy life before us. Do not sacrifice it, take back your words, Aigerim!"

In the bluish half-light, Aigerim seemed even paler than before. Saying nothing, she rose, wrapped herself in a black silk chapan and went out into the dim light of dawn, leaving Abai alone in the white yurta.

The days passed, but Aigerim was unchanged. Her outburst of grief was followed by silent torpor, and Abai could do nothing. A chill crept into their relations for the first time, and it would not melt.

Aigerim was his favourite wife and dearest friend. Their separation was unbearable, a wound that would not heal. Malicious slander had killed their happiness, and Dilda alone was the cause. For the first time in his life, Abai knew what it was to grieve over an irretrievable mistake. Why did he marry Aigerim without divorcing Dilda? Was he any better than other men who were ignorant, stupid and treacherous? He must suffer for this now and drink the poison he had mixed himself.

Tormented by remorse and loneliness, Abai spent his days and nights reading. Books were as necessary to him as breath itself. Soon he had read everything he had brought from the town and sent Baimagambet to fetch more books.

Nature itself seemed to respond to Abai's state of mind. It was a grim autumn. There was incessant rain over Yeraly and Oikodik, cold winds swept in from the steppes, and the long nights were damp and chilly.

Like a scholarly recluse, Abai hardly ever raised his eyes from his books and it was as though the chill of autumn had penetrated his heart. He seemed resigned to loneliness which he came to regard as an affliction — serious, but one to which he had become accustomed. Sometimes, towards evening, he mounted his horse and circled the herds aimlessly. When he returned after dark, he would feel that someone was waiting for him. Who could it be?

"I always feel that someone will come and dispel this gloom, but for whom am I waiting?" he thought one evening. "Perhaps Aigerim has come to life again. No. That is unlikely. Who am I waiting for then?" And suddenly he knew. "It is Yerbol — I wish he would come to spend these bleak days with me!"

On that rainy evening he felt an acute longing for his stalwart friend. Never had he appreciated Yerbol's friendship more. They had ridden the tortuous paths of life, suffering heat and cold together, and there had never been any differences between them. Only recently had they been compelled to part for long spells in winter or in summer.

When Abai married Aigerim, Yerbol, too, had celebrated his wedding with Damely, and his baby son Smagul had been born at the same time as Turash. Abai was as concerned with Yerbol's affairs as with his own. For a long time Yerbol had been dependent on Suyundik and other kinsmen, but now he had a good herd of his own and was not obliged to follow Suyundik's aul. He had united seven households into one independent aul surrounding the bright pentagonal yurta of his own family, and had enough milch and draught animals. Each time he went home after a long stay with Abai, he took back a cow or some sheep given him by his friend.

Just now Yerbol was living at the winter place in Karashoky; he had delayed leaving the hills for a time to prepare fodder and take measures against the oncoming cold. Abai had not troubled him, knowing that Yerbol would come to see him as soon as all this was seen to.

In the distant Chinghis, Yerbol must have sensed that he was needed. One evening when the lamps were being lit in the hushed yurta where Abai sat over his books, the door flew open. "Good evening," Yerbol sang out in his cheery voice.

Abai sprang up, rushed to his friend and hugged him fiercely.

"How good that you've come," he kept saying as he led Yerbol to the place of honour. "I've needed you like air itself. Take off your things. Please lay a corpeh on the floor, Aigerim, and don't forget the cushions!"

He was as pleased as a child. Even Aigerim laughed a little at the fuss he made, but quickly relapsed into silence again. She remembered how Abai used to meet her in just this manner after a day's separation. Something akin to pity stirred within her, but only for a moment.

A young heart seized with jealousy is sometimes vindictive, unjust and capable of mistaking a precious stone for a bit of worthless glass. Thus, she mistook Abai's exhilaration for something else; she thought that he was not rejoicing to see an old friend, but an accomplice in his affair with Saltanat.

She had always welcomed Yerbol as joyfully as Abai. His friendship had been a necessary part of their happiness; but now she felt that the two were linked by the very thing which separated her from Abai. "Saltanat has brought me grief and Yerbol helped to arrange their meetings. Who knows what secrets they share!"

Yerbol's arrival nonetheless dispelled the gloom that had long settled in this yurta. No sooner had he drunk his piala of kumiss than he began to joke as usual.

"Serve both tea and dinner at once, Aigerim. Nothing has passed my lips since the tea Damely gave me in Karashoky. Meanwhile, I shall pay my respects to Dilda, Alshinbai's daughter, who'll be screeching otherwise. I also want to see the children.... Are you going to stand there staring at me all day?"

Yerbol visited every one of the yurtas as though this were his own aul, everywhere greeting the elders. Soon he returned, and applying himself to the food, he told them the latest news. Preparations were underway for Umitei's wedding in Eskhozha's aul. This favourite of her clan, famous for her beauty, kindness and lovely voice, was soon to leave for the aul of Dutbai of the Kokshe.

Sure enough, the very same evening, Abai's aul received an invitation to the wedding. The women set off with Aigerim in the morning, while Abai, accompanied by Yerbol and Baimagambet, reached Eskhozha's aul in time for the midday meal.

The festivities were at their height and the Guest Yurtas were crowded with guests. The friends first went to the Great Yurta to salem Eskhozha and to wish happiness to the newlyweds. There they were invited to stay for dinner. From the yurta of the groom and his suite could be heard the songs of the girls, daughters-in-law and young men, until suddenly everything was drowned in the sound of loud

chattering voices and laughter. Something extraordinary
was afoot. Young people and children were running past
the Great Yurta and even some of the elderly folk were
contributing to the general commotion. There was a tumult
of voices.

"See, the seris have come!"

"Where have they come from?"

"Look at their dress—you can't tell whether they're
men or women. Look, some are all in red and some all in
green."

"There goes the eldest seri. See how he has decorated his
dombra. There's never been such a seri before."

The children were milling about in the crowd, screaming
with laughter.

"Look at those hats. Just like saukeleh.* They are not
seris, but a bunch of brides."

"And look at their trousers. Aren't they like skirts? And
that one's pantaloons are dragging behind like sausages."

The people were jostling each other, shouting and
laughing with excitement.

"The sals and seris have come," was the general cry.

Izgutty, who was also present in Eskhozha's yurta,
apparently, felt that it was beneath his dignity to address as
sal and seri some unknown tramps who had dared to
present themselves here with such ado.

"Who are they? Where are they from?" he asked
disapprovingly.

"They're no strangers. It's all a trick of your Amir,"
Eskhozha explained, having been forewarned, it appeared.

Abai and Yerbol had heard that several young djiguits
headed by Amir had been riding over the steppes during
the summer, visiting the auls as real sals and seris, though
no one had given them such titles.

The friends, therefore, went out to watch the antics of
Amir and saw a great crowd of young people in vivid and
motley garb heading for the three yurtas set up for the
groom.

The middle yurta was octagonal, its upper felts fringed
with red and ornamented with designs cut from red and
green cloth. The girls at the door were splendidly dressed,
wearing sable hats topped with owl feathers, and heavy
glittering sholpy in their braids. Umitei's outfit was especially conspicuous; her hat of dark otter was set at a slight angle.

---

* Saukeleh—a bride's headdress.—*Ed.*

She shone like Sholpan, the brightest of the morning stars, as she led the girls to receive the seris. Among the singers there were also some young women.

"Are there women seris too?" Baimagambet was surprised.

Yerbol had already recognised the party.

"Don't you see? Our Aigerim is among them too. They've taken our women into the secret."

On the eve of their arrival the unusual guests had sent messengers ahead — elaborately dressed youths with daggers in their belts. It was they who had raised the tumult and led a bevy of young women to meet the seris, who dismounted and walked on, their arms round the girls, and proclaiming their presence in song. The company was led by the senior seri, with a young woman on either side of him, each with a hand on his shoulder. He was the tall and handsome Baitas, the eldest of the young people. His dombra was decorated more luxuriantly than the others' with a thick tuft of owl feathers and jingling bells, as a sal-dombra* should be. He began each refrain by lifting and shaking the instrument over his head, a sign to the other seris to raise their decorated dombras as well and join in the refrain of "Zhirma-bes".

Abai and Yerbol were surprised to hear them singing in chorus. A song was usually sung by no more than two, even if a yurta was crammed with singers, and this novelty greatly appealed to them.

> Make merry while
> You're five and twenty,
> Remember, you will never be so young again!

ran the song. It was the very call of youth.

Led by Umitei, the girls sang the same song until the two processions met and finished the refrain together. Those of the girls who had been walking with the singers withdrew to the background, while each of Umitei's train took a seri by the hand. Baitas again found himself with two companions, while Umitei walked at Amir's side.

The crowd was heading for the middle yurta. The messengers dismounted and ran ahead, jestingly brandishing their ornate whips to keep the curious onlookers at a distance. The wedding yurtas were surrounded by a great throng, among which were Abai and his friends, the suite of

* Sal-dombra—a professional singer's dombra.— *Ed.*

the groom and the matchmakers. The messengers obeyed only the orders of their seris.

"Keep back! Make room!" they shouted, edging back the crowd to make way for the procession.

When someone moved forward, they would assume a ferocious attitude and roll their eyes in imitation of shabarmans. The tall batirs even gave the more venturesome a taste of their kamchas, something which no one seemed to mind, the victims laughing as they dodged the blows.

The pageant had attracted people from many auls; riders from great distances were pressing at the rear. No one had ever seen so many seris gathered at once — there were about forty of them. Their festive array, their unusual antics and their singing delighted everybody.

Tall, ruddy Baitas with a red, sharply pointed beard, stalked on with majestic disdain for the curious stares. The two girls still clung to his shoulders.

He was followed by Amir and Umitei, walking a little apart from the rest and pressing to one another like lovers after a long parting. It was they who led the chorus. Baitas was the leader of the procession, but the singing seris took their cue from these two, a handsome pair who attracted general attention and, in the language of the seris, seemed to have been painted by the hand of Allah himself.

Umitei's attire, from the owl's feathers on her fur hat to her pointed patent-leather shoes, enhanced her loveliness; she was radiant with happiness.

Amir, too, cut a dashing figure. His blue satin garb looked well on his tall figure and became his fair young face with its small moustache. He was obviously blind to all but Umitei, who seemed almost to float along on a current of joy. Their hearts already belonged to each other.

Yerbol watched the pair dubiously. Abai was also seized with foreboding. He suddenly lost all interest in the procession and began elbowing his way out of the crowd. Exclamations of surprise pursued him.

"Look at Amir and Umitei. They seem to think they're alone," an elderly woman was saying to her husband.

"Whose wedding is this — Dutbai's or Amir's?" a greying man asked, shrugging his shoulders.

The whispers running through the crowd were sure to converge into a great scandal. Abai was uneasy. He was ashamed for Amir and Umitei, ashamed before the crowd and Dutbai, Umitei's husband to be. Though a young man,

he enjoyed the respect of everybody, including Abai.
Should the talk reach him, things would go hard for him
and the other two. Abai could enjoy neither the singing nor
the merry-making, and when the djiguits mounted after
their repast and the games and races began, he found his
own horse and slipped off alone.

The faces of Amir and Umitei, aglow with passion, were
still there before his eyes. He was vexed and yet pitied them,
condemned them, yet felt that they were urged on by
something stronger than themselves, by something he had
found in books many times. Abai rode over the steppes, lost
in thought. Rhymes and rhythms vaguely came to his mind.
A new melody appeared of itself; it was slow and
melancholy, well suited to the words that were on his lips.

> The speech of lovers needs no words,
> Another tongue they seem to know.
> The eyes light up, the eyebrow curves,
> And there's the answer — yes or no.

He could not get these lines out of his mind all day and
when he returned to the aul they were still with him.

Only the first day of the festivities passed gaily and noisily
as a wedding should: but the next day was charged with
impending disaster. The gossip flew over the steppes like
fire on a windy day and spread through all the clans.
"Amir's behaviour has disgraced the Irgizbai in the eyes of
the Kokshe," hissed those who nursed a grudge against the
Irgizbai; while others, eager to settle scores with the
Karabatir, said that the youth had been led astray by Umitei.
"Sing me into marriage with your songs," she was supposed
to have said as she invited the young man to her wedding.

Be that as it may, Amir and Umitei were inseparable,
singing the whole time. Aigerim sang a great deal too, as if
releasing all those songs which had been pent up within her
for so long; they flew from her like nightingales freed from
a cage.

Dutbai was one of the cleverest, most eloquent and
famous djiguits of the Kokshe who already commanded the
respect of his kinsmen. The dubious position in which
Umitei had placed him at his own wedding was agony to a
man so proud and ambitious. At first he had cut short the
hints of his friends, then tried to persuade Umitei to
withdraw from the seris. He did not reproach her, but
Umitei would not listen to reason.

"I am taking leave of my kinsmen, perhaps for ever," she answered. "I know it is not pleasant for you but please let me make merry for the last time with the friends I grew up with!"

She knew how to get her own way, especially by coaxing, and was not used to obeying anyone.

Dutbai was a good judge of people and was sufficiently self-possessed to preserve his dignity under the circumstances. After some deliberation, he decided that direct action could only make matters worse and lead to an open rupture. He was unwilling to lose Umitei, whom he had always liked. He would, therefore, suffer the company of the seris and pay no heed to the spreading gossip.

But on the fourth day his patience was tried too far. Early in the morning he came upon Umitei and Amir, wrapped in a black chapan, standing locked in embrace beside the bride's white yurta. Dutbai tore the chapan from their heads and saw their tear-stained faces. The lovers were lost to the world in a long farewell kiss.

Dutbai ordered the horses to be fetched from the pasture at once. Everyone of his party was immediately awakened, including the chief matchmaker and the eldest kinsmen. "Let them mount their horses without so much as a sip of water," he commanded. His tone brooked no contradiction, and at sunrise the groom and his suite left Eskhozha's aul without telling anyone.

It was not only the bride who was disgraced, but the entire aul. The groom had deserted his bride, contemptuously returning her to her people. Eskhozha gathered the elders and tried to overtake Zhanatai, the chief matchmaker. "Don't fan the flames; don't invite trouble. You can say that you merely went off ahead of the general party, that everybody was asleep and no one saw you leave. We can still save the situation—we'll dismantle the wedding yurta immediately and send Umitei with you. Why should we part as enemies?"

Zhanatai spoke to Dutbai, who had already recovered his balance and agreed, having considered the inevitable consequences. Eskhozha then galloped back to the aul. The bride's yurta was dismantled and soon Umitei was sent off to the groom's aul together with an escort and the dowry caravan.

At the end of that troubled day Aigerim returned to her aul. Abai and Yerbol, who met her outside the yurta, were struck by her expression, happy and animated as in the days of old. She alighted, and handing her coat to Zlikha, asked Abai and Yerbol how things were in the aul.

"Just look at her, Yerbol. She seems to have come to life again. This is what her beloved songs have done for her." Abai regarded her with delighted surprise.

"Very true," Yerbol agreed. "She is like a red fox who has rolled in the virgin snow."

Aigerim smiled.

"Why did you leave me then, alone with my songs, and why are you now joking at my expense?"

"We're not joking, my dear. We're perfectly serious," Abai reassured her gravely. "You were born for singing and we have hooded you like a falcon. Now you look like a bird circling over the aul in the winds after a long flight. It's a shy bird at such a time, and won't easily alight on one's wrist. It has been dreaming too long of the free skies to forget its brief spell of freedom at once. Am I right, Aigerim?"

At first smiling with the two, Aigerim then added with mounting bitterness, "You're still joking. Now you call me a fox, now a falcon. What am I then? I know only that I am hooded so as to keep the truth from me." She frowned and went into the yurta.

Umitei's departure could not cool Amir's madness. When she was taken away, he set off from Eskhozha's aul with his seris by another route. As soon as the aul was out of sight, he slumped over the neck of his horse and abandoned himself to grief. The djiguits tried to console him and one of them proposed that they overtake the wedding to give Amir a chance to kiss Umitei goodbye for the last time.

Amir, who never took any notice of gossip, remained deaf to the talk even now. The mere thought of seeing Umitei once more sent his spirits soaring at once, and he sat up in the saddle again.

Even the fact that her groom left so abruptly failed to bring Umitei to her senses. She did not conceal her grief when she sobbed in Amir's arms, or now, on the way to the groom's aul. Her eyes red with tears, she wept bitterly, and every now and then glanced sorrowfully at the road behind her. Suddenly she noticed a party of riders in motley garb rapidly overtaking them. The elders at the head of the train saw them too.

"Now what has brought them here? Are they out of their minds?" said Eskhozha to Izgutty in surprise.

A lone rider led the group at a distance of an arrow's flight.

Umitei reined in her horse, certain that it was Amir.

The young man galloped to her side and pressed her to his breast, while his companions surrounded the couple, forming a living yurta of white horses around them. The seris struck up the Kozy-kosh farewell song, slowing the tempo to impart a special solemnity to the words.

> *Goodbye, my friends, my gay young friends!*
> *With you I was a youth again,*
> *But when I part with you, alas,*
> *My borrowed youth too soon will pass....*

Amir and Umitei continued to weep in each other's arms. Hurrying to them from the head of the procession, Izgutty and Eskhozha cut through the living barrier, shouting wildly:

"Stop that at once. Haven't you caused trouble enough?"

"Come to your senses, Amir. You've said your farewell and now go your way."

Izgutty seized the reins of Umitei's horse and pulled them furiously towards him, so that the pacer leapt aside and tore Umitei from Amir's arms.

"Amir!" she sobbed, trying to stop the horse. "Don't leave me! My relatives are throwing me into the fire! Take me to it. Stay with me, all of you."

Her tears were instantly dry. She swept the company with a look of despair and exclaimed with a peculiar vehemence:

"Let him go mad, if he likes. Let him dare thwart me!" She clutched at the reins of Amir's horse, drawing him on.

"Dear moon of mine," he said leaning towards her and kissing her. "I would rather die than see you set, my full moon. I'll go with you even if it costs me my life." He then addressed the seris. "We shall all go."

The party of seris surrounded Umitei and Amir, jostling Eskhozha and Izgutty out of the way. The elders and matchmakers returned to the head of the procession, helpless to alter the course of events.

The festive octagonal bride's yurta had already been taken to the groom's aul and the young kelin entered, supported by Amir and Baitas. A silken curtain was carried unfolded before her, since the seris did not wish to break the custom. The aul, however, received the party with anxiety and even hostility.

The spirit of enmity, nonetheless, did not cross the threshold of the Young Yurta with them. Both the young people and the elderly baibishes met the new kelin with best wishes, showered gifts on her in the manner usual at weddings. Nobody seemed to notice the odd fact that Amir was there.

This solemn and dignified reception was the work of Dutbai. He had taken counsel neither with the elders of the Kokshe nor with his father Alatai. Patiently and manfully, he had carried out his own decision — to turn the slander from Umitei's name and to accept her hospitably and joyfully.

On the same evening, however, he entrusted his guests to his mother, a calm and tactful woman, mounted his horse and rode to the chief of the Kokshe, his uncle Karatai, who lived in the neighbouring aul.

When he arrived, he requested everyone to leave the yurta and then told Karatai of how his pride had been insulted by Amir.

"Can you go to Kunanbai and explain all to him?" he concluded. "Let him put the curb on the boy or the friendship between the Kokshe and the Irgizbai will crumble to dust."

Karatai looked at the young man intently, thinking over his decision.

"Tell them to bring my horse," he ordered briefly. "Also ask someone to accompany me. I shall go to Kunanbai at once."

Dutbai sent a messenger to fetch his father Alatai and Bozambai, one of the leaders, requesting that they accompany Karatai.

Kunanbai's aul stood all by itself on Korik. The old Hadji had separated from the Irgizbai, who were now in the winter places in Oikodik. Nurganim had not been willing to forget the insult from Ospan and begged Kunanbai all the summer to build her a separate winter house. She wanted to be away from her rivals and their grown-up and impertinent sons. This request, it so happened, fitted in well with Kunanbai's hankering for the solitude he sought in his old age. During the summer he moved to Korik before the others, taking a party of djiguits with him to build a small winter house for himself and Nurganim. Now he was enjoying the death-like quiet he wanted.

Karatai and his companions arrived by nightfall. The aul seemed asleep, but a light burnt in Kunanbai's yurta. On hearing their horses and the ferocious barking of the dogs, Nurganim decided that the visitors must be strangers, since everyone gave the aul a wide berth even by day. Kunanbai never emerged from behind his curtain to join in wordly conversation; his guests, therefore, were usually bored and anxious to get away.

"Karatai has come," said Nurganim quietly to her husband when the men entered the yurta. She had peeped through the curtain from her place at Kunanbai's feet.

Kunanbai was sitting up in bed, propped up by pillows, and telling his beads with lowered eyes. He looked up quickly, his expression of repentance and humility vanishing in a flash. The guests had hardly reached the place of honour when Kunanbai jerked aside the curtain which had not been moved since the morning, and fixed his one bleak eye upon the visitor. Karatai was shocked by the cruel, wary and malicious look of the repenting Hadji. No one had seen Kunanbai look just that way for ten years. Karatai felt as if he had stumbled into the den of a sleeping beast of prey and awakened its occupant to instant fury.

Karatai's visit was no surprise to Kunanbai, as Aigiz had called upon him on return from Eskhozha's aul the night before. She had left the wedding in a state of righteous indignation. Eskhozha was a close kinsman of hers and she had remonstrated with him angrily before she left for allowing the seris to take such liberties and turn the wedding into a disgraceful spectacle. Eskhozha was no less indignant than she and asked her to convey his protest to Kunanbai, explaining that he had permitted Amir's presence only because the young man was Kunanbai's grandson.

Aigiz not only passed on his words to Kunanbai, but added many remarks of her own.

She relieved herself of her long pent-up hatred for those who were younger than she, and did not leave until she was satisfied that her words had struck home.

Kunanbai guessed at once that the old men had come here on behalf of the entire Kokshe clan. The late hour, the grim faces and frowns boded evil times for the Tobikty. Kunanbai was the first to speak, as he sat there, his hand crumpling the edge of the curtain.

"What evil wind has brought you here? What has happened? Speak up!"

The two old men understood each other from the slightest movement of their eyebrows. Staring at the cold angry mask of Karatai's face, Kunanbai knew that his old crony had made up his mind as stubbornly as he himself. "He has suffered a mortal injury. He has not come to make peace."

And Karatai, who in his turn read the Hadji's thoughts, felt that he could give free rein to the anger that had had him in its grip since the night before.

He told all he knew about Amir, Dutbai and Umitei.

"If it were my honour alone that were at stake! But they are disgracing our ancestors, desecrating their ashes. They are dancing on their tombs, they are besmirching us with their filth to make us appear as black as they are in the eyes of Allah. I pity you, but can no longer hold my peace. To whom else shall I complain? Who shall be my support in these wicked times? I have never brought my complaints to you nor even to the meanest dog in your aul. But now I demand that you put an end to all these outrages. It is time you passed judgement."

Further discussion was unnecessary. Kunanbai told Nurganim to accommodate the guests in a separate yurta and ordered a rich dinner. Then he summoned one of his djiguits and told him:

"Take two horses and gallop to Alatai's aul on the Sholak-Terek. Find Izgutty and give him this message. He must bring Amir to me before sunset; if he resists, then let him be brought by force, bound hand and foot, and beaten into obedience, if need be."

Kunanbai continued to sit very still with the hem of the curtain still in his hand until the very morning. The lines of his face were deepened by the cold hatred and impotent rage seething within him.

The first pale streaks of dawn became scarlet ribbons of autumn over the broad yellow plain. The first rays were flooding the yurta with crimson sunlight when Izgutty and Amir entered. Amir was deathly pale, and his eyes were dull and lifeless.

It was a long time since Kunanbai had seen his grandson. He glared at the youth in silence, and then beckoned him nearer. Amir discarded his hat and whip, approached his grandfather and kneeled before him. The old man's bony fingers suddenly released the hem of the curtain, closed round the neck of the youth and squeezed his bare throat. The aged hands had not lost their former power and the iron grip became more terrible, until Amir grew livid, gasped for breath and collapsed. Kunanbai dropped to his knees, but the iron claws gripped tighter. Another instant and everything would have been over, had not Izgutty hurled himself at Kunanbai.

"What are you doing? Even if he is a dog, he is your grandson." But he quailed at Kunanbai's look. Then Nurganim seized her husband by the hands.

"Hadji, oh light of our eyes, come to yourself! Forgive him!" she screamed, and tore Kunanbai's hands from the young man's throat by her sheer weight. But the old man thrust his knee into her chest with such violence that she sank to the ground unconscious.

At that moment the felt door was thrown back and Abai appeared. He saw Kunanbai pounce upon Amir again as Nurganim fell. In one leap he was at the old man's side.

"Stop it!" he cried tearing his father's hands from Amir's throat.

"He's an infidel," roared Kunanbai.

"I won't let you kill him!"

They stood facing each other with burning eyes, ready to fight to the death. Abai was filled with revulsion, and his words came as sharp as daggers.

"Allah is on your lips and blood is on your hands — and what for? In the name of the Sharia again? But does this Sharia forbid love? Or is it the same Sharia in the name of which you once shed innocent blood?"

Again the scene of Kodar's death flashed before Abai's eyes. He was only a boy then, but now he would not let his father repeat the crime.

"And so you're going to murder a man against the law of the Sharia now? Was your pledge of silence and prayer given in a state of humility or not? Or was it done only to conceal that vulture's heart of yours?"

Kunanbai recovered the power of speech at last.

"Get out!" he shouted. "Out of my sight!"

"I will not go!"

"Abettor of evil-doers! Seducer! Everything is on your conscience. You'll lead them all astray!"

"Be that as it may. But why should you not die in peace? This is my time, not yours, so why do you meddle in our lives?"

"Ah, so, that's how you talk! How low you have fallen..." snarled Kunanbai and suddenly stopped short.

He stretched out both hands, palms outwards, as though pushing someone away — motioning towards Abai and Amir who had only just regained consciousness. Then Kunanbai brushed his face with his knuckles — an unspoken prayer for vengeance.

Nurganim and Izgutty cried together:

"Reject his prayer, O Allah."

"Hear him not, O Lord of the Creation. Woe! Woe! He is cursing his children," they repeated in horror.

Kunanbai seemed oblivious of them. Kneeling by his bed he clearly enunciated the curse, pointing now to Abai and now to his prostrate grandson.

"On this crimson dawn and early morning, I lay my paternal curse on this tainted blood, on these two bastards of my tribe. I beseech Thee, the great and omnipotent Allah, Thou who hast not let me put him to death, to heed the prayer of Thy slave, my one and only supplication. Take the lives of these two; send Thy certain death upon them; destroy these wretches before they contaminate others!"

Once more, he raised his knuckles to his face.

"Begone!" he shouted hoarsely. "Even if in truth my blood flows in your veins, you are bastards! I shall make a sacrifice of both of you. Go to your death, and may you perish quickly. Begone!"

Abai listened, looking at his father with contempt.

"I will go. And for ever!" he said tersely.

Kunanbai drew the curtain and leaned back, his beads moving swiftly in his wiry hands — once more the Hadji had given himself up to prayer and repentance.

Amir stumbled to his feet and picked up his hat and whip, but suddenly collapsed again. Mustering all his strength, he turned towards the curtain.

"You have called for my death, but I am not afraid. I am not afraid, do you hear? Even if you burn me alive!" he cried desperately.

Abai helped him to his feet and led him into the open. How fortunate that he had come just at that moment. The alarming tidings that Izgutty had taken Amir to Kunanbai had reached him shortly before dawn. Abai, who knew his father's wicked temper, mounted his horse at once and arrived at the old Hadji's aul in the very nick of time.

2

October had come and the auls were finishing the sheep shearing. The day when they should leave the autumn pastures was drawing near, but no one seemed to be in a hurry to move to the winter place. Though much of the grass, once thick as felt, near the auls in Oïkodik had been devoured and ground to dust by the cattle, there was still abundant fodder farther on. Now that the heat had subsided the cattle seemed to be growing fatter by the hour and the thrifty aul masters decided to endure the hardships of the autumn rains and winds for a while.

The larger of the summer yurtas had been dismantled and dispatched to the winter places, and the smaller and warmer tents had been set up in their place.

The walls of Aigerim's new yurta were hung with carpets and patterned felts. The tall bed had been replaced by several thick corpehs laid on the floor. The space before the bed where meals were eaten was covered with long-haired sheepskins, while the hearth and the cauldron occupied the centre of the yurta.

One rainy day, Abai sat reading on the bed, leaning back against the folded blankets and pillows. He was wearing his winter clothes: a light fur-lined coat over his beshmet and roomy felt-lined boots. Aigerim, who sat at her husband's side as always, was well wrapped up in a light beshmet of fox paws trimmed with marten at the collar and hem. The fastenings were of red semi-precious stones, and the silver buttons were the work of a well-known handicraftsman. She was busy with embroidery as usual, while Yerbol and Baimagambet played togiz-kumalak,* leisurely sipping the autumn kumiss. The dinner was ready, the cauldron had been removed from the fire and the acrid smoke from the cinders stung the eyes and left a bitter taste in the mouth. When the hostess invited them to wash their hands and take their places around the cloth, Abai shut the book he had been reading since morning and raised his eyes to the shanrak.

"We should open the tunduk," he observed. But drizzling rain came through the crevice left as an outlet for the smoke.

"What foul weather!" he said with a frown. "When you open the tunduk, you get the rain, when you close it, you get the smoke."

Low voices could be heard outside and Shakke, Abai's nephew and Amir's elder brother, came in. He had a worried look and obviously could not wait to speak with Abai. Indeed, as soon as the meal was over, he turned to his host.

"I've come for your advice, Abai-aga. I should like to talk to you about Amir."

---

* Togiz-kumalak — "nine marbles", a Kazakh game somewhat resembling draughts. — *Ed.*

Shakke paused, and his hesitation alarmed Abai and Aigerim.

"Is he in good health?" Aigerim asked. "The poor boy lives like an outcast."

"Is he still as unhappy?" Abai asked sympathetically.

"He is a secretive sort," answered Shakke vaguely. "I don't think he is ill. He looks well enough. But he is sick at heart. That's why he's wasting away. What I'm really troubled about, Abai-aga, is this: he used to walk about like a ghost, but now, out of stubbornness perhaps, he has taken to his old ways. Without consulting his kinsmen, he yesterday summoned all his old friends, these sals and seris. They've dressed themselves up again and are preparing to do something mad. Only this morning I heard some of them say that they were going to go to the Kokshe — but that would be an open challenge, wouldn't it? What will the old Hadji say? He has just put his curse upon Amir. And the Kokshe are just waiting for a chance to revenge themselves upon Amir. I fear that they will stop at nothing, and do evil. How can I prevent it? Give me your advice."

Abai listened intently, weighing every word of these sad tidings. His decision came as a surprise to all.

"We cannot abandon Amir to his grief or let him die," he said. "If he had lived in other times, he might have been head and shoulders above the rest of us, the generation that has cursed him. I sympathise with Amir with all my heart. He has been punished enough, let him do as he pleases now. Let him at least not say that he is being driven from pillar to post by pursuers on horse and on foot. Place no obstacles in his way, Shakke. Let him go to the Kokshe if he wants to. Father will not take back the curse, no matter what Amir does. Besides, the Kokshe have calmed down. His heart may be lightened if he pours his grief out in song."

Yerbol and Shakke pondered Abai's words and agreed. Aigerim alone denied him support.

"What good are honeyed words from one's kinsmen unless they are confirmed by deeds?" she exclaimed, and turned away.

Since his return from Semipalatinsk, Abai had felt that he had lost his Aigerim. She had never been wont to say much, but had always shared his thoughts and feelings. She seemed to have lost her old ability to catch the meaning behind Abai's words. And now, in her remark he sensed estrangement and an inner coldness.

Worried as he was over Amir, Abai's sense of loneliness was intensified by this thought about Aigerim. The old happy days of warmth had given way to a grey, humdrum married life. Dreariness had come to stay in his once cheerful home. It seemed a bleak autumn of life, full of hurts, reproaches and accusations — and the cause was the innocent Saltanat.

Aigerim's words stung Abai to the quick, but he made no response and began to turn things over in his mind. "Confirmed by deeds," he mused. But hadn't he openly confronted his father to shield Amir? He recalled Kunanbai's curse and smiled bitterly; on the one hand there was his father's hatred, which had driven the old man to plead with Allah for Abai's death, and on the other there was this estrangement from Aigerim, the only person whom he had thought to be completely devoted to him. Why this estrangement? What crime had he committed? He had never betrayed their love and Aigerim was wrong to think so.

It was true that Abai often thought of Saltanat, but only with the deepest respect. He was indeed proud of the fact that he had conducted himself with discretion and was sure that he would act in the same way if he met another such as Saltanat. Was his behaviour not a newly acquired virtue, a consequence of his education, a rare instance in the Kazakh society of his time? He knew that the Russian books had taken root within him and brought forth new fruits of purity and humaneness. He was lonely, but his conscience was clear. It is not only an education I have acquired, he thought, but a new outlook too. The result is my attitude to Saltanat, an attitude which seems so ridiculous to the djiguits.

Aigerim could understand nothing of this, of course. A djiguit and a girl could not be mere friends, in her opinion. She understood things in the old way. How could he explain?

A person could only come to the viewpoint he had reached through experience, and by adopting a new attitude towards people and life. That, indeed, was the crux of the matter. "We would understand each other at once if she had a broader view. As things stand, it is impossible," he thought, recollecting how many times he had tried to heal her imaginary wound, how many times he had attempted to get her to think of Saltanat in a different light. Yet, every time he had met with silence as she withdrew into herself with a gloomy, resentful expression. They seemed to stand on the opposite banks of a river with no ford between them.

THROUGH THE PASS

1

April had come. Spring had set in early that year and everything had turned green at once. Lambing time had come and the lambs and kids were frisking about their mothers, grazing on the hills around the winter place at Akshoky. Abai's aul had not yet moved from the winter houses and only Aigerim had so far set up her yurta nearby.

Abai and Baimagambet sat on their favourite hill surrounded by eager listeners.

During the winter evenings, when Abai talked to Yerbol, the Kishkineh-Mullah and his elder children about the books he had read, Baimagambet had always listened attentively. He easily remembered the plot of every story with its host of characters and involved situations at first hearing, and could vividly and accurately render the content afterwards. His fame as a story-teller had thus spread not only over Korik and Akshoky, but throughout the whole area from the Chinghis to Semipalatinsk.

The sun was going down and the evening breeze grew cooler, but no one stirred to go. The children too were listening breathlessly; Abish, the most diligent pupil in Abai's family school, Magash, an unusually gifted youngster who was the favourite of all, and grown-up Akilbai, who had come specially from Nurganim's aul and was staying for the night to hear Baimagambet. They were all so engrossed that no one noticed the approach of a rider, until he sprang from his saddle in their very midst.

It was Asilbai, one of the herdsmen of the Great Aul, on his way back to Ulzhan's aul from Semipalatinsk. His bay was wet with foam.

"What's the news in town?" Abai asked after the exchange of salems.

"Haven't you heard?" Asilbai was genuinely surprised. "Terrible things are being said, Abai-aga. The white tsar who ruled us, they say, has died — and a violent death too. Someone killed him with a gun."

The Kishkineh-Mullah moved his lips silently as he reverently swept his face with his palms.

"Whatever happened?" Abai asked. "Where did you hear such a thing? When was he killed? And by whom?"

"Must be more than a month ago. That's all they can talk about in Semipalatinsk. The churches are full of Russians and in the mosques too they are saying the evening prayer. People have to swear allegiance to the new tsar. It's bedlam, I tell you! The tsar's son has ascended the throne and the murderer has been caught, they say. I had no time to hear more."

Abai digested the news and began to think things over. Those who had arranged the assassination of the tsar could be no ordinary murderers, he was sure. "They are the sort that cannot be restrained or intimidated," he thought. "They have a clear mind and a strong will, they will never reconcile themselves to banishment and exile. They had to do something that would shake the whole of Russia, and they did do it."

In the meantime, the Kishkineh-Mullah decided to improve their minds on the occasion.

"The Sharia teaches us to revere him who rules us and our people, no matter what his faith. A funeral prayer was held at the mosque and this means that we Moslems are also in mourning. It's a truly sorrowful event. In no books have I ever read that simple people could kill their tsar. The end of the world must be near and these are the final days."

Abai caught only the last words of his sermon.

"Wherever there is great violence, there is sure to be great hatred," he said, rising with a faint smile. "How can you who live here know what wrongs and anger prompted that hand?" He went to the yurta, beckoning Baimagambet to follow.

"Bakke," he said to him as they approached the tent. "I want you to take a letter to town tomorrow. Find out all the particulars you can."

Baimagambet left the next morning and returned in three days, bringing a basket full of books and Mikhailov's answer.

The Russian briefly cited official reports: on March 1, as the tsar was returning from a walk, a bomb was thrown at him. He was fatally wounded and died soon afterwards at the Winter Palace. The assassination had been planned in advance and some of the conspirators had been caught. The governor of Semipalatinsk had mustered the garrison and the employees of the town offices to attend a mass for the deceased tsar, after which all of them, from soldier to clerk, swore allegiance to the new tsar, Alexander III. At the end of his note, Yevgeny Petrovich said that he had been dismissed from his post by secret orders. "Such is the pass to which we have come, Ibragim Kunanbayevich," his letter concluded. "You will hardly be satisfied with the story that Baimagambet will bring you. No matter how comfortable you may be at Akshoky, it would be worth your while to come to town and get first-hand information."

The next day Abai left for Semipalatinsk, accompanied by Baimagambet. A fresh, invigorating breeze blew in their faces. The ground was dry and the uneven muddy patches were gone. The spring grass, as yet untouched by sun or dust, was bright and fresh. The low bushes of wormwood and early tulips covered the hills from Akshoky to Semipalatinsk. Even the smallest puddle was fringed with soft silky grass.

Baimagambet loved a fast drive and had three light bays, well kept and well trained, ready for the occasion. He set them at a fast trot, right from the house, and the swift ride, with the wheels rattling over the stony road, was cheering, rather than tiring. Lashing the horses with his long whip, Baimagambet continued the story, *Black Age,* that had been interrupted by Asilbai's unexpected arrival, hoping that Abai would set him right in the most tricky places.

His memory always amazed Abai. In telling the story, Baimagambet clearly expressed his own attitude to the characters, correctly judging their actions, minds and their upbringing. He recounted the complicated plot without once faltering, as if he had read the book from cover to cover several times.

Baimagambet had never studied Russian nor could he read or write in Kazakh. But he so thoroughly digested the books read by Abai that his behaviour and even his character was noticeably changing under their influence. Abai could not help seeing that the man had become somewhat different from other djiguits, unconsciously imitating the actions and speech of his favourite heroes. He was an amazing phenomenon in this environment — an educated illiterate. There was something about his prominent aquiline nose and sharp blue eyes fringed with heavy lashes that distinguished him from other djiguits. To Abai he was not like an ordinary groom, but a fellow-traveller from some unknown country.

Abai now looked at his companion as though he saw him for the first time. This was a new man indeed. Baimagambet was straightforward and truthful, unflinching in the face of danger and superior to trite gossip; he never repeated anything which might hurt anybody. He could be trusted with a secret, and as Aigerim said in fun he would not even divulge what was said between Abai and his little son, Turash.

Aigerim, who was good at qualifying people, once said: "You have told him so much about the Russians, that he is becoming like them himself: he takes the straight road, not a twisting path. I imagine a good, honest Russian is like that."

"We simply don't notice how much books do to educate us and form our characters," Abai thought. "Baimagambet is younger and shows it more than I. Looking at him, I can see as in a mirror how far my own character has changed, how far I have come from the age-old precepts."

After the riders had paused at midday to feed their horses and refresh themselves, Baimagambet resumed his *Black Age* and finished it by evening, at the very gates of Tinibai.

During this visit to town, Abai met Mikhailov even more often and had longer talks with him. Yevgeny Petrovich's time was now his own, and they saw each other whenever they pleased. At their first meeting, Mikhailov told Abai those details of the events which he had thought ill-advised to set down in a letter. There had been earlier attempts to assassinate the tsar, and Zhelyabov and the heroic Russian girl Sophia Perovskaya had recently been executed in St. Petersburg. These men and women unhesitatingly risked their freedom and their very lives for the cause of the people. This time the authorities were seriously frightened, he thought. With a smile, he observed that the manifesto of March 4 stated that the government would give its attention to economic and social problems, something hitherto unheard of.

"If such a word as 'social' has found its way into their vocabulary," he said to Abai with mock horror, "it can only mean that the throne is tottering. Yes, in St. Petersburg they are certainly frightened by the spectre of revolution."

Abai plied his friend with questions — this was a subject they had never touched on before. Mikhailov told him that the assassination had been stimulated by a broad, popular movement against the autocracy, and he drew the conclusion that Russian society was heading for revolution, led by its finest people. This raised Mikhailov still higher in Abai's estimation. Abai tried to digest what he had heard, and asked more questions to solve the fresh problems in his mind.

"You have just said that the authorities are frightened. Then why don't they do something to relieve the lot of such exiles as you? They've even dismissed you from your post, haven't they?"

Mikhailov shrugged his shoulders and laughed.

"I'm small game, I suppose, and the authorities don't think I'm worth bothering about. My wings were clipped, so to speak, when I was only in my third year at the university. And then, they tolerated me at my post not because they liked me, but because they had no alternative. Two years ago, you see, the governor received instructions from St. Petersburg to set up a statistical committee. Now the local officials had never heard of such a thing as statistics and, since I was rather good at it in the university and there was no one else, they had to put me in charge of a task which gave me little authority but a lot of trouble. I had nothing better to do just then and decided to agree. But unfortunately, I suffer from an incurable disease: I can't do anything half-heartedly, and so I plunged headlong into the subject and even acquired an inkling of the complexity of economic conditions here. But the moment the authorities heard what had happened in St. Petersburg they hastily dismissed statistician Mikhailov, who was under police surveillance, from office. Still I won't drop the work merely on that account. I may do some good to this region yet. To think what could be made of this country if one went competently about it and had the good of the people, and not the merchants and industrialists in mind."

The subject carried him away.

To facilitate their meetings, Abai took quarters not at Tinibai's, but at Karim's. The small islands in the midst of the Irtish were thick with green and the two friends often rambled along the riverside or at times boated to Colonel Island and talked for hours. Their conversations grew more and more interesting. Mikhailov was only four years older than Abai, but his crowded experiences seemed especially rich in their complexity. "It's an unwritten dastan," * thought Abai and at once corrected himself, "No, dastan is not the word. A dastan tells the story of one hero, while there are many heroes here and the dragon that they fight is a thousand years old; it's earthly God attired in gold and precious stones."

* Dastan—a lay.— *Ed.*

Abai was eager to know when and how revolutionary thought had come into being in Russia. Mikhailov told him of the origin of the struggle against the autocracy, about Pushkin, Belinsky, Hertzen and the new upsurge of the revolutionary movement stimulated by Chernyshevsky. He spoke of the latter with special reverence, and Abai decided that this man must have been the teacher of his friend.

He also learned of the unsuccessful attempt of Karakozov and his death on the gallows. The fate of Ishutin, Karakozov's cousin and the leader of the group, shocked him deeply. He had been taken to Semyonov Square in St. Petersburg on a grey autumn day and heard the death sentence read. Then, when a hood had been placed over his head and the noose around his neck, another order was read commuting the death sentence to hard labour. This was the first time that Abai heard of prisons whereby the autocracy kept itself safe. They were a hell on earth, where a man's soul was ripped out without shedding blood and his breathing was stopped without a rope and gallows — the Fortress of Schlüsselburg, the Alexeyev Ravelin, the Irkutsk Alexandrov Central Prison where Ishutin went mad, though he had lived there for a long time afterwards and people had been unable to look upon him without tears. To Abai it seemed that only a beast of prey could play with its victim so cruelly, threatening it with death and tormenting it with hope.

"Can such things be possible, Yevgeny Petrovich!" he exclaimed. "Is it possible before the eyes of all Russia to torment and humiliate a man who was prepared to die?"

Mikhailov told him that almost the same thing had been done to Chernyshevsky, whom he called the pride of advanced Russian society and the champion of free thought.

"We have but one teacher, Chernyshevsky. His ideas have been inspiring the younger generation for the past fifteen or twenty years."

Chernyshevsky, he said, was taken to Mitnaya Square in St. Petersburg on May 19, 1864, and publicly received a sentence of seven years hard labour. Though seventeen years had passed, he was still in Vilyuisk Prison in Siberia.

Another thing, too, surprised Abai. He had taken it for granted that the idea of assassination had come from Chernyshevsky, but was surprised to hear that Mikhailov's teacher had had nothing to do with the event of March 1.

"But didn't he prompt such a thing by his ideas and his teaching?"

Mikhailov had to explain at greater length.

"There is nothing of the sort either in the thoughts or the words of Chernyshevsky. The assassins were not able to comprehend Chernyshevsky's revolutionary ideas. On the contrary, this group decided everything in its own way, in a spirit quite remote from his."

Individual terrorism, even assassinating the tsar himself, Mikhailov said, was not the way to destroy the autocracy. There would be another tsar and nothing would change. According to Chernyshevsky, the peasantry, the millions of toiling people, must join the struggle against the autocracy. He told Abai about Chernyshevsky's leaflet to the peasants of Russia, the leaflet was headed: "To the Peasants of the Landlords with Compliments from Their Well-Wishers." In it the author had called upon the peasants to go into battle, axes in hand, for the people were being kept in slavery, the tsar had simply deceived them with the phantom of liberation in 1861 because he was not a people's tsar, but a landlord's tsar. Mikhailov remembered this leaflet from his university days and repeated it almost word for word to Abai: "He's pulled the wool over your eyes.... What is he if not just another landlord?... You're the serfs of the landlords and they are the serfs of the tsar. He's their landlord.... He sides with them, of course!" And then followed the words about freedom: "...that the people should be in charge of everything and that the chiefs should obey the community ... and nobody should dare to abuse the peasants." Mikhailov said with emotion that deliverance from the tsarist system lay with the axes of the people and not with the actions of four or five solitary conspirators. The assassination of a Minister or the tsar was futile.

Abai at once perceived the correctness of Chernyshevsky's view that it was the people who were the decisive force. "The real duty of the people's well-wishers is to awaken the people's minds and to call them to struggle against the hordes of evil and violence," Abai summed up his thoughts to himself.

Meeting with lawyer Akbas, a few days later, Abai spoke of Mikhailov in glowing terms.

"Mikhailov is a real man," Akbas was glad to support him. "His civic conscience awoke very early. He was already a revolutionary at the age of 20, and his entire family is like that. Didn't he tell you what his sister did at Chernyshevsky's mock execution? No, of course he didn't."

When the sentence was read a young girl elbowed her way
through the crowd and threw a bunch of flowers at
Chernyshevsky's feet, shouting, "Farewell, friend!" It was a
farewell from all decent people and also a challenge to the
autocracy. The girl was Yevgeny Petrovich's sister.

Abai was greatly impressed. This brave and fearless girl
was the sister of his friend! It was most surprising that
Mikhailov, who had told him about so many revolutionaries,
had never as much as mentioned this. He set it down to his
friend's natural modesty. Mikhailov never talked about
himself or his activities. Abai could not remember him ever
having said, "I acted thus or thus." The heroes of his stories
were always others, while he seemed somewhere dissolved
among the crowd. All Abai knew was that he had been
exiled two years before Chernyshevsky was arrested.

Mikhailov's personality appealed to him more and more
and gave him much to think about. "What a good, strong
generation this must be if there are many such as
Mikhailov," he thought. "What a force has accumulated
there! It is as mighty and yet as patient as an elephant." He
decided to get Mikhailov to talk about himself at the first
opportunity.

Abai put to him the question which had been occupying
his mind.

"I should like to ask you something, Yevgeny Petrovich,
though I'm afraid it might not be proper to ask such a thing.
What were you exiled for?"

Mikhailov answered briefly. He had been captivated by
Chernyshevsky's ideas while at the university and had
joined the circle led by Shelgunov, his elder sister's
husband. He was given some tasks to do, like others, and
was arrested at a students' demonstration which he had
organised with his friends to force the dismissal of the most
bigoted of the professors. As a result, he was exiled to
Petrozavodsk. A year later, on the advice of their comrades
in St. Petersburg, the group of exiles there wrote a petition
to the tsar, requesting mitigation of their sentences. Instead,
the group was exiled still farther away, to Siberia. Mikhailov
ultimately learned the cause from Losovsky who, in his turn,
had heard it from the governor. The tsar was favourably
impressed when he read the first page: "Such young people
too! They can't be hopelessly bad. They've been in exile for
a year and must have come to their senses by now." Then,
unfortunately, he came across a blot of ink on the last page.
It had been carefully erased by one of the petitioners and

yet it decided the matter; it was interpreted as a sign of protest and contempt. The tsar threw the paper away in disgust, ordering, "They shall not be brought back. On the contrary, let them be sent still farther away."

Mikhailov had been talking calmly, adding humorous touches, but now he spoke of a matter which must have weighed on his mind for a long time.

"The police regard me as a dangerous man and think I am preparing to murder the tsar or at least to plant a bomb under the governor's house. But what can I really do? I might have done something worthwhile if they hadn't cut me down when I was young! You, too, regard me as something of a leader of social thought and the revolutionary struggle, but that's out of friendship. Actually, I'm a man of the ranks and one who is only in reserve."

"I do understand what you must be suffering," said Abai thoughtfully. "Yet your people are fortunate. I can see that the darkness is lifting from them and that the dawn is near."

"Why do you think so?"

"If they have more men to defend them than to offend them, how can the people be unhappy?"

Abai had often shared his anxieties over the fate of the Kazakh people with Mikhailov, and today he was more sure than ever that his friend had given the problem much thought. Mikhailov sought to summarise their previous talks on the subject.

The Russians had brought both good and evil to the steppes. The evil was plain for all to see, while the good was difficult to discern. The evil lay in the local authorities and the officials, deaf and blind to anything but promotion and bribes. The good lay in Russian culture, a matter which was still a closed book to the Kazakhs, who could only see brute force in every Russian. Russia possessed a treasure of knowledge respected the world over. She had her thinkers who had won universal recognition, but the Kazakhs knew little of this — it was all so far removed from them. And yet there were perceptible stirrings among the Kazakh people. Men like Abai were already able to draw on the spiritual treasure-store of Russia. The way lay open for the entire Kazakh people, the way of enlightenment.

"It is difficult, of course, to shape your own future to a pattern, let alone an entire nation's," Mikhailov went on. "I remember a fine Kazakh proverb you once told me: 'The lone track is the birth of a road.' That's very true. It is always one who begins and many who follow. A single grain can beget an ear of grain and an ear of grain a wheat-field. 'A spark will kindle a flame.' These sayings are worth remembering. What should I advise you to do? The younger generation of Kazakhs should study, first of all. Begin with your children. Let them learn to read and write Russian. Secondly, pass on what knowledge you have. It will only be a tiny glowworm in those vast steppes, a feeble candle flickering in a lone hand, but you must carry it into the darkness. One thing more: there are many sores on the body of your people. You should learn to identify, diagnose, and incise them. In short, bold critical thought is necessary. You have a powerful weapon for that. As far as I can judge, your people are responsive to songs. I would make their dombras, legends and songs speak of their needs and the causes of their afflictions. I would glorify enlightenment and knowledge in song. Your people are fond of apt metaphors and would assimilate the essence of those songs much quicker than the sermons of the imams in the mosques of Semipalatinsk. As you know, the development of social thought in Russia has been greatly helped by our poets. True enough, we have a mighty ally which you have not, the printed word, but that would not stop me if I were you. It is necessary above all to enlighten the people, no matter how. There's a crowded programme ahead of you, as you see," concluded Mikhailov patting Abai on the shoulder.

Abai had so assimilated Mikhailov's thoughts that he was soon unable to separate his own ideas from those of his friend. They came to form his credo.

This conversation, which touched upon great, vital problems, ended with Mikhailov asking how Abai's children were taught in the aul. Abai explained that his sons Abish and Magash and daughter Gulbadan had been attending the family's Moslem school, but that he had decided to give them a Russian education. He did not know how to go about it, though.

"Bring them here and we'll arrange something. If they stayed with a Russian family, they would be sure to master the Russian language in two or three years. But let this be understood: they're not to study in order to become officials. Let them memorise these words: 'I am the first swallow and I study for the good of my people.'"

"What if Abish and Magash were to become such men as Mikhailov?" Abai suddenly thought. He imagined them not in the Kazakh dress of the Tobikty cut, but dressed as Russian townsfolk. Perhaps they would become scholars, bold defenders of the people, the leaders of the younger generation. That was a great future indeed. "If I could only live to see it!" he almost prayed. "If I could live long enough to tell them, 'I'm old and worn and must hand our cause on to you!' I would be the happiest of fathers if that were to come true."

A new arrival interrupted his thoughts. It was the lawyer Andreyev.

He brought them news from the office of the district chief. The news, indeed, concerned the whole of the Tobikty and he thought it necessary to inform Abai. The office of the district chief, the magistrate's office and even the office of the zhandaral were snowed under with complaints, decisions passed by the elders, accusations and requests from the Tobikty. The papers bore the tamga, the finger-prints of the plaintiffs, and reported cases of arson, pillage and even of "causing the miscarriages of pregnant women."

"You have no idea, Ibragim, what your volost rulers are doing," Akbas concluded. "There's inter-tribal warfare again. Or it might be a scramble for posts, since the re-elections are scheduled this year."

"Who is complaining?" Mikhailov asked Akbas when he heard the news. "The volost rulers or the people?"

"All the complaints are directed against the volost rulers," answered Andreyev, smiling ironically at Abai. "Those same volost rulers you recommended to Losovsky at the last elections. If I remember correctly, you said they would be the friends of the people," he laughed. "There's one serious complaint in the pile, however. From the poor zhataks. Some of them asked me to intercede for them: 'Take on our case and bring it to the knowledge of the authorities that the rulers are doing us a lot of harm.'"

Abai demanded to know the names of the volost rulers in question, but Akbas could not remember even one of them. He recalled, however, that he had seen a few of their statements accusing of theft those of the zhataks who had launched complaints against them.

Mikhailov interpreted this in his own way.

"Evidently the men whom Ibragim Kunanbayevich thought capable of serving the people have enjoyed their taste of power. They have forgotten about the good of the people and are only trying to get votes for themselves. An opposition party has apparently sprung into existence, and the zhataks, it seems, have joined neither the one nor the

M. AUEZOV

other. They have obviously refused to side with the present
rulers and so have been set down as thieves and bandits.
And you, Ibragim Kunanbayevich, hoped these rulers
would be the champions of the people. And there they are,
slinging mud at their own people who, you see, do not obey
the authorities. Your volost rulers are no fools, of course.
They got their posts from you and feel they have finished
with you. They know very well that it is far more important
to be on good terms with the governor and the district chief
than with you. If that's the sort of protectors your people
have, it must go hard with them! They managed to pull the
wool over your eyes, although you know all their tricks, and
they will certainly do the same to the people. And of course
they won't find it difficult to appear honest in the eyes of the
authorities. They're just the sort that the authorities need
most. The volost rulers play into their hands and the
authorities care very little for the people who will make
them neither rich nor poor."

"Poor? They'll get poorer only if the people are left to live
in peace, but if they quarrel, the authorities rake in the
bribes and are duly promoted for pacifying the populace."

Abai was both shocked and pained to learn that the men
for whom he had vouched, men he had recommended as
the protectors of the people, had turned out to be no better
than their predecessors. One of them, moreover, was his
brother, Iskhak. Abai felt as if he too had had a hand in all
the outrages.

He could not take part in this conversation. He sat
gloomily silent for a while and then left.

2

Abai stayed in Semipalatinsk longer than he had planned.
He was reluctant to leave Mikhailov and Andreyev, and his
talks with them seemed more important to him than any of
his studies.

It was midsummer when he at last set off for his aul. On
the way he visited Yeraly and spent the night with the
zhataks.

The morning tea was just over in Darkembai's yurta. With
a shabby beshmet thrown loosely over his shoulders, the
host sat facing Abai, shaking tobacco into his palm from his
yellow horn shaksha and glancing at his guest with
satisfaction. He was pleased to have a talk with such a visitor.
The hostess, a thin, elderly woman, was no less

pleased—Abai had spent the night in their yurta. As she cleared the table, she tried to catch the jests between the two and her wrinkled face broke into a smile.

"They talk to us about nothing but obedience to the atkaminers and the volost rulers," Darkembai said, resuming a conversation started the previous night. "If it's a high-born man, he speaks about his power and authority and boasts of his cunning and cleverness. If it's a poor man, he complains of his needs and woes. Now, you, Abai, have told us about brave men who killed the tsar and suffered for it. We know now that the poor have their defenders who worry about their plight, and are prepared to die for the people. Their goal is to achieve happiness for the people. They're also the protectors of the zhataks who are hiding in their holes like crippled wolves."

The old man took a pinch of tobacco, thought for a while and concluded:

"Yes, that is how it is. The strong boast of their oppression of the weak and the weak complain that they suffer at the hands of the strong."

Abai was impressed with the clarity of such reasoning.

"Well said," he exclaimed. "Your conclusion is as good as a proverb. I can see now that it is not the rich man with many herds who has the clear mind, but the poor man who has been taught to think by need."

Darkembai smiled.

"A clear mind alone is not enough to make you an elder. When a poor man is not clever, they are sure to say that he is brainless; and if he is clever and speaks well, they are sure to say that he is a windbag. No, Abai! It's not a clever tongue that helps to gain justice."

The neighbours came to the yurta one by one, among them Dandibai, Yerenai and Karekeh of the Kotibak, old men whom Abai knew. They had come to talk to Abai about the affairs of the aul, which now numbered 50 yurtas. Darkembai, too, had things to say to his guest about the wrongs done to him and his neighbours, but had not wanted to trouble Abai with them the night before, as he was obviously tired after his journey.

Abai now asked the old men about life in the aul, the sowing and the harvest.

"You have enough good, arable land. Has much been sown this year?"

"My dear Abai, which of us could sow much?" said Dandibai, shaking his head. "In our wretched life in which

we have nothing but dogs to pull our ploughs, no one has
the strength to reap even the things that God has given us.
We have nothing to boast of. The twenty yurtas which stand
near Mialy-Baigabil have hardly sown twenty lands.*"

"Has the wheat sprouted well?" asked Abai. "Sometimes
a small plot will yield a lot."

Dandibai, Yerenai and Darkembai spoke at once:

"A lot, you say!"

"Not likely!"

"A lot of nothing, I would say."

"I can't understand anything." Abai turned to his host.

Darkembai at last ventured to speak:

"Didn't you say last year, 'Don't expect good things to
come from the sky, and better work for them yourselves.'
We took you at your word and did our best. And I must say
that the results were not bad at first. Our hearts were
gladdened by the crops on Sholpan, Kindik and Mialy-
Baigabil. And what happened! Don't you remember the
trouble we had after the elections in Yeraly?"

"And didn't Takezhan and Maibasar ruin our harvests?"
interjected Yerenai. "'Don't quibble with the authorities
over your rotten yurtas,' they said. And what a harvest that
might have turned out to be! We were just going to gather it
in, when they turned the herds of five auls loose upon it."

Abai remembered it very well. The Irgizbai and Kotibak,
who had been wandering near the plots of the zhataks in the
autumn, had done this foul deed at the instigation of
Takezhan. Through the new volost ruler Asilbek, Abai had
made provision for compensation to be paid in livestock for
the damage suffered by the zhataks. He had not known,
however, that not one of the guilty auls had bothered to
make these payments.

Darkembai asked Abai's opinion as to their chances of
success if they were to send a representative bearing a
formal complaint to the inter-tribal council of the Siban,
Tobikty and Uak, which was to be held shortly.

Before answering, Abai asked whether they had any other
wrongs to complain of.

"Have they trampled down this year's crops as well? Have
any of the kinsmen helped you with horses during the
sowing and the reaping?"

The old men laughed again.

"What are you talking about, O light of my eyes?" said

_____
* A land—a square measure.—*Ed.*

Karekeh. "Help is given only to those who pay for it and not to paupers like us."

"What talk can there be of help? And are they kinsmen of ours at all?" added Dandibai. "They trampled down Karekeh's plot this spring when the first sprouts came up."

"And they've driven off our poor old nags," Darkembai interrupted bitterly. "And why don't you tell him the main thing?"

He described the fresh wrongs perpetrated by the kinsmen in Abai's absence.

When the auls of Takezhan, Maibasar, Kuntu and Karatai had wandered to this district, the zhataks had approached them with the demand for compensation still unpaid. But this had only enraged them all and when the fields were green again, the horses were turned loose on the crops as before. And complaints to influential people gained them nothing. True, they had sympathised with the zhataks, had agreed that it was an outrage, but they would not support them openly for fear of spoiling relations with the powerful auls. Their sympathy for the injured people exhausted itself in whispers at the threshold.

In desperation, the zhataks, led by Darkembai and Dandibai, had started a fight with Takezhan's herdsmen and seized two horses. On the next day a hundred djiguits armed with soeels had raided the aul, taken back their horses and very nearly thrashed Darkembai. When the zhataks tearfully complained to Takezhan and Maibasar, they were heaped with curses and sent packing. "All you do with your ploughing is spoil the pastures," Maibasar had shouted. "Beggars like you should be driven away. It was because of you dogs that I was dismissed from my post. What does it matter if we have common ancestors? You're not my kinsmen. To the devil with you!"

"And that was not the end of the matter either," Dandibai interjected. "Seven horses were stolen from our people a month ago."

"The four of us have been asked by the people to recover those horses," Darkembai went on. "And the thieves are just around the corner. They're in Akhimbet, Kzil-Moly Volost. We gave everything we had to find the thieves and the horses. And we were sure we should get the animals back. The volost ruler is your brother Iskhak and this gave us the courage to demand that they return our horses, our property, threatening them with Iskhak's name if they did not. At first, they were frightened, but then decided

to put us off: 'We did not take your horses ourselves; we
received them from your kinsman Serikbai. He was
indebted to us and gave us the horses in payment. First
bring him here.' When we returned, we found that the thief
had been living in Takezhan's aul since last year. You can be
sure Takezhan did not even let us get near the man. 'Let the
zhataks stop wagging their tongues. Serikbai is a poor man
and I won't let them hurt him.' Takezhan has suddenly
become a protector of the poor, you see! Or, to put it more
plainly, Serikbai does his stealing under Takezhan's protection. In short, the thief got away. When we returned to
Akhimbet, we found fresh troubles waiting for us;
Takezhan had sent a messenger to Iskhak: 'The zhataks are
my enemies. Don't let them have the horses and throw them
out.' And that is just what Iskhak did. He was even worse
than the others. It's no wonder we are wailing with grief.
That is why we are thinking of petitioning for payment for
the damages done this year and last, and also for the return
of the seven horses. We have no other draught horses. Is it
not true that the biys and the volost rulers are afraid of the
Russian authorities sometimes? Perhaps we shall be lucky
and justice will be done. What do you think? It is not on our
own behalf that we are telling you this, but on behalf of the
zhataks of fifty yurtas who have been robbed."

Abai sat listening, biting his lips and frowning. He was
furious with both his brothers. Vexation, shame and disgust
rose in his soul in cloudy waves. He felt as though he had
been caught in a storm of filth that poisoned his mind with
evil vapours, and through it all he seemed to hear new
words again and again. The words of a new poem? "The
clear mind will reject all that conscience has condemned."
What could shame mean to those whose conscience was
deaf, whose heart was frozen and whose maw was insatiable!
What did they care for pity and injustice!

There was a general hush.

"And this evil was done by my brothers," Abai said
finally. "And I too am guilty before you for that reason. It's
no consolation, of course, if I say that the vengeful hand is
regretted by the reproachful heart. What good would that
do you?

"I remember a good saying of yours, Darkembai: 'Those
who have a common need have a common life. Real
kinsmen are united by their common lot.' The truth of your
words came home to me when I was talking to a wise
Russian. It turns out that there are such kinsmen not only

among the Kazakhs, but also among the Russians and, though the tsar and his officials are Russians too, these poor people will never regard them as their kinsmen. The Russian zhataks in Siberia and Russia have the same thoughts as the zhataks of the Kokshe and Mamai."

Abai was pleased with his line of reasoning. Darkembai nodded approval, though much that the young man had said seemed strange to him.

"And if you take a deeper view of things," Abai went on, "you'll see that the rulers of the tribes among the Tobikty, the Kerei, the Karakesek and Naiman are the real kinsmen of the powers of Semipalatinsk, Omsk, Orenburg and St. Petersburg. They are of one tribe and have one common tribal cry. They're as thick as thieves. That is the answer to the riddle, my friends. There is a wise Russian man, one who suffers for the people as if they were his own children, who has said that only the axes that the people wield can save them. And it is time perhaps to use these axes to strike at the root of the evil in the steppes!"

Carried away, Abai had said more than he had meant to. These people had to be helped with deeds, not words.

"The gathering will be held not in Arkat, but Balkibek," he said suddenly, sweeping the four old men with grave eyes. "It may have begun already. That is what they told me in town. I was not thinking of going there, but now I will go to present your case before the chiefs. You must follow me in three days. We'll demand full compensation from Takezhan, Iskhak and Maibasar. I will speak for you, but you must help me too. You, Darkembai, will come to town and bring Dandibai with you. He is also determined and courageous."

Abai got up hurriedly.

"It's agreed then. We'll talk about the rest on the spot. But don't be late. In three days — remember! And I shall go straightaway. Harness my horse, Baimagambet!"

3

Abai and Baimagambet spent one more night on the road and by the next evening reached Baikoshkar where the auls of Ulzhan and Abai were located. As they drove past Botakan they saw a large aul, which turned out to be Takezhan's. There were herds of horses and flocks of sheep grazing nearby, and the Great Yurta was surrounded by more than a dozen servants' tents.

"We won't stop here," Abai said to Baimagambet.

The aul was still awake when they arrived in Baikoshkar, and Abai was happy to find that the children had not yet gone to bed. The clatter of the carriage wheels brought them running to meet him. Magash and Turash climbed into their father's lap, hugging him and shouting for joy, while the other children scrambled up to the driver's box or the step at the rear. Baimagambet headed for Ulzhan's yurta, knowing that Abai would want to see his mother first.

Ulzhan stood near her large bed as Abai entered with the crowd of children. She embraced and kissed her son. Aigerim, Aigiz and other women had gathered in the yurta. Ospan was also there — a huge, broad-shouldered man, wearing a light chapan trimmed with a velvet collar over his white shirt. He had brought his young wife along, pretty slender Erkezhan.

Glad to see his brother back, Ospan tried to outshout the children, wanting Abai to hear the good news at once. Three members of their family — Takezhan, Shubar and Iskhak — had been elected volost rulers, and laughing loudly he demanded that Abai should pay a suyunshi.

"I hope it will bring everyone happiness," said Abai in a low voice, looking at Ulzhan. "I see that you are all overjoyed."

Ulzhan at once understood that he was not at all pleased with the news.

"Yes, may it bring everyone happiness, my son!" she echoed.

Ospan continued his noisy rejoicing.

"I forgot to tell you. Bazaraly's been caught and the new volost rulers have written down their decision and sent him to town. They put him on a camel and fettered his hands and feet so he wouldn't run away!"

Abai turned sharply.

"Damn them. No sooner do they get to power than they turn to their old ways! A pack of snarling wolves!"

Abai knew that the stubborn and straightforward Ospan hated Bazaraly as viciously as did Takezhan. Ospan would not go in for crime, and Bazaraly's exile quite satisfied his touchy pride. As always, he responded very exuberantly to what he considered good news. His sparse black moustache and pitch-black beard bristled more than ever.

In the simplicity of his heart, he thought that the brothers owed their election to Abai.

"Our volost rulers think that the authorities have elected them for their fame and their influence. 'Don't turn up your noses,' I said to them. 'For the love of Allah! The authorities have never heard of you. Do you think that Abai has been sweltering in town and swallowing dust there from early spring to midsummer for nothing? That's the only reason all these honours have fallen upon you from the sky. He's rubbing shoulders with the big chiefs!' That shut them up!"

"Though you are nearer to me than the others, Ospan," Abai said, shaking his head, "you're as mixed up as a man lost in the dark on a moonless night. Shubar, perhaps, is not so bad. He is young and has yet to show what he is worth. He's a good djiguit, as far as I know. But how could I ever support Takezhan, who has used his office in the past to increase his herd from eighty to five hundred head? Or what could I say for Iskhak, who abets the Tobikty thieves in his Kzil-Moly Volost? I realise that you respect me so sincerely that you'd pin all sorts of honours on me, but I had nothing at all to do with these elections. You're only confusing people with your talk."

Ospan was not convinced.

"Rubbish! You won't find a single Tobikty to believe you. Three of Kunanbai's sons have become volost rulers and you mean to tell them that you had nothing to do with it, though you were living in town all that time. You had better not deny it—you may as well accept the gratitude of your brothers. I shall go on saying that it was you who did it. They enjoy great honours as volost rulers, but you deserve even greater honours since it was you who made them such. Are you your own enemy? Allah sends you honours which you reject!"

It was obvious that Ospan would stick to his view, and Abai argued no further in the presence of his mother and children. Beckoning Abish to his side, he asked the boy about his studies.

"I've been learning Russian, too," the boy said. "Ever since we left the winter place."

This bit of news had been kept by the family as a pleasant surprise for Abai.

"Is that so? But who is your teacher?" exclaimed Abai, kissing the boy's fair forehead.

"When you went to town in the spring, a young Russian djiguit came to Zhidebai," Ulzhan explained. "He had served in town as interpreter for a year. That's why they call him Bala-Tolmach.* He told me he was ill and had come to

---

* Bala-Tolmach—a boy-interpreter.—*Ed.*

the aul to heal himself with kumiss. He asked if he could live here with us and teach the children Russian. I remembered that this was just what you wanted and sent him to Akshoky. Not only Abish, but also Magash and Gulbadan are taking lessons from Bala-Tolmach Bayev."

Abai was delighted.

"And are they doing well? Are they as diligent as when they were taught by the Kishkineh-Mullah? Have you made the teacher comfortable?"

When Aigerim spoke, Abai suddenly realised how much he had missed her voice.

"The children are very enthusiastic and never missed a day, even on the way to zhailyau. And their teacher likes them too. When lessons are over, he often mounts a two-year-old to race with Abish." Aigerim smiled kindly. "How funny these Russian mullahs are! There's nothing solemn about him. He teaches the children as if it were a merry game. They love being with him."

Abai nodded approval. And then Ospan began to poke fun at his sister-in-law.

"See! She's not praising a mullah who knows the Sharia and the ways of Allah, but some Russian tolmach. Before we know it, she'll start studying Russian herself." Here he imitated Aigerim, pronouncing a few words in broken Russian. Everybody laughed, Ospan more boisterously than the rest.

Abai asked the children the Russian words for various objects in the tent and listened with pleasure to the eager clamour of their answers.

After the evening meal, he went to Aigerim's yurta with the children. Abish, Magash and Gulbadan cuddled to him, walking under his broad chapan. Abai was indeed a proud and happy father.

"Light of my eyes!" he embraced Abish. "I'm so glad you've begun to learn Russian. You've studied long enough with our Mullah, and I'm going to send you to a Russian school this year. Allah willing, you'll grow up to be an educated man. This is my greatest desire. And I'm especially glad that you've begun to study without me, that it was your own wish!" Abai raised his eyes to the full moon and silently prayed: "Let his life not be ruined, O Allah! Let my sons have the things I could not have: knowledge and all the best human qualities. Make him happy, and light his way." It was a silent, fervent prayer. He pressed his son to his heart again.

Abish did not answer, but it was obvious that he was deeply moved. Indeed, he was quite pale with emotion.

"I'm glad too, Aga," he said quietly.

"Why only Abish, Father?" Magash cried jealously, clutching at Abai's belt. "I want to go to town to study Russian too."

"Me too, Father!" Gulbadan wailed. "I want to study too. Ask Bayev. He's always saying that I'll learn to speak Russian before any of them. I'll go to the town by myself if you won't take me."

Abai smiled happily, stroking Gulbadan's head and kissing Magash's pouting lips.

"I'll take you both to town in the autumn, I'll take all of you, I promise."

Aigerim stood at the door of her yurta, watching them with a smile. She turned back the felt door to admit Abai.

AT THE CROSSROADS

1

Abai was accompanied to the gathering in Balkibek by his old friends, Yerbol, Baimagambet and Shakke. They made a stop-over at Yerbol's aul where they were joined by Asilbek, who had at the last elections lost his post of volost ruler received through Abai's intercession.

The gathering at Balkibek had been convened by four tribes: the Siban, Tobikty, Kerei and Uak, to investigate and settle quarrels, complaints, and old scores. A plot of land had to be found which did not belong to either side; the chiefs of the tribes had always availed themselves of their proximity to bring pressure to bear upon the council. Balkibek, however, was situated on the border-land between the Tobikty, Siban and Kerei and, though abounding in water and fodder, remained unoccupied year after year. Attempts by any of the tribes to take possession of it were promptly frustrated by the other three. This was the most convenient spot for the gathering.

The gathering represented the population of the nine volosts in the two districts of Semipalatinsk and Kar-karalinsk. Four of the volosts belonged to the Tobikty, two to the Siban, two to the Uak and one to the Kerei. Now the Irgizbai were more influential than ever. The news that two sons and a grandson of Kunanbai had been elected was being discussed everywhere. Those of the Tobikty who belonged to the rich and powerful auls and could therefore aspire to office were both offended and worried.

"Lucky devils, those Irgizbai!" they said enviously. "When Kunanbai was Aga-Sultan, they stood above all others and now that he has retired from worldly affairs and is resting like an old camel on the ashes of a hearth, the luck and the power have gone to his sons. They rule over three volosts! And his son-in-law Dutbai rules in a fourth, in Mukir. The whole of the Tobikty is in their hands now...."

On the way, Abai learned all this from Yerbol, who had visited the gathering a few days before, and knew the sentiments of the people. The "people" in this case meant the atkaminers, the biys and the volost rulers, vested with power and authorised to make speeches, and their immediate associates.

"There's nothing they like more than a bribe," said Yerbol. "It used to be said that they could swallow a camel alive, but this pack can do far better now, mark my word! They swallow the sheep in flocks and the horses in herds, and the town chiefs, may Allah punish them, also grab what they can. No wonder they're always remembering Takezhan. The new volost rulers are now bleeding the people to make up for their losses."

"And what about the biys. Are they corrupt too?" asked Abai.

"I wouldn't say that about all of them, but they do very well for themselves on the whole. Judge for yourself. Say, it's a quarrel between the Kerei and the Tobikty. Both sides appy to the volost rulers, who pass the matter on to the biys but let them understand that they'll be rewarded if the decision is favourable. And the biys are not saints. So they share the loot."

"Tell me frankly, is it possible that Zhirenshe and Urazbai are corrupt too?"

"Of course, they are!"

"And I regarded them as friends." Abai shook his head. "And I was responsible for them becoming biys. Perhaps you are wrong. I hope you are. I want to believe they are honest men. If these two are corrupt, who is there to trust?"

Abai fell into a moody silence. Yerbol said no more. How could he tell Abai about the dirty doings of men he called friends? He remembered Abai's words: "Slander and malice are at the bottom of all quarrels between friends and kinsmen."

There were two endless lines of yurtas on each side of the river and it took Abai and his party quite some time to find their kinsmen. Septagonal and octagonal yurtas were rare. Most of the Kazakhs gathered here had set up brand new white pentagonal and hexagonal tents adorned with embroidery and coloured cloth. Clusters of drab and sooty little yurtas stood somewhat apart — the kitchens and the servants' quarters. Many foals were tethered along the rows, the milch mares having been brought to the council together with riding and harness horses.

Abai and his friends soon came upon the triple octagonal yurtas set up for the chiefs, between smaller yurtas grouped in twos and threes. Volost rulers, biys, elders and shabarmans were bustling about. Herdsmen and curious onlookers were also shuttling to and fro. The chapans, jackets, saddles and bridles made a riot of colour. The various hats and caps showed that all tribes and clans were represented here.

Baimagambet went asking everyone where the yurtas of Kunanbai's sons had been set up. He located Takezhan's yurta and Iskhak's aul, but Abai refused to put up in either.

The brothers had set up their yurtas side by side, and next to these were the yurtas of Kunanbai's grandson Shubar, the new ruler of Chinghis Volost, who now came forward to meet Abai's party on his brown pacer. He was a tall, broad-shouldered djiguit with regular, faintly pock-marked features. He was two years too young to be a volost ruler, but the Irgizbai had put down his age as twenty-six. In spite of his youth, he was better educated than the others; he had studied with Gabitkhan for ten years and could have been a mullah himself. Not satisfied with this, however, he too had learned to speak Russian from his interpreter. He was determined, active and bold, and therefore conspicuous among the men of his age. Shubar had more than once influenced the discussions and decisions of the council, and the elders had entrusted him with the responsibility of conducting negotiations with the Russians at the elections.

He salemed his uncle and invited him in.

"Abai-aga, our yurtas are here. Do not ride past, and please stay with us."

Abai greeted him courteously, congratulated him upon having received so important an office at so young an age, but declined the invitation.

"You're an official now and are sufficiently burdened as it is. You'll have your hands full with the chiefs and the plaintiffs and petitioners and your friends. We, you see, are used to doing as we please. We go to bed early and get up late. So we'll stay with Ospan, if you don't mind."

Shubar was somewhat disappointed but did not insist.

"I would like to have a few words with you first, Abai-aga," he said, detaining his uncle while the others rode on. "When the oyaz came, we, the volost rulers, led him to the Guest Yurta and the first thing he asked was, 'Has Ibragim Kunanbayevich come to the gathering?' This heartened us considerably and I was the first to say, 'Yes, he is here and will surely come to convey his salem!'"

Shubar could not conceal his pleasure that, thanks to Abai, he had been able to bring himself to the notice of the authorities.

"It would be good if you visited him," he went on. "There are many people here, as you know, and everyone is trying to put a spoke in everyone else's wheels. It would be very important for us if you could salem the oyaz before the others."

Abai guessed that it was Losovsky who had asked for him and decided to call upon him, though not with the object that Shubar had in view. He simply wanted to see his old acquaintance.

"You needn't coax me. I'll visit him without fail," he answered and made for Ospan's yurta where his companions were waiting.

There were many guests. Though he was not a volost ruler, Ospan, the master of Kunanbai's Great Yurta, had set up five large yurtas. He had also ordered the slaughter of a grey mare with a silver-blazed forehead, the sign of truth and loyalty, as was customary on the eve of an important undertaking such as a campaign or litigation. The volost rulers of both districts had been invited to partake of the repast.

The volost ruler Zhumakan, the son of one of the most influential elders of the Siban, sat in the big octagonal yurta. The Kerei were represented by their shrewd volost ruler Toisary, and the Tobikty by the self-confident and bellicose volost ruler Moldabai, a stout, robust-looking djiguit. Takezhan, Iskhak, and other volost rulers were also present.

No words were wasted. They sat silently eyeing each other, wondering which of them would find favour with the chiefs. Deep-seated envy and hatred were thinly veiled by courtesy. The little they said was spoken in hints and implications. The case between the Siban and the Kzil-Adir was to be heard soon, perhaps even tomorrow. To put it more accurately, it would be a contest between the two volost rulers, Takezhan and Zhumakan. The next case to be heard would be that of the Motish against the Kerei. This too was to be a duel between two volost rulers, this time Moldabai and Toisary. No gathering had been held for several years and a host of complaints had accumulated. There had been reports of barimta, raids, abductions and other crimes. The biys would soon vie with one another in eloquence and each of the volost rulers was on his mettle.

Abai alone was remote from their anxieties and apprehensions. But he was curious, and asked Zhumakan and Toisary all about the case between the Kerei and Siban, a matter which had long troubled the region and was still unsettled, both sides frequently going on raids and stealing each other's horses. The case went under the heading of "Litigation of the Girl Salikha."

Toisary was evasive, but Zhumakan spoke his mind.

"With goodwill, peace could be easily restored, my dear Abai, but how can you settle a matter in court if even some chit of a girl won't obey?"

Obviously he meant the Kerei in general. The case had made bad blood between the two tribes, and Abai stopped asking questions, so as not to add fuel to the fire.

When the kumiss was served, everyone livened up, and someone suggested that this was a fitting time to hear a good song. Abai took the dombra from Shakke, who had been sitting by him leisurely strumming the instrument, and passed it on to Baikokshe, an akyn who had come from Kzil-Adir with Takezhan. The akyn lived in Ospan's yurta, but was in the habit of walking about everywhere and from time to time shared his observations with his host.

"They've stuffed their bellies full with bribes," he had said. "The volost rulers, the elders and our worthy biys. If you are not satisfied with what you have, become a volost ruler. You'll be able to skin everyone, whether innocent or guilty, and no one will dare to judge you."

Ospan had listened to the local news with great curiosity.

"How have you learned all that?" he asked the akyn. "Bribes are given and taken on the quiet; agreements are made in whispers, by winks of the eye rather than by actual words, and still you seem to know all about it! Are you a jinni or what?"

Baikokshe explained his methods.

"Don't tell anyone, but simply try to keep on good terms with the shabarmans of all the volost rulers. All the bribes that are given and taken must pass through their hands. They hide nothing from me. Besides, they know the doings of their masters from the messengers of other rulers and tell me about this too."

Baikokshe accepted the dombra and sang an extemporaneous greeting to the company. Slightly light-headed from the kumiss, the volost rulers punctuated the song with loud exclamations.

"Good for him! He's the best akyn we have nowadays."

"Sing on, nightingale! I can tell the old school at once!"

Baikokshe sang without raising his eyes, neither impressed nor flattered by the praise. After the song of greeting,

ABAI   413

he changed to another tune and other words. "You've
achieved your goal and now enjoy esteem and power. If you
are honest, do not wrong the poor, do not patronise the
villains and let them abuse the meek. Don't rob the people,
don't ruin their happiness, don't be a burden to them." He
mentioned no names, but it was clear that the words were
aimed at most of the volost rulers present.

No one complimented the akyn on this song, and the
arrogant Moldabai took it as an affront.

"This Baikokshe is by no means kokshe,* " he said
angrily. "He's a sly fellow, he'll steal up to you, and heap
filth upon everything you've done."

"The listeners are supposed to listen and say nothing,"
Asilbek retorted with a laugh. "An akyn's words show the
truth of many things."

The volost rulers tried to change the subject, talking and
laughing loudly. But Abai once more brought their
attention back to the akyn.

"That's just why Baikokshe's song should be heard. It's
not the flattery of a petitioner or the praise of a beggar, but
the keen eye and voice of the people, expressing their
thoughts before they can put them into words."

"The people have nothing to do with it," Takezhan said
with asperity. "The people never empowered him to speak
for them in such words, as bitter as poison. It's simply that
Allah has given him a spiteful nature."

Iskhak and Toisary supported him.

"Why confuse him with the people? He's liable to infect
them with his spitefulness."

"The mangy horse rubs himself wherever he can."

"No one can hear the truth without murmuring,"
commented Abai, smiling. "Your words mean in fact, 'Keep
the truth to yourself, or you'll make us angry!' If one
Baikokshe alone can make us so angry, then how can we
bear to listen to the entire people?"

"Baikokshe is not the people," Takezhan insisted.

"Oh, no, my worthy volost ruler," the akyn interrupted,
lifting his hand from the dombra he had been strumming.
"Baikokshe is, in fact, the people. To be sure it sickens you
to listen to me, but Baikokshe only repeats what the people
say."

* Kokshe—the name of a clan; the word means "obscure", "incon-
spicuous".—*Ed.*

"Now, what do the people say? Perhaps you could sing it in one verse?" scoffed Takezhan. His words were caught up by the others who joined in the jeering.

Abai looked at Baikokshe with a mischievous twinkle.

"Why not! I'll begin the song and you will finish it," said Abai.

> *The grass grows thickest in the hollows and the*
> *bog.*
> *Some men are born to make an easy life.*

The akyn half arose, humorously raised his eyebrows and finished the stanza.

> *They get promoted to a volost ruler's job,*
> *And bribes they take until they're thrown out on*
> *their ear...*

"That is what the people say," he added and laughed, looking at Takezhan. In spite of themselves, the company could not help approving the apt words of the rhyme.

"Empty chatterer!" Takezhan snorted, looking away. "May your tongue be scorched!"

Abai sat rocking with laughter.

"I'm sure Moldabai was wrong. He's not Baikokshe, but Zhaikokshe*." He rose and left the yurta, still laughing.

The volost rulers had been sadly ruffled, and looked like nothing so much as fat, terrified ducks or turkeys pressing to the ground under the shadow of a falcon.

"Enough of that! Keep quiet now!" Ospan said to Baikokshe, when he saw that the akyn's gibe had offended most of his guests. He began to refill the cups with kumiss with his own hands.

Shubar also resented the affront to his uncle and the atkaminers he had invited.

"May your tongue run dry, Baikokshe! Surely if you want to be outspoken you don't have to insult everyone? Since when have you forgotten all decency and learned to spit into the bowl you've eaten from?"

His words set Ospan off, his protruding eyes flashing angrily at the akyn.

"I've invited my kinsmen here for a ceremonial feast, to let them rest and make merry. If you are really so wise, you should remember the proverb: 'Kind words make a good half of happiness.' I expected kind words from you and

* Zhai — thunder. — *Ed.*

what have you given us instead? Don't you start any quarrels in my yurta!"

Baikokshe, Shakke and Baimagambet left the yurta one by one after this tirade from the host.

That evening Abai called upon Losovsky. The Russian met him with a smile on his sunburnt face and shook his hand warmly. After the usual exchange of pleasantries, Losovsky seated his guest and described one of the cases on hand. The table was piled with papers pertaining to an appeal drawn up by several tribes.

"All these seals and signatures," he said, "have turned out to be forgeries. I'm glad you're here, Ibragim Kunan-bayevich; you may be able to help me. This paper is an appeal to the governor from a young Kirghiz of Mukur Volost. His name is Kokpai Zhanatayev. It concerns Balki-bek. The decision on his case was taken by the rulers of six volosts interested in the land. Let me read it to you:

"'We, the volost rulers, have agreed that the land in question, known as Balkibek, has long been the property of Kokpai Zhanatayev, registered in Mukur Volost, and must be restored to the petitioner. We request, therefore, that Balkibek shall henceforth be regarded as the property of Kokpai Zhanatayev.' And it's covered with seals too. They look authentic, don't they? I thought so too. But when I looked into the matter more carefully, I found that the volost ruler of Mukur had never set his seal to it, let alone the other rulers. It's an ordinary forgery. Just look."

Losovsky began to leaf through the papers, pointing to the seals.

"The petitioner claims that these are the authentic seals of six volost rulers. Actually, they're one and the same seal of the aul elder set indistinctly on each of the papers. And to think that a young djiguit is involved in such a grave case of forgery! It is commonly said that our offices know nothing of the life in the steppes and make many mistakes, at times verging on absurdities, but who is to blame? It's just such cases as these that cause the mistakes. Now they perjure themselves or send us fabricated accusations or try to aid a robbery as in this instance. It is outrageous! I've sent someone to fetch that forger here. He'll be coming presently and, meanwhile, make yourself at home."

"Tell them to bring the tea," Losovsky said to the grey-moustached guard at the door.

The volost rulers who had been feasting in Ospan's yurta such a short time ago were now crowding outside the triple

yurta. Whenever the doors were flung open, those who
stood outside could not help seeing Abai sitting at the table
with the oyaz and looking through the papers. Some were
glad, others were envious. There were endless whispers and
nudges. But when the guard emerged and shouted for tea,
everyone was astounded.

"Is the tea for Abai?"

"The oyaz treats him as a guest!"

"He must be his friend!"

There was a hubbub of conjecture; how would this affect
one case or the other?

"It's clear now that the Tobikty will have things their own
way. Kunanbai's sons will never let anyone say anything if
Abai is so friendly with the oyaz."

When Zhumakan, Toisary and Moldabai had returned
from Ospan's yurta an hour before, they had still been
heatedly discussing the impertinence of the akyn.

"Baikokshe would never have dared to say such things on
his own. It's Abai who put him up to it."

"You're right. It's Abai's handiwork," Toisary agreed.
"He set his akyn to bark at us and then went off. Now what
was his idea?"

"Kunanbai's sons are certainly on top now," mused
Moldabai. "Surely Abai must have some plan. Or is he just
trying to frighten us? He has managed to make volost rulers
out of three of Kunanbai's brats by hob-nobbing with the
authorities winter and summer. Pride has gone to his head."

But when they came to the oyaz's yurta and learned that
Abai was having tea with the great chief himself, they
became strangely deflated. They were jealous of Abai, yet
each of them was thinking: "I must be on good terms with
Abai, if whoever else. I've got to have him on my side."

At tea, Abai said nothing at all about the affairs of the
steppes, the volost rulers or the meeting.

"I've just come to have a look at the gathering," Abai had
said to Losovsky earlier in the evening. "I've only one small
matter to attend to. I want to intercede for the poor zhataks
who have been robbed by the rich auls. I am going to try to
help them myself. Let's not talk about it just now. I've come
to see you and to hear the news from the town. I'd also like
to know how Yevgeny Petrovich and Akbas Andreyevich are
getting on."

"Splendid, Ibragim Kunanbayevich. I'm very glad you
came. You're my only interlocutor here in the steppes, you
know."

He readily told Abai all he knew about their mutual
acquaintances, and the most interesting articles in the St.
Petersburg newspapers and magazines. They were interrupted by a fat, red-faced policeman who came in and stood
at attention.

"Kokpai Zhanatayev is here, Your Excellency! Shall I bring
him in?"

"Please do."

A tall, broad-shouldered young djiguit was led in from
the outer yurta. Abai liked his clear forehead, the intent
expression of his large grey eyes, and his slightly aquiline
nose. He was especially impressed by the deep, guttural
voice when the young man said in Russian:

"Good day, Oyaz!" Noticing Abai, his eyes shone with
pleasure. "Assalau-magalaikum, Abai-aga!" he pronounced
with his hand to his heart.

The next to enter was Kokpai's interpreter.

Losovsky began his questioning, and Abai learned that
Kokpai was twenty years old, that he was a shakird who had
been studying at the madrasah of the Khazret Kamaly for
many years. He came from the Kokshe clan and was related
to Dutbai, the ruler of Mukur Volost.

"Zhanatayev," Losovsky addressed him, "all the six
rulers, including your relative Dutbai, have today testified
that the documents you have submitted are forgeries. Let's
leave aside Russian laws for a while. You're studying at a
Moslem madrasah, aren't you? What punishment should be
imposed on a liar according to the Sharia? You're very
young, but what will become of you if you take the crooked
path now? Frankly, I'm worried about you. You're not
illiterate and are very well aware of what you've done.
Lenience may be shown if a crime is committed in
ignorance, but in the present case it should be punished
twice as severely. What have you to say for yourself?"

No sooner had the interpreter finished, than Kokpai
cleared his voice, as if preparing to sing. Abai remembered
hearing a few years ago that the young man was a good
singer. Kokpai shifted his eyes now to Losovsky, now to
Abai, flushing and paling nervously.

"My guilt is heavy, Taksir, I agree. But let me explain why
I did it. I'll accept your decision as a just retribution."

"Tell us why," said Losovsky.

"Out of need. I'm a poor man of the weak tribe of
Kokshe. On the one side our neighbours are the Mamai, a
strong tribe with large lands. On the other lie the Tobikty,

another rich tribe. The best of the land belongs to them and we are as crowded together as needles in a pin-cushion, all huddled up on the bank of the Bakanas River, a stream no longer than a man's tongue. Balkibek is near at hand, nearer to us than to the Siban, the Kerei and the Tobikty. The valley lies deserted and the broad meadows too, and there's this large river. It's no farther than a flock's drive from us. And so I decided to help my kinsmen. The statement is false. No volost rulers have set their seals on my appeal. And why should they? I have nothing to bribe them with; my kinsmen are not powerful, and the rulers have nothing to gain by it. They would never consent, and so I drew up the statement on my own, not to enrich myself, but for the sake of my poor kinsmen. I have told you the whole truth. I'll take my punishment, whatever you decide. If you forgive me ... I shall pledge my heart to you."

Abai listened carefully to see that the interpreter did not distort the words. The young man's manner, boldness and dignity appealed to him, and he was determined to intercede for him if necessary. Losovsky often had to deal with petitioners. His experienced eye could size them up at once. He took an immediate liking to this djiguit. Reading Abai's mind, he said good-humouredly: "Let alone practise forgery, Zhanatayev can be his own defence lawyer. Do you think those were really the reasons which made him do it, Ibragim Kunanbayevich?"

Abai was glad that Losovsky had addressed him. It would have been awkward to interfere in an official investigation. He looked at him with a grateful smile.

"The seals are false, of course; but his explanation is genuine, I'm quite sure of it and am ready to bear him out."

"But why should he commit a crime instead of seeking justice by honest ways?"

"That was wrong, of course."

"If he begins to do such things at his age, what will he come to?"

"He'll come to a bad end. And with his intelligence, he'll be a more dangerous criminal than other men."

"Quite true. And the people must be protected from this djiguit. In other words, we've got to punish him."

"Yes. I suppose so. But I think he has been sufficiently punished already. Not by prison, but by his conscience. It is clear that he is suffering greatly. Just look at him now."

Losovsky laughed and looked at Kokpai, who had flushed to the roots of his hair.

"You're so sure of his conscience that you would vouch for him, would you?"

Kokpai suddenly spoke to Abai in Kazakh.

"A real djiguit rarely gives his oath, Abai-aga. I always tried to be a real man, and I mean what I say. I understand little Russian, but I've grasped the meaning of your words. Yes. I'm really ashamed of myself. Please vouch for me and I swear that I'll be indebted to you until my dying day."

Abai was deeply moved.

"My respected chief," he said turning quickly to Losovsky. "This djiguit has given his oath and I am ready to vouch for him. Forgive Zhanatayev and hold me responsible for any future misdeeds."

"Then listen to me, Zhanatayev," Losovsky said solemnly to the young djiguit, trying to impress him with every word. "If you do not stray from the straight road you might grow to be a good and useful man. You were on the brink of a precipice, and do not forget this. Try to be a real djiguit and follow the advice of Ibragim Kunanbayevich, who has vouched for you. He is a man of honour. And if you are a man of honour too, then let this transgression be your first and last."

Losovsky then tore the forged documents to pieces.

An even greater surprise awaited those who stood outside.

"Abai has saved me from the clutches of death. I'll never forget Abai-aga, never, to my dying day!" cried the young man as he came out.

Abai sat talking to Losovsky until late at night.

On leaving, he found Kokpai waiting for him, and he took him along to Ospan's tent.

The volost rulers had gone, each marvelling over the influence Abai had miraculously gained over the oyaz.

"To snatch a man from the threshold of prison! There's nothing Abai cannot do," they said.

They sat up all night and, as the Kazakh saying goes: "Tried to cut a cloak to the pattern of a shadow." Conjectures rose from the yurtas like flocks of frightened birds.

2

The passions of tribal rivalry ran high among the atkaminers, the biys, volost rulers, and even their messengers and servants when they gathered next morning.

"Who is to be the presiding biy?"

"There are two districts here and two oyazes. Whom will they choose?"

"It is said that the oyazes have entrusted the elders with the choice."

"It will be a fat morsel for the tribe from which the biy is chosen. Whose star is to be lucky this time, the star of the Tobikty, the Siban, the Kerei or the Uak?"

"The Tobikty are our elder brothers and the honour is to be theirs!"

Abai and his companions got up late that morning. They were neither plaintiffs nor petitioners, but merely curious onlookers. They left the yurta at noon and on their way to the gathering were joined by Baikokshe and Kokpai.

Watching the volost rulers flocking round the yurtas of the chiefs, Abai recalled how they had been standing about and peeping in at him and Losovsky the night before. The mocking words that had lurked in his mind now clamoured to be set free. Pointing to the crowd of them with his whip he began:

> *A messenger, riding his poor nag to death,*
> *Yells out the order, all out of breath:*
> *"The oyaz is coming! A meeting there'll be!*
> *Drive up your camels and slaughter your sheep,*
> *Set up the yurtas, and don't go to sleep!"*

Baikokshe, Yerbol and Kokpai laughed heartily and others joined in. Lashing his horse, Baikokshe came alongside Abai.

"Go on! What does the volost ruler say?" Abai responded with:

> *I toil for the people, my best I try,*
> *My tongue trickles honey and never runs dry.*
> *Today I'm going to lay it on thick,*
> *And if God permits I'll turn the trick.*
> *A simple lot, they easily fall*
> *For the silliest rot, and I dupe them all.*
> *No trouble at all to cook up a case*
> *With the oyaz alone in some private place.*

He finished, laughing.

Kokpai was fond of verses and was good at making up satirical ditties himself. He added his own lines:

> *I hide my secrets like a hoard of gold,*
> *On what I grab I keep a good, tight hold.*
> *Whoever's against me had better look out!*
> *No one must dare my person to flout.*

"Allah be praised, Kokpai. I didn't know that you were an akyn and not just a singer," Abai said with surprise.

"Neither did I know that you were an akyn!" Kokpai laughed.

Abai's friends surrounded him, begging for more. But as they approached the yurtas of the chiefs, they heard someone calling them. Some elderly men were sitting in a circle on the grass, with Takezhan standing in the centre and waving his hat. The riders presented their salems as they approached.

"Abai and Asilbek, give your horses to the djiguits and stay here with us," said Takezhan, still on his feet. "We're having a council of the Tobikty elders and would like to have your opinion on a certain matter."

Abai dismounted and gave the reins to his friends who withdrew.

"A good horse shows what he's worth not at the beginning of a race, but at the end," said Baigulak, the oldest man there. "We've made a good beginning and the star of the Tobikty has ascended so high that we can almost reach the moon. We now have the honour of choosing the presiding biy. The three other tribes have declined this honour in our favour, since we are the descendants of the eldest brother. We are the worthy sons of our fathers. Let us give our thanks to Takezhan, Iskhak and Shubar, our volost rulers. It is they who wrested the high honour at the conference of chiefs. We, the elders of the Tobikty, are here to talk things over. The presiding biy will take office tomorrow. We must choose a man respected by all. The oyazes will have to approve our choice. We've got to uphold the good name of our tribe. Let us find the man among us who is worthy of the office. May Allah shower his bounties upon him, amen. We've been hoping that you, Abai, who are so respected by the authorities, would go to the oyaz and name the man we have chosen. Well, kinsmen and friends, who shall that man be?"

Abai knew that every one of them was watching the others, warily biding his time. They made him laugh. The silence dragged and finally he spoke himself:

"Well, kinsmen, if Allah has blessed us with such an honour, why hang back in such a way? Speak your minds unless this talk about the star of the Tobikty and the good name of our tribe was just empty words. Why don't you name anyone?"

He stood up, arms akimbo and shoulders thrown back, and slowly eyed them one by one. Still, there was not a sound. They knew that Abai was far superior to them in eloquence, education and knowledge of law. They envied and feared him; none missed the mockery in his voice and the atkaminers preferred to lie low and wait. "What's he driving at?" they thought. "What's his trick?"

Abai decided to make the best of their silence.

"Let bygones be bygones, my dear kinsmen," he said. "Let's tell the truth for once! The office of presiding biy is more than an honour. It's a test. You've said much about the honour of the Tobikty, but that's not the only thing that the people are concerned with. It's not your personal disagreements that the presiding biy will have to think of. He'll have to deal with big matters — the injured and the insulted will expect him to reopen cases settled in the old way. He'll have to cope with the tears of the weak, the complaints of the widows and orphans, and petitions to restore what people accumulated in the sweat of their brow. To say nothing of the feuds between the tribes, between the Siban and the Tobikty, the Tobikty and the Kerei, the Uak and the Tobikty. Only he who can truly say that his law is the law of honesty and justice is fit to be the presiding biy. You haven't ventured to mention a single name and so I shall have to do so. I'll speak openly. You're probably thinking of choosing someone from the Irgizbai, or more accurately, one of Kunanbai's sons. I who am an Irgizbai and a son of Kunanbai would not name any one of them. I shall name a man who will not make the name of the Tobikty accursed, but on the contrary will enhance our fame with his honesty and fairness. This man alone I shall support before the authorities."

Everyone listened alertly.

"I name Asilbek. I advise you to choose him as the presiding biy. He is not a volost ruler or biy, but the people will be well pleased with his justice and solicitude for them. If you want my opinion, you have it now."

He had no sooner finished speaking than the Bokenshi, the kinsmen of Asilbek — Zhirenshe, Urazbai, Abraly and the resourceful Kuntu — shouted enthusiastic approval.

"Well said! So be it! No need to say any more! We thank you for your justice, Abai."

Things ran smoothly after that. Everyone was in agreement with Abai with the exception of the Irgizbai; they could not agree, but were afraid to argue.

The council then and there requested Abai to inform Losovsky that Asilbek had been proposed for the office of presiding biy.

Losovsky readily agreed, as usual, when he heard Abai's favourable opinion, and unhesitatingly gave his approval.

It was only then that Abai broached the subject of Bazaraly, presenting the case as a personal matter.

"I've been expecting you to say something about Kaumenov," Losovsky hardly let him get started. "Andreyev spoke to me about him when we were in town; he's made inquiries on your behalf. But unfortunately I am helpless here. The case has passed out of our jurisdiction. It has been filed with the case of that fugitive Oralbai, the bandit, and since his crimes were committed in both Semipalatinsk and Semirechinsk districts, the case was heard at the offices of the governor-general in Omsk. Sentence was pronounced long ago, its execution was left in abeyance pending the capture of the Kaumenovs in hiding. When we were leaving for the steppes, Kaumenov was already being marched to Omsk. His fate is sealed; fifteen years of hard labour. That's all I can tell you."

Abai was so shaken that he wandered from the yurta without remembering to say goodbye.

His blood ran cold as he thought of Takezhan, Iskhak and the other kinsmen who had betrayed Bazaraly to the authorities and had given false testimony against him. He walked on, unaware of his surroundings, seeing only Bazaraly before his eyes. It was hard to imagine this passionate, active man in chains at the mercy of men who could not understand his language or appreciate his splendid character. Tears streamed down Abai's cheeks as he tried to get away from the noisy crowd. He felt as though he had been beaten black and blue.

He was brought back to reality by a clatter of hoofs. Zhirenshe and Kuntu had been sent to learn what had come of his talk with Losovsky. Abai pulled himself together with an effort.

"Asil-aga has been approved, may it be a happy omen! Tell the news to the others," he said.

"We thank you for your justice, may Allah brighten your days!" said Zhirenshe. "You are not the son of your father, but 'the son of the people', as you've often said." Zhirenshe laughed, his eyes narrowing. "You'll be famous all over the steppes. You are not the presiding biy, but you have chosen the biy of the gathering. Let the Irgizbai be offended if they like. They don't seem to understand that they owe everything to you. Kuntu is happy for Asilbek's good luck and I am happy on your account!"

He grasped Abai by the hand. While smiling in response, Abai felt as despondent as before.

"Ah, Zhirenshe! What do I care about that? An arrow has pierced me to the heart in the oyaz's yurta. Where is my Bazaraly? I hoped to help him through Losovsky and now I've heard this terrible news. Bazaraly has been marched to Omsk and then he will be sent to serve fifteen years of hard labour. All my hopes have crashed!"

Zhirenshe was shaken by the news.

Abai walked on, feeling that there was nothing he could do if even Losovsky was helpless. But was he really? Abai suddenly remembered his dry tone when speaking of Bazaraly. It was obvious that he had wanted to wash his hands of the matter, and Mikhailov's words came to his mind: "Try to rely on him when something serious is at stake, and he will show himself for what he really is." How true this was! Losovsky could have done a great deal; he could have at least refuted the false testimony and certified that Bazaraly had nothing to do with Oralbai. What he had been ready to do for the inoffensive Kokpai he was by no means ready to do for Bazaraly, whom he suspected of being a bitter enemy of the authorities and officialdom in general. Yes, Yevgeny Petrovich had been right. He knew life and he knew people!

Joyful shouts broke in upon him.

"Isn't that Abai over there. It certainly is!"

"At last we've found you, O light of our eyes!"

Abai turned to see Darkembai and Dandibai hastening towards him.

Abai decided to take up their case at once and beckoned them to follow, asking them about their aul in Yeraly as they went along.

The new chapan fitted Darkembai's broad shoulders well and he wore a new hat. Dandibai had come in a homespun beshmet of camel hair and an old lambskin hat. This skinny, wrinkled man with the high cheek-bones protruding above his thin beard was older than Darkembai, and already beginning to stoop. He suffered from pains in his side and it was difficult for him to keep in step with his companions. He walked with his riding-whip clasped in his hands behind his back and by the side of Darkembai looked very much like an old stable hand.

Abai led them to a group of Irgizbai who were sitting somewhat apart from the crowd. Beefy Maibasar sat in the middle, stroking his beard, with Takezhan, Iskhak, Shubar, Akberdy and other atkaminers on either side of him. They had just been railing at Abai for not choosing the presiding biy from among his kinsmen. What in Allah's name had made him choose Asilbek, a Bokenshi? Maibasar was especially incensed.

As Abai and the old men approached, the two zhataks respectfully salemed the company and put the usual polite questions about the welfare of the auls. The Irgizbai responded very coolly, realising that the zhataks had not been brought here for nothing.

Abai did not greet anyone, though there were some present whom he had not yet met. He stood facing them with his hands behind his back and a cigarette in his mouth; his gaze was cold and penetrating.

"Takezhan, Iskhak and Shubar," he pronounced the names as if he were reading them off a list, as he took the cigarette from his mouth. "Come with me, all three of you. We must have a talk." Gesturing to the old men to go on, he followed them without looking back.

Shubar was the first to spring up. Takezhan and Iskhak also heaved themselves up to their feet.

"These old men, Darkembai and Dandibai, have come here on behalf of the fifty zhatak households," Abai began without preliminaries, when they had found a place to sit. "I went to Kop-Zhatak and told them to send these two to the gathering, promising my support. They have come and I want you, three volost rulers, to come to terms with them. Remember that you will be the defendants if the case is brought up at the gathering."

Abai's hard look disconcerted them. Takezhan went into attack at once, glaring at his brother.

"So we are the defendants, eh? Was it Takezhan and Iskhak who raided their auls? You would like to lay the blame at my door. You've brought them to scare me and well they might, this couple of scarecrows!"

Abai went white with anger.

"Don't pretend to be so high and mighty, Takezhan. It is true that the old men are not very well dressed, but they are strangers to evil ways, while you are just as much a stranger to the true duties of a volost ruler."

"So it is I who made beggars of them!"

"Yes, it is."

"That's a fine thing to accuse me of!"

"But that's just what I do accuse you of! If not you personally then your grandfather and his sons, Kunanbai and Maibasar. These old men came to their house as kindling wood and left as ashes. They were squeezed dry and thrown out, but they are your kinsmen nonetheless."

Abai was seething with rage. The words about the axes wielded by the people, now came to his mind.

"Don't try to wriggle out of this," he shouted. "If you don't want to be disgraced before the four tribes, settle the matter here and now. Otherwise I'll do what has to be done. Well, hurry up. Answer me!"

Abai's threats implied that he would go straight to the oyaz, Takezhan reflected, and this did frighten him. Iskhak was silent too, his eyes downcast. The sight of Darkembai had reminded him of the seven horses he had never returned. He was troubled by the thought that Abai might mention this too. He was now inclined to regard Abai as a representative of the authorities, half respectfully and half fearfully. He looked to Shubar expectantly; he was the only man to whom Abai would listen.

"Well, kinsmen, what have you come to complain of?" said Shubar to the old men. "The ice has been broken and you can carry on now by yourselves."

"We don't like a quarrel, delight of my eyes," Darkembai began confidently and boldly. "We haven't the strength for it either. We're not trying to wheedle something out of you through Abai. We only want to recover our own hard-earned property. We have come with two complaints. The first is that last autumn the herds of Takezhan and Maibasar and yours, too, my dear Shubar, trampled down five plots of wheat that was almost ripe. Your animals grazed there for four days and we did not reap a single grain. This year, too, your horses trampled down the early shoots until only black earth remained. We all but wailed with despair, my dear kinsmen. Secondly, there is a nest of thieves called Akhimbet in your Kzil-Moly Volost, my dear Iskhak. They've stolen seven horses from us. We tracked down the thieves, as you know. But what was the result? Just an endless exchange of letters and some other underhand dealings, but let bygones be bygones. In short, we went to ask for our seven horses, but returned only with tears. That is all I have to say, my worthy volost rulers. To whom should we complain if not to Abai, and where should we go if not to this gathering?"

Takezhan was seething with anger, but did not dare pounce on the zhataks in Abai's presence, and only darted murderous glances at him.

Shubar was quick to realise that if this matter reached the biys or the authorities, the three of them, volost rulers, would be in a fix, and there would be no stopping Abai.

"You stand firm as a rock today, I see!" he said with a good-humoured chuckle, speaking as to good old friends. "There's no one at this council who would dare to press the sons of Kunanbai so hard. I had a mind to defend your case myself; since you are from my volost, but I see that you do not need me. You have a powerful protector in Abai-aga. He is supported by the presiding biy on the one hand and by the oyaz on the other; your words will reach them quicker than ours and then there'll be the devil to pay. You're very lucky, old men. And so we have nothing that we can really argue about and shall have to come to terms. I heard of your complaint last year. After all, we must not forget there's a god, too...." Shubar glanced at Takezhan and Iskhak significantly.

"We don't want to appropriate the fruits of their labour, do we, brothers? Let Abai-aga tell us his decision and that will be the end of it," he said.

Abai appreciated Shubar's quick grasp of the situation. He had managed to give the conversation a fresh turn and there was no denying that he was a glib talker. "He's wiser than Takezhan and Iskhak, though younger than either," he thought. "He'll go far, but in which direction?"

Dandibai, who had said nothing, understood that Shubar was trying to persuade Takezhan to satisfy their claims, to conciliate Abai, and preserve the prestige of Kunanbai's sons. He had been listening and nodding his approval.

"If the talk is over, the horses will go to our herds," he said, after clearing his throat. "We are satisfied with your decision. You may be young, but let it be as you have said."

"Let Abai tell us his decision and we shall do as he bids," Iskhak declared.

Takezhan felt it was useless and even dangerous to argue when the two were agreed. "Abai stands so near the authorities that he can become a threat at any moment," he thought, waiting for Abai to speak.

And so the decision was announced; the zhataks were to receive two five-year-olds for each plot that had been twice trampled down, twenty head in all. The theft of the seven horses was to be made good with due allowance for their

issue, which meant that they would get ten "full-valued"*
animals.

The old men were dumbfounded, and secretly prayed
that Abai would see the matter through to the end. The
volost rulers kept silent too. Objecting to the decision they
had accepted beforehand would have been a violation of
custom.

Abai pretended not to notice their resentment.

"The decision has been made," he said firmly, "what
we've got to see to now is that the horses are actually given to
the old men. You're only pretending to agree with the
decision but will try to get out of it once the council is over.
To prevent this, I want you to give them those thirty horses
in three days. You have plenty of shabarmans to do your
bidding, so send them to fetch the horses. I'll be present
when they are being delivered and only then shall we regard
the matter as settled. Have you understood me?"

"Yes," they sighed, as though barely able to pronounce
the word.

Abai rose, lit a cigarette, and went off with the old men.

The five-year-olds were duly brought within three days
and handed over to the old men in the presence of Abai.

The old men were beside themselves with joy.

"That's more than is usually paid for such losses as ours,
more than bride money; it's a whole kun paid for murder."

"Never have the zhataks received so much. May Abai be
happy for the rest of his days!"

But there were misgivings too. The first to express them
was the cautious Dandibai.

"You've made them restore the horses, Abai-zhan," he
said to Abai, blinking with embarrassment, "but what if the
horses run back to the volost rulers? That is what my
frightened head is worrying about. We'll never get those
horses home. It's a long journey through the steppes and it
won't be hard to rob a pair of old men and lay the blame on
thieves."

Darkembai, who was the bolder, was ready to face up to
the risk.

"Why talk that way, Dandibai? What have we to be afraid
of? We'll find some companions and drive the horses safely
home."

But Abai too had misgivings and at once summoned
Baimagambet. "You will go with these old men," he told

* Full-valued animals—a strong, healthy horse, a mare with a foal, or a
cow with a calf.—Ed.

him. "First drive the horses to our aul in Baikoshkara and rest there for a day or two. Give my salem to Aigerim; let her make these aksakals as comfortable as she can and let her also give you my revolver. I keep it in the big coffer. Then choose a good horse for yourself and help the old men to bring the animals to Yeraly. Allah will be with you on your way, my old friends. Present my respects to your aul."

With the case settled, Abai could have gone on his way, but he preferred to stay and watch the proceedings. The hearing had begun of one of the most intricate cases, known as the "Litigation of the Girl Salikha". It had been dragging on since the previous year and growing like a snow-ball with mutual recriminations.

A girl by the name of Salikha of the Kerei tribe had been betrothed to a man of the Siban who had died the year before. The kalim had been paid in full and the bride's yurta and dowry had been ready. The Siban, therefore, had decided that she should be married to the elder brother of the deceased, a man of sixty who had two wives. But this had been bravely and stubbornly opposed by Salikha, who wrote a letter to the elders of the Kerei and also sent a message to them through her kinsmen: "Let us not lose our honour! I have obeyed you always. Don't ruin the youth of your daughter, blessed Kerei. Don't give me away as a third wife to a man who is older than my father."

The girl's plea had become known far and wide and the young people decided to intervene. "We cannot allow such a humiliation," they said. An old akyn had composed a song called "The Plaint of Salikha to Her Kinsmen", which was sung by everybody. A young man of the Kerei fell in love with Salikha, and she with him. Finally, this general sympathy for the girl had its effect even upon the elders and it was decided to return the kalim to the Siban and to break the wedding contract. When word of this reached the Siban, the busybodies got busy talking. "The Kerei want to show their strength and humble us. They've made a mockery of our ancestors; it's an insult to the Siban." All negotiations failed, and tribal feud ensued.

Barimta broke out when the snow melted and the first grass appeared. Both tribes began to steal each other's sheep and horses and as many as fifty djiguits were wounded in the clashes. There was no peace between the two tribes, even during the gathering; the barimta was at its height and herds of choice horses were driven off every night by raiders armed with lances. A great battle was imminent.

This was the most urgent complaint of all that had been submitted to the Karkaralinsk and Semipalatinsk chiefs, since the situation was growing graver every day. The number of people involved was enormous, and each side kept submitting one complaint after another.

Both the district chiefs received numerous appeals urging them to take a decision themselves, but they refused. But the choice of Asilbek did not suit the Kerei either. "He is too close with the Siban, and his wife comes from the aul of the horse-stealers," they said. Just then rumours of Abai's amazing fairness and honesty spread throughout Balkibek.

Meanwhile, Abai attended the meetings, forming his own opinion of the biys. On one of those days he was called to the yurta of the oyaz, where he found Asilbek the presiding biy and the Karkaralinsk district chief. Their conversation was brief. Asilbek told Abai that the Kerei and Siban wanted him to act as mediator and put an end to their feud for them. Before agreeing, Abai first made sure that the request came from the parties in question and had not been prompted by the chiefs.

The district chiefs were pleased and at once approved his appointment. The Karkaralinsk chief Sinitsin then handed him two appeals written in Arabic by the girl. Abai read them, but reserved his opinion for the time being.

On the same day he summoned three representatives from each side. The Siban were presented by Zhumakan, their volost ruler, and two elders. The Kerei sent Toisary, who was also a volost ruler, and two atkaminers. They were received by Abai, Zhirenshe and Urazbai.

"As far as I can gather, kinsmen, your quarrel has developed into open strife," Abai said. "Things have come to such a pass that you are even raiding each other's auls and stealing each other's horses. The disputed compensation was first a kalim for the bride, but has now grown to the dimensions of several kalims, to even more than a kun for murder. The man who handles your case must verify much of the information and find out all the particulars. This is too much for one person to do. 'One head is good, but two are better,' as I have read somewhere. If you do not object, I shall appoint two biys to assist me. They are here: Zhirenshe and Urazbai. They're both from the Tobikty, whom you were willing to trust."

"So be it," Zhumakan and Toisary at once agreed without consulting their kinsmen.

"It is for you to choose your helpers."

Abai bowed silently and the discussion was ended. An arbiter must be reticent, for thoughts are often betrayed by superfluous words. There were intriguers on both sides, people who were always trying to guess which way the wind was blowing and take advantage of it.

He sent his assistants to make inquiries on the spot; Zhirenshe would go to the Kerei, and Urazbai to the Siban.

"You'll have to investigate many facts, but remember that truth and the semblance of truth are two different things. Enemies are inclined to mix truth with lies, to exaggerate or conceal things. Keep your opinions to yourselves, and do not say: 'This is the truth and this is a lie!' And especially express no favour for the one side or the other and do not bind yourselves with promises. If you do, I shall be bound as well. And most important, strike no bargains. The kinsmen have chosen me because they rely on my honesty, and I beseech you to be my wings which fly only the course of truth and justice."

The investigations took more than a week and were held in three places simultaneously—among the Siban, among the Kerei and at the meeting itself, to which many petitioners and witnesses came from both sides.

Abai himself only questioned the principal plaintiff and the principal defendant: the old, would-be bridegroom Sabatar of the Siban and the girl's father, Kaldibai of the Kerei.

He ascertained the losses sustained through the breach of contract: the kalim, the gifts and the dowry.

The dead bridegroom had been the favourite son of a rich man, and the kalim had been one of the largest known in the region. When the young man had died and the girl was to marry a man so much older than herself, her father made Sabatar pay him an additional half of the previous kalim.

Kaldibai, for his part, had also sustained considerable losses. He had enlarged the dowry agreed upon. Besides the octagonal and well-furnished yurta with a silk carpet bought from a Kokand caravan for a hundred sheep, there were twenty-five fur coats, twenty-five embroidered felt carpets and twenty-five coffers. There was twenty-five of everything: dresses, linen, table-cloths, crockery, pillows, blankets and silk covers for the ivory inlaid bedstead.

The dowry had not yet been delivered, while the kalim had already been paid in full.

The Siban were especially sorry that they had paid such a large number of animals as part of the kalim, and that was

why they began stealing the horses of the Kerei immediately
after the breach of contract. The Kerei, for their part, had
also resorted to barimta to get back these horses which they
had come to regard as their own. Each side tried to capture
as many horses as it had lost in the previous raid. Strong
djiguits, experienced in barimta and raiding, fell upon their
opponents again and again. Soon every man capable of
wielding a soeel was involved in the struggle and the tangle
over the ill-starred marriage contract grew increasingly
complicated.

Abai's questioned everyone concerned in the quarrel, one
by one. And now he wanted to know what Salikha had to
say.

She had come to Balkibek to submit her complaint to the
chief of the Karkaralinsk District in person and had not yet
left the settlement. Abai invited her and her kinsmen to
Ospan's yurta, where he was living.

A tall olive-skinned girl wearing a sable hat, a silk chapan
and large silver earrings entered the yurta accompanied by
her father Kaldibai and other kinsmen. She walked in slowly
but fearlessly. The yurta was crowded, since everyone
wanted to have a look at the girl whose name was on
everybody's lips. But after Ospan had offered kumiss to
everyone, Abai gestured to the Tobikty, and the people about
him began to leave. Kaldibai also rose and led his kinsmen
outside.

Now that he was alone with her, Abai had a good look at
her face. Her dark wide-set eyes glowed with a curious fire,
the long lashes enhancing their depth. There was the
suggestion of a curve in the delicate line of her nose. Her
mouth drooped slightly at the corners and, though barely
perceptible, the premature lines on her face bespoke
anxiety and grief.

Abai had long cultivated the habit of saying little and
listening intently.

"My dear Salikha! We have never met, but I believe I
know as much about you as any of your kinsmen," he said at
last.

She blushed and smiled, her features changing instantly.
Her white teeth flashed and her face seemed suddenly
radiant, sincere and frank.

"I've read your appeal," Abai went on. "Do you still abide
by what you've written?"

Salikha frowned, and there was a flicker of annoyance in
her dark eyes.

"Abai-Mirza," she said in some dismay, "I didn't write it

only to repudiate it afterwards. I haven't changed my mind." And she smiled again.

"Then let me ask another question: when you wrote that you would never marry, did this imply that it was only old Sabatar you would never marry? Or is there no one of the Siban you would care to marry? Would you change your mind if a worthy man of the Siban tried to woo you?"

"I would never have dared to refuse if it were a man of my age. Nor would my family and my aul have let me do such a thing."

"Did you ask the kinsmen of your betrothed to name another djiguit as your groom?"

"Yes, I did. But they replied, 'The kalim has been paid and Sabatar has his rights, which have been determined by Allah. Let her stop her nonsense!'"

"Tell me another thing, my dear Salikha," Abai continued more gently. "It is no longer any secret that the kinsmen of your betrothed often say, 'She would never have refused if she had not been urged to do so by a djiguit of the Kerei. It was only when she became entangled with him that she grew so stubborn—and so the Kerei are doubly guilty before our ancestors. They've taken our kalim and dishonoured the maiden.' That is what they say. And what have you to say about it? Did you form an attachment with this djiguit before or after you refused to marry Sabatar?"

Salikha went dead pale, and then blushed. She answered without hesitation.

"What I have to say is as true as our faith itself, Abai-Mirza," she said with emotion, her silver earrings dangling. "When the Siban answered that they would not name anyone as a groom but the old man, I decided to run off with the first man who came along; and it was only then that this djiguit appeared. No living man could approach me before that. While my first betrothed was alive I regarded the Siban as a desired home," she said, brushing the tears away with her embroidered handkerchief.

"That will be all," said Abai, still looking at her.

She seemed surprised that the conversation had ended so soon. It had been quite different when she had talked to her kinsmen. The compassion she felt in Abai's words strengthened her determination.

"No one incited me to do this, Abai-Mirza!" she assured him with a sorrowful and angry frown. "The bitter thought came to me of itself. Why should I be the third wife of that death's head Sabatar? I kept asking myself. I no longer felt

alive, I seemed to be suspended between life and death.
Shall I tell you all that's in my soul? I look into the dark waters of the Balkibek every day, just as I used to look into the
Bakanas near our aul. In this river, too, there will be room
for me. I would rather the cold waters caressed my body
than old Sabatar."

Abai looked up, deeply moved. Salikha got up and walked
towards the door, but he sat still, and merely nodded a
farewell. He could see the waters part before her body, her
delicate eyebrows raised in terror beneath the still surface,
her slender hands reaching for death....

The interrogation continued for three days more.
Zhirenshe and Urazbai were back with detailed information.
The losses of both parties and their mutual claims had now
been fully assessed. The tangled case was completely in
Abai's hands, but no one knew what decision he had arrived
at.

He ordered the people of the Kerei and the Siban to
gather before the yurtas of the district chiefs. The
shabarmans accordingly rode through the settlement shouting: "The litigation of the girl Salikha! The dispute between
the Kerei and the Siban! Hearing of the case today! Decision
to be announced!"

The people flocked to the base of a small hill. The chiefs
in their brass-buttoned uniforms had also come out, surrounded by interpreters, guards and policemen, and
formed a separate compact group of their own. There was
something festive though solemn about the gathering.

As Abai approached the hill, he was intercepted by
Zhirenshe and Urazbai.

"You are holding the two ends of the reins in your hands,
Abai. The final test has come for you and for our clans,"
said Zhirenshe. "But you have not told your decision even
to us, to Urazbai and me. Couldn't we hear it now? Who is
right and who is wrong?"

Laughing, Abai squinted at his friends.

"What do you think?" he asked. "Which side should we
support?"

Neither spoke.

"Has something stuck in your throat, Zhirenshe? Speak
up."

"The sight of gold will tempt even an angel," Zhirenshe
began significantly, watching Abai's expression closely, and

trying to speak calmly and firmly. "The customs of the ancestors are law for the descendants. The Siban elders send this salem to you through us: 'Let him adjudge the daughter of the Kerei to Sabatar and he shall receive forty pedigree horses from the herds of the Siban.' This is what we wanted to tell you...."

To Abai it seemed that these were not words that were streaming from Zhirenshe's lips, but unspeakable filth. He stopped him short with an angry gesture, but instantly took hold of himself and laughed. This quick play of expression did not escape Zhirenshe and at once kindled his hopes.

Abai was still laughing and looking at them.

"Well, Urazbai? How about you? Is that what you advise as well? 'Let us take the gift and sacrifice the Kerei to the Siban.'"

Urazbai well knew Abai's attitude to such matters, but was resolved to speak his mind nonetheless:

"Yes! That's my advice too. I agree with Zhirenshe. It's as clear as day. Is there a chief who does not take bribes, or a biy who does not feather his nest? We didn't start it, and it won't end with us. It's not to 'Mecca we have come as pilgrims, but to the gathering at Balkibek."

"So that's your decision," said Abai, neither his voice nor his face betraying his thoughts.

Zhirenshe and Urazbai grew bolder.

"Yes! That is our decision."

"Let it be as the Siban wish."

"Enough of your yapping, you curs," Abai shouted hoarsely, unable to control himself any longer, and he added a few strong words.

Both of them were older than Abai and never before had he permitted himself to speak so rudely.

"You two were to have been my helpmates," he continued, his anger hardly appeased by his outburst. "My wings indeed! I might just as well have chosen Takezhan. Justice and injustice are the same to you! What do you care either for the Siban or the Kerei! But both of them are my people! You wanted to sacrifice me to your greed, to disgrace me before the gathering and all the Kazakhs. You would have done better to kill me. How could you have sunk so low? The people trusted the honour of your tribes and the spirits of your ancestors and what did you do? You reached out for a bribe from under their very shrouds. Get out of my sight!"

He strode quickly away from them.

Takezhan and Iskhak were hastening towards him.

"The chiefs are waiting for you! Where have you been, Abai?" they shouted, panting for breath.

Abai walked through the crowd and took his place on the green top of the hill. He courteously greeted the two oyazes and then presented his salems to the biys of the opposing parties.

He opened the hearing by calling upon the two biys to speak. Both finished with the following words: "We entrust our case first to Allah and next to you. Decide the matter in all justice! Let the spirits of our ancestors say the final word."

It was only then that Abai began to speak. He sat with his legs folded under him, his hand pressing his hat against his side. Beads of perspiration stood out on his broad forehead and large straight nose, he was under a great emotional stress, but his voice was clear and firm, his speech calm and fluent.

"My people, all who are gathered here! My kinsmen of the Kerei and the Siban! You have set me up between yourselves that I might seek the origins of your discord and restore peace among you. Entrusting this task to me, you said, 'May you serve as a seam to unite that which was torn asunder.' I wish to warn you that in settling this case I have been thinking of the people in general and not of individuals. But in thinking of the people in general, I thought of the younger generation first of all. Our hateful quarrels over brides have been a source of enmity between Kazakhs for many ages. As the times change, the laws grow obsolete and new ways must be evolved for settling such disputes which disturb our peace, disunite us, and bring us dishonour. Such are the thoughts with which I approached this case, and such, too, are the thoughts which have prompted my decision. My first decision concerns the girl Salikha. I do not know our ancestors judged such cases, and what they based their verdicts on, but I do know that the young do not wish to live in sorrow. New times have brought new customs and those fathers of the people who refuse to heed the demands of the young will not heal the wounds but only reopen them.

"Salikha has once shown her obedience to her parents and became the betrothed of the man they had chosen for her. But fate bereaved her of her betrothed, a man who was her proper match. There cannot be two deaths in one life; such is the law of Allah. Is not Sabatar's demand tantamount

to a second death for the girl? I know what I'm saying,
because the girl is prepared to depart from this life just to
escape the fate in store for her. All of you have sisters and
daughters, my people. Is it fair to sell a girl twice? She
surrendered her freedom once in favour of her tribe. Let
her freedom now be returned to her. Salikha is released
from the engagement. Such is my first decision."

Abai said the last words in a deliberately loud, clear voice,
and continued:

"But the Siban are not to blame for the death of the girl's
betrothed. The Siban meant well and honestly paid the
kalim. You, Kerei, have received it in full and not once, but
twice. The first kalim was large enough, costing no less than
fifty camels. Not satisfied with this, you took advantage of
the fact that Salikha was now to be the third wife of an old
man and demanded an additional kalim, which was
generously granted. Thus, you sold your own daughter a
second time, and the Siban are not to blame for this. On the
contrary, you, Kerei, are to be blamed for your avarice. And
so the Kerei are to return the kalim they received, and not
only the kalim. They must also pay compensation. They
received property valued at fifty camels as the first kalim
and at twenty-five camels as the second kalim. I have
determined that the compensation for the guilt of the Kerei
to the Siban and their own daughter shall be twenty-five
camels. In all, the Kerei must give the Siban a hundred
camels. The clan of the bride and the clan of the djiguit she
has chosen for her husband must contribute equally to this
payment. Such is my second decision.

"These last three days I have been collecting information
about the losses sustained by both sides in their conflict. The
Siban have driven away 200 horses, while the Kerei
possessed themselves of 170. Let both sides return the
horses or substitute five-year-olds for those that are gone.
This is my final decision, kinsmen, and it has been
prompted only by my desire to restore peace and unity
among the tribes. I have spoken."

The crowd was silent. Only the two oyazes, who had been
listening to their interpreters, now exchanged a few
remarks of approval. They nodded to Abai, smiling, and at
once went up to him. The crowd interpreted this as a sign
that the litigation was over.

But neither among the Kerei nor among the Siban did
one hear that animated hubbub which usually followed the
announcement of a decision: "I agree." "I don't agree."

"It can't be!" "That's a good decision." Nor was there a sound from even the Tobikty, who were disinterested observers.

The gathering drew quickly to a close. The chiefs were gone and the people were leaving for their various auls. Abai and his friends went to Baikoshkar. Zhirenshe and Urazbai were travelling the same way, but kept themselves an arrow's flight ahead.

Abai had had no opportunity to have a further talk with them, and he lashed his bay to overtake them. But when the two saw him, they exchanged glances and spurred on their own horses.

"So that's how it is, I see!" exclaimed Abai.

The two reined in their horses for an instant.

"Yes, that is how it is," Zhirenshe shouted angrily.

"And it's all the better that you should know it," added Urazbai.

The two galloped furiously off. Abai checked the pace of his horse and sadly looked after the men he had once called his friends. Both were now his enemies.

Takezhan and Maibasar returned from Balkibek amid a crowd of people who were also cursing Abai. Everybody knew about the forty horses promised by Siban.

Neither the Kerei nor the Siban had anything to say against Abai. Accepting his decision, they told both oyazes, "We agree with his decision, shall abide by it and make peace." Both sides thought highly of Abai, appreciating his courage in promoting new ideas and smashing the obsolete Kazakh traditions.

"His words were good and will bring relief to the people. The whole district will reckon with the man," they said one to another.

3

An open carriage drawn by three horses sped along the road from Akshoky to Semipalatinsk. Baimagambet, who sat on the driver's box, now and then lashed the bay to make the most of the coolness of that autumn morning. Abai and his three children, Abish, Magash and Gulbadan sat in the carriage upholstered in red morocco. Abish's thin and usually pale face was flushed with animation.

"Where shall we live when we get to town, Father?" he asked again and again. "At a Kazakh or a Russian house? Shall we be together, the three of us? I think I could do better if I lived alone in a Russian family."

"You do? Well, it's I who am going to live alone with a Russian family. They have a girl my age and I'll learn to speak Russian sooner than you," cried Gulbadan, who had always been more precocious than her brothers. Pushing Magash out of her way, she had snuggled on to her father's knees. Abai liked the boldness of his little girl and her cheerfulness, which had endured even this first separation from her mother.

"My precious carefree darling," he said, tickling her chin, "you're bolder than your brothers and you'll live with the family of an educated Russian woman who will be like a mother to you. You'll be comfortable, all of you. I'll come to town often enough, because there's nothing more important to me than your studies."

He hugged the three children with both arms and held them close. Noticing that Magash had said nothing and had apparently been saddened by his separation from home more than the others, Abai tried to distract him.

"Why don't you sing a song, Magash?"

Secretly pleased that his father had taken notice of him, the little boy's thin lips parted in a smile, revealing his small teeth.

"What song shall I sing?" he asked, brightening and clinging to his father. "I'm afraid to begin because I'll mix it all up. You'd better begin it yourself."

Gulbadan, who sensed her father's intention, joined in the game and said jokingly, "Magash never likes to begin. Whenever someone asks him to sing, he gets so frightened that he backs away like a foal."

Everybody laughed, including Baimagambet. Even Magash laughed, though he buried his face in the cushion.

"Just because a foal backs away doesn't mean that he can't go forward sometimes," Abish told his sister. "How can you know it anyway when you never ride a horse?"

Magash raised his head.

"She can't ride a sheep, let alone a foal; and my tai,* which always backs away, took first place at the baiga five times," he said, all his sadness dispelled. "You begin the song, Father."

Abai sang the *Kozy-Kosh* and the children joined in.

Throughout the two days of their journey Abai sang songs to the children, told them stories or made Abish and Gulbadan tell him what they knew. When they were sleepy,

* Tai—one-year-old colt.— *Ed*

all of them, including Baimagambet, sang together. At last they reached the town.

On Mikhailov's advice, Abai placed Magash and Gulba-dan in a boys' and a girls' school respectively, and arranged for them to live with a Russian family Andreyev had recommended. Mikhailov's advice with regard to Abish was somewhat different. This boy had already learned to read and write Arabic and was quick-witted and inquisitive. He understood spoken Russian quite well, but was overage for the first form of elementary school. And so he was boarded with an educated Russian family where he could improve his language and receive a good upbringing. Abai found an experienced private tutor for him.

Mikhailov took an interest in the boy from the start and gave Abai another bit of advice about him.

"Your eldest son, Ibragim Kunanbayevich, is capable of serious study, in my opinion. It doesn't matter that he is a little overage for school. It is even better that he has come here armed with some knowledge received in his native tongue. That will make it easier for him to study another language. Take my advice: let your Abdrakhman study with his tutor this winter and next year send him to school, but not in Semipalatinsk. Let him go to Tumen, where the schools are better. I have some good friends there, and he might live with them. Let him spend the summer in the steppes and the winter in town, where he will get a Russian education. If he keeps in good health, we may some day send him to the University in St. Petersburg!"

Abai was grateful to Mikhailov. Here was a friend who had given more thought to his children than all the kinsmen in the aul, and Abai unhesitatingly took his advice in everything.

Abai stayed all autumn and the first half of the winter in town. The children were now going to school, but he could not bring himself to leave them. He spent all the weekdays in the Gogol Library, where his reading became more and more like research work of engrossing interest. In the evenings he would retell the contents of some of the books he had read to Baimagambet, and the latter's stock of stories grew steadily.

On Saturdays Baimagambet hitched the horses to the sledge, and went off to fetch Magash, Gulbadan and Abish. This gave Abai two nights and a day with his children. He

made no other engagements then and refused to receive
visitors from the aul. He devoted every minute to his
children, talking to them, helping them with their lessons or
just playing with them or else getting Baimagambet to tell
them stories. Sometimes they sang songs together and they
spent their time happily.

He had also made some arrangements for several Kazakh
orphans—the result of a conversation with Mikhailov, who
told him that in accordance with an order received from the
Corps in Omsk, every volost was to pick a boy to be sent to
the city school. No parents could be found willing to part
with a son, although there were some who would have
agreed to send their children if they were richly compensated. The feeble light of knowledge that had reached the
auls was quickly extinguished by the age-old prejudices.
Mikhailov commented bitterly that there was not a family in
the whole of Semipalatinsk District willing to send their son
to school. And so Abai had written to some of the Tobikty
kinsmen whom he knew he could influence.

The thought of the poor zhataks continued to worry him.
Recently he had learned that not all the horses he had
adjudged to the poor at the council at Balkibek had been
delivered to them. True, the whole herd reached Yeraly
safely, but by the autumn no less than ten horses of the
thirty were gone; they had been driven away singly or in
twos by unknown horse-stealers. "Let at least some of the
zhataks receive something which cannot be stolen—knowledge," he thought when he made arrangements at the
schools for the children of the poor.

More than half of the winter was gone and it was time for
Abai to return to his aul. It was on a Saturday that he made
Baimagambet spend half the day gathering together the
little Kazakhs who were at school in the town. Abai's house
that evening rang with the songs of the children. They
played all sorts of games and Abai gave them riddles to
solve, while Baimagambet entertained them from his stock
of tales and funny sayings. Before the evening meal, when
they were tired and had calmed down, Abai collected his
little guests and his own children about him.

He produced a sheet of paper and the children stood
around expectantly. It was a new poem written that
morning:

> *I lived in ignorance and darkness as a boy,*
> *Of learning and its fruits the worth I could not know.*

You, children, are our hope, our promise and our joy,
So boldly take what we had missed those years ago.
And here is my behest: make it your goal
To study not for ranks or personal gain,
But for the benefit of people as a whole,
And then your efforts will not be in vain.

He repeated the poem several times and then said a few
words to them in farewell:

"My dear children! We, your fathers and elder brothers,
are like the grass that has wilted before it could really grow.
We did not receive an education at the right age, alas. We
used to dream of learning, but the dream never came true.
How I wish that you will do as my poem says. This is not
only my wish, but also the wish of your friends in the
steppes, of all those who expect you to help them some day.
You must study with only one thought in mind: to become
useful and honest men, defenders of your people."

Pausing for a moment, he concluded: "That is all I want
to tell you before I go away. This poem was written specially
for you by an akyn whose name is Kokpai."

During that winter Abai had often committed to paper his
cherished dreams and thoughts. But he still did not feel that
he was a real akyn and his exacting pen, for that reason,
concealed his identity under the unknown name of Kokpai.

AT THE SUMMIT

1

Several years had elapsed, years of arduous labour and searchings. But the hours he spent with a book or pen in hand seemed the happiest to Abai. To meditate and set his experiences down on paper had become the purpose of his life. The sparks of truth he found in books or learned from life found their way into his poems and songs that were unlike any written before him in Kazakh.

His name was widely known and he was aware that his poetic work was a duty to the people. A book of his verses entitled *Of People* branded the ignorant parasites, the callous rich of the steppes and the corrupt officials with ignominy. To the young he sang of beauty, making them think and feel more deeply.

Born in Akshoky, the songs were soon carried over the boundless steppes. He set them on paper and his young, enthusiastic followers quickly learned them by heart, found suitable melodies for them and spread them far and wide.

One sunny winter morning, Abai was sitting at his usual place, near his tall bedstead decorated with carved ivory, his favourite cushion at his side, his hand resting now on his knee, now on the edge of the small round table. He was lost in thought, gazing through the window at the snow-covered slopes of the Akshoky hills, lit up by the sun. How mysterious is the power emanating from those snow-covered mountains!

He had managed to get out of acting as a mediator too often that year and spent most of the winter at home. It had been a fertile year. While reading his books, writing his poems or drifting through the hours in inspired meditation, he had come to look upon those hills as old friends. Did they not respond to his melancholy in the mornings and in the gloaming of the evenings? Always austere, they seemed to conceal a deep longing — they longed for the sun on overcast days and for the spring in winter. Today their grey brows were not drawn glumly together: motley herds of cattle could be seen on their steep slopes, and the herdsman's song was all the solitary hills could hear.

Baimagambet, aware of Abai's preoccupied mood, had kept himself respectfully in the background. To pass the time, he took Abai's whip and proceeded to replace the old thong, occasionally glancing at Abai, who was now beating the air with his hand and muttering something—a curious habit he had acquired that winter. Baimagambet was sure that he would presently call for pencil and paper. This time, however, Abai said nothing, merely stretching out his left hand. Baimagambet guessed his wish and placed two thick, worn volumes on the table.

Abai opened one of them, found the page he wanted, scanned it briefly and leaned back, thinking again.

There was no one for miles about who could read these books written by two poets from a remote world, and a remote day.

Pushkin and Lermontov, both of them had lived so far from the steppes and were unknown and alien to the Kazakhs. They had expressed themselves in an alien tongue, but to Abai they seemed like kinsmen. In their sadness they seemed to say to him, "You are like us, our thoughts are the same."

Those poets were not among the living, but they were not dead. They were immortal, and the world would always remember their names. What does a man usually leave behind him? Only a grave and even that is gradually levelled by the winds. But those two would stand for ever, like the two peaks of the Akshoky.

"Blessed is a nation enlightened by knowledge," Abai thought with a sigh. "How I wish that we, the Kazakhs, had also inherited a golden treasure of knowledge from our ancestors. The memory of those two poets will serve as beacons to the future generations."

Abai began to read Tatyana's letter, a fragment from *Yevgeny Onegin*. "How skilfully those words are woven together, and as alive as breath itself in their deep tenderness," he thought, and suddenly remembered a poem he had once composed.

> *The speech of lovers needs no words,*
> *Another tongue they seem to know.*
> *The eye lights up, the eyebrow curves,*
> *And there's the answer—yes or no.*
> *Once I could also speak that tongue,*
> *I knew it well, I understood the signs.*

> *Alas, I am no longer young,*
> *I have forgotten it with time.*

He read the lines of the letter again and again.

"I have lived through this myself, but where have I ever heard it set down so wonderfully!"

Two images suddenly flashed across his mind, like two shooting stars. One was Togzhan, a symbol of radiant youth, and the other—Saltanat, an image of wistful longing. He had been thinking of them as he translated Tatyana's letter into Kazakh the night before. Like Tatyana, they, too, had listened to the voice of reason, they could not break free. Their parting words sounded in his heart.

They would feel Tatyana's words as their own, and that was why he undertook the translation. For two days he had been making Tatyana speak in an alien tongue, in the Kazakh language. Engrossed with this task, he found more and more new expressions, noble in their sadness. He compared his translation with the original and found that his own Tatyana had at times used words that were too ordinary. Still, that could not be helped, since they were written for new hearers. Even then, would they understand?

He murmured quietly, his fingers caressing the dombra, and though his eyes were fixed on the two peaks of Akshoky his gaze was turned inwards. When he went to bed the night before, he had the faint stirrings of a melody within him, but now it spoke more boldly. He tried to sing the tune; the rhythm was close to the metre of the poem.

> *The heavens meant you for my husband,*
> *To love and cherish as my own.*

Tatyana's secret, though timidly and uncertainly as yet, was beginning to sound in the melody. Abai urged his dombra on, the chords flowing one after another. The final two lines were especially elusive, but at last fell in with the melody.

Abai then sang three stanzas of Tatyana's letter and smiled contentedly. He took a fresh pinch of nasibai. He remembered the melody well.

2

There were so many guests at Abai's winter home that the large room where he used to sit after his evening tea was too small to hold them all.

Aigerim, Yerbol, Baimagambet and Kakitai, Abai's young
nephew, acted as hosts. Old Baitory, Burkitbai and
Baikadam had arrived with their wives and now sat near
Abai. Kakitai's voice could be heard all over the house.
Smiling and courteous, the young djiguit captivated
everyone with his cheerfulness and was ever ready with a
jest or friendly word. That day he was especially attentive to
the guests.

Kakitai was one of the sons of Iskhak, Abai's brother and
for the past two years he had been living with Abai as his
adopted son.

With his broad open face, large, somewhat protruding
eyes, and short, slightly upturned nose, he was the picture
of light-hearted youth. Any young woman could have
envied his full red lips. Abai especially liked the boy's clear
eyes and merry voice, which seemed to vibrate from his very
heart. This nephew was as dear to him as his own sons.

Kakitai could not be sent to study in town, but living with
Abai he studied Russian with extraordinary zeal and read
Russian books for hours on end. He also studied with Abish
when the boy came home on holidays, and shared his
knowledge with him. Kakitai never left Abai's side, accompanying him wherever he went, and took every chance he
had to ask his uncle about the Russian books he read. To all
intents and purposes, he was now equal to any of the pupils
in the town, and any teacher would have been proud of him.

The young akyns and singers had always been welcome in
Abai's house. A group of them, including Kokpai, had just
returned to the steppes on horseback and in carriages after
a few months in Semipalatinsk. These were Mukhah,
Magavya, Iskhak—the son of Irsai—Shubar and
Mukhamedjan, a relative of Abai and one of the best singers
in the district. In other years they had been accustomed to coming here often and staying long, spending their days and
nights in their happy and intimate circle.

They had only just arrived, and Kokpai addressed Abai
and Aigerim on behalf of the others.

"Abai-aga, we became real celebrities in Semipalatinsk.
No family gathering, no marriage ceremonies or any other
festivities on either side of the river were held without us.
They outdid themselves in kindness to us, and it was your
songs, that gave rise to all this, especially the *Song of Tatyana*
which Mukhamedjan brought to us. Since everyone there
agrees that we are real masters of song, let us show you what
we can do."

"But if each of you alone could entertain a great gathering, what will it be like here, with all of you singing together," said Abai smiling. "Aigerim, Kakitai, Yerbol and Baimagambet! Call in the whole aul, young and old! These singers are so swelled-headed they cannot sing to a mere four or five of us alone. Remember the saying: 'When the fare is frugal, the guest bites his tongue!' Now see that our guests don't have to do the same! See to the comfort of each of them and give them a good treat."

As twilight fell, Kakitai and Baimagambet made the rounds of all the neighbours.

While the guests were gathering, Kokpai told Abai the latest news in the town. He described how pleased Mikhailov had been with the translation of Tatyana's letter and conveyed his congratulations, without concealing the doubts expressed by Mikhailov.

Abai was pleased with his friend's insight.

"Mikhailov seems to be right, djiguits," he admitted. "My translation is not as accurate as it should be. I was carried away by my own emotions, you see."

Unwilling to say any more about the lines that had been inspired by his own memories, he spoke about his friend.

"What a fine sense of judgement he has! He does not know Kazakh well, yet he is able to detect the weaknesses in my translation. That is what learning does for a man."

It was an evening of songs and poetry, of poetic contests between akyns and singers, and it was well after midnight when the old men left. Everyone took part in the singing, both the guests and the people of the aul; only Abai and Aigerim were silent. Now it was Mukhah, Mukhamedjan and Kokpai who sang in turn, then Magavya and Kakitai sang together, and then Iskhak, Yerbol and Baimagambet joined Shubar and Kokpai. At the request of Abai and Aigerim, the best singers sang their favourite songs, both old and new. Finally, Aigerim was asked to sing by Kokpai and Mukhamedjan.

"We haven't heard her sing for such a long time. Why does she never sing? Couldn't we hear her today, Abai-aga?" they pleaded.

Abai looked at Aigerim, whose beauty seemed to glow like molten gold.

"Aigerim sings no more. She doesn't want to." His voice was sad and tinged with bitterness.

Their married life, all these last years, was based on mutual respect. That, and nothing else. The happiness they had once known did not return. Their hearts seemed chilled to one another for ever.

There was a tender reproach in Abai's voice, an echo of bygone days, and Aigerim's heart literally missed a beat. She quickly turned to Abai, her eyes deep with inquiry, her lips almost smiling. Her soft answer was like the words of a song.

"Am I to blame, Abai? Was it not you who ceased to listen to me?"

"Then do sing for us, Aigerim! Sing some new songs for us!"

He did not want to hear anyone but Aigerim now.

Glancing at Yerbol, she made an almost imperceptible sign and he understood at once. Reaching for the dombra, he moved closer and began to play. The *Song of Tatyana* filled the house with silvery ripples and everyone was still.

Abai was astonished. To his knowledge Aigerim had never once sung the poem, but she seemed to know every word and every shade of the melody. The truth was that she had learned it with Yerbol's help.

"It is Tatyana herself who is singing!" the thought flashed through the mind of every akyn there.

Abai had heard his own song for the first time when it was sung by Mukhamedjan on the day he wrote it. Now he heard it for the second time and was swept with a new wave of emotion. Aigerim gave new meaning to Tatyana's words and the song was reborn before its own creator.

To Abai, too, it seemed that he had been rejuvenated. Had he not listened to his beloved that very first time with the ardour he felt now? As always, Aigerim seemed to be more than singing — to be living the very words, the very melody! All those fervent hopes and whispers now burst into flame, a fire that burned only for him, for Abai.

> *The heavens meant you for my husband,*
> *To love and cherish as my own.*
> *But for a wife you did not want me,*
> *And left me in the darkness, all alone.*

Was that not a melancholy reproach? She was very pale. Her secret hope was revealed in every trembling word: "Am I to blame? And if so, then can't you forgive me? Can't we recover our former days of happiness?" she seemed to be asking Abai.

Aigerim seemed exhausted, as though the song had drained all strength from her. For a time no one dared to break the silence. Abai sat very still, unable to pull himself together. Then with sudden determination he put his arm about her.

"Aigerim, my precious, you have spoken to me with your song and your tears. You have come back to me!"

The guests were deeply moved.

"Oh, Tatyana, you have found yourself in the daughter of a Kazakh!" said Kokpai. "More than one heart will speak with those words."

But Abai and Aigerim could not speak. Newly awakened love needs no words and tolerates no stranger's eye.

Mukhah, Kokpai and the other djiguits rose and left.

The song had loosened the knots in the hearts of Aigerim and Abai.

Poetry had brought them together again as equals, equally inspired. Poetry did not let them betray or lose each other. Their love flared up anew...

It was thus that the great Russian akyn Alexander Pushkin first came into the Kazakh steppes in the winter of 1887. He brought his songs and his Tatyana who taught the Kazakhs to speak their love in the frank and artless language never spoken here before.

The poems and melodies born in Akshoky, taken down in writing and learnt by heart, spread far and wide. Every new word sped over the steppes like the gentle but persistent wind of the Sary-Arka. Songs never heard before were carried by the winds over the steppes bringing a long-awaited reply to a desire that had lain dormant through the centuries. The voice of a new tribe, the songs were the harbingers of a new spring. Born in the still lingering winter, they were songs for the summer that was to come, a summer that would see a fresh blossoming of life. They rang for those who were seeking a new life and fresh horizons, who had a keen mind, a responsive heart, for the strong and bold, who were concerned for the people and were ready for battle.

The poems and melodies born in Akshoky reached Yeraly. Darkembai and other zhataks made the children recite Abai's poems again and again. Moving up closer to the fortunate boy who could read, Darkembai listened eagerly.

Oh, my countrymen, Kazakhs, my poor, poor people!
You have covered your lips with your whiskers and dare not
speak out.

On your right there is virtue, on the left there is evil,
Where is justice and truth then, how`settle your doubts?

Dandibai and Yerenai would then ask the children to recite another favourite poem:

We may be old, and sad may be our thoughts,
But avarice in us seethes unabated.
Good work and noble deeds we set at nought,
Our hearts delight in jealousy and hatred!
But if our sons take after us, their fate
Will be too terrible to contemplate.

The old men were especially fond of those songs which scourged their old enemies. Not satisfied with the recited

M. AUEZOV

words alone, they wanted them to be sung. Even more impressive in the chorus of young voices, the words delighted the greybeards.

"My, how well put! Those words run through all the sixty-two veins of a man!"

"No Kazakh has ever been able to say what you have said, Abai! Only you could have said such things, the only golden poplar in this desert," said Darkembai, voicing the general feeling.

The poems and melodies born in Akshoky were copied, memorised and rendered by Mukhamedjan. He sang them one evening in the yurta of Ospan. The young people of the aul and the servants clustered round the tent in a dense throng.

Ulzhan had not seen Abai for a long time and missed him sorely. Listening to the poem, she even failed to notice that guests had arrived. Perhaps these words were addressed to her?

> *I am with you once more, I speak with you.*
> *With understanding new please hear my verses new.*

Her son denounced the old and ignorant akyns, the traders in words, those who were eager for distinction.

> *The greatest trouble-makers in the land*
> *Are the Tobikty clan.*
> *Immodest schemers, dealers all,*
> *The fathers of the people they are called!*

She was brought back to earth by the roar of Ospan's laughter. He had been listening in silence, but suddenly seized with mirth he pointed to Takezhan and his companions, who sat sedately drinking kumiss.

"There they are," he said through his laughter. "It is they whom he meant."

When Ospan saw that Takezhan, Zhirenshe and Urazbai were offended, he laughed even more heartily, for an instant becoming the mischief-maker he had been as a child.

"What's the matter with you, Ospan? Why are you guffawing like a young ass?" Zhirenshe growled.

"There are no greater intriguers in the Tobikty than you three. That is why Abai has lashed out at you. Just try to deny it, Zhirenshe!"

Ulzhan smiled, but was soon lost in thought again.

"Abai was always my world from the day he was born," she said after Mukhamedjan had recited many poems. "My gold nugget, the joy of his mother's heart. And I see that my hope has grown into a beautiful poplar and I can die in peace. I wish for nothing more, dear Allah, and am thankful."

Takezhan's anger at Ospan flared up anew, and his mother's words got his back up.

"Oi, Apa," he said to Ulzhan, "you say such things because you have given your heart to one son alone. Are there not noble and eloquent Kazakhs in our family besides him? And haven't they said so often, 'Praise be to Allah that we have brought forth not a single baksi or akyn!' Why be so pleased about Abai then? Isn't he a real baksi?"

Zhirenshe pinched Urazbai's leg, to make him look at Ulzhan. Her face was distorted with anger.

"I am sure that you think you have sprung from the same litter as he, but there is a difference between a kumai * and a mongrel. Say what you like, but remember you are not worth one of Abai's finger-nails!"

Her broad, lined face was livid, her tear-filled eyes were bloodshot.

Takezhan reached for his kamcha and timak.

"Let us go," he said testily to Zhirenshe and Urazbai. "I've heard enough!" He strode to the door.

The poems and melodies born in Akshoky, put down in writing and learnt by heart, reached Kunanbai on one of his sleepless nights. He lay tossing and turning in bed, a captive listener to a verse of some song, repeated over and over again with annoying persistence.

Karipzhan, the night watchman of the aul, was singing it. He had not remembered the whole song on first hearing, he knew only that one verse and could go on singing it forever:

> The heavens meant you for my husband,
> To love and cherish as my own,
> But for a wife you did not want me,
> And left me in the darkness all alone...

Kunanbai could not make out the words, and all he understood was that someone was left in the darkness, punished by the heavens. Unnerved by the inescapable melody and the threat he sensed in the words he called to his wife:

"Who is he cursing? Go and find out."

But Nurganim knew the song.

* Kumai — a legendary hound. — Ed.

"They say it's one of Abai's... It's on everyone's lips," she told him, and recited the verse.

Kunanbai gave a noisy sigh, and turned to the wall.

"Tell him to shut up and stop wailing! Go on! He's taken away my sleep."

When Nurganim first heard this poem, she felt unutterably sad. The words expressed her own misery. She thought of Bazaraly, the friend who had abandoned her in an hour of need, and her heart was laden with unspoken sorrow.

She called the watchman, and gave him her own instructions:

"Sing your song at the farther end of the aul, and when you come near here sing it under your breath... Your passionate song scorches the old man's heart. Your song is hotter than the hottest fire... It's not liked here," her low voice ended on a sigh.

She had told herself, not the watchman, what lay secreted in the innermost recesses of her soul...

On a quiet summer evening, Abai sat on the rocky hill of Kaska-Bulak, listening to the evening noises of the aul. His small aul had not gone to zhailyau that summer, and instead, he was spending the season in the neighbourhood of the zhataks.

Many guests had come from the zhailyau that morning. They were young akyns who had brought him glad tidings of how popular his songs were throughout the steppes. Abai's name had been on the lips of everyone at the crowded fair at Koyandin.

"A good man has appeared in the steppes and his name is Abai. He has special words and behests for us. He is a wise man, a protector of the downtrodden and enemy of the tyrants. He was born among the Tobikty, but is truly a son of all the people. We shall heed his words and behests."

It was Kokpai, Mukhah, Mukhamedjan, Magash and Kakitai who had brought the news. They had crowded round their aga-akyn, proud of their friend.

Leaving his friends in the yurta, Abai had climbed this hill to be alone with his thoughts.

His eyes searched the vast expanses of Yeraly, Oikodik and Korik. How great was the face of this world plunged into evening stillness and bathed in slanting shafts of the sun!

Abai felt as though he were in a lonely ship on a boundless sea. With sails unfurled, he was going towards strange shores, to a haven called the future. The name of his ship was "Hope and Struggle". It was forging steadily ahead.

Abai looked again towards the distant horizon, trying to visualise the course of his imaginary ship.

His momentary elation gave way to a fresh train of thought, as sullen clouds gathered over his vision of joy.

Life and struggle lay ahead and he was alone. True, he had strength and hope. His strength lay in poetry and his hope in the people, but his hope was still deep in slumber. And his strength? Would he be understood by the people? Had he the patience and willpower to go on alone?

He had reached the summit of his life. And behind him, in the past, what was there more of — losses or gains? He was not sorry for much of what he had lost. His father had become a stranger to him and so had his brother Takezhan. Many others like Takezhan had become his enemies, for instance Zhirenshe and Urazbai. Oh, well. There would be many more like them. Never mind, so long as the people were with him, so long as the torch that lighted his path to the hearts of people remained burning in his hand.

He whispered the words as a pledge.

But what had happened to that sea of his? He looked about startled.

There was no sea, just the usual plains of Yeraly with a column of dust rising in the distance, and another column and yet another. What could it be?

A rider galloped up from behind him. He came from Yeraly. Darkembai had sent him.

"Abai-aga! Do you see those clouds of dust?" he cried in a voice that shook with anger. "The robbers have fallen upon the poor herds of the zhataks. They are driving away our last horses. They are robbing us again!"

Gone were the sea and the dream. And gone was his momentary vision of joy, of consolation. Life with its bitter reality, its grim struggles, was once more calling Abai to battle.

REQUEST TO READERS

Progress Publishers would be glad to have your opinion of this book, its translation and design and any suggestions you may have for future publications.

Please send your comments to 21, Zubovsky Boulevard, Moscow, USSR.